The New Du Rose Matriarch

The Hana Du Rose Mysteries

K T BOWES

Copyright © 2013 by K T Bowes

All rights reserved.

No portion of this book may be reproduced in any form without written permission from the publisher or author.

Acknowledgements

I wish to acknowledge my long-suffering family.
Only those related to a writer can fully appreciate the frustration of living with one.
I wholeheartedly apologise for the numerous times that there has been no dinner, scant cleaning and little fulfilling conversation, while I sought to bring this novel into being.
Writing can feel like an insatiable hunger, which for those not involved may feel at times like a curse.

Would you like to be part of it?

I'm a believer in 'try before you buy.'
There's nothing worse than forking out your hard earned cash on a doozy and regretting it.
I don't want stinky reviews. I want you to love my work and feel like you got value for money.
If you'd like 4 free eBooks, you can join my mailing list at ktbowes.com
The novels will be delivered to your inbox.

Chapter 1

Hana Du Rose pushed the pram across the soccer field without seeing in front of her, willing the baby to stay asleep. A prickling sensation crept up the back of her neck, plaguing her with unease. She turned her head to survey the empty field. Nothing. Yet the sense of someone watching remained.

The child fretted in the pram, raising her tiny hands to her ears and tossing her head in quick movements. "Hush," Hana crooned, placing one foot in front of the other in a haze of misery. "I can't do this," she hissed in desperation. "It's worse than I remember."

Baby Phoenix Du Rose spent the entire night screaming, taxing Hana beyond her ability to stay sane. Reacting to her six-week inoculations, she bumped across the school field as her mother tried the last trick in her repertoire to get her to sleep. Hana shivered beneath the eerie sensation and turned her head again. Still nothing. She sighed and rubbed her eyes. "I'm so tired, I'm creating monsters," she grumbled.

Her feet turned in the direction of the school boarding house and an early dew speckled the cricket pitch. She'd been walking since before dawn and every step seemed more laboured than the one before. "Let's find your father," she murmured. "I bet he enjoyed a lovely night's sleep."

Phoenix groaned in the pram in reply and Hana rubbed at her tired green eyes again. Her eyeballs ached in their sockets. The baby brought her knees up to her chest in pain and opened her mouth, emitting a piercing wail. Hana increased her pace, distress adding itself to the guilt of failed parenting. She'd wanted to vomit as the needle penetrated the spindly little olive-toned leg, feeling a traitor as she held onto her child and allowed the atrocity. This was her punishment for the betrayal. "I'm sorry," she murmured, adding a rocking motion to the handle of the pram. "I'm rubbish at this."

The pram bumped across the crease in the centre of the cricket pitch as Hana registered a momentary stab of anger at her husband. "He promised," she hissed. "He promised it wouldn't be like this." Logan hadn't discussed taking on the extra duty as the boarding house manager as a favour to the principal. He'd announced it days after arriving back in the city. Hana ground her teeth, knowing it impacted on her more than either of them imagined. Four night duties in a row left her coping alone with a new baby. The constant sense of being watched frayed her nerves to breaking point.

"Oi!"

She turned, swinging the pram around to face the shout. A quad bike sped towards her, not slowing until the last moment. The head groundsman hurled his stumpy body from the vehicle and strode the final two metres towards her. His pocked face bulged with fury. "What do you think you're doing?" he shouted into her face, spraying spittle into the air and onto Hana's red curls.

The sleepless night caught Hana up in one overwhelming punch and she gaped, her lips producing no sound. Unsatisfied, the man jabbed a finger into her chest. "Get off the cricket pitch!" he bawled. "Wheeling your effin pram over it. Especially the effin crease!" He waved his arms and backed towards the bike, his expression showing no recognition of Hana's bedraggled state. Jumping onto the quad bike, he whirled it in an arc and drove straight over the hallowed pitch without regard, flicking up dust behind him. Hana's shoulders slumped in defeat. Her gaze strayed to the pram as Phoenix opened her eyes and let out another wail.

Hana abandoned the pram outside the dining hall of the boys' boarding house. Dating from just after the Second World War, St Bartholomew's complimented the illusion of affluence with its gabled roof and mock Tudor facade. As a private institution, The Waikato Presbyterian School for Boys commanded an appropriate price tag for the bespoke education and opportunities it promised. Hana scooped her daughter from the blankets and as Phoenix wailed again, she fought the urge to hand her off to Logan and make a run for it. Guilt coloured her cheeks pink with shame and she kissed the bobbing downy temple. "I'm sorry," she whispered. "Silly thoughts. I'm just exhausted."

The baby's face made a picture of misery as her unfocussed eyes tried to latch on to the shapes and colours whizzing past. Hana walked through the lobby and into the dining room, her eyes downcast and the set of her shoulders oozing defeat. A hundred pairs of eyes turned to watch as she appeared in the entrance. Phoenix gave a pitiful wail and Hana cringed.

"Hey Miss." A tall, dark haired boy greeted her. Dressed in a prefect's white shirt with black-and-white striped blazer, he cut an imposing figure as he separated himself from a group of younger boys.

"Hi, Acton." Hana dropped her gaze, aware of her red hair escaping from its ponytail accompanied by shapeless tracksuit bottoms and sick-stained hoodie.

"You looking for Mr Du Rose?" He smiled and Hana nodded. Phoenix stopped grizzling and her head nodded comically as she tried to focus on his face.

"She won't stop crying," Hana blurted, surprised by her spontaneous confession of failure.

The teenager reached out an olive finger and slotted it into the baby's little fist. "They do that don't they?" His face held a knowing expression. "My baby brother squalled when he came out and he's still going." His lips curved upwards. "He's fourteen now." Seeing the misery cross Hana's face, his cheeks reddened with guilt and he back pedalled. "This little girl won't be like that, she's a Du Rose."

"What does that mean?" Hana regretted the words as she sensed his confusion. Acton gulped and his gaze coasted across the dining room. He spotted Logan striding towards them and swallowed. "She wouldn't dare do half the stuff my brother has," he hissed. Twisting his lips into a quizzical smile, he retreated back to his knot of adoring fans. The younger boys fell into line behind him like a family of ducklings.

Hana's breath caught in her chest with a familiar sinking sensation as her stomach flip-flopped. Logan Du Rose's Māori heritage exuded from him in the smooth olive skin and dark wavy hair. He moved through the rows of chairs with ease, already lifting his lips in a smile at the sight of his wife and daughter. His immense personality dwarfed Hana, rendering her ragged by comparison. In a split second, she moved from relief to inadequacy.

"How is she?" Logan accompanied his words with a kiss to Hana's forehead and a matching one on his daughter's crown. Boys turned to stare and he disregarded their smutty interest. His strong arms encased his girls in safety and Hana sighed. She hid her face within the folds of his expensive jacket and heard the murmurings of teenage voices.

Phoenix's head bobbed as she searched for Logan's face, tears still drying on her cheeks. Logan smoothed them away with gentle fingers and responded to the hitch in her chest. "You still unhappy, baby?" he whispered. His grey eyes flicked upwards to regard Hana, irises the colour of slate. "Should we take her to the doctor?"

Hana shook her head. "I took her last night. He thinks it's a reaction to the jabs. I've filled her with pain syrup, but she needs to sleep." She sighed. "I can't get her to drop off, Logan. I'm exhausted." She yawned and Logan winced.

"Sorry." His lower teeth gnawed the inside of his lip. "I need to help you more."

"Mr Du Rose?" A boy spoke his name and waited to the side, twisting his fingers in expectation. When Logan turned to face him, the boy gushed out his problem. "Darren's puked up in his bed. He asked me to fetch you."

Hana sensed the wave of uncontrolled emotion rise from her chest into her throat. She tamped down the urge to shout and scream, to wrestle her husband's attention back from the seething mass of fragile male egos in his care. Her eyelashes fluttered with the effort of controlling her tears and she stared at the parquet floor while Logan dealt with the child.

"I should go," she muttered, turning away to release him. "I'm in the way."

Logan's fingers clamped around her forearm, holding her in place. "Ask Matron to take a look at him," he said, his tone impassive as he spoke to the edgy boy. "I'll go up to see him in a minute."

The child nodded with relief and Hana ached to dump her problems on someone else and run. She backed away, her daughter's cheek bumping against her chest. "Will I see you later?" she asked, the question holding more rebuke than she intended.

"I'll walk outside with you." Logan made a hand action to one of the prefects and the boy nodded. Like a well-oiled machine, the teenager assumed command of the dining room without question. A hundred pairs of eyes watched Hana leave and she sifted the sensation in her tired brain. It felt different. Curious, not hostile eyes followed her progress and instinct told her whoever watched from the shadows didn't possess teenage acne and raging hormones. She sighed and in the corridor,

Logan rested an arm around her shoulders. "You're doing great," he whispered. "I promise."

"No, I'm not!" Hana raised her voice and then swallowed. An embarrassed flush coursed up her throat and added colour to her cheeks. "I didn't agree to be a single parent, Logan. This isn't fair."

"I know, I know." Logan looked around him before drawing her through the front doors. He pulled her to the side and waited until a group of boys passed out of earshot. "It's not what we agreed, but I'm getting there, I promise. A few more weeks and we can go home once the new manager arrives."

Hana groaned and turned her face towards the brightening sky. "But it's too hard, Logan! The staff unit is uninhabitable and you're never home. The last time I had a tiny baby to care for I was twenty-five years younger."

Logan's eyelashes fluttered and Hana saw conflict flicker behind his eyes. Sighing, he reached for Phoenix, hoisting her over his shoulder in strong, tender hands which belied his physical strength. Hana felt naked without the child in her arms, not sure what to do with her hands. Her fingers twisted and writhed in front of her. Logan edged her away from the entrance. "The boys will stampede in a second. Let's get out of the way." He pressed a kiss against Hana's forehead, his brows knitting when she didn't respond.

Hana straightened her spine as the bell sounded from the main building, a raucous peal ripping through the airwaves. She held her hands out to collect the baby. "Go back to work, Logan. I'm fine." Forcing a fake smile onto her lips, she ignored his narrowing eyes and the suspicion in the line of his lips. She lay Phoenix in the pram and the child fussed before closing her eyes and pushing a tiny thumb into her mouth. Hana felt the tension ease in her shoulders at the promise of peace.

"Hana." Logan waited for her to finish releasing the pram brake and then spoke her name again, putting more force into it. "Hana?"

She rubbed her eyes and turned to face his perceptive scrutiny. "I'll see you later." With a dismissive wave, she walked away. The oppressive staff units appeared in her peripheral vision and she bit her lip against the scream bubbling into her chest.

"Hana!" Logan raised his voice and forced her to turn, his authority tugging at their tenuous connection.

"What?" After a cautious look at her sleeping daughter, Hana turned.

"I know something's going on." He kept his tone even and Hana fought the instant desire to swallow.

She clenched her jaw and shook her head with a little too much emphasis. The lie tripped off her tongue. "I'm just tired," she insisted. Forcing a smile onto her lips, she gave a final wave and left.

Shouts and jeers betrayed a fight breaking out on the first floor and Hana capitalised on Logan's distraction to push the pram away with as much confidence as she could manage. The prickling sensation returned, raising the hairs on the back of her neck. She resisted the urge to look for its source. Experience told her she wouldn't find it. Boys milled around her in obedience to the bell's summons, their presence holding no fear. Hana's knuckles showed white as she gripped the handle of the pram and she put her head down and stalked across the field.

She didn't see the shake of Logan's head before he let the front doors swing behind him. Nor did she notice the figure watching her from the boundary of the school grounds. Hana didn't see. But she felt the burn of the intense interest as she bumped the pram up the front steps and into the dilapidated staff unit.

Chapter 2

Hana tried the door handle, realising she'd rushed out without her keys. It opened under her fingers. She sighed. "A prospective burglar might feel sorry for me and leave something nice," she sniffed, wiping the back of her hand across her face and streaking sticky tears over her cheeks. The solid weight shifted in her chest at her stupidity. Leaving the pram by the door, she searched the tiny unit for intruders. Her lungs complained as she held her breath but found nobody. Everything remained as she left it, a bomb site of her own making.

Peering into the pram, Hana's relief produced a sigh as her daughter settled. The sleeping infant looked stunning, dark eyelashes fluttering over olive cheeks. "Sorry baby," Hana whispered. "I'm rubbish at this parenting thing but I promise to try harder." Pulling a blanket over the baby's legs, Hana surveyed the mess in the tiny open plan living room. The washing up from Logan's breakfast the day before still sat on the draining board and tufts of blanket fluff lay on the tatty rug near the gas fire. It demanded the last of Hana's energy and her forty-five-year-old body complained at the prospect of cleaning. "I can't do this," she said again, indulging the negative self-doubt with defeatism. She sank into the lumpy sofa instead, remembering Logan's heated phone conversation with the school principal.

"I'm not moving my family in here!" he'd exclaimed. Whatever Angus said in reply had changed his mind and Hana found herself in the dilapidated unit held together by tin and string. Alone. Logan offered no explanation and she left her neat home in the hills in mute obedience, the summer's awful events still leaden in her heart.

Ripped wallpaper overlooked the decrepit, filthy old sofa. Hana's body craved a lie on the bed, but the thought of the smelly mattress in the double room made the caved in, mustard coloured sofa seem appealing. She knew the unit challenged Logan's neat-freak tendencies, not that he spent much time there.

"What am I doing here?" Defeated, Hana reached for Logan's sweater curled over the back of the sofa and buried her face in it. She smelled his familiar, safe scent and wished for his strong arms to wrap around her tired body. Tears leaked out and droplets sat on top of the wool. Hana watched them trickle down and felt her dam grow closer to bursting.

A familiar creak made her sit up and she swallowed at her forgetfulness. She didn't lock the front door behind her. Wiping her eyes on the sleeve of the sweater, she readied herself for the kind of visitor who didn't knock first. Her gaze strayed to the pram sitting beside the opening front door and she tensed.

"Where's Logan?" Glossy lips curled backwards in a spiteful sneer as the woman's face appeared around the corner.

Hana released the held breath in a whoosh. "Get out Caroline!"

Logan's ex-fiancé stood her ground, edging closer with her sassy blonde hair windswept and artfully sexy. She wore tight fitting jeans which stressed her slender figure and Hana rose to face her. She swallowed, not daring to glance down at her rumpled, sick-stained clothes and draw attention to her unkempt state.

Caroline rested a manicured hand on her hip. "I need to see Logan," she repeated. "Where is he?"

Hana gritted her teeth. "He doesn't want to see you, so get out!" Her fists balled against her thighs and she experienced an emotional shunt as power borne of insanity coursed through her veins like burning mercury. Caroline's presence near the pram infused naked maternalism into Hana's brain and she needed her to move away from Phoenix, whatever the cost. "Get away from my baby!"

Caroline inhaled without looking into the pram. "I'm not interested in your brat! I want to see Logan."

Hana took a step forward, something dangerous lurking beneath her emerald irises at Caroline's description of Phoenix. "She's not a brat. And don't even speak my husband's name!" Another step. "He wants nothing to do with any of you. Get out!"

Caroline snorted. "That's not what he said at Reuben's tangihanga." Her eyes narrowed, attempting to throw doubt on Hana's trust in Logan. But the lie left a burning thread in the air and Hana seized it with relish.

"Liar! I saw you following him around like a love sick puppy!" she spat. Her lips crinkled back into a vicious smile. "He spent the whole funeral avoiding you, Caroline. He lost both his parents and even in his weakest moment, he still managed to avoid you." Hana laughed, disgusted at the sound of victory in the awful cackle. "Just get out."

The previous six weeks seemed to condense before her eyes. The fire which claimed two lives was followed by her daughter's traumatic birth on a mountaintop. Both memories still woke her sweating at night. Caroline's unwanted presence in her scruffy living room compounded her sense of righteous indignation. Hana snapped.

Her exhausted brain failed to filter the words which tumbled from her lips. She advanced towards Caroline's lithe shape, anger burning in her green irises. "Why are you here? Do you have another pregnancy to pass off as Logan's?" Hana moved forward, enjoying the satisfaction of watching her nemesis back away. "Or is it about money Caroline?" Her next step brought her alongside the pram and relief flooded through her veins. Still the lioness' instinct to protect her young roared like a red haze before her eyes.

Caroline backed towards the door, her hands grappling behind her. Hana advanced, cutting her baby off from a possible threat. "He hates you, Caroline!" she hissed. "Logan hates your guts! He's glad you jilted him at the altar because that one selfish act led him to me.

Temper fuelled her movements, filling her with a reserve of untapped energy. Tiredness left her body as fight replaced it.

Caroline tugged the front door open and slid through the gap, almost tripping down the narrow steps. Her lips parted but for once, no sound emerged. Hana capitalised on her win. "I'm Mrs Du Rose now and I've given Logan a child. Everything you ever wanted belongs to me. Go away and stay away." She lifted her shoulders and glared at Caroline, guilt prickling the back of her neck for mentioning the other woman's failed pregnancy. She clasped her fingers behind her spine to stop them shaking while he rational mind rebuked her unkindness.

Caroline hovered on the path outside, her movements jerky and something unreadable in her expression. Hana retreated inside the unit and slammed the door, causing the timber house to shudder on its aged piles.

Phoenix's tiny arms splayed wide in a fear reaction and she parted her rosebud lips to release a pathetic wail. The dam in Hana's chest broke and she slid down the ripped wallpaper until her bottom touched the floorboards, sobbing as though her heart might break.

Chapter 3

The child's distressed hitching ceased as Hana nursed her, tiny lungs rising and falling beneath her pink woollen cardigan. Hana curled her toes at the momentary discomfort as her baby settled at the breast. "I can't do this," she admitted, closing her eyes and feeling the tiny fingers fix around her thumb. "I've made a mistake."

Hana owned none of the dilapidated furniture in the staff unit and collected her few belongings while Phoenix fretted in her car seat by the door. "Not long now, baby," she promised. "We're leaving before I become someone I like even less." Her words to Caroline stung, knowing she'd crossed the invisible line of conduct between women. She berated herself, feeling no amount of exhaustion justified such behaviour. "A baby still died," she whispered. "Not Logan's, no. But someone's."

Self-reproach followed Hana to Ngaruawahia, trailing her up the main highway towards Culver's Cottage. With every passing kilometre between her and the staff unit, the tension eased from her shoulders. Phoenix slept next to her in the car seat, milk leaking from one side of her pursed lips. The guilt settled to a dull ache as

Hana crossed the Waipa Bridge and turned right onto Hakarimata Road.

A mountain range hugged the road, rising above it like a sentry to the west. The Waikato River snaked alongside, sticking close as Hana took her daughter home. She sighed with relief as the black metal gate slid sideways in obedience to the remote in her hand, pushing the car through the aperture and beginning the climb.

The uphill driveway meandered through a kilometre and a half of stunning native bush and Hana sensed her sanity return. At the crest of the hill, Culver's Cottage winked down at her and promised rest. Hana killed the engine and listened to the car's clicks as the mechanisms cooled. Birdsong surrounded her. No school bells, no teenage dramas. No ex fiancé watching her from the shadows.

Phoenix snored in the wide lobby as Hana inspected the rooms of her home, breathing in the scent of cleaning products and soap powder. "Why did I let him talk me into leaving?" she demanded of the empty rooms. "I'm letting him run away from his feelings again."

The late February day sent sunlight into the rooms, offering healing and warmth. Hana showered in a bathroom that didn't make her want to break out the bleach and dressed in clean clothes devoid of musty aromas. She carried her baby into the kitchen and pulled the blanket away from her gripping fingers. Phoenix snuffled and replaced her thumb between her lips, settling into the car seat with a sigh.

The empty fridge forced Hana to drink black tea and the freezer in the garage disgorged a loaf of bread. A knife separated two slices and almost her fingers and a layer of jam made the toast edible.

"Oh, bloody hell!" The telephone in the lobby gave a chirp, forerunner to a resounding ring. With a nervous glance at the baby, Hana managed to reach it before it trilled and ripped the cord from the socket in the wall. Phoenix slept on, enfolded in the peace and safety of the old house. Sighing with relief, Hana searched the baby bag for her cell phone, groaning at the memory of it sitting on the seventies style coffee table at the unit.

Futility and exhaustion washed over her and she stifled a yawn which threatened to detach her chin from her jaw. Phoenix grumbled in the car seat and Hana sighed. "At least you slept for an hour," she said, lifting her baby over her shoulder. The child wriggled, bouncing her lips against Hana's shirt as her eyes darted left and right with interest. "This is our proper home," Hana whispered. "This is where I imagined we'd live."

She changed her daughter's dirty nappy in the master bedroom, laying her on the four poster bed Logan bought before their wedding. She cleaned the squirmy body and worked to rebuild the connection damaged by tiredness and Caroline's antics.

The injection site on the child's olive leg appeared less angry and Hana fed her another dose of infant painkiller through a small plastic syringe. "You like that?" she asked in a baby voice.

Phoenix contorted her features, making Hana laugh with the combined sucking and licking she performed at the end of the syringe. Listening to the tinkling sound of her own mirth, Hana realised she hadn't laughed once since they moved into the staff house. Her mind took her back further, to the week before the fire and she sighed. "What a summer," she whispered.

Phoenix clenched her fists and beat them against the bedspread, her dark brow furrowing and her eyes squeezing into thin lines framed by lash fringes. "Are you hungry again, Bugle Bum?" Hana asked, lifting her upright and cradling her to her chest. Phoenix rooted against her shirt and made her needs more obvious.

Hana settled in the four poster bed, pillows supporting her back and neck. The luxury of privacy meant she could open her shirt and feed in comfort, her tight muscles aching as she allowed herself to relax.

She woke in a panic three hours later, alarming the baby who snuffled and jerked in her arms. Phoenix kicked her legs and waved her uncoordinated hands, staring at a fixed point on the ceiling. "You're awake," Hana said, stroking the smooth olive cheek. "And not crying."

Phoenix gurgled nonsense and pursed her lips. Her light blue eyes flickered and danced in the afternoon sunshine. Hana checked her nappy and offered the other breast, falling from a doze into a heavy sleep. She twitched as she dreamed of Miriam Du Rose, watching her mother-in-law run into the fire. The orange flames threw their arms wide in delight and Logan's birth father held his hands out towards her. His fingers beckoned Miriam but his eyes looked at Hana.

Tears ran into her hair as the familiar horror played itself out, robbing her of energy and understanding on a continuous, inescapable loop.

Chapter 4

Hana woke again and fed the stirring baby, keen to prolong their peace. When she dozed, Caroline's influence snaked its destructive fingers into her slumber. Terrifying images swirled before her and Caroline gripped a wailing Phoenix in manicured fingers. "She's mine!" she screamed. "She's Logan's and that makes her mine!" Helplessness filled Hana's world and her chest hitched with a terror which turned her inside out.

She woke with a start, grateful for the small body cradled against hers. With a shaking hand she pulled back the blanket and checked Phoenix, relieved at the sight of her closed eyes and relaxed face. Hana pushed herself back against the pillows and waited for her heart rate to slow.

Checking her watch, she saw that six hours of sleep had eaten into her day. Though her red curls stuck up like a banshee's, her mood felt better.

The sound of the front door's familiar click reignited the pounding in Hana's chest. Her body stiffened as an old fear reaction kicked in. "It's just Caroline again," she told herself. "I can deal with her." She lay the baby on the mattress and shifted sideways, ready to launch herself at the bedroom door. Footsteps walked along the hallway, setting off a series of creaky floorboards.

Hana inched backwards until her socks hit the bedside rug and she forced her feet to skirt the end of the bed. "Caroline doesn't have a key," she hissed. Her fingers gripped the post nearest the door and the green voile cascaded down in the air current.

"Hey." Logan's face peered around the door and Hana released an exaggerated exhale. His head jerked backwards. "Sorry. I didn't mean to scare you."

Hana glanced at the peaceful baby and jabbed her head towards the hallway, a finger already making its way up to cover her lips. She followed him on trembling legs, still shaken by the sudden withdrawal of adrenaline. Logan leaned against the wall and pushed his hands into the pockets of his leather trousers. His motorbike helmet sat by the front door. "Have you left me?" he asked, his voice small.

Hana released a whoosh of air. "No, Logan. I've left that awful unit. I can't stay there with a new baby."

Logan nodded, his dark fringe dropping over his eyes and shuttering his emotions. He gave a short nod. "Okay." The forced smile didn't involve his eyes. "Sorry." He reached out a tentative hand and stroked her hair away from her forehead. "I tried to ring here and your cell phone a few times. Then I went to the unit after school." His jaw worked in his cheek, creating a dimple which appeared and then receded.

"I haven't left you, Logan." Hana pressed herself into his chest, smelling motorbike oil and the warmth of the sunshine on his leather jacket. "I promise." She let his lips graze hers, sighing with relief as he pulled her closer and enfolded her in his strong arms.

"Good," he whispered. "Because then I'd have to kill you and bury you under the deck."

Hana snorted, the sound echoing around the lobby. "No interruptions, cool dark space to sleep. Sounds amazing."

Logan's smile made it to his eyes and he bumped the end of her nose with his. "Whatever, Mrs Du Rose," he replied. He noticed the loose phone cord and bent to retrieve it, tracing it back to the handset.

"Don't!" Hana stopped him plugging it in. "Just leave it."

"Why?" His eyes narrowed and he drew himself up to his massive full height. "What's really going on?"

"Nothing!" The lie tripped off her tongue and she sensed he knew. She hoped Caroline was responsible for the spooky feelings she had on the school site, but instinct told her not. Her brow furrowed. "I spent the last two days with a crying baby, Logan. She's sleeping right now. If it's all right with you, I'd appreciate her staying that way for a while longer."

Logan dropped the wire as though it contaminated him and strode towards the kitchen. Hana pushed the door closed behind her and leaned against it. "Sorry," she breathed, running a hand over her eyes. "Just tired and snappy."

Logan nodded and filled the kettle with water. "No, I'm sorry." He flicked the switch and sighed. "I let myself get trapped into something I can't get out of and I've made you feel second best along the way." He licked his lips and picked at a speck of oil on his jacket. "A few more weeks and the new guy will arrive, I'll go back to teaching and we can come home." Dumping tea bags into the chipped brown pot, he opened the fridge door and cursed. "Crap. No milk."

Hana closed her eyes and leaned the back of her head against the door. Logan's presence brought the outside world into her safe haven and tension crept into her spine. "There's nothing here," she whispered, holding onto the ready tears collecting behind her eyelids.

"Sweetheart." Logan pulled her into his side and kissed the top of her head. "What can I do?"

Hana sniffed and wiped her nose on his jacket, leaving a streak. "Quit the boarding house job right now and stay here with me." She pressed her face into his collarbone, enjoying his scent for real instead of through his abandoned clothing at the staff unit.

"This is a disaster, isn't it?" he replied. "Angus suckered me and I fell for it. I needed a challenge to take my mind off what happened at Christmas." His voice trailed off and he balanced his chin on the top of Hana's head.

"I can distract you." She slipped her fingers under the heavy jacket and parted the buttons of his work shirt. Her lips found smooth flesh. "I can take your mind off everything." She experienced a flurry of excitement when he held his breath. Glancing up, she saw his grey irises darken with desire. She reached up and stroked his cheek. "You have us, Logan," she whispered. "We love you."

"I know." His lips pressed over hers and he closed his eyes. "I love you too wahine."

Hana squeaked as Logan dipped his body and caught her beneath her thighs. He hoisted her up in one fluid movement. His taut stomach muscles pressed against her side and he carried her into the lobby. "Phoe's on the bed," she reminded him as he headed for their bedroom door and he changed direction, laying her on the red rug in the lounge. She giggled as he made an art form out of undressing her, recapturing some of her pre-pregnancy confidence beneath his gentle, solicitous touch.

The peace of the house enfolded them as they reconnected, healing each other through mutual tenderness. Logan kissed the soft skin on Hana's neck, shifting her curls aside and feeling them cascade through his fingers. His lips felt warm against hers and she responded to his gentle touch.

They lay beneath a blanket, legs tangled together on the rug. Hana leaned her cheek on her elbow and admired Logan's biceps as he snatched a cushion from the sofa for her head. "I've missed this place," she sighed.

Logan leaned back against the sofa, his expression thoughtful. He played with a strand of Hana's red hair, twisting and turning the amber tresses in fingers scarred and damaged by cuts which took longer to heal for him. Hana touched his chest, parting his open shirt to run her fingers over the rugged welt snaking across his ribs. She traced it, sensing his gaze fixed on her face and feeling tension hike in the room. His silence said it all.

Dread slipped its horrid fingers around her heart and Hana closed her eyes. Logan pulled her chin up with his index finger. "Look at me, Hana."

In response, she burst into noisy tears as her fragile peace shattered. "Hey, hey," he breathed, hunkering down and pulling her closer. "Women don't normally cry when I make love to them." His strained humour fell on deaf ears and his forehead creased in concern.

"Don't make me go back there." Hana pressed her face into Logan's chest, her tears leaving sticky tracks through the downy hair. "Please don't make me."

Phoenix squeaked from their bedroom and the moment ended without conclusion. Logan heaved in a ragged sigh and stood, hauling his shorts on and leaving Hana to wrap herself in the blanket and follow. Her breasts felt full and sore and she paused at the bedroom door with the fabric clutched at her throat. Phoenix lay in the centre of the huge bed, her legs waggling in the air. Happy sounds issued from her lips and her gaze tracked something unseen on the ceiling. Hana sniffed and wiped her nose on the blanket. "I hope she's hungry," she said.

Logan wrinkled his nose. "Probably. But she also stinks."

Hana pushed the bag of supplies towards the bottom of the bed, guiding it with her foot and watching her daughter. "Your turn," she said. Phoenix cooed up at her father, enjoying a debate only she understood. "I'll freshen up." Hana headed for the bathroom to regroup and dry her tears.

Her resolve crumbled with the click of the lock and she sank onto the lid of the toilet. "I can't go back," she sobbed into a wad of toilet roll, muffling the sounds of her misery. "I can't do this." She wrestled with her limited options, picking them over as though selecting shells on a beach. If she refused to return to the school site, she left Logan vulnerable to Caroline's charms and while she doubted he'd succumb, she couldn't take the risk. The boarding house master's role stipulated living on site and Angus wouldn't budge on that issue. With or without her, Logan needed to stay at the unit.

Hana scrubbed at her face with a cool flannel, no nearer a conclusion. "Caroline!" She spat the woman's name, hating her constant interference and the way it shaped her decisions. "Logan wouldn't cheat with her," she breathed. "He wouldn't." She believed her own words. Any doubts she'd entertained ended at Reuben and Miriam's funeral. Logan avoided Caroline with a rudeness bordering on vicious. She'd exercised one betrayal too many and he'd cut her out of his life forever. Hana's relief felt short lived, especially if Caroline had returned to Hamilton.

She recalled the sounds of the funeral and smell of the smoked taro unearthed from the hangi. The feast should have united a family over the shared meal, restoring noa and normality after the burial. Logan made a pretence of eating the smoked chicken and vegetables and chatting to the marae elders. Only Hana saw his desolation. The boarding house had become his new mission to avoid facing the damaging family secret. His father was not his father.

Hana moved to the edge of the bath and listened to him play with his daughter. His peace seemed so fragile. She mentally traced the line of his tattoo as it wound around his upper arm. The whakapapa portrayed his precious French Du Rose lineage as it intertwined with Māori. Dark and indelible, it followed the wrong line, mocking him every time he looked in the mirror.

They hadn't talked yet, not in the six weeks since the fire. A gnawing ache flooded Logan's eyes when he mentioned Alfred. He didn't speak Miriam's name anymore. She made her choice, marrying one brother whilst continuing her affair with the other.

Hana dried her face and contemplated herself in the bathroom mirror. She saw long, messy red curls spread over her shoulders and swollen green eyes, puffy from crying. "Not attractive," she chastised, comparing herself to Caroline with her polished nails and perfect makeup. Thoughts of returning to the school site sapped the rest of her energy and she tried to rally. "You lost one husband and you're sobbing through your second chance." She sighed at her reflection, squaring her shoulders and letting the blanket slither to the tiled floor. "You're not bad for your age." Her index finger prodded her abdomen and then her left breast. "Get it together, Hana."

Phoenix represented the start of something pure, a new legacy. Logan made a promise to his paternal grandmother to create something different from their deceitful, adultery-riddled heritage. Her blood still ran through his veins. And his daughter's. He could still achieve it, but not without Hana.

She freshened her appearance, damping her unruly curls and masking her puffy eyes with makeup. Smiling at herself in the mirror, she set her jaw in a determined line and arranged her features into less of a grimace. She emerged from the bathroom with a different mind-set to the bedraggled woman who went in.

Hana retrieved her clothes from the lounge rug and replaced the blanket. She followed the sound of Logan's voice to the bedroom. His conversation made her halt just outside the door. "I was fourteen when I met your mother," he said. "I'd never seen such a beautiful wahine." Phoenix kicked her legs and a tube of nappy cream flew off the side of the bed. Logan's expression seemed distant, his mind in London on a dirty tube train almost three decades earlier. He sighed and pulled himself back to the present, his lips curving into a sad smile. "Twenty-six years searching for her and now I'm losing her."

"That's not true." Hana saw Logan jump as she stepped into the room. Guilt and shame darkened his eyes. His long fingers fixed the nappy around his daughter's rounded belly and he fumbled with the press studs on her sleep suit. Hana heard the portcullis slam down over his heart.

"Will you teach her the old ways?" she asked, perching on the edge of the bed.

Logan shrugged and changed the action to a nod. "Yeah. I'll help her create her own mihi so she knows where she comes from." Hana's heart chilled as he lifted Phoenix over his shoulder and kissed her downy head. "It's important to know where you're from, baby. Otherwise you end up like me."

"Like you how, Logan?" Hana watched his jaw flex in his cheek and he refused to meet her gaze.

"The bastard son of a disgraced uncle," he replied, his tone clipped and formal. "Hanging onto a heritage that isn't mine."

Hana shook her head. "Orphaned and grieving," she whispered. Logan stood up, the movement jerky and awkward. The baby's head bounced against his neck and she rubbed her eyes with a tiny fist.

"I'm too old to be an orphan," Logan snapped, his voice hard. "And I'll save my grief for those who deserve it."

Hana sighed, the moment of candid honesty over. She inhaled and rose, brushing imaginary dust from her pants. "I'm ready," she said, snatching up the bag and reaching for a spare nappy and baby wipes. "Just let me feed Phoe and we can leave."

Logan shook his head and walked towards the door. "Not tonight," he said. The scar beneath his right eye creased as he grimaced. "I just called Angus. He's agreed to renovate the unit. You can inspect it when it's done and if you don't like it, we won't go back."

"What did you say to him?" Hana's brow furrowed. "He never caves in that easily."

Logan's eyes widened and she saw the latent fire burning in his soul. Something told her the conversation hadn't sounded pleasant. "It doesn't matter," he bit. "He sorts it out, or he finds himself another manager. That's the score."

Hana watched as the rigidity relaxed in his spine. His hand shook as he patted the baby's back and his gaze rested on her face. Irises the colour of slate carved a groove in her soul and she sensed his pain. "My girls are all I've got left, Hana. I won't take any more risks."

She exhaled after he left the room, listening to his feet pad through the lobby. She ran a hand over her face and rejoiced in her unexpected reprieve. A break from the bugs and the holes in the ceiling gave her a heady sense of relief and she sank onto the mattress. A break from Caroline's interference and from the eyes which studied her every move, whoever they belonged to.

Chapter 5

A peaceful evening followed the wretched day. Logan drove into Ngaruawahia and fetched fish and chips which they shared in front of the television.

Hana sighed and stroked her daughter's fluffy head. "It's nice to sit on the sofa without falling between the gaps in the springs."

"Yeah, I know," Logan tutted. "I'm sorry." He slipped his arm around her shoulders and stroked Phoenix's feet.

Hana saw the blackness descend and nudged him. "What are you thinking about?"

Logan shook his head and gnawed on his bottom lip. "I'm wondering what to call my father," he said. Hana's heart clenched in her chest at the sadness in his voice. "Do I call him Pa still, or Alfred?" Sighing, he squeezed the bridge of his nose between finger and thumb, smiling at the way Phoenix kicked her legs in protest.

"You stopped your massage." Hana smirked. "Boy, you're whipped!" Her expression grew serious. "What do you want to call him?"

Logan stiffened. "Nothing right now. Please, can we not talk about it?"

Hana experienced a spark of irritation, but knew pressing him achieved nothing except an argument.

"Why did you tell Phoe about how we met?" she asked instead. "She won't remember." Her teeth worried at her lower lip. "You won't tell her I was eighteen and pregnant, will you?"

Logan shrugged. "Not if you don't want me to. I'd like her to grow up knowing her heritage. It will shape who she becomes." He silenced, the dark spectre back in position over his chest, forcing him to take stock of what he'd lost.

"I guess." Hana's mind wandered back twenty-six years as she snuggled into his side. Logan's striking grey eyes stared at her from an olive, boyish face. She remembered the wet tears on her cheeks and his mother passing her a handkerchief as the tube train gobbled up another underground station. Miriam. Hana closed her eyes and released a sigh.

"Promise you won't tell Phoenix why I was crying?" She tensed, wondering why it bothered her so much still. Logan shot her an odd, sideways glance.

"I won't, Hana. When have you known me betray someone else's secret?"

"Thanks." Hana released her held breath. "I'm not sure Bodie ever worked it out. Vik never celebrated our wedding anniversary, so hopefully he'll never guess." She sighed. "He wasn't big on marriage vows either."

"Hey." Logan pulled her in tighter. "Don't rake over old coals, babe. There's no point."

When they went to bed, Hana stood in the bedroom cradling the baby and casting around. "The cot's still at the unit," she whispered. "What should I do?"

Logan yanked his empty bottom drawer from the cabinet and snatched up a blanket. "Put her in here," he said, laying it on the rug. Deft fingers created a nest from the blanket and he slipped his warm tee shirt over his head. "Give her here."

"You can't do that!" Hana twisted her body to shield the child. "It's a drawer."

Logan rose and claimed his daughter. "It's how I started out, Hana." His eyes darkened with pain. "Not that it's any kind of endorsement."

Hana relinquished the child and watched Logan lay her in the drawer. He swaddled her in his tee shirt, allowing enough room for her to poke her thumb between her lips. Glancing up at his wife, he broke into a smile. "I wasn't born six foot four, Hana. It'll work out for tonight."

"Thank goodness she's stopped crying," she said, rubbing her eyes and yawning. "I made a terrible mess of coping. I thought I'd be better at it this time around, but I'm just older and more knackered."

Logan wrapped his arms around her, his brow furrowing. "I miss your pregnancy curves," he whispered. "You're getting skinny. I liked you with bigger boobs."

Hana pushed his hands away, her lips quirking into a smile. Logan caught her again, trapping her arms and kissing her neck. "Let me say it one more time and then I'll stop," he whispered, frowning at Hana's confused expression. "I'm sorry for allowing Angus to browbeat me into helping him out. It was a big mistake, given our horrific summer. We needed time to heal and didn't get it. I'm sorry." He sighed into Hana's hair and she snuggled closer.

She possessed no magic words to take his pain away. Instead, she pushed her hands inside his shirt. "How about I distract you while Phoe's asleep?" she offered and Logan smiled.

"I could be persuaded."

Hana slipped her sweatshirt over her head, revealing the maternity bra beneath. "Oh." She looked down in disappointment, her sexy image dissipating before her eyes. Logan's lips curved upwards in anticipation and he bit his lower lip.

"And the rest," he whispered. The desire in his face emboldened Hana, folding her in a haze of desirability and she shed the rest of her clothing in a series of sexy shimmies.

"You're gorgeous," Logan sighed, grabbing her around her waist and edging her backwards onto the bed. He removed his clothes, making Hana wait while he revealed his muscular olive chest and the dusting of dark hair. She followed the line down his stomach, her pupils dilating as it disappeared into his boxer shorts. When he joined her on the bed she reached for him, pulling him on top of her and seeking his lips with urgency.

Some of the pain left Logan's eyes as they cuddled later. Hana ran her hand between his pectorals, making him shudder as she dragged her finger across his nipple. The baby slept in the drawer, gentle snores punctuated by the sound of thumb sucking.

"She got so distressed after the injection." Hana stopped herself stepping back into yesterday's misery, the endless, painful crying and sense of utter powerlessness. "I took her back to the clinic and they gave her pain relief. She cried until after we saw you this morning. Actually, she cried until we arrived here."

Logan took Hana's roving fingers in his wide palm and pulled her onto his chest. "You're a great mum, Hana. Stop being so hard on yourself." He placed a finger over her lips and she heard the cry of his heart in the whispered words, "We both love her, Hana. She already has more than we ever did."

Phoenix woke twice in the night, feeding with enthusiasm to help her little body cope with the inoculations. In between, she slept, allowing Hana to shuck her own exhaustion.

"I feel so much better," she exclaimed next morning, saner and ready to deal with the day. After a six o'clock feed, Hana washed the baby in the shower, handing her out to Logan so she could soap herself.

He stumbled around in his towel, fumbling with a tiny sleep suit and nappy as Phoenix wriggled on the bed. He swore as his cell phone vibrated on the bedside table and reached across to retrieve it. Phoenix sent the tube of nappy cream spinning across the bed with a well-aimed kick.

"Who was that?" Suspicion laced Hana's voice as she entered wearing a towel, her hair pulled back into a ponytail.

Logan finished speaking and frowned, disconnecting the call and fixing a steady gaze on Hana's face. "Who do you think, Hana?" His eyes narrowed and he tugged Phoenix's foot away from her mouth.

"I don't know." She put irritation into her tone and jerked her shoulder upward, wondering if he'd tell her the truth. Doubt crept back into her marriage, infiltrating by degrees with Caroline's appearance.

"Angus employed contractors last night. They're working on the unit over the next week." Logan sounded tired, rubbing his hand over his face.

"He got onto that fast." Hana swallowed. "He must really want you at the boarding house."

"Yep." Logan fastened his buttons while the baby kicked on the bed next to him. He blew a raspberry on her soft stomach and she jerked in surprise. "You can stay here until it's finished."

"What about you?" Rebellion raised her tone. "I won't stay here without you." She set her jaw in determination and pushed away the sassy image of Caroline.

Logan winced. "I'm rostered on for another night duty."

"Again?" Hana felt the muscles in her back bunch and panic ramped up its game in her heart. Her fingers fluttered over the knotted towel at her breast. "I don't understand."

"What don't you understand?" Logan fitted socks over his feet and eyed her sideways. "We can't leave the boys without supervision, Hana. It's my job."

"But it's not just yours. There are other boarding house staff, Logan. The duties are shared. I don't understand why it always falls to you."

Logan sighed. "I'm sorry."

Hana saw his jaw working in his cheek and felt the falling sensation creep back into her psyche. "You're avoiding me, aren't you?" She asked the question whilst knowing he would dodge it, her little world tilting to one side as fear took hold. Wrenching the knotted towel apart, she reached for her underwear. "You didn't think I'd grow suspicious when Caroline turned up yesterday after you've spent most nights at the boarding house." She closed her eyes and blew out through pursed lips. "I'm such a bloody idiot!" Her bra shook in her fingers and the clasp resisted her.

"She did what?" Logan snarled the question and his body took on a painful rigidity. The darkness in his eyes made Hana gulp. His jaw tightened, spitting out the words like bullets. "You think I'm having an affair with her?"

"I don't know." Hana finished fastening her bra and hauled her knickers over her hips. "I don't know what to think about anything anymore." Snatching a summer dress from the wardrobe, she pushed her head through the hole and let the fabric muffle her voice. "I know I can't go on like this much longer."

Logan exhaled. "Geez, Hana." He rubbed a hand over the bristles on his chin. "Go on like what?"

Hana lifted her daughter from the bed and carried her to the armchair by the ranch slider. She dressed the jerky, rag-doll body in a knitted cardigan. Logan stood and he appeared wooden as he pulled on his work trousers and tucked in his shirt.

"I'm not having an affair with Caroline or anyone else." His tone softened and Hana felt tears well up her throat and make their way into her forehead. She struggled to hold onto them. "Hana." He said her name, compelling her to look into his mesmerising grey eyes.

"Fine." She kept her voice light as she popped a bonnet over the baby's dark hair. Phoenix blinked and her eyes widened as she searched Hana's face. Her thumb strayed into her mouth and Hana kissed her soft cheek and tried to drown out the turmoil.

Logan followed her to the lobby and watched as she fitted the baby into her car seat. He waited until she stood up straight and then captured her around the waist, dragging her into his chest. "You don't believe me." He said it like a statement of fact and Hana shrugged. Logan inhaled, temper vying for airspace. "What did the crazy bitch say to make you think that?"

Hana shook her head. "Nothing, Logan. She asked where you were and said she needed to see you. I said some spiteful things and she left." She bit her lip, not wanting to admit quite how spiteful.

Logan sighed. "She wanted permission to stay at the motel with Nev and his family. I told her no way. She left."

Hana's eyes narrowed and she leaned back so she could see his face. He kept an even grip on her waist. "And?"

Logan tutted. "And she tried to kiss me. And she made threats. And then she left."

Hana shook her head. "Would you have said anything if I hadn't mentioned it?"

Logan's brow furrowed and he appeared to give it serious thought. "I don't know." His honesty stung. "I don't think so. Things were okay between us. Now they're not."

Hana closed her eyes. "Things were not okay, Logan." She freed her arms and pushed against his chest. "We call the occasional truce when we're both too exhausted to fight, but that's not okay."

Logan released her, taking a step backwards as hurt slithered across his face. "I thought things were good."

Hana snorted and bent to push her feet into her sneakers, wrinkling her nose at the pretty dress paired with comfortable shoes. "You're never around, Logan," she said, tying the laces with shaking fingers. "How would you know?" She glanced up to witness him clenching his teeth. When she stood, she picked her words with care and aimed them to cause deliberate hurt. Something had to give and she'd grown tired of it being her. "We both watched your mother die, Logan. She committed suicide and chose death with her lover over life with her family." Hana stuck her chin in the air. "Bottling it up won't make the pain go away and nor will spending your life at work. If you won't talk to me, at least talk to someone. Angus. Anyone." Hana flapped her hand towards his ashen face. "I'm done with the hard-man act, Logan. Do I wonder why you're not at home with me and our daughter? Yes. All the bloody time. Do I think you'd go back to your ex fiancé? Probably." Logan's eyes widened and his lips parted, ready indignation ready to rain on her fire. Hana sighed and bent to seize the car seat's handle. "Right now you're a loaded gun and I have no idea what will make you pull the trigger." Her chin wobbled as emotion threatened to spill out. "It sure as hell makes you unpredictable and I'm tired of raising our daughter alone. It wasn't what I signed up for."

Hana left while Logan remained speechless. She closed the door behind her, sensing guilt follow her down the porch steps. Loading up the car seat, she left. "I know you're suffering," she breathed as she joined the rush hour traffic. "But I can't help you if you won't let me."

Chapter 6

Hana used her card to access the rear gate. The barrier rose and she entered the school site with deliberate slowness. Boarders spilled over the private road. She pressed her foot to the brake as a group ran in front of her, their faces grimacing in panic as the bell tolled from the main building.

A wave of misery buried her beneath self-pity as she turned onto the narrow road between St Bart's and the staff units. Joined in twos, they presented a picture of dereliction and filth. Hana pulled alongside the unit allocated to Logan and lowered the passenger window enough to hear Phoenix cry. She readied herself for a quick in and out visit. "Two minutes," she promised, drawing in a fortifying. "I don't plan to stick around long."

The narrow access road forced Hana to park with centimetres to spare between her passenger wing mirror and the kitchen window. She grumbled as she squeezed her body around the truck and climbed the steps. A rusty key ground in the lock and she entered holding her breath. It looked just as she abandoned it, suitcases open on the dressing table. In the family's absence, the musty smell had reoccupied the space, permeating the loose clothing and filling the rooms with its damp odour.

"Come on girl, get out of here," Hana breathed, snatching up the bedding from Phoenix's cot. It took minutes to clear up the dirty crockery and she watched her sleeping daughter through the window. A shiny brown cockroach darted from the cupboard as she opened it to put a plate inside and she screamed and abandoned the task. In the bedroom, she slammed the suitcases closed, grateful they'd avoided filling the rickety drawers and borer infested wardrobe. Negotiating the car's wing mirror with her arms full, she shoved the load onto the back seat. Then she returned for more. She hefted the suitcase into the boot and slammed it closed.

Phoenix slept through the decamping process and Hana sighed with relief. She'd forgotten how hard life became with a car seat, child and related paraphernalia. Locking up the unit, she wrinkled her nose at the peeling paint on the front door and slipped around the vehicle. "Home," she whispered. "Thank goodness."

"Hana, wait!" She turned, her hand in the act of pulling on the driver's door handle. The shout made her start and she jumped and let go. Not Caroline. The sports teacher called her name again and she paused and forced composure onto her face. "Hey, wait up." Chris Carter jogged towards her and Hana stiffened. Caroline's former lover wore a wide smile on his cocky face. "I wanted to speak to you."

"I'm just leaving." Hana worked hard to keep the barb from her voice. "I'm in a hurry."

The man's smile wavered and he eyed the belongings strewn across the back seat. "Oh. Didn't you move in a few weeks ago? I hoped it might be a permanent thing."

"Not to my knowledge." Hana kept her response terse, showing little tolerance for a man who'd cheated on his pregnant wife. "A temporary arrangement."

"How are things?" he asked and Hana's brow knitted in confusion. Chris Carter made no secret of his dislike for Logan, especially after bedding his ex-fiancé.

"Fine thanks." She nodded and grappled with the door handle, comforted by the warm metal beneath her fingers. Imminent escape beckoned.

"Hey, wait." Carter's tone became slippery as he placed a large hand over hers. "Are you coming back?" Good looking with striking blue eyes and a perfectly proportioned face, he used his assets to his advantage. His reputation preceded him and Hana sensed him trying to win her round. "It's good to have neighbours." He indicated the unit attached to hers before dropping his eyes to her lips. His fingers moved over Hana's in a stroking motion and she withdrew her hand, acknowledging another reason to dig her heels in and refuse her return to the unit.

She shoved her hands behind her back and Carter's gaze roved over her full breasts instead. A step back did nothing to discourage the twitch of his lips. He sighed and gave her a lascivious wink which turned Hana's stomach. She felt old enough to be his grandmother. Carter continued the one-sided conversation and ignored Hana's hungry glances towards the safety of her car. "Angus is renovating our unit at the same time as yours. Amanda's living at her parents' place with the baby and she'll come back when this place is nicer. Then I'll move back in."

Hana noticed a thin line appear beneath his brows and heard the indecision in his voice. Perhaps Amanda had no intention of returning or allowing her errant husband back into her bed. She made no comment and an awkward silence filled the airwaves. Carter breathed out in a snuffing sound and leaned forward to stare into the car seat. He screwed his head sideways and bent his knees to see, bringing his face mere centimetres from Hana's. "Your baby's pretty, what's her name?"

"Phoenix." She took a step backwards, the door handle moving out of reach.

He nodded. "I remember it sounded unusual." He waved his arm at the building behind them, encompassing both units. "Do you think they can make these any better?"

Hana held her breath as he took another step forward. Calculating and practiced, he had his overbearing seduction technique honed into a fine art. "I don't know. They can't make them any worse. Ours is horrid." Another step back.

Carter nodded and rested his fingers on the roof of Hana's car. "Yeah. Amanda got depressed living here with the baby." He sniffed and wrinkled his nose, leaving out the other glaringly obvious cause. Adulterous husbands and their wives' depression spent significant time holding hands. "She'll love having someone else here with a baby."

Hana nodded and smiled although it didn't reach her eyes. Carter edged closer, putting a large hand on her left shoulder. She tried not to panic as he leaned in and lowered his voice. "Caroline's looking for your husband. I wanted to warn you. She's trouble."

Hana held her breath, aware if she exhaled her breasts would touch his shirt. A cloud of cheap aftershave whirled around her head and she batted at his fingers. "I need to go," she gasped. A sense of violation enveloped her, yet she sensed a recount of the moment would make her sound paranoid. Or egotistical. He'd done nothing and yet the whole incident felt inappropriate and dirty.

She heard Logan's motorbike before she saw it. It roared into the narrow street from the soccer fields. Logan wore no helmet and his hair blew back from his forehead. She watched his grey eyes narrow and instant fury consume his expression.

"Oh, shit!" Carter dropped his hands to his sides and panic sent him in the wrong direction. He stepped into Hana for protection, instead of having the sense to move away. Her right leg shot out behind her for balance and she gave him a hearty shove with both hands.

Logan's bike gave a meaty roar and he drove straight at them. Carter struggled to keep his footing as he dived sideways, his hands grappling in mid-air. Hana seized hold of the car's wing mirror and held on as Logan threw himself sideways, catching Carter by the throat before his bike hit the ground. In seconds, he had the younger man shoved up against the wall of St Bart's, Carter's trainers dangling off the ground. The expensive motorbike lay on its side rumbling to itself, protesting as black smoke funnelled from the exhaust.

"What are you playing at?" Logan shouted into Carter's face. His opponent didn't answer, his eyes bugging and his cheeks turning a hideous shade of red.

Hana collapsed into the driver's seat of the Honda and covered her eyes with her hands. Chris Carter's shiny white trainers dangled in her peripheral vision. Logan glanced back at her as she banged her head against the steering wheel, causing the horn to let out a series of frustrated beeps. He dropped Carter to the ground and snarled into his face. "You touch my wife again and I'll snap every one of your greasy fingers off! Consider yourself warned!" His irises flashed slate grey, obscured by black pupils fuelled by anger. Carter picked himself up and his fingers coasted over his throat as though checking everything still worked.

Muscles bulging, Logan hauled his bike upright. A long scratch marked the paintwork and his fury hiked further. Yanking it onto its stand, he shook his head at the gouge and shot a look containing daggers at Carter. "Bugger off!" he snapped, pointing towards the main building in the distance. "Do some work for a change!" Livid anger fizzed the air surrounding him.

He strode across to Hana and squatted next to the car. "You all right?" he demanded.

She nodded with deliberate slowness, her pulse rate fighting for equilibrium. "You didn't have to do that!"

Hurt infused Logan's face. "Oh." His fringe hung over his right eye. "You liked him coming onto you?"

"I was handling it," Hana lied. "It's all an act. I'm old enough to be his granny."

Logan snorted. "You weren't and you aren't. His kind don't understand the word no, Hana. If he touches you again, I'll kill him."

Hana sighed. "I don't think he'll ever speak to me again." She ran a hand over her face. "Which is probably a blessing." She closed her eyes and pinched the bridge of her nose between finger and thumb. "You're right. I didn't handle it well. He took me by surprise but I would've got there without you beating him up and getting yourself fired." Her lips quirked upwards at the unbidden bright spot. "Mind you, getting fired might also be a blessing in disguise." She swallowed and her mind flicked back to the sense of subtle violation. "Thank you."

"For what?" Logan reached out a hand and lay it over her thigh. His thumb coasted over her skin and brought relief. Hana felt her leg shake and admitted to herself that Carter had freaked her out more than she realised.

"I'm glad you arrived when you did."

Logan nodded and glanced towards the field. Carter jogged away in the distance, one hand still rubbing his throat. "Yeah?" He sounded both relieved and doubtful.

"He said Caroline wanted to see you. Said he was warning me." Hana's lower lip wobbled. "She's everywhere, Logan. I can't get rid of her."

"No, she isn't." Logan pulled her writhing fingers up to his lips and kissed them. "She wanted to ask if she could stay in the motel, I said no and she left. Trust me, she's gone."

Hana gave a slight shake of her head. "I think she's been spying on me," she whispered, looking around at the empty street. "But perhaps I've imagined it. I don't feel spooked right now."

"Spying on you?" Logan's eyes narrowed and his tone sounded sharp. "What do you mean?"

"Nothing." Hana brushed away her unfounded paranoia. "I'm just jumpy. I'll feel better at Culver's Cottage." She turned and peeked at the baby in the car seat next to her. Phoenix still slumbered, having missed her father assaulting a colleague. "You'll be in trouble if someone reports you to Angus. An accusation of physical assault could end your career."

Logan snorted. "Don't care. I defended my wife against the local lothario. That guy's got one foot out the door anyway for exactly that kind of behaviour." He rose and leaned against the Honda, resting his left arm along the roof. He looked sorry for himself with the anger dissipated. His fingers picked at a flake of rust on the roof trim and Hana sensed herself melting with compassion. She clambered from the driver's seat and pressed her cheek against his chest, feeling him exhale with relief as she slipped her arms around his waist. He kissed the top of her head and she felt one of his shirt buttons dig into her nose. "Hana?" His voice sounded gentle but alarm bells went off in Hana's head. "Babe, we need to talk."

She grimaced and stamped her foot in a childish reaction. "I don't want to move back here." She pressed her face into his shirt and inhaled his scent. He smelled delicious and she let her fingers rove until they slipped into the waistband of his trousers.

Logan laughed and pulled her hands in front of him, clasping her wrists in his fingers. "Loving the distraction technique, Mrs Du Rose, but I don't have time. Besides, we need to face some things coming up. Like the court case."

Hana put her fingers in her ears and refused to listen. The court case loomed ahead in her vision, presenting logistical nightmares she couldn't filter out. "I can't think about it now, Logan," she protested. "Please, one thing at a time."

Logan pulled her hands away. "I know this is hard, Hana. He hounded you for more than a year and tried to kill me. The cops need to make sure he stays in prison." He massaged her hands with tender strokes and leaned in to kiss her neck. "Babe, we need to get stuff straight. I want to talk about how we manage the baby while we're both in court. There are things going on at the hotel I need to tell you about and then this crap with the boarding house. I need to decide if it's worth the effort to help Angus out. There's also something else."

Hana opened her mouth to speak, Logan's final sentence creating intrigue. But the arrival of a white van halted further talk. It parked behind the Honda and three men piled out. Logan stiffened and moved to block Hana. His reaction caused fear to bud in her chest. The men wore white overalls covered in splatters of different coloured paint. They formed a rough line in front of the unit. One scratched his head while his companion scratched his groin. The third spun on the spot as though surprised at his location. "Is this the place we're renovating?" He pointed at the front door behind Hana's car and she saw the tension leave Logan's spine.

"Yeah, these two." Logan dug into his trouser pocket and hauled out a key. "Hand this back to the receptionist when you're done. She'll have a spare key for this one." He jerked his head towards Carter's unit. Glancing back at Hana, he gave a reassuring smile. "You should move the car," he said. He straddled his bike and revved the engine, satisfied at the puff of cleaner exhaust it spat out. "Just oil," he said, answering Hana's unasked question. "From lying on its side."

"We can talk tonight," she promised.

Logan smiled and his grey eyes glittered as he registered her reluctance. He leaned sideways to kiss her temple. "For sure," he replied. "You can't keep running."

"Says you!" Hana snorted. She drove along Maui Street to the rest home where Father Sinbad had lived for the last fifteen years. Blind and no longer able to leave the complex, he loved Hana's visits. She sat on his bed and fed Phoenix while voicing her fears about the looming court case. The old man slumped in his wheelchair, lifting his face to draw comfort from the early rays of sunshine.

"Do ye have a date yet me darlin'?" he asked in his thick, Irish brogue.

Hana shook her head, remembering at the last moment he couldn't see her. "No, not yet. But it can't be too far off. Laval's on remand, but very unwell so he needs to be declared fit enough to stand trial. The cops caught two of his newer guys but they pleaded guilty. Logan says Flick's still hiding up at the hotel." She sighed. "I have this feeling I've missed something important."

The Catholic priest put his head back against the headrest of his wheelchair and smiled, the sunshine warming his lined face. "What does yer man, Bodie think?" he asked. "He'll have the police view of things, won't he?"

Hana sighed. "I never know what my son's thinking, Father. You should know that. The prosecution will call him as a witness, so he's careful not to discuss the case with me. Besides, it's just a feeling and I don't want to keep going over it all before I need to."

"Remind me who Flick is again?" Father Sinbad asked. Crinkled fingers tapped out a tune on the arm of his wheelchair.

"Laval killed his stepmother. So Flick infiltrated Laval's organisation and came after me, believing I had the deeds to her property. Logan offered him a lifeline after hearing his story and hid him on the mountain."

"How do you feel about that?"

Hana exhaled and Phoenix stopped feeding and stared at her. "I'm not happy. Flick hurt me and I'm afraid of him."

"Does yer husband know this?" Sinbad turned his head in Hana's direction, waiting for her reply. His blind eyes flicked from side to side.

"Yes. But Flick's proved loyal so far. I guess I need to get used to it. Logan seems to know what he's doing. He wants to talk about the court case and I'm avoiding it." She sat the baby upright to wind her, patting her fragile back and holding up her tiny head as it wobbled against her palm. "I think someone's watching me, Father."

The old man's brow crinkled. "Why? What's happened?"

Hana sighed. "Nothing. That's the trouble. I have no evidence other than a spooky feeling." She shivered and smiled as Phoenix gave a dignified burp.

"You must tell dat handsome husband of yourn," Father Sinbad said, his tone urgent. "Talk to him."

Hana swallowed and considered her new method of avoiding discussion. "We don't do much talking when we're alone." She smirked and the conversation trailed off.

Sinbad gave a sharp laugh. "I spent enough years on de other side of da confessional to know what dat silence means."

Hana gave a haughty sniff. "You have a filthy mind, Father."

Phoenix produced another burp. This one might have induced a cheer from a more uncouth audience. Hana pulled a face at her daughter who returned a beatific smile in reply. "Piggy." She patted her back. "What should I do, Father?"

"Stop patting her back and she won't burp," he replied, his lips quirked upwards. "Or are you referring to your distraction technique? Being a priest, I can't help you wit dat kind of information."

Hana rolled her eyes. "I meant about the feeling someone's watching me. Should I set a trap?"

Sinbad sighed. "No, Hana. Don't do dat! Ask Logan to put de word out amongst his underworld friends. They'll know."

"No!" Hana recoiled and Phoenix jumped. "He isn't in contact with the Triads anymore. It's all behind him. Everything's open and above board. He promised." Hana chewed her lip and worried. "But he did say he wanted to talk about something else."

Sinbad nodded. "Well den, let's ask our Holy Father in Heaven to intervene. Surely he knows de whys and wherefores of dis whole situation. He loves ye Hana and he'll keep ye and your wee one safe."

Hana closed her eyes and laid her head back, allowing the gentle prayers of the intercessor to wash over her.

When he lapsed into Latin, the lyrical cadence of his words brought reassurance.

An hour passed before Hana realised it. The Father had been silent for some time and she lay with her head against the pillows, enjoying the tick of the wall clock and the welcome sense of divine weightlessness. "Please let everything be okay," she whispered. "Please."

Chapter 7

Hana drove back to the school with Phoenix awake in the car seat. She parked in the visitors' car park outside the main reception, ignoring the old Mazda in her former space outside the Chapel. Life at the school had moved on without her, its surface sealing over as though she hadn't donated fifteen years of her life to its insatiable cause.

She carried the baby seat into the reception, already feeling like an outsider. The receptionist stopped her halfway across the lobby. "You need a name tag," she bit. "You can't come and go as you please."

Hana swallowed and turned to face her. "I live on site," she replied. "You know who I am."

The woman shook her greying head and clipped a plastic tag to the front of Hana's jacket. "It's health and safety," she insisted, patting the enormous letters downgrading Hana to a visitor.

"But I only went on maternity leave a few months ago," she grumbled. "I know everyone here."

"Not everyone. We have some new teachers this year." The receptionist swished back to her desk in her voluminous floral print skirt.

A few of the older students remembered Hana and gave her that special flick of the head which showed acceptance. It cheered her as she wrestled the heavy car seat up the familiar double staircase to the first floor. In the common room, a group of Year 13s endured a study period, supervised by a teacher Hana didn't know. An overwhelming sense of misery bit her, mirroring the sadness she experienced whenever she visited the former home which she rented to the new biology teacher.

Hana's shoulders sagged as she reached the closed door of the student centre. She'd hoped to sneak in and visit her old colleagues without knocking like a stranger.

"Miss, Miss," a voice cried behind her and the floorboards shook with the slap of sandaled feet. Hana squeaked as the large Korean student wrapped his arms around her neck and swayed as though to the beat of slow dance music. The study teacher rose to his feet and widened his eyes in concern. Hana shook her head before sitting the car seat on a nearby table. "James," she croaked through the choke hold. "How are you?" She used both hands to peel his arms from around her.

"Awful!" he gushed, placing both hands over his eyes in a dramatic flourish. "I miss you so." He rocked from foot to foot, oblivious of over a hundred pairs of eyes watching him in fascination. "In the Chapel this morning, I shit my eyes and do big one."

Hana swallowed and lowered her voice. "A big what, James?"

"Pray!" he squealed, "And here you are!"

Sniggers loosed around the common room and the study teacher mobilised. He set off towards the back of the class and Hana felt his irritation at the disturbance. "Are you still working at the fast food place?" she whispered.

James waved his arms around like a windmill, shouting in his over exuberance, "No! I want to go Bugger King. I need your help."

More boys tittered, ignoring the study teacher's feeble attempts to hush them. All eyes turned towards Hana as James squealed again. "This is baby?" He pointed to Phoenix and she eyed him though knitted brows. Her expression channelled pure Logan. "Lurvely!" he gushed, clasping his hands to his chest. His brown eyes flickered with a hunger for affection which sent a knot of pain through Hana's chest. "I hold?" he demanded, jabbing a finger at the child. "She like sister. I miss sister and four brother."

"I know you do." Hana reached out and touched the olive skinned arm. "If I'm still here at interval, you can have a cuddle with her."

James nodded and grinned, his eyes narrowing to slender arcs. A snigger from a group to his left drew his attention and he pointed at the playing cards in the process of changing hands. "That not allowed," he stated. Before the group could react, James waved at the study teacher and made a shuffling motion with his fingers. The man's eyes widened and he set off walking towards Hana. She imagined the boys daring to play cards in one of Logan's study classes but the picture ended in bloodshed. Her husband had eyes in the back of his head.

"Oh," James added, turning back to Hana, "lady in der is wicked woman! No nice. She not help me like you. Too busy!" He jabbed his finger at the student centre door, punctuating his words. "No. Like!"

"She's nasty," a boy near Hana murmured. "She doesn't know what she's doing." He lifted his blonde head to give her a hopeful smile. "When are you coming back, Miss?"

Hana paused to watch James return to his seat. He high fived the other boys on his route and the teacher closed his eyes as though wishing James might disappear by the time he reopened them. "I'm not sure," Hana lied to the student. Seeking escape, she picked up her daughter, knocked on the student centre door and then pushed it open.

A war zone greeted her. The door hit a table wedged behind it and Hana pressed her face through the gap to peer inside. Paperwork littered the floor and a steaming bucket of water sat on a low shelf. The cloth floating inside it wore a coat of brown scum. An acidic stench filled the room and Hana glanced down at her baby. "Maybe now's not a good time," she whispered. Phoenix pushed a big toe into her mouth for a lick and then stared at it in surprise.

"Hana's here!" a male voice shouted. Everyone in the study centre turned towards the noise. Hana cringed and mouthed her apologies to the study teacher. "Move this table. I want to see the baby." Peter North appeared in Hana's view, his skinny arms flailing at the table.

"Get out of the way!" A blonde head joined his and a scuffle began.

"No, Sheila! I'm moving it!"

"I'll come back," Hana whispered. "Or use the back door."

"You can't!" Pete yelled. "She's got us trapped in here."

Hana shook her head to stop Pete and Sheila fighting over the table. "It's fine. I'm leaving," she hissed through the gap.

The sound of tearing carpet accompanied a series of wooden clunks and the door flung open. Pete buried Hana's face in his flaccid chest. "Please tell me you're coming back?" he begged, refusing to let go.

Hana's former boss elbowed him in the ribs. "My turn!" Sheila slapped the top of Pete's head and he released Hana with a grunt of pain. A cloud of expensive perfume shrouded her and Pete backed away so she could enfold Hana into it.

"No need to push!" he grumbled.

"Hi, Hana." Rory spoke from his desk next to the radiator and Hana leaned across to kiss his cheek. "Nothing's changed, as I'm sure you've gathered." He jerked his head toward Pete and Sheila as they argued over which one got first cuddle of the baby.

"What's happening to the room?" Hana asked, staring at the devastation. Sheila and Pete spoke at once and Rory hid his eyes behind his hands. Sheila shoved Pete to shut him up and his hands itched to do it back.

Phoenix stopped sucking her toe and looked up at Hana, alarm in the widening of her eyes.

"Will she come to me?" Rory asked. He stood up and before Sheila or Pete noticed, took the handle of the car seat and absconded to the staffroom with Hana's daughter.

Hana waited for the bickering to stop. Sheila pouted at having lost her cuddle with Phoenix, but Pete dipped a knobbly finger into his trouser pocket and yanked out a black, plastic comb. He ran it through his sparse, fluffy hair from crown to fringe. Hana watched as it rose in two tufty clumps either side of his head. She looked him up and down, noticing the smart new shoes and the absence of Pete's filthy school tracksuit. "You're looking smart, Pete," she commented.

"Don't mention it!" Sheila hissed too late.

Pete rose to his spindly height and pushed out his chest with comical pride. "Henrietta gave me a makeover," he said. His hands fluttered in mid-air as though stroking his girlfriend's mountainous curves. "Look." He yanked up the hem of his trousers, pulling until they passed over his knobbly knee. "She bought me new socks to go with my shirt and trousers."

Fluorescent orange socks blinded Hana as she marvelled at their availability in a knee high option. "Very nice, Pete," she complimented, blinking in surprise.

He whipped off the shiny, black patent shoe and wrenched the sock off his foot. "I love them, but they do this, look."

Sheila groaned and made puking sounds behind her hand. In between each of Pete's disgusting hairy toes and yellow toenails, nestled a ball of orange fluff. Hana curled her lip and looked away as he hauled the bucket off the shelf and plunged his foot into the steaming water. "It stings a bit," he said.

"The fluff stings?" Hana asked, staring at his long white toes wiggling in the bucket.

Pete shook his head. "No. The water." He leaned forward and Hana got a bird's-eye view of his hair. She'd never seen someone with an actual rear-parting. Not on purpose.

The study teacher arrived in the doorway and slotted himself through the gap, making a line for Sheila. His face channelled irritation and Hana winced, waiting for him to complain about the ruckus. Sheila turned her back on him and trying to feign a casual air, he took a swig from the coffee mug in his hand. Salvaging the last of his dignity, he faced the man wearing the bucket on his foot.

Pete glanced up and saw Hana watching him as he relocated orange fluff from his toes into the water. "You like my hair, Hana?"

"I love it," she replied. "You look like Julius Caesar."

Coffee blossomed from the study teacher's mouth, shooting a film of brown spray into the air. Hana dodged backwards and avoided the worst. "Julius Caesar," he wheezed. "Julius Caesar."

"It's not that funny!" Pete shot upright and hauled a handkerchief from his trouser pocket. "You soaked me!" He dabbed at his shirt in exaggerated movements, his brow furrowing in anger. The study teacher wiped his mouth on the cuff of his sleeve, colour flushing his cheeks and neck. "You stained my new shirt!" Pete protested. He took a fateful step forward.

Murky water gushed from the upturned bucket and Pete lurched, one foot still wedged inside. He landed with his face in the study teacher's stomach and the man tipped the rest of his coffee down Pete's back. "Ow! Hot! Hot!" Pete wailed as the coffee soaked through his shirt. He rose upwards like a coiled spring and grappled with the waistband of his trousers. "Not these too!" he yelled, dropping them with such speed, Hana wondered if they were elasticated.

The student centre door clanged against the table to reveal a woman Hana didn't recognise. She clutched a cup of steaming tea in her hand and gaped at the scene.

Pete stood in a pool of filthy water and Hana caught the distinctive whiff of vinegar, finally naming the elusive odour and reason for his stinging foot. A collective gasp from the common room signified the gathered boys had moved for a better view.

Pete jabbed at his crotch with a knobbly finger, his lips widening into a foolish grin. He shuffled towards Hana with his trousers around his ankles. "Look!" he announced, "what do you think?"

Hana swallowed and gave a polite nod as Pete waddled over to an equally horrified Sheila. Water soaked into the carpet as he showcased Henrietta's latest purchase with an inappropriate thrust of his hips. An enormous 'S' graced the crotch of his lurid red and blue underwear and he scowled at the study teacher. "It's a good job you didn't ruin my favourite Superman undies!" he snapped.

Chapter 8

The room's new entrant froze in the doorway, lips parted to display a neat row of white teeth topped by a pair of disbelieving brown eyes. Her cup of coffee tilted at a dangerous angle so the liquid dripped onto the floor. Her hand shook and her face morphed into deep disapproval tinged with dismay. "You're all mental!" she hissed, tears filling her eyes. "I can't take any more of it."

Hana cast around looking for someone to defend the apparent madness. Pete bent double, inspecting a dubious stain in the middle of his Superman 'S' and sighing. Sheila shrugged and disappeared into her office, slamming the door after muttering, "Who cares?"

The woman's head bobbled on her shoulders as she pushed past Hana. With a trembling hand she laid her dripping coffee on what used to be Hana's desk before it situated itself on a jaunty angle behind Rory's. Hana watched her pick up the phone. "I want to speak to Angus!" she snapped into the receiver and Hana cringed. "Tell him I refuse to work in this madhouse any longer."

Pete slipped his trousers up with as much speed as he downed them, peering at his toes wiggling on the dirty, wet carpet. "What's in this water?" he asked.

The woman put a hand over the phone before hissing, "Vinegar!"

Pete gave a shriek and lifted his foot off the carpet. "It stings!" he squealed and Hana saw the woman's shoulders tense and slump.

"I should leave now. I have things to do." Hana waved her hand in a feckless movement and made her escape. Rory met her in the common room as the bell rang. He'd already lost Phoenix to James. "Have they stopped spring cleaning yet?" Rory asked, straightening the baby's cardigan as she grinned at James' fake sneeze.

"I don't think so." Hana winced. "It looks terminal."

Rory rolled his eyes. "Another attempt by Angus to right a wrong. Heather's husband ran off with a neighbour and took their joint business and house with him. He declared bankruptcy and left her with nothing. Angus is trying to give her an income." Rory waggled his eyebrows. "I suspect he fancies her."

Hana pursed her lips and her brow furrowed. She couldn't imagine Angus fancying anyone. Rory kissed her cheek and returned to the student centre, leaving James to entertain her.

"She smiles," he gushed, producing another fake sneeze for Phoenix. She grinned, opening her whole mouth as though intending to take a bite out of him. Her eyes squeezed closed. "Eyes change soon," James predicted. He bent his knees to squint into Hana's face. "Not like you though," he said, shaking his head.

A crowd gathered around them as some of the boarding house boys arrived early for the next study period. Feeling protective over Logan's daughter, they stuck close and filled the air with testosterone fuelled machoism. Hana alternated between watching James with her baby and ogling her husband on interval duty in the courtyard. She eyed him from the floor length window, seeing him as other women did with his muscular build and sex appeal.

Sheila's new assistant made several trips to the staffroom with her bucket, pausing on the last run to ask Hana a question. "How did you stand it?" she demanded, her voice wavering. "Peter North is completely idle,

Sheila is chaotic and Rory's passive-aggressiveness leaves me frequently at a loss."

"Oh." Hana nodded to James and reclaimed her daughter as the bell rang. She took time to slot her back into the car seat. She rose, picking her words with care. "This school community has been very good to me over the years. Perhaps give it more of a chance."

The woman's brow knitted and her eyes filled with tears. "I thought cleaning the office might help me settle. They managed to screw even that up for me."

Hana sighed. "Sheila likes to work in a mess. I kept my desk clean but she frequently ransacked it for something she'd lost. I found that keeping another set of records worked for me."

The woman's eyes widened. "Oh. That makes sense. I found duplicates in the filing cabinet by the back door." She pulled a lace handkerchief from inside her sleeve and dabbed at her eyes. "I'm Heather, by the way. We didn't get properly introduced."

Hana smiled and nodded. "Nice to meet you, Heather." Her expression softened. "The people here were my friends, family and for a while there, my only source of sanity. I journeyed through some of my hardest times in this place. Give them a chance and they'll do the same for you." She smirked. "Oh, you should get used to seeing a lot of Pete naked and when Sheila walks in and slams her handbag on the table, find some brochure racks to tidy in another department."

"Okay." Heather blinked and her expression filled with doubt. Hana walked away before she could ask questions about Pete's nakedness.

On the way through the front doors, Hana heard her name and paused. Angus leaned against his secretary's door frame watching her. "Do you have a minute?" he asked.

Hana glanced at the baby and nodded. She followed him into his office.

"Take a seat." Angus indicated his visitor's chair and Hana put the car seat on the floor next to her as she sat.

It brought back memories of being called in to discuss her teenage son's behaviour. "Would you like some tea?" he asked and Hana worried at her bottom lip.

"Am I likely to need some?" she asked.

Angus called his assistant on the intercom and demanded a pot of tea for two. They listened to her grumbling in the office next door as she slammed the handset down and stamped upstairs to the staffroom. Hana watched Angus' face break into a wide smile and shook her head. "You knew she wanted to listen to our conversation."

"She listens at doors." Angus steepled his fingers beneath his chin. "And now she can't. How are things?" He pushed his bifocals along his nose to observe her over the top.

Hana felt the guard crash down over her expression. "Okay," she lied.

Angus raised a ginger eyebrow and sat back in his chair. "I apologise for the unfortunate state of the staff accommodation. I confess, I haven't visited those units for years." He looked through the narrow window, silent for a moment. "My dear wife and I undertook the renovations more than two decades ago. It's not somewhere I would usually venture unless invited and I left their maintenance to the grounds staff."

Hana swallowed and her eyes widened in realisation. "I didn't know Iris helped you." She sighed. "Nobody's touched them for years, Angus. They're rotting on their piles."

"I should have paid more attention."

Hana pursed her lips. "Logan dragged you over there?"

Angus shrugged. "Yes. I admit to feeling rather shocked at the state of them." His expression grew wistful. "Iris spent days making curtains and choosing paint. I've reprimanded Larry Collins for his neglect and am attempting to put it right. The contractors will renovate yours first."

Iris died the same year as Vik. Hana imagined her choosing the curtain fabric in the staff unit and cringed.

Mould decorated the pastel blooms and the tracks hung from their anchors. She wouldn't recognise it. Angus cleared his throat to regain her attention. "Do you think Logan can sort it out for me?"

Hana shrugged. "Maybe. He's got a good eye for colour, but I'm not sure where he'll find the time. He's working almost every night at St Bart's." Her gaze flicked to Angus. "That's not what you meant, is it?"

Angus sighed and leaned back in his seat, peering at her over his glasses. "Hmmn," he said. "I assumed he'd told you."

Anger bridled in Hana's heart and she felt her jaw grow tight enough to begin a headache. Phoenix stretched her tiny arms above her head and bent her body outwards in a graceful arc, her legs retracting upwards into her baby suit. Hana turned to Angus. "If you need my help, you'll have to start talking because this child is gonna blow!"

Chapter 9

Angus' personal assistant used her bum to open the principal's door, backing into the room with her tea tray resting high on her bosom. The stench hit her nostrils before she could turn around and the principal stood by the open window gagging. She clattered the tray onto his desk and waved, not daring to open her mouth.

"I've never known her so quiet." Hana smirked from behind Angus' desk, putting the finishing touches to Phoenix's vile nappy. She used baby wipes to restore the dirty bottom back to its rightful pink.

"The child or my assistant?" Angus spoke from behind his hand.

"Your assistant." Hana smirked. "Perhaps making rotten smells is the way to curb her nosiness."

"Perish the thought." Angus turned and pushed his face through the small gap, heaving in fresh air and cursing the adjoining building which robbed him of view and air current. He groaned and Hana glanced up. "I bet she thinks I made the smell," he grumbled.

Hana grinned, bouncing the nappy in the palm of her hand. Phoenix kicked her legs on the change mat. "You should feel proud then. Logan calls that a ten pointer."

Angus groaned and pressed his fingers over his chest, desperate to hold on to his breakfast cornflakes. "Stop playing with it," he urged. "Please!"

"Sorry. We had fish and chips last night. I'm guessing it didn't agree with her."

Angus made a sound and pushed his face back through the window. "Stick it in the fire," he demanded.

Hana finished dressing her daughter and shook her head. "No, you really wouldn't want me to do that. I'll take it away with me." She hefted Phoenix into her arms and watched the tired baby's head loll. "Why do you need the fire lit anyway? It's still summer."

"I'm drying out the water damage." Angus pointed to a dirty patch on the ceiling. "And it felt cold when I arrived at the crack of dawn."

Hana wrinkled her nose. "It's an odd room for a headmaster and I have noticed it's always cold in here. Like a windowless cell with that tiny slither of glass. You should ask the board for an upgrade."

Angus sighed. "I have. Every year for the last twenty and the answer is always the same. I can meet visitors in the board room which makes a fancy office non-essential."

Hana shrugged and cleared up her belongings. She sat the car seat on the desk and stuffed the dirty nappy into it. "I'm guessing we're not staying for tea now."

"No! I need to evacuate," Angus grumbled.

"I'll grab this on the way back to the car after our walk. Are you ready?" She walked towards the door and Angus peeled himself away from the window and followed. On an impulse, he snatched up the nappy and lobbed it into the grate, congratulating himself on his bowling arm. The package smouldered as the plastic melted on the logs and dripped like blue snot. The white cotton insides turned brown as they burned. Angus slammed the door on his way out.

"What a transformation!" Hana exclaimed later, staring around the dreaded staff unit. The musty lounge furniture sat outside in a skip, stacked on the double bed and its noxious mattress. "It's bigger than I thought."

Angus nodded. "I'll do the semi-detached units two at a time." He peered at the freshly painted lounge ceiling as another truck arrived outside. "Next door is empty at the moment so it's a perfect time."

Cracking sounds came from the kitchenette as a man crawled over the counter and ripped out the dilapidated cupboards.

Hana gaped at Angus. "You're doing the kitchen as well?"

He nodded. "Your husband insisted. He helped me pick out furniture and kitchen units from catalogues."

"Oh." Hana winced. "You know he has expensive taste, don't you?" She peered at the principal as his colour faded and patted him on the arm. "I'm sure it'll be fine. You did agree a price."

Angus gulped. "I didn't see any prices."

Hana wrinkled her nose. "Oh dear."

Phoenix jumped in panic and wailed as the contractor dropped his hammer on the kitchen floor. Hana moved outside to comfort her and untangle her hair from the tiny coiled fingers.

"Let me hold her?" Angus asked, his voice wistful. Hana handed her daughter over, saddened by the look of longing in his eyes. "My Iris wanted children, but they never came along," he crooned to Phoenix, his voice low and conspiratorial. "She'd have adored you."

Phoenix settled into his arms with a sigh and closed her eyes. They walked back to the main building, taking their time to watch a sports class toss around a giant rubber ball and dive on top of it and each other.

"So," Angus asked as they reached the steps up to the reception, "do you think Logan can help us?"

Hana sighed and considered Angus' convoluted explanation. The boarding house finances needed more than a man with a good head for numbers. "It sounds complicated," she said. "I don't know."

Angus kicked at a loose stone, sending it skittering onto the soccer pitch. "It's ceased to be viable as a business. St Bart's is in danger of closing unless I can find the leak without involving the authorities. The public scandal will have repercussions for the whole school."

"The previous manager quit because his father got sick, didn't he?" Hana asked. "Had the issue already begun then?"

Angus nodded. "Yes, unfortunately. He was amazing with the boys but less so with the books. It's been happening for a while. I can't seem to get to the bottom of it. I've been over the accounts so many times and whatever's happening just isn't obvious." His Scots lilt sounded tired. "The books balance, Hana. But there's no profit. It makes no sense at all."

"Could you put the price up for new boarders?"

"Not until next year. And how high? We can't increase it beyond what's reasonable, or we'll lose the new boys. I've abandoned one of the scholarships already because the school can't sustain it. The new manager arrives soon, but I need Logan to stick around and help him sort it out. The accounts are with the auditors and I'm not looking forward to meeting them when they're finished." He sighed.

"And you just gave my husband a blank cheque to renovate the staff units." Hana winced. "Bad timing."

Angus rolled his eyes. "I can take that out of a different pot as it's technically maintenance. Larry Collins will have his budget reduced with immediate effect. Stupid man. I really must look into what he actually does all day."

"Shouts at anyone on the cricket pitch," Hana muttered and Angus pursed his lips.

"I need your support, Hana," he said. "It's why I wanted to see you. I have to get this sorted out. And soon."

"You think someone's stealing, don't you?" She lowered her voice to pass a class of younger boys waiting outside the library.

Angus nodded and gritted his teeth. "Yes."

"Logan's great with numbers," Hana conceded. "If anyone can work it out, he can." A distant banging and crashing came from the staff unit, cutting over the hum of the boys like a claxon. "Maybe we could live at home and he could drive in every day, like before?"

"I need him here." Angus studied Hana as he handed the baby back, his ginger brows narrowing into a single fluffy line. "I feel sure the deception is happening on site, not in the accounts."

"I don't know." Hana shrugged in defeat. "I'll let Logan decide for both of us." She didn't add that she'd try everything to sway his decision.

Angus nodded and thanked her as they reached the front steps. He held the door open and waited while she carried her precious bundle over the threshold. "I'll just grab my stuff from the office," Hana said, smiling down at her sleeping daughter.

"Oh, bloody hell!" Angus hissed and Hana looked up to see Peter North reading a woman's magazine in the waiting area. He had his shoes and orange socks off and reclined on the sofa like a movie star. He leapt to his feet with the sound of ripping paper as the flimsy magazine cover detached itself. A photograph slithered to the ground, disfigured by the twisting of the staples in the centrefold.

"I need to see you, Angus!" Pete exclaimed, bending to pick up his shoes and socks before hurrying after the principal. Hana glanced back and saw him pushing the torn edges of a photograph into his trouser pocket.

"What?" he demanded as she jerked her head towards his pilfered goodies. "Oh." Rachel Hunter's pretty face distorted as he shoved it further in.

"Any urgent calls?" Angus begged his assistant as the three adults stood over her desk. "Anyone I have to call back right this second?"

The woman gave him a calculating smile and exacted her revenge for the earlier banishment. "No, Mr Blair," she answered with a benign smile. "Mr North is desperate to see you regarding that staffroom complaint about him."

"I didn't mean to fart in her face," Pete began. "I had a bad biryani the night before and bent over to pick up my shoe." He looked to Hana for support and she shook her head.

"Don't look at me," she whispered. "I'm just grabbing my stuff and then I'm going home."

Angus pushed his office door and halted in the opening. Sandwiched between him and Pete, it took Hana a second to appreciate the full effects of the nappy Angus lobbed into the grate. Its pressure cooked contents had filled the room with something akin to Pete's biryani backside.

Angus gagged. His assistant shot around her desk and disappeared into reception, one hand over her mouth and the other snatching at the door handle to outside. Her retching echoed off the wood panelled walls.

Hana slipped past Angus and slung her bag over her arm. She balanced the infant and the car seat somehow and made an apologetic exit from the fumes of baby excrement. Nodding to the chairman of the school board as he held the outside door open for her, she made a dash for safety, hearing Pete demanding from the office, "Who's been cooking shite in here?"

Chapter 10

Hana walked towards the Honda as the car seat grew heavy in her arms, the sun glinting off the red highlights in her hair. She bypassed Angus' assistant who sat on a bench heaving in great gulps of fresh air. "You should be lighter after that nappy," Hana grumbled to her daughter.

A low wall bordered the visitors' car park, decorated with ceramic tiles made by decades of leavers cemented to the brick. Colourful and bright, they danced and reflected the sunlight. Hana belted the car seat into the passenger side and Phoenix waved her little arms and opened and closed her mouth. "Funny girl," Hana told her. "Little Miss Bugle-bum." She kissed the soft forehead and closed the door, jangling her keys as she walked around to the driver's side.

A man waited between her car and a sleek black Mercedes, his smart backside resting against the wall. Hana started in fright. "Sorry," she said, backing out of his way. He gave a casual smile but didn't move, his weight resting on one leg and his arms folded.

Hana heard Phoenix squeaking in the car and blowing bubbles. She waited, sensing a wave of unease as the man observed her. He turned his head and his gaze strayed across the steering wheel at the helpless baby. "Nice kid," he said with a smirk.

Hana's fingers shook as she pressed the key fob, activating the central locking. The man smiled but continued his watching vigil. His dark business suit seemed incongruous with his behaviour, fooling the alarm bells in Hana's brain. His tailored black shoes looked expensive and someone cut his blonde hair into an office style. He looked familiar and Hana convinced herself she'd misunderstood. He meant her no harm and she'd overreacted. She ignored the pounding in her chest and stepped towards her car door. "Are you waiting for someone?"

He smiled, revealing even, white teeth. "Yes," he replied. "You." Hana realised her mistake as she grabbed at her locked door handle and the tall vehicles shielded her from the car park. He seized her arms and dragged her into his chest. Then he spun her so her spine pressed against the Honda, gripping her forearms hard enough to keep them by her sides. Last year's nasty elbow break registered pain. A stretching, dragging sensation began where the muscles and tendons still felt tender. Hana inhaled and tried not to panic. A similar height, the man pushed himself close enough to stand nose to nose. His breath smelled of mints and her brain told her lies. He wouldn't hurt her in a school car park surrounded by six hundred boys. He just wouldn't.

The man portrayed a jarring paradox. Apart from his behaviour, he appeared plausible. His clothes screamed business and his accent oozed class. Under other circumstances, Hana might have bought life insurance from him. His coal brown irises glinted, shot through with lighter specks of hazel. "What do you want?" she demanded, willing her voice not to waver.

His eyes softened as he smiled and stared at her lips. "I've wanted to meet you for a long time, Mrs Du Rose." He said her name like an insult and Hana's eyes widened in fear. The fantasy of mistaken identity abandoned her.

"Who are you?" she hissed. "How do you know me?"

He smiled, his tongue showing through his cheek while he decided if he would enlighten her. Squinting against the sunshine caused laugh lines to appear at the outer corners of his eyes. "I'm Michael Laval." He cocked his head to gauge her reaction.

Hana shook her head and pressed herself against the car door. The metal flexed beneath her. Her heart beat in painful strokes against her chest wall. "No." Confusion creased her forehead. "He's in prison. He's a dying old man."

The man released a snort of derision, but didn't relax the pressure of his body against hers. "I'll take that as a compliment. But you're referring to my father."

A gasp escaped Hana's lips and he laughed, cocking his head and staring at her lips. Hana swallowed and the action bisected her words. "Logan was right," she stammered. "He said the cops wanted someone else."

"And they did!" Laval grinned, enjoying her discomfort. "My father's low-grade criminal activity kept them busy for a while. Very entertaining. He's nasty enough to want your husband drowned in the lake, but not high enough up the food chain for his arrest to call for a round of drinks. I hear the detectives felt a little flat after their big night. What did they call it? Operation Waltz?"

"I don't know." Fear prickled in Hana's chest and she prayed for the empty car park to fill with help.

Laval's fingers stroked the front of her blouse in a covetous action, but he kept his gaze on hers. "What a pity they wasted so much time. Father enjoys tea dances and the odd waltz. It's where he picks up his rich grannies. It's not my scene."

"What do you want?" Hana demanded, aware Phoenix had stopped squeaking. Laval used his free hand to brush a strand of her red hair from her cheek, letting his fingers trail down the side of her neck in a seductive motion.

"You won't give evidence against my father in court," he said. "I expect you to withdraw your witness statement."

Hana shook her head. "It's too late. The hearing can't be far off. They won't let me."

"But you'll do it, anyway." His voice held quiet menace and he leaned closer to make his point. "I haven't done my own dirty work for years, Hana. But I wanted to meet you myself. It's true. You're delightful."

Hana squirmed, writhing away from him. Bodie's self-defence classes seemed too long ago for her to remember the moves. She hadn't practiced and her limbs forgot what to do. Her addled brain rendered her feeble and pathetic before the terrifying new threat. Laval's eyes sparkled with danger and Phoenix gave a wail of discontent. Hana stiffened and forced herself not to look at her baby. Laval pressed his body against Hana and stroked her cheek. "Do as you're told, Hana. Unless you want me to restore your worst nightmare."

Rational thought crept back into Hana's brain. She shook her head, tilting her chin in defiance. "You know nothing about me! This is a school. You can't hurt me here." Maternalism emboldened her, urging her to draw him away from her child and out into the open. She tried to take a sideways step but Laval blocked the motion with his leg. His fingers dug into her upper arm until it hurt. In the scuffle, the car keys hit the ground with a tinkle of metal.

He leaned so close, she smelled the coffee on his breath. "What's your worst nightmare, Hana?" he whispered.

She snorted, an angry, insolent sound. "You think I'd tell you?" she snarled. She fought to free her wrist, feeling his grip relax. Her brain screamed at her to move but her feet didn't understand the message.

"I don't need you to tell me," he crooned. "I know everything about you, Hana Du Rose."

In a moment of clarity, Logan's surname galvanised Hana's courage. She freed her wrist and pushed her fist forward in an impressive jab which caught Laval in the right eye. The pressure of his body lessened as he took a step backwards and Hana used the leverage to drag the sole of her shoe down his shin. Laval hissed in pain, overbalanced and slammed against the passenger door of the Mercedes. In the tiny space, Hana remembered to turn her right hand palm upwards and raise it, slamming the heel of her hand into the underside of his chin.

Laval swore as blood dribbled over his lips from a bitten tongue. But his reflexes proved faster than hers and he grabbed her around the back of the neck as she tried to run, hitting her face against the car window and causing her to cry out. She bumped her forehead and Phoenix jumped at the sound, the child's lips parting in a wail of alarm.

Laval's hiss emerged through blood stained teeth. "Your worst nightmare, Hana, is another dead husband!" He released her and pulled his smart jacket back into place, still breathing in shallow puffs. Long fingers brushed a speck of dust from his trousers with a casual air and he smiled at Hana as she turned. Shock ran riot in her brain and her body refused to obey any warning messages. Laval smoothed the back of his hand across his bleeding mouth and inspected the blood. He bowed, an odd movement under the circumstances. Admiration glowed in his eyes as though he considered her a reasonable opponent. He backed away, walking to the driver's side of the Mercedes and opening the door. "See you soon, Hana," he said, the words carrying his veiled threat.

The throaty engine roared to life and galvanised Hana. She snatched up the keys, fumbled with the fob and opened her door. Shaking legs propelled her into the driver's seat and she pressed the switch for the central locking. Laval's car reversed next to her with a screech of tyres. Hana spun in her seat to watch through the window, hoping he drove away. "Just go," she muttered under her breath. "Just go."

The expensive car's brake lights flashed for a moment as Laval paused and Hana watched the passenger window ease down. Laval leaned forward until his gaze met hers and then he smiled. His eyes resembled bottomless pits of spite and the sight took her breath away. He gave a pointed, seductive wink before depressing the accelerator, driving away with brash confidence as though leaving a lunchtime tryst.

Spots of light danced before Hana's eyes and she released the held breath. Her mind went into free fall. She gasped, trying to control her lungs without success as dizziness attacked her. Phoenix wailed, shocking Hana back into reality and she pressed her hand against her pounding heart. "Sorry, baby," she apologised, her voice wobbling. She patted the child's thigh, not trusting the accuracy of her fingers with any other action. "We're going now," she promised, firing up the engine.

Hana's plans for the day melted against the force of the threat. She bolted, covering the half an hour drive to Ngaruawahia faster than usual. Her cell phone registered a text, but she ignored it, a sense of isolation descending on her like a lead weight.

At Culver's Cottage, she closed the gates behind her but didn't relax until she reached the house and locked the front door. Phoenix fretted for her next feed and Hana hid in the lounge with the curtains closed, hunkering on the floor to oblige. Hungry, but aware of Hana's anxiety, the baby fed poorly, getting herself into a state before crying herself to sleep. Hana changed her nappy, bound her in Logan's tee shirt and settled her in the drawer. Only when the little legs stopped fighting the constriction and her face relaxed, could Hana let her mind run rampant. She paced the kitchen, knowing she should tell Logan but dreading it.

Digging in her bag revealed her cell phone and Hana unlocked the screen and prepared to call her husband. A missed message grabbed her attention and she opened it.

'Tell anyone and Logan dies.'

Hana inhaled, the unrecognised number showing as private. It didn't matter. She knew who sent it.

Her stomach roiled as she read the text twice more. The previous year's misery washed over her like an unwelcome douse of freezing water. "Not again," she breathed. "I can't do this again."

The phone bleeped and another message envelope showed. Hana bit her lower lip as she opened it.

'This is your first warning.'

Hana dropped the phone. The threat tore at her sanity like nails on a blackboard. She needed to tell Logan. She didn't have a choice.

The day disappeared from beneath her in a haze of fretting and taking care of Phoenix. It frightened her how much Michael Laval knew about her life. As she cooked dinner later, she wondered how he knew she'd lost a husband previously and that it had destroyed her. A lump rose into her throat at the memories, not just of his loss, but the aftermath of mopping up the mess Vikram Singh Johal left behind him.

The landline trilled around the time Hana expected Logan home and she answered, not speaking until the caller did. Logan's voice sounded capable and tears sparked tears behind Hana's eyes. "What's up, babe? You didn't answer your cell phone."

"Sorry," Hana gulped, her voice croaking. "I put it down somewhere." She paused. "Why are you ringing? Aren't you on your way home?" Panic caused a red mist to blur her vision of the bush beyond the lobby window.

"Heads of department have an after school meeting." Logan sighed. "I forgot. I've switched night duty with someone else, so I'll be home as soon as I can get away."

"Logan!" Hana called into the phone as he started to disconnect, hearing him pause. "Please be careful?"

"Always, babe," he replied, "I'll be home soon."

Hana lowered the oven setting on the casserole and resisted turning her phone back on to see if it bore another threat. Dark and foreboding, it sat on the counter like a time bomb and the realisation came to her. She couldn't tell Logan anything. She'd told Sinbad she didn't want him reconnecting with the Triads or his other nefarious contacts but the real reason was his mother. Her death hung over them still, dripping with bitterness because of the revelations it brought. Ominous and dirty, they'd unpicked Logan's understanding of his history, his whakapapa and the effects scored his psyche like knife wounds. "I can't add this to his load," she whispered. "It's too cruel. He can distract himself with sorting out the boarding house finances. This other problem will go away by itself."

Hana rang her son's phone number hoping to speak to her grandson. Jas babbled for a while about his new school. "I'm five," he told her, as though she didn't know. "Can't I go back to kindy?"

"No," Hana answered with caution. The precarious child had a habit of spinning life on its head. "Why?"

"I don't like school," he announced. "It's shit."

"Jas!" Hana's horror mirrored his mother's in the background. She heard Amy trying to take the phone away.

"Well, it is," he maintained. "My teacher says if we're naughty, she'll sit on us." Accepting the humorous threat as reality, he sounded indignant. "If she sits on me, Dad will never get me out! He'll need to send the dogs in to find me again." His mother snatched the phone, denying him the pleasure of describing the part of his teacher's anatomy which made him most fearful.

"Hey, Hana." Amy sounded rattled, in a way only Jas could achieve. "What's the matter?"

"Nothing," Hana replied, hearing the sharpness of her tone. "Why should there be anything the matter?"

"You sound a little up tight," Amy replied, her police sergeant's brain working overtime.

"I'm fine," Hana lied. "Just wanted to speak to Jas. Is school that bad?"

"Not sure yet. You know Jas. Able to make a drama into a crisis. It's probably too early to tell, but he's not a fan."

"Oh, I'm sorry." Hana chewed her lower lip. "You remember those self-defence moves Bodie taught me over the summer?"

Amy coughed to cover a laugh. "Absolutely. They're ingrained on my brain and his shins."

Hana huffed with indignation, remembering the disastrous lessons. They tended to result in her hurting herself, hurting her son or him wanting to hurt her in frustration. "I've forgotten some of the moves. Do you think he could give me a recap soon?"

"I'll ask him." Amy smirked, imagining Bodie's horror at the thought.

"Tonight?" Hana pressed and Amy hissed through her teeth with instant unease.

"Has something happened, Hana? What's the urgency?"

Hana squirmed at the ease of the lie, disliking relying on mistruths and hating Laval for making her. "I need a distraction," she replied. "The court case is hanging over me and I wanted something else to think about."

"You could take up knitting again," Amy joked and Hana pursed her lips. Amy reacted to the silence and conceded defeat. "I'll talk to Bo. He's on night duty but he'll ring you tomorrow and sort something out."

Hana thanked her and engaged in another chat with Jas, trying to convince him his teacher wouldn't actually sit on him. Knowing he responded best to fact and evidence, she suggested he researched how many children had died in such an event. She left him pestering Amy to log him onto the Internet.

She took a long bath with her daughter, laying back in the old tub so the baby could loll on her stomach and kick her knees in the water. It was fun until the child peed and the bath turned into an unexpected shower. Hana tried to push away thoughts of Laval's sinister son. His persona represented a complete paradox. Well-presented and professional, he appeared polar opposite to a man who would threaten her husband's life and her sanity. Her mind went there anyway and then to memories of Flick. Laval Senior's sidekick terrified her, but his stalker tactics seemed clumsy and thuggish compared to the new threat. Laval Junior possessed an unhinged quality. He induced a sense of vulnerability and violation. The testament to his strange predilections came in the enjoyment the fight seemed to give him as though he delighted in Hana's spark of defiance. Hana shivered and drew a towel around herself and her baby.

Her son's status as a police officer should have offered sanctuary, but his suspicion of Logan drove a wedge between them. Bodie left Hana in no doubt his career came first. If Logan put a foot wrong, he'd be there waiting with the handcuffs. Hana realised her stupidity in requesting more of the fateful lessons, suspecting Bodie Singh Johal would help his chances of promotion before he assisted her.

She decided she needed to get rid of her mobile phone. Laval knew the number, so it needed to disappear from the equation. Fine-tuned to deceit after his engagement to Caroline, Logan would become suspicious if Hana received and deleted random text messages.

"Sink?" she mused, staring into the porcelain. "Or toilet?" She held the device in her hand and shook her head. "Logan will find a way to dry it out." In a moment of pure stupidity, she dropped it out of the bathroom window, hearing it smash on the concrete two floors below. Satisfaction coursed through her and ran to the top of the stairs, determined to stomp on its remains before clearing it up and claiming she lost it.

The gate alarm sounded in the hallway, sending her into a panic. Thoughts of Laval's menace made her twitchy and she convinced herself of an imminent invasion. Hana ran to the bedroom to hide the baby, abandoning that plan in favour of grabbing a weapon from the kitchen. Clattering in a drawer, her fingers settled over the rolling pin and she clutched Phoenix close. Hefting the wood in her other hand, she took a few practice swipes through the air.

The guttural sound of Logan's motorbike making its last surge up the slope, sent a curious weakness through Hana's body. She met her husband at the front door, the rolling pin replaced and a relieved smile plastered onto her face. "You're early," she said, tugging the baby's cardigan closed against the evening breeze.

"Something smells awesome; I'm starving," Logan remarked. Tiredness left dark lines around his eyes.

"Good meeting?" Hana asked, closing the door as her husband removed his boots. She noticed his eye roll and curiosity budded. "What happened?"

"Everard quit." Logan washed his hands and then took Phoenix, his brows knitting at the sight of the single bowl. He balanced the baby on his knee and ate one handed. "You not eating?"

Hana shook her head. "Not hungry." She noticed how the truth sounded more convincing.

"Did you find your phone?" Logan asked. "I texted to say I was on my way."

Hana swallowed. "I don't know where it's gone," she lied, sensing Logan's narrowed eyes studying her over his spoon. She gulped and searched for a distraction. "So, why did Everard quit?"

Logan shrugged. "Dunno. There's been some kind of fall out behind the scenes."

"But he's taught biology there forever." Hana shook her head. "That's sad."

"He stormed out and Alan Dobbs went after him. He came back alone."

"Maybe Dobbs going after him proved the final straw!" Uncharacteristic spite glossed the statement and Logan's eyes flashed.

"Hana, what's the matter?"

"Nothing! I'm fine. I just don't like the man." Hana stood and leaned against the counter, finding it difficult to keep still as she squirmed beneath Logan's perceptive gaze. Thoughts of Laval rushed unbidden into her head as she filtered the mess in her brain, looking for a rescue angle.

"Hana!" Logan stopped eating and stared at her.

She jumped and sat at the table, knocking over the salt in her fright. "Sorry."

"I asked you a question, babe," he said, laying his spoon down and reaching for her tangled fingers. Phoenix yawned and closed her eyes. "Is she ready for bed?" Logan smiled down at his daughter and Hana nodded.

"Give her a kiss and I'll put her in the drawer." Hana smirked at the connotations of the sentence. "That sounds awful."

Logan handed his daughter over and Hana escaped, taking time to wrap the baby and settle her in the unconventional bed. When she returned to the kitchen, Logan finished putting his bowl in the dishwasher and held out his arms to her. Hana sighed into his neck and wrapped her arms around his broad chest, hungry for reassurance and security.

Logan smoothed his fingers down her back, his body rigid and unyielding. "You're keeping something from me," he whispered into her hair. Playing the long game, he waited for her usual eager confession. When she didn't yield, he kissed the top of Hana's head and gripped her shoulders, pushing her far enough back to study her face for guilt. If he saw it glaring there like a beacon, she felt relieved when he didn't comment.

"We need to talk," he said, his voice level and without challenge. "Remember?"

Hana feigned innocence and Logan edged her towards the table, reclaiming the chair and pulling her into his lap. Hana avoided eye contact, snuggling into her husband's neck and praying her slack tongue didn't let something slip to put him on alert. "I don't want to talk about court until we have a date," she insisted. "I'll face it when I have to."

"Not that," he said, pushing her upright and forcing her to face him. "I wanted to ask you about something else. Something we haven't talked about."

Hana nodded, relief flooding her features as she felt herself on more secure footing. It proved a mistake. Logan licked his lips. "After Ma died and I found out who my father was, I realised everyone knew. They kept it from me."

Hana gulped and sent her gaze towards the window. The mountain stared back at her, reflecting her betrayal. Logan used a scarred index finger to bring her chin down. "You didn't react, Hana. During that whole nasty scene, you didn't even look shocked." He swallowed. "Who told you? And more importantly, why didn't you tell me?"

Hana sighed, remembering the fateful day in glorious technicolour. It haunted her at night when she lay next to him, feeding her baby and listening to Logan's soft breathing. Miriam ran into the fire on a sickening film loop, always meeting the orange glare with sure steps and the same screech of agony.

"Well," Logan continued, nudging her forearm. "You knew Alfred wasn't my father but said nothing."

Hana swallowed. "How could I, Logan? You loved Alfred and he raised you. Would you have believed me?"

Logan shrugged and ran a tired hand across his bristled chin. "I don't know, Hana. How did you find out?"

She exhaled, her memory dragging her back into Logan's old room with the handsome man and his magnetic smile. "I met him," she said. "I met Reuben."

Logan's face grew tired and pinched. "Where?"

"Your bedroom at the hotel used to be his. I turned around and he was just standing there. People talk about your mana and his presence felt the same. It was like he could do anything he chose. He had your hands, your hair and your face expressions. I wondered why you didn't see it for yourself."

Logan gulped and closed his eyes and shook his head. "I met him a handful of times and he was always drunk." His jaw worked in his cheek. "He frightened you?"

"No. The whole experience was surreal. He helped me up and his fingers looked scarred, like yours. He touched my stomach and the baby moved." Logan's eyes narrowed and Hana saw his eyes flare with temper. "He didn't hurt me," she promised. "I sensed Phoenix knew him and saw he thought the same. He removed his hand, smiled at me and left."

Logan let out a ragged breath and guilt wracked Hana's soul. She sniffed and her eyes pricked with tears at what he'd lost. "They should have told me," he whispered. "I can't forgive them for that."

"What about me?" Hana's lower lip wobbled. "Can you forgive me?"

Logan reached for his default setting. He pushed his fingers inside her tee shirt, connecting with the soft skin and searching for a distraction to dull the pain. Hana kissed his neck, watching as her silent tears stained the cloth of his shirt darker. "I forgive you," he breathed. "But not them."

Hana sighed, her relief tempered by the hatred in his voice. "They had their reasons, Logan. Reuben's boys kept that secret for years."

Logan shook his head. "Kane meant to hurt me!" he spat. "They hadn't carried Reuben's body off the mountain before he broke his neck to tell me."

"He was in pain. He lost his father, Logan!" Hana saw her mistake as his pupils flared a dangerous slate grey. His thigh muscles tensed beneath her.

"Yeah." The single word condemned her along with his family.

"Logan," Hana breathed. "I know you lost out too. You lost both parents and your relationship with Alfred is now strained."

"Strained!" Logan snorted the word, his teeth gritted. "It's destroyed."

"I'm sorry, I'm sorry." Hana stroked his cheeks with her fingers, seeing the agony blossoming in his eyes. "How can I make it better? What can I do?"

Logan cupped the back of her neck in his hand, pulling her close so he could kiss her. "Make me forget," he whispered, reaching for her bra clasp with the other hand. He pressed his face into the soft skin of her neck and sighed with relief at the familiar tightness in his trousers, glad not every part of him was broken.

"No more secrets," he breathed as he slipped Hana's tee shirt over her head and bowed to kiss the soft curve of her breasts. "Promise?"

Chapter 11

"Caroline came to see me again." Logan spoke the words into the darkness, the kitchen chair rejected in favour of the wide four-poster bed. Hana tensed next to him, acid churning her stomach with instant nausea.

"Why?" She tried to speak through gritted teeth, the effect producing a strange muffling of her voice.

Logan sighed. "She still wants to stay in the motel units with Nev's family. I told her no."

Hana breathed in through her nose and out through her mouth. She'd heard it assisted stress relief but saw no immediate relief. "I assume she dressed to kill and made another pass at you." Her tone sounded flat.

"Yep. You remember her well." Hana sensed his confusion, the confession not eliciting the desired response. He wanted praise for his honesty, receiving antagonism instead. She rallied, making her voice sound less threatened and more confident.

"Thanks for telling me," she managed.

"The insurance company is building a new homestead at the bottom of the mountain. Nobody wants to live on the old site. It's still tapu."

Hana nodded against Logan's shoulder, her mind straying to the Māori prayers said over the fire site.

Death made it sacred and the local kaumatua had walked the area with Logan, blessing it and offering comfort. "I thought the old man removed it," she mused, remembering his crinkled olive face and kind eyes.

Logan shook his head and his hair made a sound against the pillow. "I want it to remain sacred," he replied. "I need somewhere to grieve."

Hana sensed his tension and rolled onto her stomach. Her fingers strayed to the downy hair on his chest. "You argued with Caroline, didn't you?"

"Yep. She always knew, Hana. All those years, she knew he was my dad. I almost married her. She's such a liar!"

"What did she say?" Hana didn't want the verbatim account, but Logan's candidness wouldn't last and she sought to extend it.

"She called Reuben, Dad." His teeth ground in the darkness. "He wasn't her dad."

Hana closed her eyes and swallowed. She understood his need for cruelty, but regretted him venting it. "You said that?"

"Yeah. But don't worry about her feelings, Hana. She said it honoured her that he chose to raise her and didn't do likewise for me."

"Ouch." Hana winced, relieved she hadn't witnessed the clash of two formidable forces of nature. "Why does she want to stay with Nev so badly?"

Logan snorted. "She doesn't. She gives Kane the occasional shag to keep him sweet, Hana. She always has, but that's another thing I proved too stupid to see." He shivered. "If you ever doubt my intentions towards her, just imagine how it feels knowing I unwittingly shared her with two of my brothers. If that doesn't knock you sick, I don't know what will."

"Logan stop," Hana breathed. "Stop torturing yourself. You have me now. And Phoe. Let the past go or it will eat you alive. I know that because I've given mine way too much power and it didn't deserve so much control."

Logan kissed her temple and played with a lock of red hair. "I love everything about you," he mused and she snickered. "No, I do, Hana. Please believe me for once. I'm grateful I stumbled across you twenty-six years after first seeing you. I wish I hadn't wasted years of my life scouring England, but having you now makes it worth it." Logan fixated on the lock of hair as it glistened and changed colour in the lamplight.

"Well, you looked in the wrong place," Hana sighed. "You should've just come home sooner."

Logan shook his head, remembering the wasted hours riding the London tube trains and dreaming of life with his soul mate. "Ain't that the truth," he whispered.

"I went back to the unit again," Hana said, feeling him descend into sadness. Her baby nestled into her breast and fed herself to sleep.

Logan caressed Hana's upper arm with his fingers and felt the spark begin again. "Can you put Phoe down?" His voice sounded husky and Hana smirked.

"In a minute. I said I went to the unit today."

"How's it going?" Logan tried to sound interested, scooping Hana's hair behind her neck and running his fingers up the back of her head in a gentle massage.

"Good." Hana moaned as his lips worked the soft skin beneath her ear. "What do you think's going on there?"

"They should've ripped out the furniture and started on the fittings," he whispered into the shell of her ear.

"Not that. I mean the trouble with the boarding house finances. What do you think's happening?"

"Someone's got their fingers in the cash register," he breathed.

"That's what Angus suggested. He said the books are with the auditors so I guess he'll know soon."

"Hana, the baby's asleep." Logan pressed his lips over hers. "Put her to bed."

"Okay." Hana's eyelashes fluttered against her cheeks. She tipped the child from her breast, leaving the supple roundness exposed. Logan groaned.

"And hurry up."

The telephone trilled from the hallway and Phoenix disturbed with a wail of indignation. Her arms flung out wide in alarm. Logan swore and stalked towards the door. He returned with the handset and passed it to Hana. He raised his eyebrows as she reached for it with a shaking hand.

"Hello?" She turned away, praying it wasn't Laval. Having failed to reach her on her cell phone, it stood to reason he'd try the house.

"Hey." Her son's voice sent the adrenaline in retreat and left her knees knocking. She sat on the bed, aware of her watchful husband behind her.

"Oh, Bo," gushed Hana, her answer high and forced. "I'm glad it's you. How are Jas and Amy?"

The baby's head lolled back and a line of milk ran from the corner of her mouth into the neck of her cardigan. Logan scooped her up and put her over his shoulder, patting her back to bring up the wind. She settled, nestling her soft face into his neck. He whispered to her in Māori, ensuring the continuance of his legacy and his private gift to her. "Parangia, little one," he whispered. "Sleep time. I have a date with your mama."

"Hang on." Hana used the opportunity to pull on a robe and escape to the lounge. The last thing she needed was Logan hearing her beg for self-defence lessons.

Bodie sounded tired and irritated. "Why are you asking about Jas and Amy? You just talked to them. I'm sure you got the same story I did about disappearing up his teacher's butt. Hurry up, Mum. I'm on a break and Amy left a message saying you wanted to talk."

"Sorry, reflex action." Hana pursed her lips and felt her heart rate rise. "Sorry," she said again.

Logan clattered around in the kitchen and Hana heard him making tea. She seized her moment as Bodie finished a Jas type tale about a work situation. "So I arrested him," he concluded and Hana toyed with the idea of clapping, though she didn't know who he'd arrested or why. She bit her lip and launched.

"I'd love more self-defence lessons," she began, pausing to make herself sound more casual. "I enjoyed them and am keen to continue."

Bodie let out a snort. "You said I almost broke your wrist and called me a rubbish teacher!"

Hana winced. "Yeah, but it turns out you were pretty thorough. I'd like some more." Her mind flashed to the effective shin stomp and the move with the heel of her hand. She needed to protect her husband and child. Somehow. Even if her hand felt a little bruised afterwards. The overwhelming need to confide in her son reared its head, promising an end to her isolation. But Laval's threat resonated again. The man's evil electricity seemed to stretch out to reach her as she recalled the piercing brown eyes which stunned her into immobility. He was a deceiver and a master craftsman.

Bodie sighed on the other end of the line. "Is something wrong, Mum? Amy said I should call you and not wait until tomorrow."

"I'm fine." Hana forced brightness into her voice. "It's okay if you don't want to do it."

"I'll do it." Bodie forced a sigh. "But I want witnesses to your brutality this time." He made the joke but Hana barely cracked a smile.

"Thank you," she whispered. "I should help Logan with the baby," she lied.

Logan made Hana forget her problems, teasing her until she reached overload. His skilled hands and lips enjoyed her, banishing her frightened thoughts. "Nobody ever made me feel like you do," he breathed, pulling her on top of him.

"Good!" She giggled. "Let's keep it that way." Her lips sought his and she caressed his tongue with hers, feeling his body tense. His muscular arms pinned her to his body, enjoying her soft curves and exploring with gentle fingers. Hana squeaked as he rolled her over, crushed beneath him.

But her brain went into overdrive afterwards, keeping her awake long after Logan slept. She made and discarded plans, ran scenarios through her mind and mostly fretted. None of her careful set ups seemed feasible and she fell asleep disappointed with her progress. Phoenix woke once for a feed, but when Hana heard the alarm clock chirp at six o'clock, it was as though her head only just touched the pillow.

"Ugh! You've got cold hands," Logan complained as Hana ran soft fingers over his brawny torso and rubbed her icy feet against his legs. "Stop it, wahine," he groaned. Logan turned over in the small space at the edge of the bed, falling backwards as he overestimated and landed on the cold wooden floor.

"Logan! I'm sorry!" Hana peeped over the edge of the mattress to find him sprawled on the bedside rug. When he didn't move, she panicked, darting from the bed naked and throwing herself on the floorboards next to him. "Logan!" her voice emerged as a strangled wail. "Logan, please talk to me!" She ran her hands over his head, the dangers of injury for a haemophiliac trooping past as a list on the conveyor belt in her brain.

"Got ya!" Logan grabbed her shoulders and pulled her down, kissing her hard on the mouth. She felt his lips curling into a smirk and temper flared to replace the fear.

"Not funny!" she snapped, tears pricking behind her eyelids. "I thought you were hurt." She crawled back under the duvet, lying longwise across the bed and pressing the palms of her hands into her eyes.

"Sorry." Logan sounded chastened. "Let me make it up to you." He ran a hand beneath the sheets to snake up the inside of her thigh.

Hana brushed him away. "No!" Her voice hitched. "You'll be late for work." She battled the awful sensation of loss as the adrenaline withdrew to leave her shaking. The silly trick reminded her of Laval's threats and she knew with a certainty she couldn't bear to lose her husband.

"It was a stupid joke, Hana. Sorry." Logan's footsteps pattered away and Hana heard him speaking to his daughter. She pressed her face into Logan's pillow, recognising the fragrance of her fruity conditioner overlaying his masculine summery scent.

Hana pulled herself together before he reappeared in the bedroom. He carried a cup of tea in one hand and a stinky, singing baby balanced over his shoulder. "Chuck her here and I'll feed her," she said, plumping pillows behind her and pushing herself upright.

Logan shook his head. "Na," he said, "she stinks. It's gone up her back, look." He spun Phoenix around and Hana saw the greenish stripe up the back of her sleep-suit. "You can grab the first shower." He smiled, bed tussled and handsome as he offered her an olive branch. Hana snatched it and retreated to despair in peace under the hot water.

By the time she reappeared, Logan had dressed Phoenix and attempted to button his shirt as she grizzled on the bed. Guilt sent darts of pain into Hana's chest as she faced the consequences of the extra time she'd taken. "Sorry," she huffed, stuffing her feet into knickers and dropping her damp towel on the floor near the door. Hearing her voice, Phoenix ramped up the grizzling to a pitiful wail as her food source ignored her.

Hana curbed her irritation as she yanked a cotton tee shirt over her head and felt her wet hair create a damp patch between her shoulder blades. She settled herself against the headboard and reached for the child, feeling Logan's gaze burning into her flesh. "What?" she snapped. "I wanted to wash my hair, so I took a little longer. I said I'm sorry."

Logan watched as his daughter bashed her tiny face against Hana's breast until she found the nipple. She stilled the instant the first milk released. He rested a hand on the bedpost nearest Hana, drawing his free thumb across the space above his top lip. "Are you mad at me?" His brows knitted at the swift shake of her head. His jaw tightened and he studied Hana with his intense, smoke grey eyes. "Hana!" She jumped and the baby's arms flung wide in a fear reflex. Hana swallowed, unable to meet Logan's expert inquisitorial gaze. Laval's threats bubbled up in her chest and she sensed the whole thing preparing to spill out like a burst dam.

"No. I'm fine," she lied.

"So, we're good?" he probed. "You're happy with me."

Hana swallowed. "Why would you even ask that? Don't I seem happy?" She fixed a fake grin on her face and saw the doubt in his eyes.

"Not really." He raised a hand to pre-empt the inevitable complaints about the staff unit. "We'll get the unit fixed and I'll sort out the boarding house. That's nothing. As long as we're okay."

Hana released her held breath and squared her shoulders. "We're good, Logan. I just feel a little wrong footed sometimes. It's not how I imagined my forties would be, but I'm not sorry. I'm grateful."

Logan gave his characteristic lopsided smile and the vulnerability Hana saw there hardened her resolve to deal with Laval alone. "I never expected to have children." Logan's busy fingers picked at a knot in the wood. "I sometimes wish I'd delivered an instruction manual instead of a placenta."

Hana winced at the memory of Phoenix's mountain top birth. "You'd have buried that under the kauri tree too. Then where would we be?"

Logan kept his gaze fixed on the side of her face and she suspected he saw right through her pretence. "Jack said my grandmother buried mine right there in the same spot. He rode up with her. Weird and spooky, huh?"

"Are we talking about the instruction manual or the placenta?" Hana joked. "Because if it's the manual, it explains a lot."

Logan stretched, reaching his long arms high and gripping the side of the canopy above Hana's head. "Placenta," he replied, as though he believed she wanted an answer. Thoughts of his birth took him to memories of his mother and his expression darkened.

"You should speak to Alfred," Hana whispered. "He'd probably appreciate the opportunity to talk."

"Na, thanks." Logan tucked his shirt into his pants and buckled his belt. "He had the summer to do that and chose not to. I thought he loved me, but maybe he's just glad the pretence is over. If his agenda was to keep Reuben away from me, he succeeded. My father's dead and I'll never know how he felt about me, thanks to Alfred."

Hana winced. "It's possible he and Miriam did what they believed was best."

"I'll be fine." Logan ground his teeth and faked bravado. "I've got my own family. That's all I need."

Hana nodded, a wave of terror riding her soul. "You ran into the fire," she whispered. "What if you'd died too?" Her chin wobbled and she squeezed her eyes shut to stem the burgeoning tears.

"Sorry." Logan soothed. He crouched down next to her. "It was a gut reaction thing. I saw Ma running towards the flames and took off after her." He ran a hand over his eyes and squeezed the bridge of his nose. "The irony kills me, Hana. Every bloody day. She ran to him and away from us. Just like always. Why didn't I ever see it?"

"Stop." Hana wrapped an arm around his neck and kissed his temple. "They caused this but we'll find a way through it." She knew she should let him talk and that recollection might bring healing. But the clenching of her heart willed him to stop. She didn't want her mind to return to the sound of cracking timber and his mother's final screams. For the first time in their marriage, she resisted the baring of Logan's soul, the irony not wasted on her.

"Get on with your breakfast, nosey." Logan grinned at his daughter as she popped her head from underneath Hana's shirt. He stood and the painful moment died.

In the kitchen, Hana balanced her daughter in one arm and shovelled toast into her mouth with her free hand. "There's a festival on at Hamilton Gardens this weekend," she mumbled. "You must be due a free weekend. Wanna go?"

Logan shook his head. "I need to go back to the hotel."

"Oh." She swallowed, feeling her lightness of soul diminish. "Why?"

"Dad." He paused and corrected himself. "Alfred didn't take the beef to market last week, so I lost a heap of money. I need to talk to Jack and Toby and create a contingency plan."

"Okay." Hana drew the word out as her mind whirred. She could withdraw her witness statement against Laval and then skip town. Easy. "I've got errands to run. If you leave me the Honda, I'll make sure I'm ready to leave as soon as you get home."

"I don't feel like using the bike today." Logan wrinkled his nose and Hana held her ground. She needed to drive to the police station.

"What about your truck?" She ditched the last of her toast into the dustbin as her appetite receded. "You said you'd get it fixed."

Logan shrugged. "I don't want to think about it." A vein ticked in his neck and Hana narrowed her eyes.

"Is it because it broke down right when you needed it?" she asked, remembering Logan's fury as a major part blew up and left him stranded on the Hamilton expressway during their first week back.

He ground his teeth and ignored the question, the answer straying too near the issue of the inanimate object's betrayal. It went on the long list of things and people who'd let him down. "Please can you drop me at school?" he asked. "But I need to leave soon."

Hana nodded and glanced down at the baby. She'd fallen asleep on the breast and her head lolled back, a contented expression on her olive face. "I'm almost ready, look. Mrs Bugle-bum's done."

Logan nodded and let his toast slide off the plate and into the bin. "Thanks. Ready whenever you are."

Hana saw the action and her heart tightened in her chest. The urge to tell him about Michael Laval's threats reared its head and then faded. A smattering of grey hair in Logan's sideburns became more pronounced with each passing day, the stress of Miriam's lies and subsequent death seeming to unleash time on his physical appearance. He ate little, exercised like a maniac and yet peace still eluded him. Hana sighed. "Take the baby and I'll grab a bag with some bits for her."

She dragged her feet, snatching up nappies and wipes and stuffing them into the huge bag she used for baby paraphernalia. The clock ticked on and the moment arrived, demanding she visit the police station and wreak a havoc she couldn't avoid.

Logan drove to school and parked in the front car park. Hana eyed the space beside them, jumping when Logan repeated his question. "I asked if you wanted to meet at lunchtime," he said. "We can sit in the staffroom or go to my office."

Hana didn't want to hang around her former workplace like a reject groupie, but the sadness in Logan's face pricked her conscience and she agreed to meet him for the start of lunch at a quarter to one. He smiled and leaned across to kiss her, lingering as though he didn't want to leave. Hana stroked his cheek and tried to infuse him with love and sincerity. "Have a good day, babe. Go change some lives."

Logan left the vehicle, closing the door with a click. Hana waved and climbed across the centre gap, checking her baby in the back seat. Phoenix slept, her full tummy rising and falling under the restraint straps. Hana smiled at her gentle snores. She settled into the driver's seat and started the engine, changing the mirrors and seat position after Logan's long-legs. A gentle breeze coasted through her open window and promised another balmy day. Reversing out of the space, she pushed the gear lever into drive.

An oncoming vehicle nosed into the gap between Hana's car and the narrow exit, blocking her way. It eased through, wing mirrors almost touching. Hana slammed on the brakes, unable to see the driver through the tinted windows of the expensive SUV but cursing him, anyway. The driver's window slid open. Hana stared into Michael Laval's face and her breath caught in her throat. "Hey gorgeous," he mouthed, winking at her in a guise of friendship. "Ready to play?"

Hana gaped, words abandoning her. She scrabbled at the switch to raise the glass between them, her fingers missing in her haste and lowering the back window instead. Laval looked handsome, his suit and tie deceptively innocuous. The light grey pinstripe oozed no-expense-spared and his shirt collar looked crisply ironed. "Move your car!" she hissed, glancing around the empty car park.

He smiled. "Don't be like that, beautiful. When do you plan to do as you were told?" His words and facial expression didn't match. They contained a threat, yet his eyes appraised her in the same way she'd seen Logan assess a new foal. Interest. Curiosity. Reserving judgement.

Hana pressed the gas pedal and revved the engine, inching her car towards his expensive side panel. Laval held her gaze, almost daring her to crunch her bumper into the side of the gleaming metal work. At the last moment, he grinned and spun his vehicle forward. It nosed into a vacant space marked as belonging to the deputy principal and Hana panicked as the white reverse lights flashed.

Not giving him another opportunity to roast her further, she floored the gas pedal and the wheels scrabbled on the hot surface. They squealed and gained traction, shooting her towards the gate house and the main road. Two plodding boys leapt out of her way and she fled onto Maui Street without checking the road. A bus driver honked his horn and she apologised with a shaking hand. "He's crazy," she hissed to herself as her fingers found the button to raise the side window.

Hana drove to the police station in central Hamilton. She banged the steering wheel in frustration as a smaller car nipped into the last parking spot out front. Calming herself in a side road, she braved the rush hour traffic and drove back across the river bridge to park behind a popular cafe. Dragging her pram from the boot, she fixed the car seat containing the sleeping baby into the frame. "Stay asleep please Phoe," she begged her daughter. She covered her with a blanket to stop the early morning coolness disturbing her. The hands on her watch predicted she'd arrive too early to find Detective Sergeant Odering at his desk and a sign in front of her vehicle informed her only customers could leave their cars.

Relenting, Hana treated herself to a coffee, got permission to leave her vehicle for an hour and then pushed the pram across the bridge into town. The cars passed her in a steady stream of heat and exhaust fumes and her flesh crept at the thought Laval probably had her under surveillance. Using the ramp to the main doors and with her nerves frayed after a torturous walk, Hana clattered into the empty waiting area. A uniformed officer sat at the front desk behind protective glass and Hana asked to see Odering. The woman muttered something and she dipped closer to the holes in the glass. "I'm sorry, I can't hear you." She raised her voice as the woman's lips moved. "Please can I see Detective Sergeant Odering? It's urgent."

The woman humphed. "He's not answering his phone," she mouthed and Hana bridled.

"You haven't tried it yet!" Defeated, she turned away and sat on the uncomfortable plastic seating. A ripped poster fluttered in the breeze from an overhead fan. Rocking the pram to encourage Phoenix to stay asleep, Hana felt her heart rate hike as the minutes ticked past.

"Well, this is a lovely surprise." Odering appeared from a security door and greeted her with warmth. "How can I help you, Mrs Du Rose?"

Hana glanced at the woman behind the glass and saw her pushing paperwork towards a couple leaned against the counter. She licked her lips and paused. "Is there somewhere we can talk?" she whispered.

Odering frowned and nodded. He turned and led her through the heavy door and into the bowels of the police headquarters. Hana lost count of the number of corridors they crossed. "Take a seat," he said, waiting for her to settle the pram in his tiny office. He pushed the door closed. He walked behind a desk littered with paperwork and folded himself into a chair which spun as he sat. "How can I help you?" he asked, his voice light and pleasant.

Hana blanched at his kindness, knowing she would ruin his day and possibly even his year. She took a deep breath and released the words she'd practiced in her head. "I'm withdrawing my witness statement from last year." She folded her top lip under her teeth and tried not to show her terror. Inside her chest, her heart beat an unhealthy tattoo and her vision swam.

Odering leaned back in his seat and studied her long enough for it to become uncomfortable. The creak of his chair provided the only sound in the stuffy room. Hana fiddled with a clip on the pram and braced herself for the detective to start shouting. She knew he would and tensed, waiting.

Odering didn't shout. His face expression remained the same, his head cocked to offer a hint of suspicion. When Hana peeked from beneath her eyelashes, she found him still reviewing her through eyes which contained far too much perception. Claustrophobia hit her, bringing breathlessness with it. The window behind Odering faced the brick wall of another building and the strip lighting cast harsh, unforgiving tones across her pale complexion. Hana stood, keeping her hand on the pram handle. "My parking is running out. Just give me something to sign and let me go, please?"

She worked her jaw until it ached, seeing Odering lean forward in his seat and still waiting for the rebuke. He reached beneath the paperwork mountain and his fingers emerged with a pack of bright pink post-it notes. He leaned across and slapped it in front of her, adding a pen he found in a drawer. Hana's breath came in heaves as he smiled at her. She couldn't read his expression.

"Pop your signature on there then," he said, "and I'll deal with it."

Hana eyed him with wariness before seizing the pen and scribbling her signature on the pink paper. Her hand shook and the nib slipped against the shiny surface. It didn't look like her name and she swallowed and dropped the pen. Her fingers trembled on the pram handle and she edged it towards the door. "Please can you show me how to get back to the reception area?" she asked, her voice over loud in the small room.

Odering remained seated, observing her as though she was a specimen under a microscope. Hana jumped as he leaned across the desk and seized the pad and pen. He said her name, "Hana Du Rose," but nothing else. He threw the pen back into the desk drawer as though he'd like to bury her with it and then studied her signature on the pad with frightening intensity.

She drew in a sharp intake of breath as he screwed it into a tight ball and lobbed it into a dustbin next to the door. It bounced once against the metal frame and then rolled inside. Hana swallowed again, hearing the dryness of her throat. Her hand shook on the pram handle and desperation coursed through her blood. "I need to go," she croaked.

The memory of Laval's casual smile invaded her brain and Hana squeezed her eyes closed. She lectured herself inside her head, urging herself to get a grip and stop giving her fear away to the last person who should see it. Odering startled her, leaning back with a grunt and clasping his hands behind his head. His rolled shirt sleeves displayed tanned forearms. "Please," she pleaded, "I have to do this."

Odering popped forward in his chair, resting his forearms on the desk. "Should I get someone from Witness Protection to talk to you?" His voice sounded gentle and Hana's insides quailed. She didn't deserve his kindness. He was asking her if she needed help and everything inside her screamed yes.

Instead, she stamped her foot like a child, a flush of embarrassment gracing her cheeks at her irrational behaviour. Laval would hurt Logan. Hana didn't doubt he'd keep his promise. "No! I need to retract my statement. I can't give evidence against Laval. Won't! I won't do it!" She changed the wording too late and heard Odering sigh.

Phoenix moved in the pram and Hana looked down at her. Her daughter stared back, her eyes focussed and knowing. With irises as grey as the colour of grit, she studied her mother and pursed her lips. Hana gasped, wondering when they changed from blue to the characteristic Du Rose grey. Logan stared at her from his daughter's face and a wave of terror lit Hana from the inside out. She'd failed. At everything.

Gritting her teeth, she wrenched open the door. Odering's expression morphed into a sneer and she couldn't contain her misery. She pushed the pram too hard and it slammed into the wall opposite the door. A lump of plaster cascaded to the worn carpet, taking a shower of dust with it. Hana held her breath and yanked on the handle, seeing her daughter wobble in the seat and spread her arms in alarm.

"Hana." She tried to shake off the hand on her shoulder, but Odering's grip proved solid. The fingers of his other hand closed over hers and he tugged the pram handle. "Don't make me arrest you," he breathed. "You know I will."

Her heart froze and her breathing hitched as the next influx of oxygen seemed too little to keep her brain functioning. Odering's iron grip crushed her fingers against the pram handle and pulled her back into the office. He closed the door and faced her. "What's going on, Hana?" he demanded. He waved a hand towards the chair opposite his desk, but she shook her head and refused to sit.

"I need to go," she breathed. "Please, let me go."

"No." He shook his head and folded his arms.

"You don't understand," Hana repeated. "I have to do this!" She shot a glance at the pram as Phoenix waved her arms and let out a tiny wail.

"It's not that simple," Odering persisted. "The prosecution will still call you as a witness, but they'll treat you as hostile. That's all that will change."

Hana ran her hand over her face. "It's not fair," she gasped. "You don't understand!"

"Then help me!" Odering shouted, snapping at last. He towered over Hana, his height threatening. "Help me, Hana!"

She stood still, her fingers itching to pick up Phoenix as she opened her tiny mouth to protest. "No, just let me go." A sob punctuated her sentence. "You can't keep me here."

"Let's play twenty questions," Odering suggested. He took a step back to lessen the sense of aggression. "If you don't want to answer, you can pass, but then you have to answer the following one. Deal?"

Hana ran her free hand over her forehead, sweating despite the chill in her bones. Phoenix thrashed around in the pram. She nodded, darting a glance at the door and weighing up her chance of escape before the car clampers towed her car.

"Okay." Odering folded his arms across his chest and moved aside, perching his backside on the corner of his desk. Hana tracked his movements with her eyes and put both hands on the pram handle as though under starter's orders. "First question, does Logan know you're here?"

Hana shook her head, her eyes wide with fear. "No!" she shrieked. "And he mustn't!"

"Okay," countered Odering. He sniffed like a dog scenting the air. "Are you in danger?"

"Yes," Hana replied. "No." She revised her answer. "Not yet."

Odering nodded. "Is someone else in danger?"

She cringed and listened to the sounds of the police station. Doors banged and people chatted in the corridor. The floor plan presented itself like a maze in her mind and panic rose to the fore. Her knuckles whitened on the pram handle and she floundered, finding she couldn't answer.

"You can pass if you want," Odering offered, his trap complete.

Hana's green eyes glared at him, projecting enough anger to melt him on the spot. "But then you'll ask it another way round and make me tell you. And I can't!" Hysteria filled her chest and the walls closed in until she couldn't breathe. "You can't help me. Nobody can!"

Chapter 12

Despite having held it together for the last twenty-four hours, Hana fought tears rubbing near the surface of her eyelids and her resolve snapped. Keeping Phoenix over her shoulder, she wrenched the door open and rammed the pram through, hitting the wall on the other side of the hallway. She wheeled from the room trying to retrace her steps but getting lost inside the enormous police station. "Please, can you help me find the exit?" she sniffed to a male police officer in full anti-stab vest and a tool belt.

"Sure, love," he said with a pleasant smile. He led her to the main office, letting her out through the heavy door into the waiting area.

Hana looked back as she shoved the pram down the steep ramp and saw Odering watching her through the glass security door. He studied her, his face unreadable and his hands stuffed into his trouser pockets. He looked like a man casually waiting for a bus, not someone watching his star witness running away from her responsibility.

"Sorry," Hana whispered as a tear escaped onto her cheek. She brushed it away and jogged back along the bridge after settling Phoenix in the pram. The baby lay on her side beneath a light blanket, a thumb in her mouth and her left hand balled under her cheek. She embodied pure innocence and her fragility terrified Hana.

The cafe looked empty and Hana ordered herself another coffee, too shaky to drive. She tucked the pram into the corner and rocked it with her foot. The waitress cleaned the tables after the morning rush and Hana watched, desperate to distract herself from the misery and embarrassment of the last hour. Her coffee arrived and she burned her mouth in her haste. She pressed her fingers against the bridge of her nose, taking stock of her disastrous trip to the police station.

"Are you all right?" the waitress asked.

Hana jumped. "Yes thanks." She sniffed and dabbed her nose with a scratchy napkin. "I just made a dreadful mess of something."

The door opened and closed. Hana sensed a draught of warm air as someone entered. The waitress gave her a sympathetic look and dashed back to the counter. Embarrassed, Hana focussed on her coffee, resting her foot on the rung of the chair next to her. She gasped as the chair jerked backwards and took her leg with it. Her elbow knocked her cup, slopping coffee onto the table.

"So sorry," Laval whispered. His voice bounced with joviality and no hint of sorrow. Hana held her breath as he set the chair perpendicular with hers and sat.

"What are you doing?" Hana gasped. "Leave me alone." She searched the cafe for help. The pram blocked one escape route and Laval the other. He reached forward and with precise movements, mopped up her coffee spill with another napkin stolen from around the cutlery in the centre of the table.

"My apologies." He waved to the waitress and pointed to Hana's cup. "And a flat white for me, please," he asked, his voice silky smooth.

"Go away!" Hana hissed again when his stunning smile turned to her. He cocked his head to one side as though offended. When he reached out for her shaking hand,

Hana shoved his fingers away. She raised her voice, "Touch me and I'll scream!"

"Hana, Hana, Hana," he soothed, his blonde fringe sliding into his eyes. "Let's play nice." He opened his hands, palms upwards to negate the threat in his eyes. The moment felt surreal, as though Hana had stumbled into a strange dream she couldn't escape.

"Please, let me go?" she pleaded, her eyes wide. "Leave us alone."

"Where's the fun in that, darling?" He used the term of endearment as the waitress appeared with Hana's fresh coffee. The girl glanced at them both with a look of sympathy and Hana's heart sank.

A couple stepped into the cafe, keeping the door open as they took their time entering. The man looked familiar and Hana swallowed. Her brain slowed and the necessary words grew muddled in her head. She needed help, but fear of making a scene overrode good sense. The waitress returned with Laval's coffee. She whipped away Hana's spilled cup and its coffee filled saucer. Laval winked at her and the girl blushed. "Excuse me," Hana faltered, forcing the words onto her lips. "Please could you..."

"Fetch her a cookie," Laval interjected, hauling Hana's reluctant body into his side. He slid an arm around her shoulders. "She's hungry." He flashed his winning smile and fished in his jacket pocket with his spare hand. A twenty dollar note dropped onto the table. "Keep the change," he said.

The girl nodded and collected the note as Hana gave up hope of rescue. "Careful now, Hana," Laval whispered and placed a gentle kiss on her temple. Expensive aftershave shrouded her in a heady mix of musk and flora.

Hana stilled. His proximity terrified her and she wondered why nobody else in the cafe sensed the waves of misery emanating from her corner. The world seemed to stall as everyone else got on with their lives. The waitress let off steam from the coffee maker and the new couple chatted at a table nearby, their voices low and unhurried. Hana blinked as the waitress handed each of them coffee in a take away cup. She focussed on them as they continued to sit, sensing they might be her last hope. The pram rocked as she removed her foot from the axle and set it on the floor. Her fingers gripped the handle until her knuckles showed white. Laval gave her shoulder a squeeze and released it, believing the imminent danger gone.

He spoke in long sentences, but Hana didn't listen. She kept her gaze focussed on the table top and watched the couple in her peripheral vision. When they rose to leave, she intended to go too. Laval could either make a fuss or let her go. They continued to sit and with each passing moment, she lost a little more hope.

Hana jumped as the waitress delivered the cookie. She opened her mouth to speak but the girl focussed on Laval as he complimented her on the colour of her hair. Blushing, she hurried away. Laval smirked and placed a predatory hand on Hana's thigh under the table. Sex appeal oozed from him in waves and confused her. She became unsure of his real agenda and thoughts of Logan caused her to panic. "What do you want?" she hissed, pushing his hand off her thigh. He quirked an eyebrow as though appreciative of her spirit and Hana sensed she'd made things worse. Logan wooed and caressed the new horses before he placed the unwelcome saddle on their backs. If that was Laval's game, she'd watched it too often to let it break her.

"What do I want?" He cocked his head as he repeated her question. "What are you offering?"

"Nothing!" she hissed. Her fingers flexed on the pram handle and she decided not to wait for the couple to leave. Laval would win them over, like he did the waitress. A wink and a large tip. Sometimes that's all it took.

"You ignored my text." He placed his cup into its saucer and leaned back in his chair. Reaching out a hand, he placed it along the back of her chair and flicked a long, red curl. Hana leaned forward to avoid contact, realising too late he'd captured it and held on. The strand tugged at the roots and hurt. "Don't ignore me, Hana."

Panic surged into her throat and constricted her breathing. Even if she escaped with the pram, it required dismantling to get it into the car. He'd come after her. If she tried to run, she'd stand out and look like she'd stolen someone's baby. Her vision blurred as terror set in. "Leave me alone," she repeated. Her voice matched the tremor running through her body.

"What happened at the station?" Laval kept hold of her hair, his arm laid casually across the back of her chair. With his other hand, he reached for his coffee. "I hope you didn't report our little conversation."

Hana gritted her teeth. She'd had enough. "God help me," she muttered under her breath. She stood in a sudden rush, sacrificing the curl and feeling the burn as her head yanked backwards with the force of Laval's grip. Her fingers gripped the pram handle as she shoved it forward, crashing through the chairs and sending the table slewing sideways. Laval's coffee slopped onto his trousers and Hana heard him hiss with pain as the hot liquid bit his skin. The chairs scraped across the polished floor and Hana shoved her way through, keeping her focus on the door.

It opened inward as she reached it and she sent up a silent prayer for forgiveness as she kept going. A woman leapt back with an angry shout as the pram wheels just missed her toes. "Watch it!" she snapped, but Hana kept going. Once the wheels hit the car park, she ran.

With the click of a few buttons, the car seat detached. Hana contemplated abandoning the pram chassis. She depressed the button on her key fob, hearing the passenger door click as it unlocked. Phoenix woke as Hana shoved the car seat inside. She slammed the door without making the seat secure and glanced back at the cafe, relieved to see Laval hadn't followed. The couple had gone across to assist him and she saw him push the woman's hands away as she waved napkins in front of his face. His gaze strayed to Hana through the glass and she saw fury in his eyes.

The pram chassis went into the boot on its side, the wheels still spinning. Hana slammed the door and made it into the driver's seat, activating the central locking. Her chest heaved with exertion. The car started without fuss and the tyres squealed as she shot out of the car park into rush hour traffic. Turning left, she joined the fastest moving stream and crossed the bridge back into town. The car seat wobbled next to her and she put out a shaking hand to steady it. "I'm sorry, I'm sorry," she panted, seeing her daughter's dark brow furrow. Phoenix pushed a slender thumb into her mouth and sucked.

Hana passed the police station and the lights stopped her. She used the delay to lean across and fasten the belt around Phoenix's car seat. The filter light turned green and the cars next to her turned, giving her enough time to wrench her own into place. Her heart still pounded and adrenaline gave her a peculiar high. The hand which rubbed her eyes shook. "I can't do this," she hissed to herself. "I can't do it."

Hana drove around town for a while, hiding in a side street to fix the catches around the car seat properly. Ten o'clock found her hiding in a car park by the river to feed Phoenix. The sunshine heated the windscreen and flushed their cheeks, but Hana felt too scared to open the windows or leave the safety of the vehicle. She clambered over the gear stick to change the baby's nappy on the back seat and then cuddled her daughter, calmed by the child's steady breathing and the gentle thud of the tiny heart against Hana's shoulder. Without her phone she felt vulnerable and alone, outclassed and unable to summon help. "Who would I call, anyway?" she whispered into the side of her daughter's temple. No ready option presented itself.

Desperation drove her back to the school site. She'd promised to meet Logan during his lunch hour, so couldn't drive back to Culver's Cottage. The staff unit seemed the only sensible place to wait and Hana squeezed the car into the lane, hiding it between a kitchen fitter's truck and the painter's van. The sound of the rear gate sliding back into position behind her increased the sense of safety.

Phoenix slumped over her shoulder as Hana stepped through the open door. Her own stupidity slapped her in the face. The decrepit furniture had gone, tipped into a skip behind the unit. The walls and ceiling wore a pleasant ivory tint and the lingering smell of paint made her eyes water. "We can't stay here," she whispered.

"Oh." The voice behind her sent a shock wave through Hana's body and she jumped and screamed. Phoenix lifted her head and wailed without opening her eyes.

"Sorry." The painter took a step forward and raised his hand, putting it back by his side in response to the fear in Hana's expression. She swallowed and blinked, trying to relax the muscles of her face into a smile. She failed. "Don't you like it?" the man asked. He picked at a fleck of dried blue paint on his overalls and frowned. "Your husband said you would."

"I do. I do," Hana stammered. "I love it."

"But you still don't want to stay?" The man looked disappointed, his bushy brows furrowing into a heavy line. He seemed emotionally invested in her happiness, as though his involvement was more than just another painting job. Hana's heart fluttered and she could almost hear her husband's warning. Do a good job or else.

Hana struggled for control and ran a shaking hand over her eyes. "It's fine, I shouldn't be here. It's not your fault. I meant I can't stay here now. I'm just killing time between appointments." Killing time. Even the familiar cliché sent darts of warning through her nerve endings. "It's beautiful. I love it." She gave the man a fake smile and left, stumbling down the small steps onto the road. Outside, she lifted her face to the sky and forced herself to breathe.

"What do you think?" The voice came from behind her and Hana jumped again. Her tolerance at an end, Phoenix stuck out her bottom lip and wailed. Wet tears ran over her cheeks and Hana cuddled her close, resisting the urge to join in.

"Don't cry, baby, I'm sorry," she whispered. "I'm such a bad mother."

"I don't think so." Angus lowered his head to stare into Hana's face. His gaze sought an explanation for her jumpiness and she avoided his eyes, unable to offer the truth. "Take tea with me," he ordered. "I've some lovely wee Scottish shortbreads I'm willing to share." He slipped an arm around her shoulders and took a step towards the main building in the distance. Hana dug her heels in and resisted.

"I can't, Angus. Don't make me go over there at the moment. Please, I just can't."

Angus narrowed his eyes and gave a cursory nod. He turned towards St Bart's main entrance and nudged Hana along beside him. He nodded to the boys who passed them and glared at Chris Carter as the teacher admired his face in the mirrored glass surrounding the office. "Lazy git!" he snarled under his breath.

Once inside the safety of the boarding house, Hana relaxed. She allowed Angus to lead her to the upstairs level and the staff restroom which overlooked the gully behind the school. Sighing, she sank into a rickety sofa and felt her muscles ache as she breathed out the tension. The cushion tilted forward as though wanting to tip her off.

Angus dragged two mugs from a low cupboard and inspected them for stains. His nose wrinkled but he spooned coffee into one and stuffed a teabag into the other. Hana gazed around the room, comforted by the homely sounds of Angus clattering spoons and opening the fridge for milk.

"I've only been up here a few times," Hana remarked, patting Phoenix's back as the child settled over her shoulder with a sigh. "It hasn't changed much."

"You mean it's as bad as the staff units?" Angus huffed out a breath and set Hana's drink on a coffee table in front of her. He sank into a narrow sofa and winced. "Yes, it is."

"I thought you'd renovated it recently." Hana reached forward to hook her finger through the mug handle and gasped as it popped off in her hand. A glance at Angus saw him inspecting a dubious stain on the ceiling.

"We painted the dormitories over the summer." He flicked at a speck on the arm of the sofa and then peered at his fingernail with a look of disgust. Hana tried not to notice as he wiped his finger along the side panel. "The current financial difficulties halted work on the staff restroom."

Hana pursed her lips and touched the side of her mug, finding it too hot to hold without the handle. "I'm sorry, Angus. You've worked so hard to make this school the best in the north island. You must feel cheated."

He ran a hand through his red hair and winced. "That's a good word for it. Cheated. Yes, that's how it feels. I'm sure our Logan can uncover the root of the problem." His eyes narrowed and he focussed on Hana. "I'm sorry for the strain this situation has put you under."

She blinked and avoided his gaze. "What happens in those rooms?" Hana jabbed a finger towards three bedrooms with open doors. She saw the end of a single bed, noticeboard and desk in each.

"The staff on night duty use them. Two staff members do four-hour rotations." Angus sipped his tea and wrinkled his regal nose. "I do believe there are bits in this milk," he mused.

"Logan's rooms then." Hana heard the bite in her words and grimaced as Angus stared at her. "I don't imagine he gets much sleep."

"I'm sorry, Hana," he replied, understanding her inference. "He's proved kind enough to oblige me, yes."

"By living here every night?" Hana snorted out a bitter laugh. "Very obliging. It's not fair, Angus. You're breaking all kinds of laws, especially when you expect him to teach the next day."

"Matron helps." Angus frowned. "I know it's not ideal." As though summoned, the matron appeared. A gentle, motherly woman in her fifties, she winked at Hana and walked through the middle door. Fabric rustled as she changed the bed sheets and tidied the room. Hana heard a tut of irritation and saw her snatch the bin liner from the pail beneath the desk. She tied a knot in the top and left it by the door. Leaving with a bundle of laundry and the bag, she raised an eyebrow at Angus. He responded with a nod and Hana wondered at the hidden conversation behind their body language which evaded her. Something about the room had displeased the matron.

Angus leaned forward in his seat. The springs twanged at the movement. "What's wrong, Hana?" he demanded. As she opened her mouth to speak, he raised a hand still bearing a gold band on his ring finger. "I know things are tough with the staff unit and the tragedy with Logan's mother. But I also know you. I haven't seen you this twitchy since all that business last year with the man who kept following you. What was his name? Flick?"

Hana looked away, fixing her attention on the water heater attached to the kitchen wall. The red light on its cover shone on and off like a lighthouse as it reached temperature. "There's nothing else," she lied. The kindness in his expression forced guilt into her throat and her eyes watered.

"And Logan?" Angus pushed, his tone gentle. Bushy red eyebrows shrouded the understanding in his eyes.

At the thought of Logan, Hana cracked. He hadn't grieved for Miriam, keeping his emotions in a heart locked tighter than Pandora's box. She pursed her lips to keep the bubble of air in her chest from escaping but failed. Logan couldn't know about Laval's threats. She promised herself that she would fix things.

"Oh, Hana." Angus shifted to sit next to her and fixed an arm around her shoulders. "I can see you're struggling with something."

"Please don't ask me," she breathed. A tear slipped onto her cheek and she brushed it away. "I'm sorting it out myself."

"Can I help?" He bowed his head and reached forward to stroke the baby's soft cheek. "I'm quite unshakable."

Hana sniffed and allowed her lips to curve upwards in a smile. "I think Bodie and Marcus made sure of it." She wiped the back of her hand across her eyes.

"I've never felt so glad to shake hands with two leavers." Angus withdrew his arm and patted Hana's shoulder. "Little buggers." He rose to his feet and straightened his jacket. Concern still narrowed his eyes. "What about Logan. Have you spoken to him?"

"No!" Hana's eyes widened in alarm. "He mustn't know." She gathered the child to her and pushed herself from the sofa. The cushion listed in protest and sucked her in further. With a brave but undignified lurch, Hana dug herself out.

"We've been friends a long time." Angus scratched his chin and inhaled through flared nostrils. "I'd like to believe you could trust me."

"I do." Hana ground her teeth together and eyed the flashing fire exit sign above the doorway. It winked once more and then went out. "It's something I must fix myself. Nothing to worry about." She pushed aside thoughts of Michael Laval Junior and his terrifying brand of charm. "Everything will be fine," she promised, as much to convince herself as Angus.

"You'll like Amanda," Angus said, changing the conversation as they walked down the stairs. "I think you'll be great company for each other."

"Who's Amanda?" Hana hurried as a group of older boys waited at the bottom to pass.

"Chris Carter's wife. She's moving back in next door."

"Oh, yes." Hana winced at the memory of Logan splatting Chris Carter against the boarding house wall.

The noise level in the building rose as boys returned for morning interval. Male bodies poured through the front door, making it impossible for Hana to exit with a baby without creating a bottleneck. Angus cut a track through them and led Hana to the office. They took refuge inside and Hana sighed with relief at the absence of Chris Carter.

"This is clever." Hana spun in a circle to admire the four glass walls. Each offered a view of the boys' activities without them realising. The queue for the dining hall lengthened and several boys used the mirrored glass on the outside to straighten their hair or poke at their spots. Angus watched an older boy tuck a long, stringy piece of hair into his collar. "They must know we can see them."

"They get comfortable and forget. Such is the weakness of the human ego." He pointed at the boy with the string of hair as he pulled up his collar and hid the offending item inside. "I see Mr Yates is growing a rat's tail hairdo. That can come off before the end of today."

"It looks long." Hana moved closer to inspect the scene and Angus raised an eyebrow.

"I agree. Such contraventions remind me very much of trying to educate your husband."

Hana screwed up her pretty features. "I can't imagine Logan with a rat's tail."

Angus waggled his eyebrows. "No, but he broke just about every other rule. Apart from smoking, I hasten to add. Unless I never caught him."

Hana glanced at the nearest desk and smiled at the neat piles of paperwork. Logan's slanted writing adorned a sticky note. She reached out a hand and stroked the pen abandoned uppermost. Phoenix sighed and bobbed her head as Hana turned, both girls sensing the presence of Logan even before he walked into view.

He took even strides, his body language calm and unhurried. The two Year 10 boys who flanked him wore faces infused with rage and their steps appeared jerky and constrained. Logan's gaze moved towards the office, unaware of his audience behind the mirrored glass. They halted outside the dining room. Angus stood next to Hana and they watched as Logan bent towards the two sullen faces. His lips moved and he asked them a question. Both boys shrugged and Logan stood up straight. The boys watched through shuttered eyelashes as he leaned against the wall opposite. After a casual glance at his watch and a smile, Logan bent his left knee, placed the sole of his cowboy boot against the exposed brick and dug a stick of chewing gum from his jacket. Unwrapping it with meticulous care, he pushed the empty wrapper into his trouser pocket and slid the gum into his mouth. He checked his watch one more time, folded his arms, leaned his head back against the wall and closed his eyes. Only his jaw moved as he chewed.

"What is he doing?" Hana looked sideways at Angus for an answer and the principal grinned.

"Just watch," he replied.

The scene remained unchanged. Boys walked past them and Logan opened his eyes to acknowledge their greetings. His body position didn't change and he appeared as though prepared to stay there all day. His dark hair flopped into his eyes and Hana saw his muscles flex through the sleeves of his expensive fitted jacket. Logan Du Rose was a paradox, both casual and dangerous. Hana pitied the two boys as they shifted on their feet and showed too much interest in the various snacks drifting past their noses. Other boys gave them a wide berth and as the crowd dwindled, one waved his sumptuous cookie and shook his head. Hana read his lips well enough to know they were all gone. Logan remained in position, chewing his gum and staring at the ceiling.

He checked his watch as one boy's lips moved. Hana estimated no more than three minutes had passed and the cookie had something to do with the sudden urgency. The other boy opened his mouth in protest and Hana watched their hands wave at a furious rate. Logan watched them with indifference. She heard Angus give a low chuckle and turned. "How did he do that?" she demanded. "They cracked really fast. Bodie could hold out for weeks."

Angus regarded her with the expression of a benevolent uncle. "He's Logan Du Rose, Hana. Invincible, unfathomable and quite possibly a sociopath. He's doing what Logan does best; getting the answers he wants without fuss."

Hana frowned. "Do they teach that at training college then?" she asked, Angus' diagnosis of her husband's personality type nagging at her loyalty.

Angus put his head back and roared, his laughter making the baby jump and whimper. "I don't think so, my dear. He learned that trick from me!"

Chapter 13

Angus walked with Hana to the staff unit as the bell rang to mark the end of the morning interval. Boys poured from St Bart's and ran the few hundred metres to the main school, rucksacks bouncing on their backs as they shoved food into their mouths. They crossed the orchard like locusts and disappeared.

"What did you mean by your comment?" Hana asked, watching the exodus from the safety of the lane next to her car. Phoenix snoozed over her shoulder.

Angus leaned against Hana's car and smiled at a distant memory. "I once withdrew Logan from class during his time at the North Shore Grammar school. It was one of many such events. I'd heard rumours among the hostel staff and wanted the truth. As the Year 11 dean, I pulled the same moves you just witnessed. I hadn't realised Logan took so much notice of my strategies. It worked. He's obviously spent the last twenty years honing it to perfection. I must admit, I hadn't nailed the sexy element quite as well as him." Angus chuckled, his eyes glinting with pride.

"Why did you withdraw Logan from class?"

Angus' forehead creased in concentration and he pushed his bifocals higher up his pointed nose. "Let's see," he said, his Scots accent leaking through as a slow lilt. "Ah yes, I remember. His mother sent a bag of confectionary for his birthday, accompanied by a rather large cake. A man wearing a cowboy hat delivered it with a note. He created something of a scene, demanding to see Logan."

"Who was he?" Hana's eyes widened at the list of possibilities.

Angus shrugged. "Can't remember. Something biblical beginning with R if I recall. But every much a Du Rose as the rest of them."

"Reuben." Hana cringed. "The cake wasn't from his mother."

"No matter." Angus ploughed on, enjoying a chance to relive his youth. "There were strict rules about contacting home and unexpected visits didn't fit into their criteria. But that's not why he got into trouble. Instead of sharing his windfall appropriately, Logan sold everything piece by piece and made a profit." He sniggered. "Our Mr Du Rose has a head for enterprise. It wasn't a crime in itself, but a boy with a nasty wheat allergy ended up in the infirmary."

"Hardly Logan's fault." Hana bridled at the injustice. Her heart ached at Rueben's feeble attempt to contact his son.

"That's what Logan said." Angus waggled his eyebrows. "But no food should be consumed in the dormitories." He jabbed a finger in the air between them. "Rules are rules. I remember asking him why he needed the money. He said he intended to go back to England and mumbled something about a girl on a train. I got nothing else from him." Angus raised his eyebrows and observed Hana sideways.

"Oh." She sighed at the memory of the gangly teenager who fell in love with her on a tube train, even though she barely noticed him. Hana stared at the baby in her arms who twenty-six years later inherited those same intense grey eyes. Her voice sounded strained as she asked, "Did you punish him?"

Angus made a noise with his lips and ran a hand over his forehead. "Not that time," he said. "But it got our Mr Du Rose onto something of a business streak. He worked out the valuable commodities within our little community and then he sold them."

"What's wrong with that?" Hana screwed up her face in confusion.

"When you've marked the same person's homework under thirty different names, it stops being enterprising and becomes an irritant." The maths-teacher-turned-school-principal knitted his brows. "I drew the line at selling assignments. He was the most intelligent boy I've ever taught. He soaked up information like a sponge. It was little effort for him to write other people's homework as long as they paid the fee. Poetic letters to other boys' girlfriends became a specialty, I believe. I'm sure there were many young ladies in love with your husband, instead of the bumbling spotty young men who returned to them for the holidays!"

He laughed again and Hana smirked. "He's certainly progressed from selling cake."

"Yes, but what to?" Angus narrowed his eyes. "He didn't learn his business acumen. It's in his blood. Misdirected it can go very wrong. But you seem to have straightened him out at last." He turned to leave, waving behind him as he set off for the main school.

"Angus," Hana called, seeing him turn at the end of the lane. "How long did you wait before Logan cracked?"

Angus pulled a face and called back, "Four hours and forty-five bloody long minutes. I had a cramp in my legs by the end. I believe to this day he only gave in because he wanted his dinner." He set off walking and Hana heard him laugh to himself as he reached the green grass of the manicured cricket field. She bet the groundsman didn't rebuke him for traipsing over it.

"Not on the bloody crease!" she muttered in Larry Collins' deep voice.

With an hour to kill before she met Logan, Hana wasn't sure where to go. Another vehicle sat behind the painter's van. The front door of the adjacent unit stood wide open. A baby's car seat blocked the narrow hallway. Hana called out and knocked on the doorjamb. "Hello? Anyone home?"

A dark haired woman appeared, her eyes narrowed in suspicion. She had a pretty face but carried too much weight for her slender frame. Long eyelashes fluttered nervously at the sight of Hana. "What do you want?" she demanded, her tone hostile.

Hana swallowed and the ready smile faded from her lips. "Hi Amanda," she said, deciding Angus must be mistaken about them becoming friends. "I'm Hana Du Rose. My husband and I will move back in next door when it's finished. Angus told me to call and say hi." Hana's voice trailed away and she turned to leave, sensing the waves of unease coming from the other woman. "I'll come back another day. I can see you're busy."

The woman let out a huge breath and clasped her hands before her chest. "Sorry," she said, "I thought you might have been that bloody woman. Chris said she'd been hanging around. I don't think I can face her at the moment."

"Face who?" Hana asked, regretting the question the moment it left her mouth. Caroline. "Actually," she said with a wince, "don't answer that. I know who you mean."

"Come in, please." Amanda moved the car seat and pushed three suitcases aside. Clothing spewed from them as though they'd exploded in the centre of the small lounge. Hana stepped through the mess, waving away Amanda's excuses. "I'm still unpacking, but I'm sure I saw a set of mugs in here somewhere."

The car seat contained a baby girl of around a year old and she slept on the fringes of the mayhem. A blanket lay on the new laminate floor near a gas fire and a jungle gym arched over it. "Why don't you lay your baby underneath the gym? She's little but she might show an interest in the shapes and colours," Amanda suggested, indicating the yellow bridge with its dangly objects.

Phoenix woke as Hana laid her on the blanket. She stared at the shapes and waved her arms but they evaded her. She lost interest and closed her eyes again. Hana covered her sleeping baby with her cardigan before staring at the detritus strewn across the floor. "Why don't I help you?" she offered. "I've a spare hour before I need to leave." She knelt next to one of the open suitcases and began sorting baby clothes from adult-wear. After Amanda retreated along the hall, Hana rose and locked the front door, not wanting a visit from Caroline or Laval while her baby lay defenceless on the floor. Once she'd ordered the clothes into piles, she carried them to the bedroom for Amanda to put away. Then she went to work on the boxes of kitchen items. She unearthed the mugs, wrapped in bedding and towels.

"It looks like a home now," Amanda commented as they finished straightening the furniture. "It was such a dump when I left."

Hana slumped onto the comfy sofa, admiring the bold black pattern on a cream background. "Did you pick this?" she asked. "It looks expensive."

"No," Amanda answered, shaking her head. "Angus said your husband ordered everything. He has good taste. It must have cost a fortune. The bed's new and feels wonderful after that other disgusting thing." She paused in her task of filling the kettle. "We've unpacked the sheets, but I still need to make the bed before tonight. Otherwise I'll get busy with Millie and discover it still unmade just as I'm ready to fall into it."

"I'll do it," Hana offered, checking Phoenix and finding her still sleeping.

"Thanks." Amanda switched the kettle on to boil and retrieved the sheets and duvet cover from the back of an armchair. "It'll be quicker with your help."

"I met Chris yesterday," Hana said as they fitted pillowcases over the plump new pillows.

Amanda met her gaze with a look of sadness and betrayal. Her lips turned down at the corners. "I suppose you know what he did?" she said.

Hana shook her head. "I know what I've heard he did," she replied, "but I'm also aware of what a liar Caroline Marsh is!"

Amanda's eyes widened at the acid in Hana's tone. "Not you too," she said with a sigh. "She wasn't here long but I know of two other marriages she ruined."

"No." Hana grimaced. "But not because she didn't try. Logan knocked her back, so she caused other issues instead."

"I wish Chris had knocked her back." Amanda sighed. "I guess siding with his wife and new daughter proved too difficult for him."

Hana saw the rawness of her emotional scars in the way Amanda's body seemed to slump as she talked about the affair. She recognised them and knew they'd take longer to heal than any physical discomfort. She turned the conversation to cheerier things. "Angus spoke kindly of you. He sounded glad to have you moving back."

Amanda nodded. "Yes. He's a nice man. He didn't have to let me live here, not as Chris and I are still separated."

Hana agreed. "I've known him a long time and he's proved a loyal friend."

Amanda cocked her head like a pretty bird. "What's your story, Hana? How did you meet Logan and wind up living here?"

Hana shook her head. "I'd worked at the school for years before Logan arrived. We began a relationship, but then Caroline arrived in hot pursuit of him and did everything she could think of to wreck it."

They straightened the sheets and stood back to admire the room. Amanda touched Hana's elbow. "You deserve that cup of tea now." They returned to the kitchen and she boiled the kettle again, probing Hana for more information.

Hana sipped her drink and watched her baby sleep the slumber of the just. "I married young and my first husband died nine years ago in a road accident. Angus proved supportive back then and we stayed friends. He listened to my complaints when Caroline worked in my office and she tried to make life difficult. He gave me a fair hearing and I'm grateful for that."

"What sort of things did she do?" Amanda asked, settling on the floor with her back against the armchair. "Did she threaten you?"

Hana shook her head. "Not physically, although once it got close. But I saw her put her hands on Logan in the car park one night and they drove off together. I jumped to conclusions and assumed we'd finished. I bought a new car and a house. Then I got on with my life."

"Wow!" Amanda choked on her tea. "That was some shopping spree! Isn't he scared of upsetting you now?"

Hana laughed. "No. I spent my own money." Her brows narrowed at the memory of how she'd believed the worst of Logan. "I felt an idiot," she confessed. "I thought he'd strung me along."

"So, fast forward to now?" Amanda demanded. "You're married, with a baby."

"That's a really long story." Hana shook her head. "Logan's a persuasive man and doesn't take rejection well. Caroline proved to be a liar and I got over it."

Amanda's brows knitted and she gnawed her bottom lip. "I heard Logan got her pregnant," she whispered. "Please don't tell me it was Chris."

"No." Hana swallowed. "It wasn't. And the child didn't survive."

"Why is she back?" Amanda's voice sounded strained. "There's no hope for me and Chris if she's hanging about."

"If it's any comfort, she wants something from Logan. I think Chris is safe from her." Hana set her mug on the table.

Amanda shook her head. "Sorry, I don't know why I'm splurging my guts to you; we only just met."

Hana wrinkled her nose. "It's lonely here if you don't have a good friend. I know what it's like."

Amanda smiled. "Yeah well, everyone on site knows my business and I'm sure they still gossip about Chris and Caroline. It makes it hard to move forward."

"Just remember you can't believe everything you hear from Caroline," Hana replied. "She's a fantasist. Maybe Chris didn't do everything she said."

Amanda shook her head. "I've never met her. Chris got an official letter from the Board of Trustees just after I gave birth to Millie. It was a written warning because of his extramarital relations and claimed he'd contravened his contract. They called it, *'behaviour unbecoming a member of staff at a church school.'* It devastated me. I thought it was a bill and opened it. When he got home, we had a massive argument and he stormed. He didn't come back for days. Then he turned up with a love-bite on his neck and I left him. I've been living back with my parents in their two-bedroom unit. Chris didn't bother trying to see us for the first month."

Hana gave a sharp intake of breath. "What a git!"

"Yep," Amanda said with a nod. "You can say that again."

Hana smiled, desperate to lighten the mood. "What will you do?" she asked. "Will you forgive him?"

Amanda sighed. "I don't know. Angus offered me the unit during a visit a few days' ago. He's stayed in touch and called to see me every couple of months. I'd had an argument with my father when he turned up and he could see I'd been crying. He suggested I move back here once they finished the unit. But if my marriage is over, I've no reason to stay. Chris should be the one to live on site and I must find somewhere else to go. I don't want to get back with him for the wrong reasons. He hurt me so much. I'll never understand how he could do something so mean. Millie was premature and ill for the first few months. It makes me sick to think what he was up to while I struggled."

Hana nodded. "For what it's worth, Logan says Caroline can be very persuasive."

"Aren't you worried about her going after him again?"

"Yes," Hana admitted. "I am. But he seems genuinely revolted by her. He behaves as though he hates her. At a family funeral in the holidays, she tried to hug him in front of everyone. He looked like he wanted to vomit and shoved her away. I thought she'd get the message, but then she turned up here a few days ago and the uncertainty began again in the pit of my stomach."

Amanda laughed and covered her mouth with her hand. "You know what? Chris popped in to see Millie yesterday. He told me to stay away from you and Logan. He said you were trouble." Her brown eyes glittered in the sunlight. "I'm glad I ignored him. You seem like nice people. I'll love having you just next door."

Hana winced, figuring Chris hadn't told Amanda the full story of how Logan splatted him against the side of St Bart's. She glanced at her watch and her eyes widened in horror. "Oh no! I should have met Logan quarter of an hour ago!"

Amanda shrugged. "Can't you text him?"

"No," said Hana, guilt rising into her chest like a hard lump. "I lost my phone."

Amanda dug around in her handbag and pulled out hers. "Here," she said, "use mine."

A few minutes later, Amanda opened the door to the handsome Māori. He smiled and nodded to her, bending to get through the door and into the hallway. His shirt looked crisp and white and his trousers well-fitted. Hana's brow furrowed as her new friend checked him out with eyes which looked a little too hungry.

Logan's fringe hung over his eyes as he removed his cowboy boots and Amanda admired him from behind. Hana felt the shine of her new friendship dulling. Logan remained oblivious, kissing Hana's cheek and caressing her shoulder with his slender fingers. "Where's your phone, wahine?" he asked, his voice soft. "You stood me up."

"Sorry. I can't find it." Hana wrinkled her nose beneath his scrutiny. She fought the desire to bury herself in his arms and hide from Laval and the lies he forced her to tell. Her hands shook and she pushed them behind her back. "I've dropped it somewhere." She bit her lip against the half-truth. She'd dropped it, but missed out the important fact she did it on purpose. Logan shook his head in feigned irritation and smiled at Amanda.

Hana noticed Amanda appeared star struck, gaping like a fish as she watched Logan. It made her nervous and edgy. "Can I make you coffee?" Amanda offered and Logan turned his stunning grey eyes on her and nodded his acceptance.

"Thanks," he said with a smile.

Phoenix and Millie woke at the same time. Millie crawled around the floor, bouncing on her knees and whining for Amanda to cuddle her. She eyed the newcomers with suspicion, not convinced they wouldn't separate her from her only source of security.

Logan changed his daughter's dirty nappy, teasing Phoenix and making her smile. He blew raspberries on her tummy and rubbed her feet along his jaw line, rasping the stubble against her delicate skin. "Gorgeous kōtiro." He laughed as she screeched and pumped her fists.

Amanda stepped into a whole new world of trouble, falling in love with Logan Du Rose in under half an hour. She studied the stunning grey eyes which changed colour from smoke to grit depending on his mood and coveted his muscular physique. The whitening hairs in his sideburns made him appear distinguished and she imagined herself in Hana's place. Millie sat on Amanda's knee at the new dining room table, eating a sandwich while her mother picked at a slice of bread.

"You've gone very quiet," Hana said. She sat on the sofa breastfeeding Phoenix.

"Just thinking," Amanda replied. Logan's presence set her heart racing. She opened her mouth several times to speak, but nothing sensible emerged. Logan sat next to Hana and drank his coffee with increasing discomfort, not enjoying the female scrutiny. His presence filled the tiny unit as though his mana forced the walls to bulge outwards. Amanda tried to make small talk, but her conversation became self-deprecating. She referred to herself in negative terms as overweight, unsexy and stupid. Hana cringed at the familiar lack of confidence and sensed Logan looking for an easy escape.

"I'll head off," he said, pressing a kiss to Hana's forehead. "Thanks for the coffee." He put his cup in the sink and smiled at Amanda, dodging around her to grab his shoes and open the door. Amanda remained tongue-tied and offered a goofy wave of her hand in response.

Hana followed Logan to the front door, winding the baby over her shoulder. "See you later, babe," she whispered, raising her lips for a kiss. "Sorry about the phone."

"And standing me up!" He faked offence but ruined it with the twinkle in his eye.

"Yep, that too," Hana conceded. "I'm a rubbish wife."

"Liar! You're a gorgeous wife," he whispered. "I'll show you later."

"Aren't we leaving as soon as we get our stuff together?" Hana asked, knitting her brow and hoping he hadn't changed his mind about the hotel visit.

"Maybe," he replied and winked. He kissed Phoenix on the top of her fluffy head and grinned at Hana. "Think you can manage not to forget to pick me up at three thirty?"

Hana wrinkled her nose. "I didn't forget you, idiot! I got busy. You do it all the time."

"I love you," Logan whispered in her ear and kissed the side of her face. Hana held the baby one handed and used the other to trace the line of his shirt buttons. He whispered something sultry in her ear and raised his eyebrow. She giggled and kissed him again.

"You're a worry!" she chastised. With a covetous smile, Logan left.

Amanda seemed sombre as she sat at the dining table. Hana gave her an encouraging smile but sensed it was wasted. Eventually, Amanda jerked her head towards the front door. "Logan really loves you guys, doesn't he?"

"Yes, he does," Hana replied. She gazed down at her sleeping baby. "But our history stretches back over twenty-six years and it's complicated. We endured more in our first year together than many people do in a lifetime. Falling pregnant at forty-five is just a small part of the story."

Amanda nodded. "I'm thirty-seven and old enough to know better. I look at how Logan behaves with you and the fact is, I don't believe Chris ever loved me that much. Perhaps I'm wasting my time holding out any hope for my marriage."

Hana sighed. "Can't help you with that, sorry. Only you know the answer."

"I don't suppose Logan has a brother you could introduce me to?"

Hana took a gulp of air and gave a definitive shake of her head. "Michael Du Rose makes Chris' cheating look like a part-time hobby. And Kane? Don't even go there!"

Amanda turned towards her with a look of desperation widening her eyes. "Pity. I need to find a way to feel better about myself. Would you consider going for walks during the week? I can't face the school gym with Chris working there and I'd love to get fit with someone else." She glanced at Hana's slender figure and sighed, "Not that you need it."

Hana watched Amanda's animation grow. The woman sought solidarity with the hunger of the tide seeking the land. "Okay," she agreed. "I need the exercise. Having Phoe seems to have robbed my stamina. I find myself breathless after getting off the sofa." She grinned. "Let's start now."

The walk proved more sweaty than invigorating as the summer sun sapped their energy and left them panting. Humidity plastered their hair to their foreheads. Amanda showered in her new bathroom while Hana watched the babies, emerging pink and refreshed. "That new showerhead feels like a massage," she sighed. "Are you sure you don't want to borrow a towel?"

"No, thanks." Hana shook her head. "I won't want to get back into sweaty clothes."

"Can we go again on Monday?" Amanda asked and Hana agreed. She hid her pique at the larger woman's faster recovery time, putting the anomaly down to her age.

Phoenix snoozed in her car seat after a feed and Hana laid her head back against the driver's seat. She'd parked the nose of the car against the chapel wall to avoid drawing attention and used the seclusion to close her eyes for a moment. Logan knocking on the window made her start in alarm. Her heart felt like it might lurch from her chest. Shaking fingers pressed the button to deactivate the central locking.

Logan shoved his briefcase into the boot and slammed the door. Hana met him behind the vehicle. "Why did you lock it?" he asked, smoothing her brow with his thumb. A group of boys wolf whistled as he pressed his palm against her waist and kissed her with soft, gentle lips.

"By accident." Hana jerked her head towards the open driver's door. "Can you drive home? I walked with Amanda and the heat made me tired."

"I'm not surprised." Logan dragged his tie from his collar and undid the top button of his shirt. "It's airless." He climbed into the driver's seat and reached for his seatbelt. His gaze ran over Hana's flustered appearance. "You okay?"

"Fine. Just eager to get to the hotel." She reached for the air-conditioning vent as Logan fired up the engine, turning the blast into her face.

Logan steered onto the main road and pressed the gas pedal. "Amanda doesn't say much, does she?"

Hana sighed and watched Maui Street drift past. "Not when you're around, no. Like most women and female horses, she's bowled over by your animal magnetism and sex appeal."

Logan winked at her. "I can't help it, babe. That's perfection for ya."

Hana snorted and slapped his leg, choosing to ignore the arrogance intended to rile her. She closed her eyes but jerked as Logan stroked her thigh with his free hand. "I need to work next weekend," he said, his soothing tone meant to placate her.

Hana's heart sank and she felt the familiar constriction. "I'll stay at Culver's Cottage," she sighed, deciding in the moment. The gates and mountain would protect her.

"Nope." Logan shook his head and turned onto the expressway north. "The unit is almost finished. You can move back."

Hana groaned and Logan squeezed her thigh. "Don't make me," she begged.

"You've got a new buddy now. And the weekends are easy. We can have lunch together and I'll nip home for breaks."

Hana curled her lip back in annoyance. "Don't treat me like a child, Logan!"

"I didn't!" His eyes widened. "I'm just saying."

"Well, don't!" Hana turned her face to the window and stared at the countryside moving past at speed. The endless possibilities for Laval's interference ran through her mind like a horror movie.

At Culver's Cottage, Phoenix slept in her car seat while the adults shoved clean clothes into a suitcase. "I'll feed her before we leave," Hana said, stripping off her damp clothes and gathering them into a ball. "I can't believe I'm more unfit than Amanda," she sighed. Dumping the clothes into the laundry basket, she reached for her robe. Logan's fingers closed around hers.

"Wahine, you expect me to watch you run around naked and still listen to what you're saying?" He growled and nipped her neck. His shirt creased as he pulled her body against his.

"No, I stink!" she squeaked and Logan ignored her protest. He picked her up and tipped her onto the four-poster bed.

"Don't care," he whispered, stripping off his shirt. "A promise is a promise, Hana Du Rose." His fringe tickled her delicate skin as he dragged his lips over the soft curve of her stomach. She arched her back and moaned. Laval's threats lost their poignance for a moment as Logan distracted her with gentle lips and fingers.

"I love you so much," he breathed as they lay sated, arms and legs tangled on the bed. He kissed her bare neck and wrapped an arm around her waist. "You know that, don't you?"

Hana nodded, the euphoria of the temporary interlude slipping through her fingers like a mist. She hid her fear by pressing her face into Logan's chest and allowing the solidity of his torso to soothe her.

"I bought you something." He placed his fingers beneath her chin to lift her head. He reached towards the floor, groping around in the left pocket of his discarded trousers. A small velvet box nestled in his palm as he rose.

"What is it?" Hana rose, hauling a sheet around her nakedness.

"Open it." Logan lay next to her, propping his head on his hand. She pried open the clasp on the box with shaking fingers. Inside the cushioned folds lay a gold ring, encrusted with a line of sparkling diamonds.

"Logan!" Hana gasped. "It's expensive; I can't keep this!" She fingered the glittering stones and fought the growing lump in her throat. At the centre, a large diamond rose above the others. The late sunshine danced over its surface.

Logan's face lost its smile of expectation. "You don't like it?" he stated, his voice flat.

"I do." Hana blew out through pursed lips. "But I don't deserve it." Dread snaked cool fingers around her heart. She'd become a liar and the purest of motives did little to dull the ache.

"Sweetheart," Logan crooned, pulling himself upright. His arms cradled her head. "Remember when we bought the wedding rings and the lady in the shop said you should have an engagement ring? You didn't want one, but she suggested we got an eternity ring when we had our first baby. You said I could."

"I assumed we wouldn't have babies." Hana's voice cracked and she swallowed the lump in her throat. "I didn't want you to spend the money."

"Well, we had a baby, Hana. So, I bought you the ring. I love you and I want to spend eternity with you." He took her hand, easing the gold band over her knuckle and sliding it until it touched her wedding ring. Her chest hitched and his brows furrowed. "Babe, what's wrong?" he demanded, urgency in his tone. "This is about more than a gift, sweetheart. What's happened?"

Hana turned her face away from his scrutiny and fought for control over her angst. "Nothing," she lied, feeling the window for truth closing on her. "It's beautiful. I don't deserve you or the ring."

"Yeah, you do." Logan kissed her lips and she felt his lips curve into a smile. "Not the bad parts though."

"Ignore me," she whispered. "Blame the baby-hormones. It's your birthday this weekend and yet you've given me a gift."

Logan wrinkled his nose. Hana sensed his thoughts run to the absence of his mother and ground her teeth. Her birthday gift seemed to morph from a great idea to a disaster. She hesitated. "I got you something, but on second thoughts, perhaps you'll hate it."

"I doubt that, Hana." He forced his lips into a smile.

Hana slipped from the bed and shimmied into a loose shirt of Logan's. She reached into her underwear drawer and heard him release a groan of frustration. "What?" She turned, the wrapped gift in her palm.

"You know that makes it worse, don't you?" His expression became coy. "You wearing one of my old shirts is just as sexy as you wearing nothing." He snagged her waist as she reached the bed, rising to kiss the swell of her breast as it arced beneath the neckline.

"Behave and open your present." Hana pressed the gift into his chest. She held her breath as he fumbled with the tape. He withdrew a folded parcel of floral tissue paper, his brows knitting as a familiar object slithered onto the bed. The pocket-handkerchief lay there like a stark reminder of his loss. Logan's fingers stilled and he stared at it.

"I'm sorry. It seemed like a good idea at the time." Hana reached to snatch it back, her cheeks flaming with a guilty hue.

Logan grabbed it first, fingering the delicate fabric of his mother's handkerchief. She'd given it to the sobbing girl on the London train a lifetime ago. Hana watched a vein tick in Logan's temple. He lifted it to his nose and inhaled, his lips forming a sad smile. "It's smells of you," he whispered. "I'm glad." The tiny kiwi birds did their familiar quickstep around the edge, formed with navy blue stitches on a pale blue background. Logan's jaw worked, but his shoulders relaxed. "You pulled it from your pocket the day I invited you back for dinner. I felt so sure you wouldn't have it anymore, yet there it was." He turned it over in his hand, feeling the crisp lines where Hana ironed it into a triangle. "I bought the set for Mum's birthday when I was fourteen. She kept the pink and green ones but gave the blue one to you on the train. As five years stretched into ten and then twenty, I dreamed you still had it, though I thought you probably didn't."

Logan opened the handkerchief and a gold chain slithered onto the bed. He retrieved it, running it through his fingers. A pendant depicting St Christopher dangled from the end, its gold surface polished and free of dark soot.

"I lost it," he breathed. "During the fire."

Hana nodded. "Toby found it while they were clearing the site over the summer. He brought it to me in case you weren't ready to see it again. The chain had snapped. I bought a new one and asked the jeweller to repair the dents and clean the pendant."

Logan's fingers trembled as he lifted the treasured disk and peered at the gentle face of St Christopher. "Hana, it's me who doesn't deserve you," he breathed.

As he bent his head to kiss her, the phone trilled from the hallway. Phoenix squawked as it woke her and the moment ended, lost in the busyness of life.

Chapter 14

The Honda kicked up dry dust on the final descent towards the hotel. The sun set on a glorious day and the manicured grounds put on their best show for the returning master. Through the open windows, the air reverberated with the lazy chatter of tui flitting through myriad shades of green bush.

Hana noticed Logan's shoulders tense as they covered the last kilometres of undulating New Zealand countryside. His slender fingers flexed and released on the steering wheel. "I know it hurts, babe," she said, resting her hand on his knee. "It's like having your tent pegs ripped up and tossed away in a gale force wind."

Logan shrugged as though not caring, but Hana sensed him drinking in her wisdom. She saw him shift in his seat and pressed on like a moth to a flame. "I remember receiving my brother's letter after my mother died. It said he and Dad didn't want me at the funeral. I don't recall ever feeling more devastated." Logan's jaw clenched. Hana felt her chest tighten, but her tongue ran away with the story. "I read about my father's death in a church magazine. The article lauded his work as a vicar among the poor in inner city Birmingham. It made me realise I never knew him at all."

"Please, stop!" Logan's voice sounded wooden and he spoke through gritted teeth.

"Sorry. I didn't mean to make it about myself." Hana clasped her fingers in her lap and turned to watch the landscape unfurl around her as the car tackled the final hairpin bend. If not for Laval's sudden appearance in her life, she realised she'd rather be anywhere but at the hotel. The citrus orange and yellow of the sunset faded into a blur as her mind returned to the fire. Miriam's screams haunted her still and the sight of the hotel nestling in the crook of the valley brought it back. The memories of smoke and the sight of pure, unadulterated misery filled Hana's soul with dread.

"Who was on the phone?" she asked, her voice sounding loud in the silence. She sought the distraction and glanced sideways in time to see Logan's brows draw into a line. "Before we left; somebody rang the house."

"Oh that. Nobody important," Logan answered. His jaw tightened and Hana sighed. She resisted the temptation to quiz him. Instead of parking in front of the hotel as usual, Logan drove into the car park reserved for staff. His fingers gripped the steering wheel as he killed the engine. Closing his eyes, he rested his head against the seat. "I can't do this anymore," he breathed.

"Yes, you can." Hana unfastened her seatbelt and reached across. Her reaction stunned her. No emotional or financial interest governed her words. Yet the thought of Logan selling his hotel seemed to render the past pointless "You'd regret letting all this go," she soothed. "Your grandmother's legacy is tied up in this land. Let's go inside before we lose the light."

Hana got out first and assembled the pram on the gravel. She pulled out the travel cot and rested it against the rear bumper. "Can you get Phoe?" she asked Logan as he appeared next to her.

"Yeah." His footsteps crunched in the gravel as he walked around to the passenger side. Hana pushed a heavy bag into the tray beneath the pram to save time. She shoved some other small items around it and stood, expecting to see Logan wielding the car seat. Phoenix grumbled from inside the vehicle and Hana's brows knitted. The door stood open with no sign of Logan.

"Where's Daddy?" Hana walked to face the baby, spinning to look around her. Then she swore. Stiff-legged with the body language of an angry bull, Logan strode in the opposite direction. The sight of his rigid spine sounded an alarm in Hana's brain. "No, no, no!" she breathed.

The straps of the car seat pinged open as Hana pressed the central button. Phoenix whimpered but nestled over Hana's shoulder and grabbed a handful of red curls. She pushed her fist between her lips and sucked, screwing up her face at the unpleasant texture of hair in her mouth. Her body bounced against Hana's as her mother picked up speed.

In the distance, Kane Du Rose leaned over the balcony rail which wrapped around the motel units. A lighted cigarette hung from his fingers. His actions mocked the sign mounted on a nearby post as it declared the site a no smoking area. A fire hazard board below showed the chance of fire from a naked flame as high. Logan's long strides cut down the distance between himself and his half-brother in record time. Hana's pace increased to a jog and she cupped the back of Phoenix's bouncing head with a steadying hand. Forty-one years of feud and secrets fuelled the coming storm and her heart hammered out a nauseating tattoo. "Not again!" she puffed. "Not again."

"Put the bloody cigarette out!" Logan's shout cut through the chatter of the nesting tui and Hana cringed.

"Piss off," Kane replied, his tone dismissive. He turned his gaze away from Logan and took a leisurely drag of tobacco smoke. Furthering his defiance, he flicked ash over the rail.

"The cigarette or you," Logan snarled. "You put it out or I'll put you out." He halted at the end of the ramp to the wraparound porch, giving Hana time to catch up to him. Kane pushed his Jakaroo hat back on his dark head to reveal stunning grey Du Rose eyes. He stood up straight and faced Logan. Hana inhaled. She'd seen Kane once, the likeness to Logan glaringly obvious to everyone but her husband. The features were Reuben's, trapping the men in an old hatred neither of them understood.

The set of Logan's body declared war as his splayed legs and balled fists made the challenge. Hana covered the last of the distance and paused, catching her breath and retrieving her hair from the baby's hand. Then Kane Du Rose lit the touch paper and something nasty unravelled, spewing into the atmosphere and sucking out the oxygen. The cigarette hit the deck and lay smouldering against the wood. It smoked to itself on the tinder dry surface. Hana held her breath and watched Kane's lips curve upward in a lazy smile. He wanted to watch Logan's life swallowed up in the same flaming misery as his own. "It's all your fault," he hissed. His fingers dug into his jeans pocket and hauled out a lighter. He threw it up in the air and caught it. "This is on you." Kane threw it again, catching without looking. "My family lived in a tent for a year while yours played happy families in our dad's house. I hate you!" He flicked the lighter with a skilled thumb and an orange flame danced beneath the valve. Four decades of undimmed hatred mirrored it in Kane's eyes.

Hana gulped at the reference to Reuben's expulsion from the Du Rose mansion. His affair with his brother's wife and the resulting child left no choice. Kane moved towards the edge of the deck, shoving the lighter into his pocket and lifting his tee shirt over his head. "Come on then te hākoro makau," he hissed. "Let's settle this, tēina, to the death." Dark tattoos wrapped Kane's muscular torso in an inked embrace. "Shame." He pointed to the genealogy snaking around his upper arm. "Mine's legitimate."

Hana's eyes widened in horror. Logan accepted the challenge without words. In seconds, his tee shirt lay discarded on the gravel. Every muscle in his torso rippled with anticipation and Hana watched the tension ease in his profile. He settled, as though an unseen hand rested over his heart and breathed inevitability into his ear. "Come on then," he hissed. His fists balled at his sides. "Why are you waiting?"

Stockmen gathered behind Hana, filtering in as word of the fight rippled around the farm. She turned to the man nearest, her voice wavering. "What did he say?" she demanded. "What do those Māori words mean?"

The man swallowed and gazed at the others around him for help. They looked away as one.

"Tell her!" The voice sounded sharp and authoritative. Hana turned to see Flick standing at a safe distance. His body language oozed menace and she shivered.

"Kane called him, *father's favourite* and *brother*." The stockman gulped, shifting on his cowboy boots and kicking up dust.

"Oh no!" Hana breathed.

Kane sauntered down the ramp as though savouring a moment he'd spent his entire life imagining. Every fight with Logan brought anger from Reuben and the welts on Kane's body showed the beatings to prove it. "My pa's obsession with youse killed his spirit years ago, long before the fire licked the flesh from his bones." He spat on the ground to accentuate his point. His left index finger jabbed at the long scar stretching from Logan's armpit. The raised tissue disappeared into his waistband and Kane's eyes flickered with the hunger of a psychopath. Hana sensed he yearned to reopen the wound and pull out the stuff the surgeons sewed back inside.

Hana heard footsteps crunch on the gravel behind her. She whipped round, relieved to spot Tama's lean body running towards the gathering crowd. "Tama, stop them!" she hissed. The surrounding men shifted to make room for him.

Logan's nephew watched the two men squaring up and shook his head. "No way! They'll kill each other. I don't want a piece of that action."

Air brakes sounded in the main car park as a tourist bus arrived. Hana held her breath as she imagined guests mingling with locals to watch the fight of the century. On the deck, another crowd gathered. A tall, olive skinned man held a small boy in his arms and a woman peeked from behind him. His likeness to Logan identified him as Nev Du Rose, the eldest of Reuben's boys. Tama's refusal stunned her with the realisation that nobody would intervene. The old feud took hold again, threatening another generation with its violence. Hana turned to Tama, angry tears pricking her eyelids. "Logan stood on that mountain and named our baby. He promised it would be different!"

Tama's shrug reflected powerlessness and the futility of intervention. "Buggered if I'm separating those two," he breathed. A collective hum added the agreement of the other males.

Fury built in Hana's chest and disappointment fuelled the bitter metallic taste in her mouth. Hoisting Phoenix free, she dumped her in Tama's arms like a sack of potatoes. "Hold her!" she snarled. His face showed surprise, but he took his cousin in his strong arms and faced her outwards as though showing her something interesting. Phoenix made no sound, watching her mother with an astounding sense of awareness in her grey eyes.

Hana stepped into the middle of the problem, a tiny dot of femininity amid raging testosterone. "Stop!" She threw her voice, hearing it echo off the mountain range and reverberate back to her. Her glare took in both men without prejudice. "Enough!"

Logan's eyes widened. Then a heady rage settled over his features. His irises turned the colour of slate and his attention flicked from Kane to Hana. She swallowed, realising too late what it must feel like to eyeball a charging bull. Distracted, she forgot about Kane.

Logan glanced up and Hana saw shock break from beneath the mask of anger. Remembering Kane, she turned in time to see his fist draw back towards his shoulder and then aim for her face. Logan reacted, but not fast enough.

Bodie's teaching flooded into Hana's brain, too late for her altercation with Laval but perfect timing for the unscrupulous Du Rose. She ducked, so he overbalanced and then dragged her boot sole down his shin, hearing his exhaled hiss of pain. Her flimsy dress shimmied around her thighs as she landed a neat uppercut beneath his chin with her right fist. When he lowered his head, she finished with a perfect left to his eye. "Shit!" he gasped as her new ring buried itself into his flesh, drawing blood from his eyebrow before exiting.

Hana took a step back as he reeled, determination hardening her features. She gave his arm a hefty shove and dodged around him. Her boots clattered against the porch as she reached the burning cigarette and crushed it beneath her sole. Kane swore up a storm below as Hana faced Nev with a withering glare. "What's wrong with you?" she demanded. "Haven't you seen enough fire for one lifetime?"

She whirled around, red hair and white dress twirling with the movement. A hush surrounded the building as she descended the ramp. Her legs trembled beneath her and Hana fought to maintain her composure. She paused to speak to Kane as he wiped blood and snot onto his bare arm. "My husband told you to leave," she hissed. "So, leave!"

The male crowd parted to admit her, closing behind her like the wake of a ship. Hana kept walking without looking back. Footsteps followed and Tama matched her stride. "Wait up!" he hissed. "You forgot your kid."

"Bitch!" Kane's insult drifted on the breeze and Tama halted. Hana snatched at his sleeve as he turned. Phoenix gurgled in his arms.

"She hit me with her handbag once," the teenager shouted. He waggled his dark eyebrows. "You wanna do what she says." All bravado vanished from his expression as Kane slid a gimlet-eyed glare in his direction.

Hana held her breath as Logan's laugh carried. Other male voices joined it. She licked her lips and tugging on Tama's sleeve, kept walking. "I've done it now," she muttered to herself. "He'll kill me. And I didn't forget my baby. I'm just shaking too much to risk carrying her."

"Logan won't kill ya." Tama lifted Phoenix, so she nestled over his shoulder. Her head bobbed as she watched the scene behind him. "Well done for stopping that scrap though. They're both haemophiliac. This family doesn't need another bloodbath."

Hana groaned. "I made a haemophiliac bleed? Just shoot me now." She picked up the pace, eager to leave the scene of her crime. In the car park, she found the Honda sitting where she left it. A bee buzzed around the open passenger door and the pram had tipped over sideways. "Please fix all that for me?" she begged. Tama nodded and handed the child back. He dug his hands into his jeans pockets and loped towards the car.

The main doors of the hotel stood open, cool air swirling around the lobby. Hana's knees supported her up the front steps but threatened to give way as she stepped over the threshold. The reception desk looked empty and she spun around. "Anyone home?" she called, her voice echoing.

Voices sounded from the top of the sweeping staircase and Hana imagined the receptionist showing the bus load of tourists to their rooms. The rumble of suitcase wheels vibrated overhead. She avoided the accusing glare of Kuia Du Rose's portrait as the old Māori woman surveyed her through knowing grey eyes. The spectre of Miriam seemed to occupy the space, seeping discontent and sadness into the furniture and ornate wallpaper. Hana shuddered.

"Youse came back!" The housekeeper's voice rose with excitement at the end of her sentence. The floorboards creaked as she made a beeline for Hana. "Mrs Du Rose, I didn't think we'd ever see you again after all that nasty business."

"Hi, Leslie." Hana grunted as the woman manhandled Phoenix from her shoulder and thrust her between a large pair of breasts. An arm enveloped both mother and child in a stranglehold.

"I thought you'd gone for good," Leslie exclaimed. Tears pricked behind her eyelids and she blinked. "With Miriam and Rueben dying an' all, we figured Mr Logan would sell." Her complexion paled. "Is that why you're here?"

"No." Hana shook her head and banked on Logan having a change of heart. "My husband needed to sort out some issues with the farm."

Leslie beamed and her upper layer of false teeth detached from her gums. "Thank you," she gushed. "We all got so worried about our jobs."

With the regal determination of her Māori heritage, Leslie ruled the Du Rose empire with a rod of iron. She'd stepped in for Miriam during the worst of her Bi-polar episodes and continued after her death. Hana pursed her lips at the realisation Logan had done nothing to formalise the arrangement, yet Leslie had poured herself into the needs of the hotel without reserve. "How long have you worked here?" she asked.

Leslie bugged her eyes and shrugged. "Fifty-three years last April." Her head bobbled on her neck with pride and then doubt furrowed her brows into a pencilled line. "I don't want to retire though," she said. "Youse won't get rid of me, will you?"

"No." Hana shook her head. "It's Logan's decision, but he's said nothing about getting rid of anyone." She experienced a pang of guilt for the troubled set of Leslie's jaw and wished she'd avoided small talk.

Leslie chucked Phoenix under the chin, beaming as the baby moved her head to follow her hand. "Hello my moko, how are youse doin'?"

Her use of the Māori word for grandchild left Hana confused. "How's Alfred?" she hedged, desperate to move onto a less controversial conversation. She realised as the question left her lips, she'd failed.

Leslie raised her apron to her eyes and mopped away instant tears. "Ah, it's too sad, Miss," she whispered. "Too sad."

Hana's jaw dropped open in surprise and then panic. "What's happened?"

"He's not dead!" Leslie patted her shoulder. "But he won't leave the apartment. He thought Miriam stopped her fling with his brother years ago. After he taitamaiti was born. It's all been a terrible shock."

Hana raised her hand to ward off Leslie's budding tirade. She remembered Alfred's kindness after the fire and sought to repay it. The old man's predicament mirrored what happened with her first husband and gave them a shared understanding. It also gave her somewhere to hide from Logan. She imagined his rebuke for hitting Kane and shuddered. "Youse cold?" Leslie demanded, dandling Phoenix over her shoulder. "Come to the kitchen."

"I'll see Alfred first." Hana held her arms out to reclaim her daughter. "We'll cheer him up."

"I doubt that." Leslie waggled her eyebrows and watched Phoenix settle in Hana's arms with naked maternal hunger. "But you're a good girl to try." She patted Hana's shoulder. "Come to see me after."

Hana walked up the wide staircase to the first floor, smoothing her palm along the baby's spine. The new guests squealed with excitement as they explored each other's rooms. Hana climbed to the next level and then cut through a passageway to the private west wing. The door to the attic apartment faced her, closed and forbidding. "Come on, Bugle-bum, let's go find Grandpa," she mused.

When the handle depressed beneath her fingers, she expected to find Alfred home. She also thought he'd be pleased to see her but couldn't have been more wrong. The heavy fire door clicked shut behind her. Hana climbed the staircase to the first dogleg and then took another short flight of steps to the attic. The apartment opened out at the top, nestled beneath the slanted roof of the old house. Partitions denoted the kitchen, a living room and bedrooms. To her left were myriad sash windows and the last of the setting sun turned everything citrus orange. "Hello?" she called. "Alfred?"

A foreboding silence enveloped the apartment. The baby's breathing sounded loud in her ear. Plates and cups littered the draining board, stacked to a precarious height. Hana paused to determine if they looked clean or dirty but identified an unhealthy mixture of both. Women's clothing spewed from black dustbin sacks and Hana winced as she recognised one of Miriam's floral blouses. The apartment looked as though it had suffered a burglary lasting days. A grubby duvet clung to the side of the lounge sofa, the liner greying and the cover missing. Hana's footsteps grew heavy as she contemplated what she might find in the master bedroom at the end of the long space. She regretted bringing Phoenix. "Alfred?" She rounded the last partition and held her breath. "It's Hana."

The old man stood at the floor to ceiling window set into the gable end of the wing. He turned to face her and his eyes appeared glassy and faraway. The window offered a spectacular view of the landscape as it stretched into the bush. Hana gulped, seeing the boundary line and the track up to Reuben's burnt-out house. Something about Alfred's timeless stance told her he'd spent hours standing in the same spot.

"So, youse came back?" He inhaled and Hana heard his chest rattle. "They never stopped," he said, without turning around. "Miriam and my brother. She lied to me for over forty years. They all knew, them downstairs. They all knew. She should've married him, not me." His emaciated frame shook with undefined emotion.

"I brought the baby, Alfred," Hana soothed. "Come and sit with us for a while."

Alfred snorted, his mind still in the past. "You once told me you didn't understand why Reuben denied Aroha access to Tama after she left Kane. Does it all make sense to youse now?" Cruelty laced his voice. "An eye for an eye, a tooth for a tooth. And a child for a child. Tama's my blood and my brother kept him as a ransom for Logan."

Hana swallowed. "I'm sorry, Alfred.

The old man turned and Hana shuttered her eyes to hide her shock. Alfred's expression was spectral and his eyes cold and lifeless. Thin and stooped, he'd lost half his body weight in the few weeks since Logan took his family back to Hamilton. He'd opted out of living. "Hey Grandpa." she said. The ill-advised words sounded less catastrophic in her head. "Look who's here. Somebody came to see you."

Alfred glanced at the baby and Hana watched the shutters slam over his heart. He turned away. "I'm not her poppa," he said, his voice dripping with bitterness. "Her poppa's dead!"

Hana's reaction proved instantaneous, served in defence at the slight to her daughter. She experienced the same wave of fury she'd meted out to Kane and Logan. "Don't you dare take it out on my baby!" she snapped. Phoenix let out a frightened wail as though to underline the trauma and Hana bridled. "You're a bunch of pathetic little men with massive egos and tired grievances."

Alfred ran a hand through the bird's nest on his head and seemed surprised to find his sideburns joining a beard beneath his chin. His fingers stroked at the loose bristles. "I mean no harm," he muttered.

"Too bad!" Hana snarled. "You raised my husband and that makes you his father. This is your grandchild whether you like the fact or not." She jabbed a finger at the devastation at her feet. "Get yourself and this place tidied up, so we can visit again tomorrow. Your granddaughter would like a cuddle."

Clattering down the wooden steps to the floor below, Hana shook with anger. "Bloody, selfish Du Rose males," she raged. "When will they ever learn?" Her footsteps took her to Logan's childhood bedroom on the floor below. She readied herself for the wrath of another Du

Rose man, expecting an argument. "God help me," she prayed, demanding divine assistance in the situation, whether Logan's whānau wanted it there or not.

Her fire dissipated at the sight of the closed bedroom door. She tapped her thigh and tried to remember the numbers for the keypad. Temper had erased the four necessary digits and with great reluctance, she lifted her fist and knocked on the wood. The door opened as though wrenched off its hinges and Logan held it open without speaking.

Hana stamped past him with her nose in the air and faked her bravado. The contents of the car turned the bedroom into a carbon copy of Alfred's apartment and she tripped over the travel cot. Logan observed her, slamming the door with his foot and continuing to suck a bleeding index finger. "Mind that," he said, putting enough sarcasm into the statement to set her blood back on to the boil.

"Great job." Hana stood in the centre of the room and observed the mess. Phoenix grumbled over her shoulder. "Did you do this by yourself or did Tama help?"

Logan leaned against the door and rested one arm across his stomach. The other stayed in his mouth and she saw blood seep onto his lip. "You should have seen it before," he muttered. Hana sighed as the precious red fluid, deficient in Factor 8, pooled on his lower lip.

"How did you cut yourself?" she asked, sounding tired.

Logan jerked his head towards the travel cot. "It's savage," he concluded.

Phoenix made sucking noises and pushed a fist into her mouth. She whimpered and Hana heard the threat of a wail behind it. Picking a route through the debris, she found an armchair next to the window and tipped off a plastic bag containing her walking shoes. She lowered herself down with a sigh of exhaustion and released the buttons on her bodice. Phoenix kicked her legs and ramped up her impatience.

Logan watched from the door, his dark eyes smouldering. Hana rested her head against the chair to avoid his gaze. "Just say it," she breathed. "Let's get it over with." She waited, but he didn't reply. Instead, he moved around the room sorting out their belongings. Hana heard the travel cot kicked out of the way and the sound of a drawer grinding as he pulled it free.

"She can sleep in here." Logan tapped the bottom. Hana groaned as her spare knickers and socks tumbled onto the carpet. She chose not to take the bait and closed her eyes. Phoenix fed and Hana dozed, letting the day's events wash out of her psyche. Laval's threats contained less bite with the enforced distance between them and she allowed herself to relax.

She jumped as the weight of the chair altered, grabbing the baby and sensing the steady sucking cease. Phoenix paused and then continued. Logan sat on the arm of the chair, a long arm stretched across the back. "I suppose you want me to tell you not to be such a dumb ass again?" he said, his voice soft.

Hana rolled her eyes at the reluctant concession. "Not really," she replied. "Unless you'd rather talk about how you lapsed from a doting father to brawling thug in under sixty seconds."

Logan leaned forward and peered at his cowboy boots. He watched them move up and down as the heels beat a tattoo on the floorboards. Hana ignored the irritating sound. When the chair shifted and he stood, she knew what came next.

"Don't you dare run away!" she snarled. She rose and placed the sleeping baby in the centre of the double bed. Phoenix lolled in the wide space, her tummy rising and falling like a well-fed puppy's. Logan's eyes flashed the colour of grit as Hana beat him to the door and stood in front of it. "I don't need to see inside your head, Logan." She raised a hand and pressed it to his hard chest. "But that doesn't give you an excuse to run from the issue. We promised not to resort to old patterns, remember?"

Logan peered at his oozing finger like a child and Hana snatched his hand. "Where are the plasters?" she demanded.

She found her handy box of medical tape in a pocket of the suitcase. Logan ran his finger under the cold tap in the bathroom and returned with the wound wrapped in toilet paper. Hana examined the depth of the cut before fixing tape around it and holding the finger upright. Logan stared at the plaster with a frown. "Want me to draw a smiley face on it?" she asked.

Logan smirked and looked away. Hana jabbed him in the ribs, making him grunt. "Where's your spray?" she asked and he pointed towards the suitcase.

"I can't find it in there," he replied. His lips pursed and Hana resisted the urge to kiss them. She unearthed the medical inhalant from inside a sock and waited while Logan inhaled the vile smelling spray. Her sudden urge to mother him mirrored the emotions she felt towards the sad old man in the upstairs apartment. She relented. "I know you're angry I got between you and Kane," she said, "but you promised things would be different. I refuse to hold your daughter while her father knocks the snot out of his half-brother." Logan turned his face away and Hana saw the smirk light his regal features. "What's funny?"

He shrugged and his eyelashes fluttered. "You knew I'd win then?"

"Yes, I knew you'd win!" Hana snapped. "He was smoking dope. His eyes focussed in different directions."

"Oh." Logan released a loud exhale. "Thanks. I think."

Hana shook her head. "Look, he took advantage, Logan. But you fell for it. I think he lit that cigarette when he saw you because he wanted to fight. He'd smoked plenty more before that one, but I know what length a roll up starts. He lit that seconds before you started walking. You should have ignored him."

Logan's eyes narrowed and Hana appreciated how intimidating he might appear to others. She released his finger and he towered over her. His thumb traced a gentle line along her jaw. Hana shivered as his fingers pushed up through the hair at the nape of her neck. "You're scary," he whispered, dipping his head to kiss the tender skin on her neck. "But I don't need you to fight my battles." Another set of soft kisses rained on her cheeks and face, a paradox to the threat in his voice. "If you ever do anything that stupid again, we'll fall out!"

"Logan?" Hana interrupted, remembering something with sudden clarity as he tugged at the sleeves of her dress. "Caroline's here."

"What?" His head shot up and dismay flashed in his eyes. "She can't be!" His lip curled back in a snarl and his face set in a dreadful mask of stone.

Hana paused, determination budding in her heart. "She is." She pulled her dress back into place and her fingers fumbled with the buttons. "Stay here with Phoenix. I'll deal with everything." She stalked from the bedroom before Logan could stop her, knowing he couldn't follow without bringing Phoenix. The door clicked shut behind her.

Downstairs, Tama leaned across the reception desk. His eyelashes fluttered as he flirted with the girl manning the phone. Hana appeared from the corridor leading to the spiral staircase and took him by surprise. "I'm just checking something," he lied, running a nervous finger over his upper lip. The girl's cheeks flushed pink.

"I bet you were," Hana retorted. "And if you don't want me to tell Logan what else you were checking, you'll do a job for me."

The conversation lasted mere seconds, but Hana doubted her wisdom in sending Tama to find Flick. The former career criminal's terrifying lack of conscience swayed her decision, making him perfect for evicting both Kane and Caroline. She knew he'd get the job done, as he almost had with her. Or die trying.

Logan opened the bedroom door with worry etched into his features. "What happened?" he demanded. "You can't just take over like that."

"Can and did." Hana narrowed her eyes. "You always tell me we're in this together. It's my hotel as much as yours. Isn't that what you always say?"

"Yes." Logan swallowed and ran a hand through his hair. Phoenix snored in the drawer on top of the dressing table. "So, what happened?"

"It doesn't matter; it's dealt with." Hana shrugged. "What did you want to tell me about the hotel?" She sat on the bed, hiding her trembling hands underneath her bottom.

"What?" Logan chewed his lower lip. The stiffness of his body language made him appear edgy as though he fought the desire to challenge her for power over his empire. Hana saw the conflict in his eyes.

"A couple of nights ago, you wanted to talk about the hotel, but we didn't finish the conversation."

Realisation lightened Logan's face. "Oh yeah," he said, his focus changing. "I wanted to talk to you about the land at the top of the mountain." He halted, looking shy. Lowering his head, he observed her through his lashes. When he sat on the bed next to Hana and took her hand, she panicked. "No, sorry, it's nothing bad," he promised, gripping her hand. "I've got planning permission to build our house."

"A house? For us?" Hana swallowed. Her world tipped at the thought of permanent residence on the mountain. She held her breath and prepared to hear him out.

Logan became animated, his lips creasing into a smile. "I want to build a house," he said and his eyes shone. "I commissioned an architect and he's sent through the plans. You should decide where things go." He halted at Hana's look of confusion. "We don't need to live here full-time, Hana. But we need somewhere private when we visit. I'm sick of this room. It feels like we're living in a goldfish bowl. The staff gossip about everything. It's time to get our own place."

"Like a holiday home?" Hana forced a lightness into her tone. "I'd love that. Can I choose colours and fittings?"

"Yeah." Logan's thumb caressed her cheek. "Decor is your department." He exhaled and Hana felt the tension lift.

"This is your kuia's dream, isn't it? A house on top of the mountain."

Logan nodded. "I always believed that was her message. Now, I think she meant me to rebuild the family." He shrugged. "But I've dreamed of building a house on that spot since I was five years old. We may as well see it through."

Hana reached up to kiss his lips. "It's exciting," she admitted. "I've never been part of building a house."

Logan's expression grew serious and a furrow showed in his forehead. "Sorry about before," he whispered. "Thanks for stopping me."

Hana sighed and rested her head against his shoulder. "I hope I didn't humiliate you."

"I'll get over it." Logan kissed the top of her head. "Just don't do it again."

"Again?" Hana raised her head to glare into his face. "I'm hoping I never need to."

"You won't." Logan pushed his other hand behind his back and crossed his fingers. "Nice left hook though, babe. Great moves."

"Thanks." Hana closed her eyes and enjoyed the sensation of Logan's fingers kneading her scalp. Her mind drifted to Laval and the recaptured moment of peace dissipated with the memory of his arrogant smile.

Chapter 15

Logan responded to a knock on the door, swinging it open in frustration. Phoenix sighed in her drawer and her tiny fists flailed. Alfred braced himself against the doorframe outside, his hair wet and slicked flat on his crown. Tufts stuck up at the back where it needed cutting. The beard had gone and specks of blood marked the areas where his razor won the battle.

Hana rose and called to him. "Hey, come in, Grandpa. I'll make tea."

"Hi," Alfred said. He reached out a hand to touch Logan and then withdrew it. Hana winced, missing the friendly hongi of greetings before the fire. She saw Logan's brow knit and recognised his craving for affection. She wished Alfred had clasped him and pressed his nose and forehead to Logan's just like always. Sighing, she walked to the en-suite to fill the kettle, wishing she could turn back the clock for them.

"Hi Dad." Logan's tone sounded soft and Hana felt her shoulders relax. Her husband talked a big fight, but sometimes natural compassion won through, anyway. She returned to the bedroom and sat the kettle on its stand, flicking the switch to heat the water. Alfred's bones dug through his clothing and he'd adopted a defeated shuffle. He walked to the drawer and gazed at the sleeping baby. Gnarled, arthritic fingers rested on the side and he smiled.

"She'll grow into a stunner," he whispered. "Just like Miriam." He stopped himself saying more, clearing his throat and turning towards the window. "This weather should break soon. The last thing we need is a drought."

Logan stared, fists bunching and flexing as he sifted through his thoughts. Hana pretended not to notice. While the kettle grew louder on the credenza, she joined Alfred to admire the hotel grounds through the window. They stood in silence and watched a couple of guests bounce their suitcases across the gravel. Her eyes widened as they kissed before climbing into separate vehicles and waving goodbye. A latent anger stirred in her breast, overriding the gentle spirit which urged her to avoid judgement when she didn't know the facts. Instead, she imagined her first husband and his mistress cosying up in someone else's hotel. As she battled to control the dragon unleashing itself from her soul, she saw a real and present danger arriving to draw her wrath.

The woman parked her car and strode across the gravel, her attractive face screwed into a snarl. Expensive red shoes which Hana had recognised outside Kane's motel unit stamped through the gritty surface, their heels catching in the stones. The long legs glided like a swan's, negotiating fast currents and debris without affecting movement above the water.

Hana's insides performed a flip-flop of fear and then she righted herself, squaring her shoulders and focussing her anger and hurt. She recalled a bible verse from one of Pastor Allen's sermons. *'For God has not given us a spirit of fear, but of power and of love and of a sound mind.'*

"I won't be a minute." Hana strode across the room and heard the door click behind her as she ran down the corridor. Power surged through her veins, eclipsing the spirit of fear and unfortunately also banishing the love and a sound mind. She hurtled down the spiral staircase, almost tripping in her hurried descent.

Caroline entered the lobby in a cloud of floral perfume and formaldehyde. "I demand to see Logan!" Her voice projected along the corridor to reach Hana, strong and grasping.

"Miss, you can't go that way! It's private! Those rooms belong to the family." Hana heard the male receptionist set off in pursuit as Caroline's high heels clicked along the tiles towards the kitchen. "That's private!" he exclaimed as her hand settled on the kitchen door. The receptionist heard Hana's running feet and turned towards her as she arrived behind him. He retreated in response to the authoritative jerk of her head. Caroline pushed the door.

"Caroline!" Hana shouted. "This corridor is for family only. And you're not."

The shock on Caroline's face morphed into a sneer, rendering her features distorted and ugly. She dropped her hand and advanced on Hana. "I need to see Logan. Where is he?"

"Not this again!" Hana took a deep breath and dragged her failing courage from the depths of her stomach. The false bravado which carried her from upstairs cooled like the dregs of a teacup. Power, love and a sound mind. Where had they gone? "You can't see my husband." Unexpected calm radiated from her, making her blink in surprise at the strength in her voice.

Caroline's jaw worked beneath her cheeks and she stalked to meet Hana, heels clacking and echoing in the narrow space. "You won't stop me," she said, adding a spiteful laugh. "He'll wake up eventually and realise how lame and pathetic you are."

Hana shook her head, her sense of calm unnerving Caroline. She put her hands behind her back and clasped her trembling fingers, willing her body not to betray her. "He doesn't love you. And you know that deep down inside."

Caroline's eyes flashed at the unexpected kindness in Hana's tone. She swallowed and masked her uncertainty. "He's my soul mate," she hissed.

Hana stared at her, seeing something she'd never noticed. Behind the facade of couture and perfection lurked deep cracks in Caroline's soul which leaked misery and bile. Though by her own admission, the concept of a sound mind evaded Hana most of the time, Caroline hadn't even inherited the gene. Hana forced her lips upward in sympathy and delivered the body blow with courage and determination. "No," she said. "Logan became my soulmate at fourteen years old. He kept that faith for over two decades. God doesn't make mistakes, Caroline. Logan is mine and we both know it."

Caroline's heels scraped against the tiles. She jumped as though Hana struck her. She'd expected hysteria, not a calm woman clasping all the aces. Hana opened her arms, hands palm upwards. She appeared gracious and gentle yet radiated a force which sucked the air from the corridor. "We all need love," she said, "You're looking in the wrong place."

"Don't give me your religious crap!" Caroline spat. "It's not true!" She pressed the strap of her handbag back over her shoulder and battled to regain her composure by hurling out insults.

Hana shrugged. "I wouldn't waste my time, Caroline. You don't want to hear it. Can't you understand, we're getting too old for this? Why are you wasting valuable energy on someone who isn't interested? It's become a habit and it must stop. Find something else to focus your efforts. The man who really loves you spends his life destroying himself because you don't see. Open your eyes, Caroline. Real love is not about being powerful, it's about rendering yourself powerless."

Caroline's face paled and her hand shook as she tucked a lock of short blonde hair behind her ear. The rage left her demeanour and grief settled over her shoulders. Hana felt pity, but not enough to risk moving any closer. The alligator's flicking tail could inflict a nasty injury as it turned to flee. Caroline staggered along the corridor, her heels losing their confident click. She ignored Hana as she passed, edging by as though afraid of contamination.

She reached the open space of the lobby before Hana spoke, her voice filled with authority. "Caroline?" She turned with exaggerated slowness and Hana waited for eye contact. "Stay away from us, do you understand?"

Defeated by a force she couldn't comprehend, Caroline nodded. The tall, blonde silhouette of Flick appeared in the doorway, his hands buried in his jeans pockets. He looked menacing and immovable. Back lit by the last vestiges of sunset, he held his hand out to Caroline, indicating the driveway and sweeping his arm towards it like a gallant gentleman. His tone held an overt threat, "This is the last time I ask you to leave nicely, Miss. The next time won't be pleasant."

Caroline shuffled down the steps, her fight gone. Flick looked back at Hana, searching her face for approval. She summoned it with a sheer force of will. "Thank you, Flick," she responded, masking the wobble in her voice with a tight smile. The last of the sunset streamed inside, lighting her in beams of yellow, orange and red. It turned her hair into burnished gold. Lithe and pretty, the glow of motherhood rested on her like a gentle blush. The ex-career criminal gaped. Hana remembered his hands around her throat and swallowed, forcing herself to trust him. Logan did and it needed to be enough. She put more effort into her smile and saw him falter beneath the sense of restitution. Then he followed Caroline across the car park.

Hana watched Flick take a step back as Caroline's vehicle roared past him in a hail of grit. Kane sat in the passenger seat and raised his middle finger to the stockman. Ignoring him, Flick brushed the dust from his shirt and glanced back at the front door of the hotel. Hana stood in the open doorway, her gaze fixed on the departing dust cloud. The fingers of her right hand flickered across her heart and then she smiled. A crash and the sound of breaking glass sounded in the lobby and Flick ran, taking the stairs two at a time.

The receptionist's fingers covered his mouth and as he turned, his wide eyes carried fear. "She fell down," he breathed. "The Kuia just fell off the wall!"

Hana glanced up to see the large picture hook bent at a downward angle. The receptionist lifted the heavy wooden frame and heaved a sigh of relief. "I can't believe the frame didn't smash," he marvelled. "Good job oil paintings don't have glass."

Hana nodded and backed away as Flick stepped forward and tipped the painting. His fingers lifted the broken wire. "I'll fix it," he offered, his cheeks flushing as his blue eyes settled over Hana's face.

"Thank you, Flick," she replied. "I'd appreciate that." With a nod of acceptance, Hana turned and walked towards the corridor and the kitchen beyond. The men fussed over the painting, propping the original Phoenix Du Rose upright and facing her against the wall. Flick left to find a ladder and didn't see Logan standing in the passage leading to the spiral staircase.

Hana's husband remained unseen in the shadows, his muscular frame leaned against the wall and his hands pushed deep into his pockets. He shook his head. "Well, well, well," he whispered. "Look who found her mana."

More beautiful to Logan than she'd ever looked and without a single Māori bone in her English body, Hana had radiated the essence of authority like a twisting silver thread of light above her. She exuded all that was good and kind and gracious, but it never occurred to Logan Du Rose until that moment; she was also powerful.

Chapter 16

Hana pushed the kitchen door open and sank into a chair at the worn wooden table. She put her face in her hands. Her fingers shook. Leslie wiped the sink with a cloth until the aluminium shone, jerking her head back towards Hana. "Tea, Miss?" Her gnarled brown hands gripped the cloth and scrubbed.

Hana nodded and muttered grateful thanks. She felt trapped in a Jane Austen novel every time the staff rushed to perform some minor task she could do for herself. She'd noticed how they referred to her husband as Mr Logan but resented not escaping the deference. Her palms patted the table-top. "Who moved this?" she asked. "Didn't it used to sit nearer the centre of the room?" Hana swallowed, regretting the question as soon as it hit the air. Miriam kept the table in the heart of the kitchen but could no longer control its placement.

"Health inspectors came, Miss," Leslie answered. She leaned over to fill a teapot from a new zip heater on the wall. "Just their usual visit, but this time he brought his boss. He said we can't cook for guests while the family sit here in their farm clothes. Said he'd told Mrs Du Rose, but she ignored him." Leslie's lips pursed in accusation. "Miriam listened to nobody if she didn't wanna." Leslie made the sign of the cross on her chest and finished with a prod to her forehead.

Hana nodded. "It's a fair point. What will you do?"

"Talk to Mr Logan." Leslie fiddled with her apron pocket and shifted her feet. "He's gonna shout. This kitchen is the same as it was when Kuia Phoenix ruled the roost. Miriam ain't been gone more than a few weeks. But the inspector is making an extra visit next month. He gave me an infringement notice." Leslie wrung her hands in the apron pocket. "He didn't care about the fire or what happened. He said the whānau can't sit here in their muck while we cook for the public."

"Logan's a businessman," Hana replied, her brow knitting as she chewed over the problem. "I'm happy to talk to him, if you'd rather." She examined a wall to the left of the heavy fire door. The welcome distraction helped her to calm the involuntary shake in her delicate fingers. A butler's pantry interrupted the wall half way along. Dry ingredients stood on shelves in sealed containers, their labels facing the door. Hana stood and walked across the kitchen, stroking the wall with her hand. "What's behind here?"

Leslie waved her arm and wrinkled her nose. "Just a storeroom, Miss. You access it from a door in the hallway. Mr Logan took part of the room for the pantry back in 1995." She winced. "You know about him taking over when his pa got into trouble, don't you?"

Hana nodded. She suspected she knew less than she should. "So, next door is a storeroom?"

"Yup. It's a mess. The extra tables from the old ballroom get shoved in there. And the broken stuff. Mr Logan didn't clear it out. He just told the builders to wall it off." She shrugged. "Then he went back to England."

"Can I see?" Hana asked. Leslie's brow furrowed, but she took a set of keys from her apron pocket and walked towards the door.

The service corridor was dark and quiet, dinner finished and cleared away. Through the open dining-room door, Hana watched two hotel staff set the tables for breakfast. An elderly couple shuffled through the parallel hallway between the dining room and courtyard and she saw them stop to look at the flowers.

Leslie's keys clattered against the wood and the sound echoed in the corridor. Hana touched the brass plate with an index finger. "Is this an unused bedroom," she asked. "I assumed so because of this."

"Once." Leslie opened the door. "When Logan's grandfather got sick, Kuia Phoenix opened it up for him, so he didn't need to climb the stairs. No lifts in those days." She smiled. "Before that, it was the morning room. It faces east and gets the early sunshine."

Drawn roman blinds covered huge sash windows, hiding the room from outside. A veneer of grey dust covered everything. Broken furniture filled every corner.

"Did the inspectors see this?"

"No, Miss!" Leslie's eyes widened in horror.

"Just as well," Hana replied. "It's a fire hazard next to the kitchen. I'm amazed they didn't ask to see."

"They inspected the food preparation and serving areas, Miss. And the main bathrooms on all floors." Leslie's face blanched. "They just highlighted shortcomings with the kitchen and family arrangements."

Hana patted her hand. "You don't feel you have Logan's favour?"

Leslie rewarded her perception with a slow shake of her head. Her brown bun wobbled on top like a cherry. "No, Miss. And I won't get it. I can't lose my job. It's all I have left now my girls are gone. I've worked here my whole life." She lifted a hand to her mouth and Hana sighed.

"I'll talk to Logan," she promised. She waved a hand at the wall to the left. "If we put a doorway behind those tables, this could be the family dining area. Nobody would need to eat in the kitchen. I'll look online at the rules."

Leslie beamed and clapped her hands together. "I knew you'd think of something. I pushed the table to the side for the inspection, but Mr Alfred moved it back. He almost dropped it on the inspector's toe." Her cheeks reddened and she flapped a hand in front of her face.

"Alfred sabotaged the inspection?" Hana swallowed. "Perhaps don't tell Logan that part."

Leslie shrugged. "I don't think he meant to. But he insists on sitting right in the middle of everything to watch me do his wife's job. He doesn't eat, just sits there. The girls hate it. Then he goes up to the apartment and doesn't come down for days."

Hana exhaled. "Poor Alfred. I'll talk to Logan about the inspection and suggest extending into this room." Her smile faded at the thought of telling her husband how to run his hotel.

Leslie missed her sudden reticence and ushered her into the corridor, locking the room behind them. "Thanks, Miss," she said, drawing Hana into her copious bosom with a sigh. "You've taken a weight off my shoulders."

Hana waved goodbye as Leslie waddled into the dining room through the back entrance. Then she released a groan which echoed around her. "I took it off your shoulders and plonked it on my own."

Logan opened the bedroom door in response to her gentle knock and raised an eyebrow. "We spent the summer here," he whispered. "How can you just forget the number?"

"Stress." Hana ran a hand over her face.

"Over what?" Logan enfolded her in his arms and kissed the top of her head. He leaned back to watch her expression.

"Life." Hana pushed her face into his armpit and avoided his perceptive gaze. Laval rose like a spectre in her memory and she squeezed her eyes closed. "Where's Alfred?"

"Gone back upstairs." Logan sighed. "Said he needed to tidy up in case you visit again without warning."

Hana smiled into his tee shirt and released a gentle breath.

"Do you have an irrational urge for red wine and chocolate?" Logan's chin rested on her head, moving as she nodded.

"I do actually." She pulled away and looked up at him. The abandoned teapot sat steeping in the kitchen, its lure paling against a sweet red. "You're a mind reader."

Logan grinned. "Give me five minutes."

Hana shook her head and threw herself on the bed. "If you step outside this room, you'll get waylaid and not come back at all."

"Five minutes!" The door clicked behind him and Hana groaned.

Logan arrived back in four, horrified to discover Hana snoozing face down on the bed. He opened the wine in the en-suite and slapped a haul of chocolate bars on the bed next to her. Hana rolled onto her back. "Is it morning?" she grumbled and he laughed.

"Four minutes, Hana," he scoffed. "I almost broke my neck on the stairs."

Her deft fingers reached for a bar of milk chocolate and she tore the wrapper, her pupils dilating at the sight of the luscious contents. "You raided the reception cupboard," she moaned, filling her mouth.

"I left a note." Logan's brow furrowed. "It's technically mine, but Leslie needs to know for stock taking."

"Yep," Hana mumbled. "You definitely took the stock." She sat up and slurped her wine.

"Haha." Logan lay on his back and stared at the ceiling. "Is everything okay, Hana?"

Nerves made her take another gulp of the wine and swallow before answering. "I'm fine," she lied. She placed her glass on the bedside table and snuggled into his side. "But I enjoy being in bed with the boss." She reached across and fumbled with the buttons of his jeans.

Logan snorted and pushed her hands away. He sat up and pulled his tee shirt over his head. His fingers made light work of his jeans and he smiled down at her. "I should fire you for drinking on the job then, shouldn't I?"

Hana smirked. "You can try."

She woke with a pounding headache at six o'clock the next morning. The empty bottle of wine paid homage to her overindulgence. Phoenix grumbled in the drawer and Hana saw a woolly arm waving over the side. She winced with guilt at the thought of giving her second hand alcohol. The baby grinned at the sight of Hana before her brow furrowed at her stomach's reminder. "Hey baby." Hana lifted her free and carried her to the bed, plumping the pillows and leaning back against them. "Mama got pickled last night, so your milk has an unhealthy marinade today."

The child fed anyway, stopping to let Hana pat her back and change her nappy. When she continued to snore, Hana wrapped her in a blanket and snuggled her back in the drawer. Logan stayed asleep and she settled next to him, listening to his steady, even breaths. He laid on his stomach with his forehead resting on his arms and Hana stared at the tattoo on his shoulder. Her finger traced the line of a koru arcing around his arm, following the detail in the coil of the baby silver fern. She jumped as she glanced up and found Logan watching her.

"Is this a real ta moko?" she asked, maintaining the soft movement across his skin.

Logan shook his head without breaking eye contact. "No," he replied. "True ta moko is scribed the traditional way, chiselling out the skin with a sharp bone and inserting the ink. Mine is kirituhi, which is more like writing on skin. Whakapapa is unique to each person. Only my family can share this pattern." He shifted and covered Hana's movement with his other hand. His fingers felt hard and forced her to stop. She saw the blackness descend over his soul. "It's wrong, Hana. This is not my whakapapa. It's Michael's." He swallowed. She glimpsed his agony, a useless bystander as he forced himself to push the demons aside.

Hana ached for him. The livid scar along his torso meant he rarely stripped off his shirt in front of others. She'd noticed of late that he kept his arms covered, even in front of her.

"I love it," she whispered. "It's part of you. My favourite piece is the way the koru wraps around your arm. The koru stands for new beginnings, doesn't it?"

Logan nodded and rested his forehead against his arm. His fingers released hers. She'd spent the previous year trying to learn when to shut her mouth and figured this was as good a time as any.

Hana lay on her back and stared at the ceiling, relieved when Logan's hand snaked across the empty space and rested on her thigh. Phoenix grunted in the drawer and she winced. "I've intoxicated your daughter," she whispered. "I'm even more rubbish at this now than twenty-five years ago. You think I'd know better."

"Don't." Logan pulled her into his side. "You're a great mum. Don't keep doubting yourself." He sighed. "You're already a million times better than mine." Hana opened her mouth to speak and Logan silenced her with his lips. He smoothed his fingers along her spine and distracted her.

They took time showering and getting dressed, savouring the time to go at their own pace. The industrial kitchen buzzed with the activity of late breakfast orders and Hana dodged the women to grab slices of toast and a pot of tea. They ate, taking it in turns to hold the baby.

"Why's the bloody table over here?" Logan snapped, banging his elbow on the wall while shifting Phoenix into his other arm. "There's no room."

The women looked straight at Leslie, who grabbed a tray and fled to the dining room. She shot an accusing glance at Hana before the door slammed behind her.

Hana swallowed her mouthful and gave a rueful smile. "About that," she began.

Logan listened to her plan without interruption, eating one handed and holding Phoenix over his shoulder. The staff moved around the kitchen in silence and Hana sensed them straining to hear the conversation. "Sounds like a good idea," Logan said after a while, indicating the blank wall with a wave of his toast. "I remember it coming up in the inspection report last year." He paused and the hair lifted on the back of Hana's arms as though Miriam's ghost set up an ethereal protest. Logan squeezed his eyes closed and shook his head. "It doesn't matter. Now is a good time to sort it out."

Hana nodded and left the subject. She watched the familiar process of Logan's mental planning as he glanced across at the wall and furrowed his brow. So much in this place threatened to defeat him with memories, leaving him haggard and diminished as he fought each battle and lost. She left him to scheme and plot, enjoying the temporary relief it offered.

Hana went upstairs with Phoenix for a nappy change, leaving Logan in the kitchen. His mind worked a series of numbers as he scribbled with a pen on a napkin. Leslie met her in the corridor. "Well done!" she gasped, her eyes bulging in their sockets. "The girls said you won him round."

Hana cringed and shook her head. "I don't understand why you're all so scared of him," she said. Her hand patted Phoenix's back in a gentle rubbing motion. "He likes being offered solutions alongside the problem, that's all. It's not difficult." Her words condemned her as a fraud even as she spoke them.

Leslie waggled her eyebrows. "I wiped that boy's ass and bandaged his cuts. I ain't no nearer to understanding his serious expression than I was then. It's best we all leave it to you from now on." Her tone held a note of triumph and Hana's heart sank. She'd walked into the role of staff spokesperson without realising. Her feet dragged her up the spiral staircase to the bedroom.

Logan arrived an hour later, brandishing a dusty old acoustic guitar and strumming it with his long fingers. Hana smirked. "Where did you get that, Casanova?" she joked.

"In the room next to the kitchen." Logan grinned. "It's my old guitar. Ma drove me to lessons for a couple of years. Every Friday night." His eyes narrowed. "She stopped when we came back from London and she got sick. I didn't take it with me when I went to high school, frightened it might get stolen or damaged. But the dorms were fine and I'd had enough fights in the first term to make sure no one touched my stuff. I came home for the holidays and couldn't find it. I never saw it again." He wrinkled his nose and thrummed his fingers across the strings. Hana jumped in shock at the sound of an almighty twang. The snapped string curled around either end of the bridge like spaghetti. "Oh." Logan sounded disappointed. "The strings are brittle. I'll ask someone in the music department at work to restring it for me." He propped the guitar against the wall and bounced on the bed next to Phoenix, firing her upwards and making her giggle. She lay on a plastic change-mat with her bottom out, a natural exhibitionist. She kicked her legs and sang. Logan blew a raspberry on her tummy and she opened her mouth wide in a smile.

"So cute!" Hana breathed. "Mrs Bugle-bum is a daddy's girl."

Hana responded to a knock on the door and found Alfred standing outside. He shuffled in with a nod and sat on the bed. Logan greeted him with a smile but continued to play with Phoenix. The old man appeared less unkempt though his hair still dangled behind his ears like curtains. Hana boiled the kettle and offered tea, wondering if he'd remain long enough to drink it this time. Alfred accepted in a tight, rasping voice. Then his attention turned to Phoenix.

Hana saw her reflection in the window, noticing the rigidity of her spine. She forced herself to relax and focussed on the sunshine blazing through the net curtains as they billowed in the breeze. "Will you go for a walk with me later?" she asked, keeping her voice light. "Logan is riding up the mountain to see Toby after lunch. I've brought the baby sling, so I can explore."

Alfred nodded, but without enthusiasm. "Okay," he conceded.

"Great," Hana muttered. The atmosphere weighed her down and turned her feet to lead. She poured tea and passed the mug to Alfred. His gnarled fingers fixed around the handle but he didn't thank her. "What time would you like to meet?" she asked. "Does two o'clock suit you in the front car park?"

Alfred nodded. "Yep," he said. "If ya want." He rose as though his visit had ticked something off a list. He hadn't touched his tea and he placed the mug on the credenza. Logan sat up to watch him, a look of irritation crossing his face. Alfred gave Hana a curt nod and she quailed inside, secretly dreading an arduous walk up the mountain with a man sworn to silence. "See ya then," he said. He turned to leave and Hana watched his body freeze in position. She tracked his gaze to the guitar. It leaned at a jaunty angle, dust covering the wooden surface and Logan's handprints leaving shiny spaces. Alfred's body slumped like a balloon with the air let out.

"What's that thing doing here?" he spat.

Logan's expression narrowed in confusion. "It's mine," he replied. "I found it this morning in that room next to the kitchen. Did you know it was there?"

"No!" Alfred's grey eyes blazed fury and his balled fists shook by his sides. "She wouldn't let me burn the blasted thing, but I should've done it, anyway. She promised she got rid of it!"

Logan rose, towering over his father and Hana. His jaw tightened. "Ma took me for lessons. She knew I loved it. Why would she hide something I wanted?"

"All that money and you never replaced it," Alfred snarled. "I thought you would."

Logan shook his head. "I liked that one. The tone fitted what I wanted."

Alfred snorted, the sound filled with aggression. Phoenix wailed on the bed, not happy with being ignored. She lifted her feet and reached for her toes, silencing as her fingers clasped around them.

Foreboding filled Hana's heart. A hideous knowledge entered her mind as though whispered to her in warning. She sensed she needed to shut the conversation down but wasn't fast enough.

"Why would she hide it when you bought it for me?" Logan asked, innocence in his eyes. "Ma said you knew the man who made it specially for me. It always felt perfect."

Alfred shook his head, the action slowed as though for a film reel. His complexion appeared ashen and waxy. Hana moved towards the guitar, sensing his intention before his conscious mind could act upon it. Hatred burned in his eyes as she thwarted his aim. "I didn't buy it," he snarled. "And I never knew about the lessons." His body moved with robotic precision as Alfred Du Rose stalked from the room. He banged his elbow on the heavy fire door but kept walking as though he hadn't noticed. Hana's gaze strayed to Logan's handsome face, stricken by the blank and empty expression he wore.

As the door clicked closed, Logan sank onto the bed. He pressed his face into his hands. "Shit, shit, shit!" he groaned.

Hana stuffed a nappy between Phoenix's legs and lifted her, sitting so close to Logan their knees touched. "It's okay," she soothed, knowing it wasn't but praying it could be. "It's okay."

"How can it ever be okay?" Logan sounded as broken as she'd ever heard him. More wracked with grief and turmoil than the night Miriam ran into the fire. "How can anything ever be okay again?"

"It just will," she promised. "It just will."

Logan shook his head. He inhaled and then rose, his aftershave surrounding Hana in a haze of his essence. "I'm going out," he stated. "I don't know when I'll get back."

"So, Reuben got you the guitar," she said. Her legs wobbled as she stood. "Was he the guitar teacher?"

Logan's colour hiked, sending a flush of anger into his cheeks and neck. "I don't know," he hissed.

Uncharacteristic tears pricked behind his lids and made his irises appear glassy. "Māori guy, Ma's age, called me son." His teeth ground in his cheek. "What do you think?" His breath came in short, agonised rasps. He backed towards the door. "I'm going out," he repeated.

"No!" Hana placed herself between the door and her husband. "Please don't run. You always do this, Logan. You promised!"

Logan fumbled through his awful eureka moment, his body twitching with involuntary muscle reactions. The grey of his eyes resembled a stormy, turbulent sea and his face set in a mask of unreadable emotion. "I need to get out," he whispered. His voice caught on the last syllable. "My own mother caused this. I don't know what to do. Let me go, Hana."

Despite the voice of alarm screaming in her head, Hana took a step away from the door. Phoenix squeaked and released a fountain of pee which missed the nappy and coursed down Hana's jeans. Logan didn't even notice. He edged towards the door, his escape within reach. Hana ground her jaw. "Ride Sacha," she ordered. "She'll keep you safe."

Logan nodded and his fingers closed around the door handle. His gaze moved to the guitar and then back to Hana. She nodded, giving him a clear run towards freedom and acknowledging she couldn't help him. But she delivered a warning as the door opened. "Don't disappear for hours, Logan. I've booked a table for eight o'clock at your cousin's restaurant. Leslie agreed to mind Phoenix at her place. It's your birthday dinner and I expect you there."

"Birthday dinner." The words seemed to choke him and Hana nodded.

"Just us," she promised. "No one else. Don't be late. I want you home, showered and ready to leave by seven."

Logan's head wobbled in a shaky nod. Hana held his gaze, returning it with defiance. Their connection felt as solid as an iron bar extending from soul to soul and for once, he submitted to her authority.

The door closed behind him and Hana's shoulders sagged. She leaned against the wall and cringed as the offending guitar slipped sideways and clanged against the floorboards. Her lips pressed against Phoenix's downy head and she rested a moment to collect herself. The pee soaked through her jeans, making the fabric cling to her skin. "Odds on your grandpa turning up for our walk," she murmured, gratified by the baby's upturned smile. "Yeah, zero." Hana sighed and looked down at the mess. "Looks like it's just you and me, kid. Let's hope Daddy doesn't break his neck." Phoenix gave a happy screech and pressed her gums over her fists. Hana turned and headed for the en-suite bathroom.

Chapter 17

Hana waited outside for Alfred long enough to know he wasn't coming. Using a map from reception, she changed her mind about her destination and found her way to the bunkhouse using the lower mountain track. Phoenix slept in the baby sling, her legs dangling as Hana walked. The sun beat on them without mercy. Sweat welded her shirt to her sides and discomfort oozed from every pore when she finally found Flick. He walked a sick gelding around a pen in wide circles. The horse groaned with colic, its tired steps wooden and forced as the stockman prevented it lying down and drowning in liquid from its own lungs. Hana stopped at the fence. "Will he die?" she asked, her tone sombre.

Flick shook his head. "Apparently not. Jack gave him some stuff and he's improving already. Just tired now."

Hana looked doubtful, patting the baby's back with a shaking hand. "Thanks for dealing with Kane and Caroline last night," she said.

Flick pursed his lips and waved a hand in dismissal. "You didn't walk all the way up here to say that."

Hana swallowed. "You don't know why I'm here."

He halted by the fence and the horse blew out a breath laced with warm beads of water. Reaching for his belt, Flick produced a radio. "The receptionist radioed me and said he'd directed you here." He clipped it back onto his belt and resumed walking. "So, Mrs Du Rose, what do you want?"

"Your real name is Robert Dressler?" She fiddled with the straps of the sling and let the name roll off her tongue. It used to fill her with terror.

"Yep." Flick kept walking. "Newsflash."

Hana huffed out a breath of exasperation. She picked up his pace and followed him around the pen, the fence between them. "I need your help," she said. "And I don't want to call you Flick. It brings back bad memories." Her brow furrowed. "But your real name has the same effect."

Flick continued to pace, lengthening the lead rope as the horse let its head droop lower. He scratched his head and glanced sideways at Hana. "My stepma called me Bobby," he said. "You can call me that."

"Bobby." Hana tried the name on her lips and smiled. "Okay. I like that."

Flick gave a shake of his head and rolled his eyes. He clasped one hand over his heart. "I'm so glad about that, Miss. Because otherwise I couldn't sleep at night."

Hana tutted and matched his pace. The point of her visit hung over her like a weight about to fall on her head. "I met Michael Laval Junior," she blurted, the words half shouted into the clearing.

Robert Dressler halted and his irises darkened. "Oh shit!" he replied.

The conversation went downhill after that. Hana described her interactions with Laval and Flick became more agitated with each revelation. The horse paced with less uneven strides and the humans followed. "You don't know who you're dealing with!" Flick snapped for the sixth time. "He's real bad news, Mrs Du Rose."

"But you won't tell me anything!" Hana stopped and stamped her foot, her eyes widening as Phoenix stirred. Her heart beat like a hammer in the heat and thirst stuck her tongue to the roof of her mouth. "How can I beat him if you won't help me?"

"Tell your husband," he insisted. "He needs to know he's under threat."

"No!" Hana pleaded. "You don't understand. I'll take care of it myself."

Flick snorted and shook his head. "You can't. This guy is lethal."

"How do you know him?" Hana persisted. "You worked for his father."

Flick slowed the horse and it closed its eyes and relaxed into a steady plod. He ran a hand across his week-old beard. "Laval Senior is a crafty old man. He killed my stepma when he missed out on the land, but the son is something else. He's dangerous."

"More dangerous than murdering a defenceless woman?" Hana's voice rose. She flapped a hand in front of her face. "He's confusing. I tried to withdraw my witness statement but Odering wouldn't let me. I told Laval Junior and he didn't listen."

Flick stopped and faced her. The gelding nuzzled the back of his shirt and released another sigh which came from his fetlocks. "He's beyond nasty, Mrs Du Rose. Trust me." His brow furrowed at the use of the words, realising too late that he epitomised the last person on the planet Hana might find trustworthy. "He sent us to the school on the night of your event." His blue eyes softened. "The younger Laval gave the orders and I know he took Huang aside and told him to finish me. Probably gave him the gun too." Flick rubbed sweat from his forehead using the sleeve of his shirt and clicked his tongue to tell the horse to walk again. "He's the real deal, Mrs Du Rose. Tell your husband!"

Hana shook her head. "No." She stuck her chin in the air and stopped walking, watching as Flick made another turn of the pen. "I won't and nor will you."

Flick groaned and halted opposite her again. "Has it occurred to you that he might have wanted Logan the whole time?"

Hana shook her head. "No. You came after me before I met Logan. How can it be about him?"

Flick squeezed the bridge of his nose between thumb and forefinger, his answer so soft Hana leaned forward to hear it. "Logan knows him," he replied. "And he knows Logan."

"What?" Hana stiffened. "My husband would have told me."

Flick shrugged. "I don't know then.

"Why do you think that?" Hana persisted. She ran after Flick as he moved away. "Bobby, please tell me!"

Her use of the name he'd offered seemed to shock him and he stopped. The horse walked into his back and the clearing rang with the sound of hoof hitting boot. Flick's shoulders slumped. "Laval Junior called Logan his old friend." He shook his head at the memory as though it still puzzled him.

"Did you ask Logan about it?" she breathed.

He nodded. "Yes. He said he knew no one called Laval apart from the old guy hunting you for the property deeds in that box."

Hana's nod felt slowed down. "You think he's lying?"

"I don't know." Flick sighed. "I came here because I had nowhere else to go. If I set foot off this mountain, the cops will pick me up straight away and I'll do more jail time. I'm not complaining; I deserve it." He stopped and turned towards Hana. "I didn't expect to like it here, Mrs Du Rose. But it's the first place I've felt settled since I was a kid. And I like your husband and the way he runs his business. I've no way of knowing if he'll turn me over one day or let me work here until I'm an old man, but I'm out of options."

Hana held his gaze and heard a ring of truth in his words. She offered him a weak smile. "Logan is a man of his word. If he says you're safe here, it's because he believes it. As for Michael Laval Junior? I'll sort it out."

"No way." Flick resumed his determined pacing. The horse plodded after him, looking less sorry for itself. "Logan needs to know."

Hana narrowed her eyes and delivered her threat. "If you betray me, I'll tell Odering where you are." She jutted her chin upwards and saw the shock in his face. "I didn't walk up here to get your opposition. I needed your help."

Flick gave a groan of exasperation and kicked a loose stone. It skittered to the side and the horse bobbed its head. "Whatever!" he snarled.

Hana took it as agreement and walked back to the hotel.

Logan reappeared five minutes after the agreed time as though pushing Hana's boundaries. Orange mud from the mountain coated his shirt and jeans and Hana's eyes narrowed in suspicion. "Good ride?" she asked, noting the stiffness of his movements.

"Yep," Logan snapped. "I used one of the new mares and she threw me, then buggered off."

Hana frowned. "Is Sacha not ready for riding yet?"

Logan shrugged and kicked his cowboy boots off, showering the floorboards with dust and bush debris. He swore. "Yes, but she's up the mountain still. I thought taking a stable horse would be quicker."

Hana touched his arm and felt the electrical pulse of his anger shoot through her fingers. "Leave the mess," she urged. "I'll clean it. Get ready to go out."

"Okay." He pouted like a child and Hana masked her smirk with her hand. "Did you have your meeting with Toby?" She retrieved a dustpan and brush from the cupboard under the sink.

Logan's face twisted into a scowl. "No. The mare dumped me before the ridge. It's taken me all afternoon to walk home." He ran a hand through his hair, raking it without care and grimacing as his fingers caught in the longer lengths of fringe. "Jack thought it was hilarious. He barfed up a lung. And the horse stood there happy after a nice groom and a bucket of feed. I'm shooting it tomorrow." Logan shucked off his filthy jeans and boxers and Hana forced herself to ignore the gentle arch of his buttocks as he walked towards the ensuite. He left his shirt on, yanking at the buttons as he marched away.

"No, you won't." She shook her head and laughed as the door closed with a click.

By the time Logan emerged from the shower, Hana had dressed and applied a liberal amount of makeup. Red lipstick matched her short dress and she'd repaired the damage done by Phoenix grabbing at the eyeshadow brush. Logan's eyes widened with appreciation as she fastened the buttons of the dress while the baby lay across her lap with a line of milk dribbling into her cardigan. "She's fed to bursting." Hana smiled. Her brow furrowed at the livid black bruise protruding from beneath Logan's tee shirt sleeve. She said nothing.

"I'm nearly ready." Logan hauled on clean jeans and socks. He caught sight of the guitar leaned against the dressing table. Its wooden veneer shone and a discarded cloth lay on the floor nearby. His fingers twitched and then ceased as he occupied them with his belt buckle. "You look stunning," he conceded, allowing a smile to tug at his lips. "Marry me?"

"No thanks." Hana rose and sat her sleeping daughter in the car seat. "You're too late. I'm already married."

"Too bad." Logan's eyes narrowed and he caught her on her way to the ensuite. His lips nuzzled her neck. "Because I know we could be good together."

Hana wriggled free. "Behave. And hurry. Leslie's waiting."

Logan rolled his eyes. "Why her?" He snatched up a clean pair of cowboy boots and inspected the toes.

"Why don't you like her?" Hana demanded. She picked up a handbag and put her head through the strap, laying the bag over her hip.

Logan snorted. "You'd need years to hear the whole story and I'm not going over it all again."

"Then stop brooding on it." Hana lifted the car seat handle. "Is that why you didn't give her the job of housekeeper? Because you don't like her?"

Logan rose to his full height and Hana shrugged off the warning in his eyes. He lowered his voice to a growl.

"No, Hana. I didn't give her the job yet because I've had other things on my mind."

Hana shook her head. "Then get on with it. It's mean. She's doing the work and accepting the responsibility, so give her a proper contract and pay her."

Logan's lips tightened and then he grinned. "Okay. But you have to do something for me."

"What?" Hana paused at the bedroom door and Logan leaned down to whisper something in her ear. She shook her head as though she might refuse and then her eyes softened and she smiled.

"Mr Du Rose," she simpered. "Kinky."

Chapter 18

Logan carried the car seat up the porch steps and Hana glanced back with a frown. His spine appeared rigid and his body language hostile. She shook her head, picking her way past broken garden furniture and lifting her hand to knock on the door. Paint peeled and flakes danced to the floor of the deck as she tapped gently. The light bulb above the front door remained dark.

"Hana!" Logan's sharp rebuke made her jump. She glanced back in irritation and saw him jerk his head towards a huge hole to her left. Spiteful jagged edges made it look as though someone once fell through. A curtain whisked back from the front door to reveal light around the frame where it didn't fit the door jamb.

"Hey, Mrs Hana." Leslie beamed as she opened the door but Hana detected a shake in the hand which reached for her. They pressed noses and Leslie's breath smelled of peppery kawakawa leaves. Logan prodded Hana in the back to galvanise her. She moved sideways and his giant frame filled the doorway. He bent his head to avoid hitting it on the lintel and stepped into the tiny lounge.

The room contained little furniture. A worn and faded armchair sat opposite a dark, fireless grate. One rickety table hugged its side. An old portable television perched on a stack of telephone books. Its bulging screen revealed images moving through a snowstorm. The single picture above the fireplace showed a group of children, their happy faces smiling into the empty room.

"Mr Logan." Leslie offered her hand and Logan took it, their contact brief and formal. Hana cringed at the atmosphere of discomfort shrouding them both, realising she'd caused it. Leslie reached out to take the car seat and Logan released it with reluctance.

Leslie cooed to the sleeping baby, "We'll be fine for a few hours won't we, wee one?"

"Who are the children?" Hana asked, pointing to the photograph. Logan's eyes widened in a silent message of desperation and she winced. But Leslie's face lit up with enthusiasm.

"Those are my mokopuna, my grandchildren," she said. She hugged the car seat to her large bosoms and drew herself more upright. "They're the light of my life. My eldest daughter moved to Australia so I see them only through the eye of the camera." She stroked the photograph, moving her brown finger over the face of a tiny child with a mop of dark hair. Her eyes dimmed.

Hana swallowed and shot a nervous glance at Logan. He rolled his eyes and jerked his thumb towards the door. Pursing her lips, Hana obeyed his request. "I've fed Phoe to bursting. If she cries, it's probably wind. I wrote Logan's mobile number on the notepad in the left pocket of the bag. There are nappies in there too." She smiled and took a hesitant step towards the door. "I haven't left her with anyone." Hana swallowed. "This is the first time."

"Oh." Leslie set the car seat on the bare floorboards and clasped her hands to her chest. "I'm honoured, Missus. I'll take good care of her."

"Thanks." Hana's feet pointed towards the open door but her body remained fixed in her daughter's direction. "Promise you'll phone if you need me?"

Leslie swallowed and looked conflicted. Her eyes widened. "I got no phone, Missus. I can't."

Hana's paused and she felt Logan losing his patience. He tapped her on the shoulder and sighed. "Leave yours," he ordered. "Then she can call mine."

Hana baulked, the jerk of guilt in her brain giving her a physical jolt. "I can't," she whispered. "I lost it, remember?"

Logan exhaled and Hana's brow furrowed as she detected the swearword uttered beneath the breath. He reached in his pocket and pulled out his own, laying it on the mantle over the bare fire. "Use mine and call the restaurant," he barked. "The code to unlock the phone is 0102 and use the number for Alex." He shook his head and turned towards the door, holding out his hand for Hana to follow. "Look after my daughter," he said, issuing the words like a challenge laden with threat.

He pointed the car towards Rangiriri but said nothing throughout the journey. Hana's nerves increased as they made the winding turns which took them away from her daughter. "Let's get Phoenix and go home," she pleaded as Logan nosed the car into the restaurant car park. "This is a mistake. I'm sorry."

"What?" Logan's brow furrowed with confusion. "Aren't you hungry?"

Hana shook her head and exhaled. "I wanted this to feel special. You're about as much company as a bowl of porridge! It's a disaster. Please drive us back to Leslie's and I'll just pay her what I promised."

Logan sighed and his fingers twisted the wedding band on his left hand. A cloud of misery shrouded him and he shook his head as though not knowing how to banish it. He ran a hand over his face. "Sorry," he said, "I really am." He leaned across and put his hand over hers. Her fingers slipped through his as she tried to ground him and pull him back to her.

"What's wrong, Logan?" she whispered. "You've frozen me out and I hate it."

Logan put his arm around her and pulled her into his side. He kissed her temple. "I don't mean to," he replied. "I'll try harder."

The driver's door slammed behind him and he walked around to Hana. He tugged her hand, forcing her to leave the safety of the vehicle. He didn't step back as she landed in the gravel next to him, her eyes level with his chin. His lips gave the faintest tremble. "I love you," he whispered. "Don't forget that."

Hana reached up to kiss him and then smiled as she pulled away. A finger drifted up to remove the traces of scarlet lipstick from his mouth. Logan gave her his lopsided smile, eyes narrowing as he blinked with deliberate slowness. She sighed, wrapping her arms around his waist and leaning against him. "It's such a mess, isn't it?"

"Yeah," he said with a sigh of resignation. "Coming back here makes it more overwhelming. I don't know who I am anymore."

Logan sounded so vulnerable and fragile that Hana squashed any desire to confess about Laval. Flick insisted she should, but he didn't see Logan's pain. He saw the facade of courage and indifference. He saw ability where she saw open wounds. Hana straightened her spine and pushed away thoughts of the venomous blond man. She promised herself she would fix things.

Logan rubbed her back and kissed the top of her head. Then he took her hand and led her towards the busy restaurant door. "Come on. I'm starving," he said.

The French-style cafe had changed since Hana's last visit, expanding to add live music and a bar. Couples milled around a reception desk hoping to get a table. The packed restaurant offered standing room only and many of the hungry hopefuls looked disappointed. Hana glanced back at Logan in confusion. "I didn't know it was this popular," she hissed.

Logan nodded and leaned closer to her ear. "Alex wanted to expand," he said. "It's doubled his profits as there's nothing else this fancy south of Auckland."

He gave her a knowing nod and Hana pursed her lips, looking for reassurance and receiving an accountant's summary.

They battled the line to the reception desk and a man dressed in black greeted them with a tired smile. "Do you have a booking?" he asked, expecting her to reply in the negative.

Hana nodded. "Yes. Hana Du Rose," she replied. The name acted as a catalyst for action. Where other couples dressed in their best received a polite rebuff, Hana and Logan found the opposite. The man rounded his lectern to greet them with smiles and an affected bow.

"Come this way," he said, waving a menu at Hana and urging her to follow. The rejected couples crowding around the doors and seated in the waiting area glared at them. Oblivious, the front-of-house manager steered them through the bodies like a tug towing a ship. A secluded, candlelit corner of the room awaited them.

A woman tugged on his arm and drew him to a temporary halt. "Excuse me, but we have a booking and they arrived after us."

The man gave her a nod and answered, "I'll be back in just a moment."

"This is embarrassing," Hana whispered to Logan as a waiter appeared to pull out chairs and lay menus before them with a flourish. Logan shrugged as though he expected nothing less. He reached across and caressed her fingers.

"Would Sir and Madam like time to peruse the menu?" the waiter asked.

Hana swallowed and nodded, watching Logan's lips turn upward at the corners. He waited until they were alone to give her a reassuring wink. "Nice table, babe. You did good."

Hana gave up trying to read the menu after the fifth attempt and settled into a depressed funk. Logan nudged her foot beneath the table. "Don't," she grumbled. "I didn't know it would be in stupid French."

"Stupid French!" Logan jerked his head back in mock horror and clasped both hands over his heart. "My ancestors are turning in their graves right now."

Hana raised an eyebrow and leaned forward, poking her chin over the top of the menu. "We jumped the queue and if that isn't bad enough, I studied German at school. I don't know what any of this stuff means. What if I end up with snails or some poor frog's kneecaps?"

Logan snorted and looked more like his old self as his lips quirked into a grin. "I'll order for you," he offered, but his sideways glance contained mischief.

Hana pushed her feet further under the table and found Logan's cowboy boot. She wrapped her ankles around his and pulled, laughing as he slipped towards the table. "Play nice!" she warned him.

"Frog's legs for you," he muttered.

"I'm assuming you still own shares in this restaurant," Hana mused, frowning as the wait staff pointed at her and whispered behind their hands. "I thought you sold them last year, but judging by the speed at which we got a seat I think you kept them."

Logan wrinkled his nose. "Yeah," he replied. "I'm a sleeping partner and I do the accounts. Alex wanted to mix things up a bit and I'm glad I agreed. It's turning over a fantastic profit."

Hana looked around, taking in the chandeliers and shabby-chic decor. A picture of Napoleon graced one wall in a white wooden frame brushed with a gilt effect. She wrinkled her nose and winced, wondering if marrying a man with French ancestry betrayed her British heritage. Logan laughed out loud at her obvious conflict. "What would your father say?" he mused. "If he objected to an Indian, what would he think about a brown skinned Māori of French descent?"

"He's probably spinning in his grave right now," Hana replied, adding under her breath, "wherever that is."

"Speaking of fathers," Logan said, leaning forward, so he didn't spread his personal business the length and breadth of Rangiriri, "what should I do about mine?"

"Alfred?" Hana asked. "In what way?"

Logan shook his head. "He's had over forty years to get used to Reuben being my father, yet now he seems crushed. Why? And what should I do about it?"

Hana thought about her reply, flattered he'd asked her opinion and not wanting to mess it up. She pursed her lips before answering. "It looks to me like he never intended you to find out. That was his worst nightmare. Now you have and he doesn't know how to deal with it. He's also lost his wife and brother. If it's any consolation, he's angriest most at your mother. He didn't know she kept seeing Reuben until the night of the fire. And you're the last person on earth he can vent to. He's had shock after shock and he's an old man. I'm not sure I'd cope any better. His entire world has changed in all the ways he's spent the last forty years dreading."

"Do you think he's spent my whole life worrying about me finding out?" Logan leaned back in his chair and a light went on in his eyes. It blazed for a moment before the darkness extinguished it.

Hana nodded with exaggerated enthusiasm. "I do. He accepted you so he could keep Miriam, but then he fell in love with you. Somewhere along the way, you became the favourite son. Maybe that's something he didn't bank on. He once told me that when you were born he held you and worried he couldn't keep you safe. Perhaps keeping you safe involved keeping you for himself." Hana picked at the crusty bread roll the waiter delivered with a flourish. She tried not to notice the devastation she saw in Logan's eyes. Her fingers reached for the pitcher of ice water and she almost toppled it in her nervousness. Ice and lemon slices clanked together in the top and she sighed. "This was a terrible idea. Would you like to leave?"

Logan's eyes resembled dark pits of despair and he reached for Hana's fingers, lifting them to his lips. "No. Let's celebrate my birthday like you wanted. But for tonight, let's not talk about either of our fathers. I'm a proud husband and daddy which I wasn't this time last year. Let's concentrate on that."

Hana smiled. "This time last year, you lived in a rented house with a gambler and an idiot."

"And then I met my girl from the train." Logan squeezed her fingers in his strong hand. "You were hiding in the last place I ever thought to look. Twenty-six years of searching for you and just as I gave up, there you were in front of me." He raised an eyebrow and his humour returned. "Geez though woman, I never expected you to be so bloody clumsy!"

Hana laughed and slapped his hand, giving him a look of fake disgust. The waiter appeared, gazing down on them with indulgence. "Is it a special occasion?" he asked and Logan gave Hana the slightest shake of his head.

"No," she replied. "Just nice to be back in town."

He took their order and Hana's eyes widened as Logan read from the menu in perfectly accented French. "Le cassoulet avec aligot," he said and the waiter wrote on his pad and turned away. Hana waited for him to move out of earshot before leaning over and tapping Logan's hand. He dropped his bread roll onto the plate and crumbs scattered onto the tablecloth.

"Did you just order alligator?" she stage whispered. "If you did, I won't be able to eat it."

"Too chewy for you?" Logan quirked an eyebrow and picked up his bread.

When the main course arrived, Hana sighed with relief at the bean casserole with cheesy mashed potatoes. Logan grinned as she remarked on the exquisite taste. "Gosh, this is nice." She dabbed at her lips with a napkin. "Why didn't you want anyone to know it's your birthday?"

"Just don't." Logan's eyes flashed a warning and Hana grinned.

"Should I cancel the cake and the choir?"

Logan's eyes narrowed. "I think they've learned enough about my personal life this summer." His fork dug into his potato with less enthusiasm and Hana felt a stab of regret.

"Fair enough," she conceded.

Alex appeared at their table as the waiter cleared the plates away. A black apron strained at its ties around his waist and he gripped Hana in a bear hug. Her toes scrabbled to stay on the ground as he placed a wet kiss on each cheek. "I'm so glad you decided to try our restaurant," he gushed. "I'm flattered!" He pressed his forehead to Logan's in a hongi and slapped his back with a giant hand. "How's the kai?" He squatted next to Hana, resting both elbows on the table. "Any good?"

"Wonderful." Hana blushed and patted her stomach. "I don't think I can manage dessert."

"Aw, just let your belt out a notch," Alex joked. "Try the sorbet. It's marvellous."

Having drawn attention from every quarter of the restaurant, he left them in peace. Hana avoided the renewed stares of the other patrons and waited for her heart rate to subside to normal speed. She looked at her watch and winced. "We should get back to Phoe soon," she said. "I didn't leave a bottle."

Logan nodded and pushed back his chair, but the reappearance of the waiter interrupted. He laid a bowl of red sorbet between them and two long stemmed spoons. "Compliments of the chef," he said with a bow.

Hana waited for him to move away and then chewed her lower lip. "I don't think I can stuff anymore in," she whispered.

Logan shrugged. "Just a mouthful to please Alex," he suggested. "He wants to impress you."

The ice moistened her lips and cleansed her palate. Hana found herself digging the spoon in for a second time. "What do you know about Leslie's circumstances?" she asked, swallowing. "They seem pretty dire."

Logan's brow furrowed. "I dunno. The state of her place took me by surprise, aye?"

Hana nodded. "She owns nothing."

Logan leaned across and stroked her fingers. "You want me to ask around?"

Hana gave him a smile of appreciation and saw the pleasure spark in Logan's eyes at her approval. "Yes please. Something isn't right there. She told me she'd worked for your family for decades. She must earn more than minimum wage."

"Yeah, she does." Logan swallowed a spoonful of sorbet. "I'll talk to her about the housekeeper's job and put her wage up."

"Thanks babe." Hana gave him a wink and he straightened his shoulders and placed his spoon in the bowl. He indicated to their waiter they would like the bill and the man strode off towards the cash register. When he hadn't returned minutes later, Hana felt the pressure building in her breasts as her baby's next feeding time loomed.

"Start the car, babe," she said as Logan shrugged his muscular shoulders into his jacket. "I'll get the bill." She walked to the counter and stood there, fidgeting as the wait staff avoided her eye. "Excuse me, I need to pay," she said, leaning across the counter. "I have to leave."

Confusion reigned as the cashier tallied her order and Hana's waiter rushed up to stop her. Hana tried to hand over her bank card, growing annoyed as they refused. "I need to leave," she hissed, raising her voice and attracting attention. "What's the problem?" She saw Logan gather his wallet and car keys and turn to face her. His dark eyes assessed the situation and registered the distress in Hana's body language. He pocketed the keys and picked his way towards her, navigating tables and chairs.

Alex appeared before her, sweat beading his brow and sauce decorating his apron. Irritation burgeoned in his eyes at being pulled away from the kitchen. "What's going on?" he hissed to the cashier.

"Mrs Du Rose wants to pay." The waiter chewed his lower lip and watched Alex's brow draw into a frown.

He turned to Hana. "There's no charge," he said, as though concluding a discussion they hadn't had.

Hana's jaw hung slack and she shook her head. "Thank you but no." She held out her bank card. "It's my treat to my husband and I'd like to settle. Please take my card so I can get back to my baby."

"What's wrong?" Logan appeared at her shoulder and Hana cringed. Her confidence sagged.

"They won't let me pay." She sounded defeated and saw Logan's jaw tighten.

"Take the card," he snapped to the cashier and Hana saw the conflict in the girl's eyes as she glanced between the two powerful men. Alex leaned across the counter and shook his head.

"It's a tax write off," he hissed. "What's the point?"

Hana closed her eyes and let the disappointment wash over her. Her planned night out became an accounting term and she wished she hadn't bothered. A vein ticked in Logan's neck and she felt the atmosphere spark. She placed a hand on his arm. "Leave it," she said with a shake of her head. "This was a stupid idea."

Alex's eyes grew round like saucers and he read the misery etched into Hana's petite features. He relented, flapping his hands and reaching for her card. "Madam can settle up," he gushed. He punched numbers into the cash register and came up with an amount way below the actual. Hana accepted the middle ground and pressed the code for her bank card into the machine. Logan placed a protective arm around her shoulder.

"Thanks babe," he whispered into her ear. "It's one of the things I love about you. You've never taken the money for granted."

Hana's fingers shook as she tucked her bank card into her purse. She saw the moment understanding reached Alex's eyes. Anyone knowing Logan's financial status would expect him to pay for everything yet Hana hadn't. She'd spent the last year fighting to maintain her independence from his fortune. She never intended to let herself feel like an appendage to another partner and a drain on their resources. Once in a lifetime was enough.

Alex gave Hana a small smile and nodded in a movement which conveyed respect. He sighed as a waitress tugged on his sleeve. "Aunty says you need to get back to the kitchen," she said. Alex rolled his eyes and nodded, waving her away with a giant hand. Hana felt his gaze burning into her spine as she stepped past couples waiting for tables. She sensed she'd made a statement without meaning to.

Hana drove to Leslie's house, picking her way along unfamiliar roads. The beam of the headlights glared against the front of the house. It appeared derelict in the darkness. Phoenix's mood changed from contented to frantic as she scented Hana's presence within seconds. Leslie rocked her to no avail. Anxiety sent a flush of colour shooting from Hana's neck to her cheeks as she faced the inevitable. "I'm sorry, I'll have to feed her," she said, cringing with discomfort.

"No matter." Leslie waved off her awkwardness. "Babies want what babies want." She gazed at the squalling child with affection. "She's impatient like her daddy."

Logan's eyes widened and Hana bit her lip. She swallowed the instant reference to her husband and breasts which leapt from brain to mouth and almost escaped. Biting her tongue, she released the buttons of her dress and settled in the only armchair to feed her daughter. Logan draped his jacket around her shoulders to protect a little of her modesty. She grumbled to the baby as Leslie left the room and Logan followed her into the small kitchen. "Couldn't you have waited?" Phoenix found her nipple and silenced, feeding as though starved for days. Hana relaxed and listened to the lowered voices coming from the kitchen.

"I'll make tea for the missus but I've no milk." Leslie sounded apologetic.

"That's fine, she can drink it black," Logan replied. Hana heard his boots as he turned to view the kitchen. "Where's your fridge?"

"Don't have one." Leslie sounded sharp as though resenting the question and a sense of foreboding jarred Hana's nerve endings.

"What's going on, Leslie?" Logan's voice sounded kind and it took Hana by surprise. She heard the other woman swallow and her reply sounded emotional.

"I can't tell youse." Her voice wavered. "So, don't ask me nothing else, please Mr Logan."

Hana heard her husband sigh and the sound of his boot soles scraping against the worn lino. "Okay," he said. "But if you're in trouble, I'd like to think you could come to me."

Leslie didn't reply.

Hana tickled Phoenix's feet to keep her awake and feeding, managing to fill the tiny belly until she slept. Logan helped bundle the baby into the car seat and they said their goodbyes. Hana pressed a hundred dollars into Leslie's hand, surprised to see the old woman push the two fifties deep into her bra. "That's double what we agreed," she grumbled, but didn't attempt to give any back.

"Thank you," Hana whispered, placing a kiss on the woman's crinkled cheek.

"See you tomorrow." Logan offered Leslie a smile and Hana saw her falter as though his kindness meant more to her than the cash.

"Night Mr Logan," she replied.

The front door slammed behind them as Hana and Logan picked their way along the rickety porch to the steps. Glancing behind her, Hana saw the shape of Leslie's back leaned against the glass. "What do you think?" she whispered as Logan belted the car seat into the Honda.

"Not sure yet."

Hana started the engine and pulled into the street, slamming on the brakes as a car careened along the centre of the road. She held her breath as it passed, loud beat music vibrating the airwaves. Logan placed a hand over hers on the steering wheel.

"Pull over here," he ordered, his tone hushed. "Kill the engine and turn off the lights." The urgency in his tone alarmed Hana, but she obeyed. The street descended into darkness.

"What's going on?" she whispered as Logan released his seatbelt and twisted himself around to stare through the back window. He raised a finger to his lips and Hana froze. Beat music thudded along the street, slowing as it reached Leslie's house. The light in Leslie's kitchen winked out and threw the house into darkness as though she sensed the attention. The car stopped at the end of her driveway and Hana saw a glittering object spin from the driver's side and hit the front door. Splintering wood and breaking glass echoed in the street but no one emerged from Leslie's house or from any of the others. "What should we do?" Hana raised her voice and Logan placed a finger over her lips. "Call the cops!"

"No." Logan's tone sounded sharp and she held her breath. "That's not how we do things here." He twisted back around and reached for his seatbelt. With a blast of an altered exhaust system, the car revved and screeched away. Leslie's house remained in darkness. "Let's get back to the hotel." Logan reached across and placed a comforting hand on Hana's trembling thigh. "Nothing else will happen tonight. I'll sort it out tomorrow."

"What did they do?" Hana's fingers shook and the keys jangled as she wrenched on the ignition. "What was the noise?"

"They threw a bottle at the front door. That's what smashed." Logan flicked at the indicator stalk and the headlights flooded the road before them. "Want me to drive?"

Hana almost accepted, but the thought of switching places in the darkened street filled her with terror. She shook her head and activated the central locking. She pressed on the gas and the car pulled away from the curb. "Do you know those people?" she asked, relieved when they reached the winding rural road and she could put her foot down and speed.

"Yeah." Logan nodded and Hana saw his brows furrow in his eerie reflection in the windscreen. "Yeah, I know them. This won't be as easy to fix as I'd hoped."

Leslie settled on the blanket she'd laid over the hard floorboards. She kept her clothes on and added an overcoat. She separated the two fifty dollars Hana gave her, placing one beneath each breast. The old woman didn't put it past the two thugs to pay her a visit in the middle of the night. It wouldn't be the first time.

Chapter 19

Hana drove home, struggling with the breakneck drive through the mountains to the hotel. Low lights traced out a path to the front door and Logan carried the baby up the spiral staircase to their private floor.

Hana rubbed her bare arms as he laid Phoenix in her drawer and covered her in a blanket. "Autumn is coming," she whispered, her voice containing a faint sadness. Phoenix snuggled after stretching her tiny body backwards and raising her arms above her head. Hana watched, stroking her cheek. "She's perfect. We're so lucky." She pulled the blanket back over the baby's arms. Logan turned the main lights off and Hana slipped out of her dress and climbed into bed. "The end of summer makes me miserable," she mused, burrowing beneath the blankets.

"Hell of a summer." Logan stripped to his boxers and crawled in next to her. "I'm glad to see the back of it." He wrapped an arm around her and pulled her close. "You looked beautiful tonight." He slipped searching fingers inside Hana's underwear and his eyes glinted in the moonlight. "At the risk of sounding cheesy, I know a great way for warming up."

Hana giggled and shushed him, giving no resistance as he tugged at her bra one-handed. He moaned with pleasure at the silky breasts it disgorged. Logan's touch on her body proved light but insistent and they huddled beneath the sheets and warmed each other.

Phoenix woke early the next day, ensuring her mother did as well. Hana fed her and took her downstairs to make Logan breakfast in bed. It proved difficult one-handed. Phoenix kept throwing her head back to watch the kitchen staff and making Hana jerk. Carrying the tray upstairs whilst holding her was a mission. Hana used the spiral staircase but regretted it halfway up when forced to lay the tray down to hitch the baby further up her hip. She repeated the process numerous times, including outside the bedroom. By the time a tousled Logan sat up to view it, the toast clung to the plate by sheer force of will and the butter congealed on the fried egg, so it sported a violent yellow fringe. "It's not supposed to look like that," Hana mused. "It looks radioactive."

Producing cutlery from her jeans pocket, she sat on the bed and continued her litany of apologies. Logan reached for her hand, his olive chest smooth and inviting with its dusting of dark hair. "It looks fantastic," he reassured her. "This is my first breakfast in bed, so as far as I'm concerned, it's meant to look this way."

"Oh." Hana's jaw dropped and her face crumpled with sorrow. "That's so sad. Never?"

Logan shook his head and tucked into the abomination on his plate. He separated the bacon from the tomato ketchup moat surrounding it. Hana fed the dozing baby, perched sideways on the bed. "You brought me food in bed heaps of times," she said. "I feel ashamed now." She sighed and promised herself she'd work on being less selfish. The coffee ran around the tray and dripped from the mug as Logan lifted it to drink. Hana winced. "Sorry about that. I had a moment where I needed to decide whether to drop the baby or the breakfast. The baby won."

Logan smiled, smacking his lips as he finished the messy feast. He leaned back against the pillows and laid a hand on Hana's thigh. She met his gaze and tried to communicate her love without words. Guilt and fear pricked behind her smile and she looked away. "Happy birthday," she said.

Logan sighed. "The fire put things into perspective, really. My parents never celebrated my birthday and at least now I know why." His brow furrowed. "It's the day I arrived looking nothing like Alfred. I guess nobody wanted to remember that every year. Not even Reuben."

"That's where you're wrong, Logan." Hana reached for his fingers. "He went to a lot of trouble to give you the guitar, remember?"

"Yeah." Logan ran a hand across his rough chin and he shook his head. "So many lies, Hana." His eyes glittered and he fixed his gaze on her face.

"Angus told me you'd sold a birthday cake at school. Wasn't it yours?"

Logan shook his head. "Michael's. He wanted fifty percent, but I beat him down to thirty."

"Beat him?" Hana's brow furrowed and Logan grinned.

"Yep. He's got a little scar on his forehead. That was his twenty percent right there." He sighed. "I don't know what I'd do without you, babe. I'm so grateful you're always straight with me." He leaned across to kiss her and her heart dropped into her stomach. Laval's image drifted across her inner vision and she shivered. She wasn't straight at all. Laval had made a liar of her. Hana opened her mouth to speak, the truth ready to tumble from her lips. Logan spoke first and the impetus died a strangled death. "I'm fed up of it, Hana. It feels like problem after problem at the moment." His right hand rested over his chest. "I'm just heart sick of all of it. We'll fix what's wrong at the boarding house and then have a rethink of everything." He smiled up at her and his face brightened. "It's a big world out there. Let's show some of it to our daughter."

Phoenix woke, flapping her arms and legs and making cute happy noises. Logan reached out to take her, gazing down at his daughter with ultimate indulgence. Hana wrestled herself back from the verge of tears. She wouldn't let him lose what he'd waited so long for. She'd deal with Laval herself, if it was her last gift to Logan.

Logan surprised her later with a request to ride up to the section of land at the top of the mountain. She made a face and pointed to the suckling baby. "Leslie's here," he said. "I asked her and she doesn't mind."

Hana squirmed. "We can't keep abusing her goodwill, Logan, it's not fair. Did you speak to her about the housekeeping job?"

"I'll do it before we leave. Please Hana?" He looked hurt by her reluctance. "If we ride hard, we can be back in three hours. She'll manage for that long."

"Even if we leave the second she finishes her feed, it'll take ages to tack the horses. That's an hour before we're mounted and then three more."

Logan threw himself on the bed next to her. The baby stopped feeding and squirmed sideways to look at him. "Please?" he begged. "I'll tack up now and have everything waiting. I promise."

"Fine," Hana agreed. She wagged a finger at him. "Only if you have that conversation with Leslie and promise we can get back in time. I don't want to walk in on a hysterical baby!"

Logan's face lit up like a child's watching the Christmas tree lights first turned on. He rushed from the bedroom, returning a few minutes later from his sister's room next door. Liza's jodhpurs and chaps dangled from his hand and he threw them on the bed. "Hop into these when you're done and I'll be outside the front." He grinned.

"Hop?" Hana snorted. "I just gave birth. Don't you mean wrestle into them?"

"They'll fit." Logan's smile sagged. "Won't they?" His voice held a begging edge.

"Don't hassle me though Loge," Hana warned as he turned to leave. "Feeding Phoe will take as long as it takes."

He nodded and left with his familiar swagger and Hana lay on the bed and watched her child feed. Half an hour later after a nappy change and another feed, Phoenix lay in her drawer in the middle of the kitchen table. Leslie bustled around her, dealing with the day's menu and whispering orders to the wait staff. It seemed calm and orderly in the industrial kitchen, but Hana wondered what the health inspector would say if he ever saw the sleeping baby in the middle of the offending table.

Logan's face split into a grin as she emerged on the front steps. Liza's clothes felt snug and she'd appropriated her sister-in-law's boots from the mudroom. Two horses stood on the pristine lawn and one had already delivered a shovel full of manure to Miriam's prize roses. Logan lifted a Jillaroo hat from his saddle horn and turned with uncharacteristic shyness before handing it to Hana. She took it and admired the brown leather replica of his Jackaroo. Smaller and daintier, it looked like one she'd seen in the tack shed once before. "I want you to have this," he said with ceremony. "It was Ma's. I bought it for her when I got my first month's wages mustering. She didn't ride much after that summer, so it's almost new. I saddle soaped it yesterday. Would you like it?"

Logan's fingers shook, his heart seeming raw and open. Hana took the hat with reverence and popped it on her head. She pulled the cord underneath her chin and poked her fringe inside. "Do I look like a McLeod's Daughter now?" she asked.

Logan put his hands around her waist and kissed her under the brim of the hat. "You look like a Du Rose daughter now," he said, approving.

It took seconds for him to help her fit the leather chaps over her calves. His fingers moved with sensuous precision against her muscles and Hana felt a flush of desire which flustered her. Logan winked as he took her hand and dragged her to the huge Appaloosa gelding. He gave her a leg up, sorted her girth and stirrups and then mounted his mare. "You remember Digger, don't you?" he called behind him as his mare wheeled round and took off towards the yard gate. Hana didn't have time to answer as her horse set off after him at a trot. While Logan opened the gate and closed it behind her, Hana caught her breath enough to ask a question.

"How hard do you intend to ride, Logan?" she demanded. "I don't want to fall."

"You won't." He spun his mare around with the merest flick of the reins. "That's why you're riding Digger."

"Great," Hana groaned, the words ripped from her lips as the horses took off.

They climbed the mountain, Logan negotiating the gates without dismounting. Hana let her horse lead the way, suspecting he knew where they were going. On the fluffy green slopes, Digger galloped hard at the prospect of Logan's mare catching up after closing each gate. Her hooves thundered behind and Hana felt as though she flew. The cooling air and rising dust robbed the breath from her lungs. Logan cut through the bush on what seemed like a circuitous route, but they reached the mountain top in half an hour. Hana's chest heaved with exhilaration, her backside still in the saddle and her hat clamped on her head. Logan laughed at her pink cheeks. "There's nothing like a good gallop to blow the cobwebs away, aye?"

"I can see the attraction," she admitted.

Sunlight bathed Logan's prized paddock at the summit, bright after the shade of the bush. The gate stood wide open, the number coded padlock gone. The horses wandered in and Logan dismounted and pulled the gate shut behind them. It creaked on its hinges as though forgetting it spent years fortifying the land against Reuben's family until recently. Logan untacked the horses, allowing them to graze and cool off. He stacked the tack on the fence near the gate for a quick getaway.

Hana pursed her lips and Logan's brow furrowed. "They'll come when I whistle," he reassured her. "Trust me."

Hana narrowed her eyes and groaned. "Those words are guaranteed to make me worry." She sensed his tension and grew quiet as he rested his arm across her shoulders. They often referred to the paddock as Serious Hill. It had been the site of many catalyst discussions in their relationship. Logan kept a tight hold on his wife as he walked her to the cliff top and she breathed in the salty scent of the Tasman Sea. Hazy buildings in the distance marked out Port Waikato. "It's so beautiful up here," she whispered.

"That's what I wanted to talk to you about," Logan said, pressing her into his side. "I told you I got planning permission for a change of usage to residential, but I want to know where to put the house and what sort of building you envisage. We could truck Culver's Cottage up here if that's what you want, but it will need to come in pieces. I want this to be our place, not just yours or mine."

He stopped and that familiar awkwardness descended. Hana hadn't seen it for a while and her heart clenched. "Culver's Cottage wouldn't cope with the extreme weather up here," she said. "I think you're right, we need to start again with something we create together."

Logan sighed with relief. They discussed where the best site would be, Hana relying on her husband's knowledge of the land. He knew where the sun rose and set and where the worst of the sea breezes would batter a potential dwelling. Logan stepped out an area, measuring with long strides to plan the footprint of the house. Hana paused as a familiar sound reached her ears, transporting her back seven weeks. She saw herself grovelling on her hands and knees in the dirt, sweat pouring from her forehead as she heaved her premature daughter into the world. The tui bird cackled, laughing now as it did then.

"Where are you going?" Logan called as Hana jogged to the gate and let herself out. She halted beneath a group of ancient kauri trees which towered above her. Looking up into the branches, she spied the bird, his blue-black feathers and his little white bow tie glinting in the late morning sun. He cocked his head to one side and eyed her from his great height. Then he cackled and made a grunting sound.

Hana giggled, putting her hand over her mouth. "Are you mimicking the sound of my labour?" She shook her fist at him and he fluffed his feathers and called again.

"Hana?" Logan showed concern as he arrived behind her, looking up in confusion. He took her arm and pulled her away from the bottom of the widest tree. "It's tapu here," he said, his voice serious. "Sacred."

"Oh, sorry." Hana stepped back. "I didn't know."

Logan pointed further up the trunk of the enormous tree to writing etched into the peeled wood. Hana squinted and shielded her eyes against the sun, trying to read what it said. "Names?" she asked her husband and he nodded.

Someone had carved each into the bark with a sharp object. Over twenty names spread out to include Reuben, Alfred and Logan's. They cascaded to form a living and well-documented family tree. Attached to each carved name was an image. Hana cocked her head and frowned in confusion. She pointed to the name Phoenix above Logan's.

He shook his head. "My maternal grandmother," he said. "Kuia Phoenix. Remember?" He repeated her name with reverence and awe. Hana nodded and withdrew her hand, letting her finger rest by her side. She felt guilty knowing she should have remembered without prompting.

The faded words looked bleached against the wood grain. Logan's name sat beneath Alfred's, but his carving straddled both lines of the family. Hana pointed again and Logan shrugged. "A clue I missed," he said, his tone sad. "I assumed they ran out of space to fit me in next to

Barry, Liza and Michael." He shielded his eyes. "See how my name runs up against Neville and Kane's?" He tapped a finger against his temple. "I always felt as though neither side had enough room for me. Now I know why."

"Don't." Hana pulled his hand down and linked their fingers. "Phoenix and I have room for you." She sighed and looked around at the smattering of sunlight bleeding through the trees. "We should head back."

Logan's lips curved upward and he wrapped his arms around Hana, pulling her backwards into his chest. Lifting her chin, he pointed to the image carved beneath his name. "Don't you want to know what my drawing means?"

Hana narrowed her eyes and peered at the tiki. "He's a good luck charm," she replied. "The first mortal born to the gods."

"Impressive." Logan kissed the top of her head. "What else?"

"I don't know." She squirmed free and walked towards the gate. "We need to go."

Logan caught her around the waist and the squeal left Hana's lungs. He kissed her neck and she giggled. "He's a fertility symbol," he breathed in her ear. "For years I believed they got it wrong."

"He gives the bearer clarity of thought and great inner knowledge." Hana laughed as he tickled her ribs.

"You're quoting Wikipedia! That's dangerous." Logan spun her to face him and stroked a finger along her cheek. "I love you, Hana Du Rose."

Hana snorted. "You think I didn't notice the massive phallus between its legs? Don't even think about it."

"Are you saying it doesn't represent me?" Mock horror showed in Logan's grey eyes and Hana shook her head.

"I'm saying you needn't prove it."

"But I do now. You've cast doubt."

The tui let out a cackle which echoed in the canopy. Hana allowed herself another peek at the image and shook her head. "Why do they need to be so graphic? It's enormous."

Logan laughed and the tui joined in, an air of mockery surrounding them. "You didn't see what I wanted you to," he said, his tone becoming serious. He took Hana's hand and led her around the side of the tree. Bending his knees, he pointed from her level so she could follow his direction. "Look."

"Oh." Hana gasped. "You started again."

Logan nodded. "Yep."

The slanted script stood out against the bark, engraved with precision. Logan had repeated his own name and added Hana's next to it, the lines running into Phoenix Du Rose underneath.

"It's beautiful." Hana shuddered. "Are you allowed to change things like that?"

Logan shrugged and his jaw clenched. "My land, my tree, my decision." His eyes became hard. "My legacy. I buried Phoenix's afterbirth under the tree because it felt like the right thing to do. Jack told me afterwards that my kuia buried mine here too and he buried Reuben's. I don't feel like adding Reuben's name above mine yet, but I will one day."

"Is that why you're so tied to this land?" Hana asked. She lowered her voice to a whisper. "Tangata whenua, the people of the land."

"Yeah, I think so." Logan sighed. "It's why I can't sell."

Hana swallowed. "So now you've tied Phoenix to it too?" A wave of superstition disquieted her soul. She looked up at the tree, regretting her inability to absorb her husband's beliefs. Her British ways distanced her from the tikanga and kawa, customs and protocols of Māori. Beauty and awe gave way to misgivings.

"How will we get to the new house?" she asked, glancing back towards the gate. "You can't yell at people for driving over tapu land every time they visit."

"It's fine." Logan released her. "They shouldn't stomp around the bottom of the tree. It's outside the gate."

Hana shook her head, attempting to lighten the heavy mood. "I can't cope with driving past a caricature of my husband with an enormous willy every time I arrive home. Imagine giving someone directions and having to say, 'Drive through the gate at the top of the hill without hitting the afterbirth and turn left at the tiki with the giant thing between its legs.'"

"Idiot." Logan reached forward and cupped her swollen breasts. "Hey," he said, breathing into her ear. "We've got an hour and a half left."

They emerged from the bush half an hour later. Hana's hair stuck up at a jaunty angle and her hat looked squashed. Half a silver fern hung from her shirt collar and her face creased at the horrid feeling in her jeans. "I think something crawled into my knickers," she said, her expression a grimace.

"Yep," Logan confirmed, without humour. "Me."

"No, really. Like a bug!" Hana hopped around, pulling ferns from her underwear. "Oh no!" she cried, pointing at the open gate. "You didn't shut it!"

"I thought you were last out," Logan replied, fixing a look of innocence on his rugged features.

Hana rounded on him, anger flashing in her eyes. "No! I came out first and you followed! Gosh farm-boy, don't you know how to shut gates?" Hana stomped into the paddock and shaded her eyes from the sunshine. She couldn't see the horses. "Walking back will take hours and hours. You promised!" she ranted.

Logan leaned on the fence and watched Hana rage around the paddock. A mission to get an earwig out of her shirt punctuated her frantic search for their ride home. She screamed and flailed, yanking her shirt over her head and not putting it back on until sure it was uninhabited. Then she put it on inside out. "You finished?" Logan pushed his hat back on his head with an index finger and waited for Hana to glare at him. When she put her hands on her hips, he placed two fingers into his mouth and released a shrill whistle. Within seconds, the horses appeared on the horizon in answer to his call.

Hana jutted her chin in the air. "How did you know they didn't leave the paddock?" she demanded.

Logan rolled his eyes. "Why would they? This fallow, ungrazed paddock hardly compares to bark chippings and silver fern. It's not much of a contest is it? And I told you I'd whistle them when we wanted to leave."

Hana hung her head and felt stupid. "Fine," she conceded. "I'm sorry."

The horses stood while Logan tacked them up. He gave Hana a leg up into the saddle and enjoyed her discomfort. "Farm-boy," he muttered under his breath, turning away when she cringed. After he concluded she'd suffered enough, he gave her a wink, laughing when she stuck her tongue out.

"Do you know what it means when a Māori woman sticks her tongue out?" he asked, his hand still on her leg.

"War?" Hana asked.

Logan shook his head and his eyes narrowed. "That's the men. For wahine it's the opposite."

Hana almost did it again, but put it back into her mouth. He didn't need an excuse to roll her in the undergrowth again and she wanted to get back to her child. The free morning merged into an enforced absence alongside the urge to feed Phoenix. The figurative umbilical cord stretched across the kilometres between them, tugging and pulling. Anxiety lit her eyes and Logan turned his horse for home.

Digger plodded behind Logan's mount, nodding his head in time to the relentless beat of his hooves. Hana lay back in her saddle to balance him out, slowing him from a canter to a trot as the going got tougher.

Logan turned off the original track, making a detour. Hana griped at the delay until they came to a familiar section of land. At the bottom of a steep slope she saw a flat, scarred piece of burnt ground. It looked half-cleared and a yellow earth mover sat beside a bulldozer, both idle for the weekend. The huge machines slept. Only the sound of the bush, the birds calling and the wind in the trees disturbed their peace. The old boundary fence still lay flat on the ground and

Hana shivered, reminded of the sights and sounds of that terrible night. She put her fingers to her lips and squeezed her eyes shut as Miriam's screams filled her mind.

"Hey, don't." Logan pulled her hand from her lips and caressed her fingers. His skin felt coarse and work worn and she clung to them. The horses stamped and crunched their teeth on metal bits as Hana faced the charred earth. "I've bought it." Logan said and she looked at him in confusion. He turned towards her, his face a mask of sadness as his horse's tack clanked beneath him. "I've bought Reuben's half of the mountain. The family didn't want to build here again and I understand. It's cursed now."

"What will you do with it?" Hana asked. Her voice sounded loud in the silence and her lower lip trembled. An icy chill seemed to wrap around her body.

"I want to create a memorial garden for them," he said. "What do you think?"

Hana nodded. "Yeah," she breathed. "That's a great idea. We can't leave it like this."

Logan nodded and squeezed her fingers before letting go. "Thanks," he whispered. Then the shutters crashed down over his soul and the moment of vulnerability ceased. Logan clicked his tongue and his horse moved off along the track. Hana followed, allowing herself only one quick glance back towards the scorched earth.

In her mind's eye she saw Reuben's face, a mirror image of Logan's. He smiled at her as her unborn baby kicked against his scarred hand.

Chapter 20

"She didn't even miss me!" Hana folded her arms and glanced sideways into the car seat. "It's the longest I've left her and she didn't care."

Logan shook his head and stared at Hana in the rear-view mirror. "So, let me get this right, you didn't want to arrive back to a hysterical baby, but a happy, gurgling baby wasn't right either?"

Hana focussed on the view through the side window and pursed her lips. "I knew you wouldn't understand," she grumbled.

"Oh, Angus texted me," Logan said. "We can move back into the unit tomorrow. He kept the tradies at it all weekend and they've finished."

Hana pulled a face. "Fantastic. I can't wait." Her brow furrowed and a smile spread across her lips. "It hardly seems worth it. The new manager arrives in a week's time and then we'll move out again. I'll stay at home and you can travel in like we used to." A smug smile of satisfaction reached her eyes.

"No." Logan peered at her through the rear-view mirror. "We're all going. I'm meeting with Angus first thing in the morning. He thinks the new manager is delayed."

"What a surprise!" The pout swallowed Hana's finer features. "I don't believe there ever was a new manager. Just a ruse to appeal to your superhero complex."

"Well, we'll find out tomorrow, won't we?" Logan ground his teeth and didn't bother refuting the superhero accusation.

Hana fretted. Laval could get to her at the school with ease. Flick's revelations about his character offered no comfort. Hana tapped a finger against her thigh. "Did you give Leslie the job?" she asked.

"No."

Logan's response made her eyes roll back in her head and she ground her teeth. "Why? Logan, you promised!"

"I've got Toby making enquiries, Hana. Something's not right. I won't give her the keys to the kingdom until I find out what."

Hana groaned and pressed her head back against the seat. A sense of powerlessness enveloped her. How could she help Leslie when she couldn't even help herself?

A pan of hot soup simmered on the stove as a welcome, courtesy of their neighbour Maihi. She stayed long enough to coo over Phoenix and then left. "Youse looking tired, kōtiro," she whispered in Hana's ear.

Hana kissed her weathered olive cheek and nodded, waving her off. They ate and she fed the baby, becoming tenser as the evening progressed. Laval would come for her again, jumping out like a dreadful jack-in-the-box and scaring her witless. "I won't bother to unpack," she whined. "I'll wash everything at the unit. We'll go back to living out of suitcases until we can go home."

Logan noticed how on edge she was and clasped her round the waist as she folded extra baby clothes and thumped them into the suitcase. He ran his fingers up the side of her neck, overwhelming her with his sex appeal and sensing her escaping from under his spell. "Hey, babe. I'm sorry you don't want to go back on site. I hate how unhappy it makes you to be trapped there, but unless we live separate lives, it's the only solution."

Hana grunted and accepted Logan's hug. "Have you spoken to Odering lately?" she asked, making the question sound casual.

Logan's body stiffened. "No. Why would I?"

"I just wondered. Oh why can't I stay here?" Hana pleaded, pushing her face into his shirt. "You'll only be away one or two nights; I'll be happier here."

"No," Logan replied, settling his lips on hers to stop the conversation escalating. Phoenix snored as he undressed his wife, distracting her from the whiney protests and making her need him. "I have to live on site," he whispered as Hana reached a breaking point in their lovemaking. "So you're coming with me."

She groaned and conceded, knowing he'd played a dirty game and won, but needing him to finish what he started. "I hate you," she hissed as she reached her climax and heard Logan snuff into her hair.

"No, you don't."

Next morning they rose early. Hana hated tumbling from the bed, knowing the school site held danger for her family. The hot water heater failed, spraying Logan with freezing cold jets of water. "Bloody hell!" he screamed and jumped from the shower naked. Phoenix thrashed her arms in response. He hopped back in to wash off the soap.

"I'm not going out without a shower!" Hana protested.

"Get one at the unit!" Logan argued. "Because you're not staying here." He poked his head around the curtain, sending Phoenix into another thrashing frenzy. "Nice try though."

"I didn't cause it!" Hana waited for him to finish before climbing under the freezing jets and pretending it didn't bother her. "You're just a big baby," she mocked. "It's not that cold." Behind the safety of the shower curtain she shivered through her wash.

Hana sent Maihi a text on the way into town, begging her to ask her builder-husband to fix the heater and invoice Logan. "Ugh!" she said in the car, piling wet hair into a high pony tail. "It feels disgusting on my back."

Logan drove the Honda through the back entrance of the school site and parked it outside their unit. Two empty spaces marked the absence of the builder and decorator's trucks. The joined units matched like twins, the window frames sanded and painted in fresh white. The front door shone with a coat of red and as Logan unlocked and pushed it open, it didn't make the dreadful creaking sound. "Wow, this is different," he said. "Doesn't look like the same place."

"Feels the same though," Hana grumbled. "It's still a shoe box."

Logan held the baby and inspected the bedrooms. Hana listened to his sounds of approval, standing next to the fireplace with a grimace marring her pretty features. A note on the kitchen counter from Amanda explained she'd helped set the furniture out and hoped it suited them. It was a carbon copy of her unit next door, with slight differences in the curtain material and sofa colour.

Hana sighed as Logan handed Phoenix back. He kissed the tiny upturned face before leaning in to kiss Hana. "I've an eight o'clock meeting with Himself," he said, referring to Angus. "I'll unload the car before I go." He turned, dragging the car keys from his pocket. "Hana..." He stopped and bit his lip. "Be careful, hey?"

Hana knitted her brow and her eyes widened. She cocked her head as her eyes demanded an explanation. "Why wouldn't I be?" Her chin rose in a gesture of defiance.

"With the court case coming up." Logan qualified his comment. "Laval might exert an influence even from remand prison."

Hana's jaw worked in her cheek as she fought for control. She saw the regret in Logan's eyes. "We'll be fine," he said and kissed her forehead. "Sorry for mentioning it. The old guy didn't look like he could tie his own shoes, let alone come after us. It's just a silly thought."

Hana stood where he left her, guilt wrapping her soul in a stranglehold. It didn't matter whether Laval Senior could get to her from prison or not. He didn't have to when his son could do it for him.

Phoenix slept in her cot in the back bedroom while Hana made up the double bed with a new duvet cover and sheets. "Angus won't be smiling when he gets the bill for this lot," she smirked, savouring the high quality of the fabric. "You've had an online shopping spree, Mr Du Rose and there's a home wares store ready to send you flowers at Christmas."

A loud rapping made her heart freeze. It restarted only as she navigated the suitcases in the hallway and heard someone call her name. Yanking open the front door, Hana poked her head out into the narrow street and then put her hands on her hips. "What are you doing here?"

"Hey," Tama cried, flinging his arms wide. "Give us a cuddle!"

Hana stood aside to admit his lithe, teenage body. "Absolutely not. Answer me. What are you doing here?"

Tama stepped between Hana and the doorframe, sliding himself through the gap. A large suitcase followed him in and banged against her shins. He indicated the smart new sofa. "My bed I presume, unless Uncle is interested in a threesome."

Hana opened her mouth and Tama placed an olive palm over it. "I've cleared it with Uncle Logan and he spoke to Mr Blair. I can stay."

"But why? You said you'd never come back here."

Tama shrugged. "I remember. I said I'd only come back if my shorts were on fire." Hana shifted her gaze to his neat backside and he hooted with laughter. "I knew you'd look. Hey, no hard feelings. When you shag the school typist, you can't expect to stay."

Hana eyed her nephew with suspicion, his philosophical attitude out of character. "What are you up to?" she demanded. "You're starting agricultural college in a few weeks and I'm not sure I can keep you out of trouble for that long. There are too many females over forty in this place and I can't protect them all. Do I need to ring Logan and check you're telling the truth?"

"Nope," Tama said with confidence. "I spoke to Uncle, but you can check if you must." He sank into the voluptuous folds of the new sofa and patted the arm nearest him. "But if you get me a beer, I'll tell you what Flick said."

Hana froze. "There's no beer. And why do I care what he said?"

"Because he told me to look after you," Tama replied, his grey eyes narrowing.

Hana shook her head. "Don't lie! Damn that man. He told you everything! I knew I shouldn't have trusted him!"

Tama cringed. "I told him you'd guess straight away. Yeah, he told me. We figured because I know what Laval looks like, I'd be the best person to keep you safe. Like a bodyguard, only way hotter."

"Why would Bobby betray me?" Hana complained. "He promised he'd wait."

"Bobby? Oh, Flick. He wanted to make things right with you. He couldn't come himself or the cops would be on him like a rash, so he sent me."

"What else did he say?" Hana snapped.

Tama quailed. "He said if I screw up and something happens to you, Phoenix or Logan, he'll come after me and make it hurt."

Hana sank onto the sofa next to Tama, trying to process the new development. He put his long arm around her shoulders. "You're pleased I'm here. I can tell."

She frowned and slapped his thigh. "Don't be ridiculous. I can handle it myself."

"Well, now you don't need to. Tama's here to save the day."

"Save the day?" Hana edged away from him, forcing herself against the opposite arm of the sofa. She raised a finger and jabbed his ribs. "If you as much as blink in the presence of a female, I will throw you out!"

"I know, I know," replied Tama. "Uncle already gave me the no sex talk! What's for lunch?"

Hana stood and ran a hand through her fringe. The presence of the teenager drew attention to the emptiness of the new fridge. "Nothing yet. Look, make yourself useful for half an hour. Mind Phoe while I get some shopping. I just put her down for a nap, so she shouldn't wake. Settle in, but don't leave the house and make sure you keep the doors locked. Promise?"

Tama nodded and practiced his reliable face. "I'll guard her with my life," he swore and Hana almost believed him. She wavered in the tiny space between the lounge and the front door, one shoe on her foot and the other in her hand. Tama picked up the remote control for the television and flicked through a few channels. He didn't look up at Hana but she saw his self-satisfied smirk. "Go, Aunty!" he told her. "I'd need longer than half an hour to get into mischief."

Hana shot out the front door and locked it behind her. She extracted the Honda from in front of Tama's battered ute and sped to the nearest supermarket.

Tama wrinkled his nose at the infomercials. Then he checked his watch. On the farm he would have been at work for hours already, fixing a fence or checking stock. He leaned back and hauled his phone from his pocket, unlocking the screen and starting a game. Twenty minutes later, a knock on the front door made him jump and a zombie ate his little soldier. "Ah, shit!" he grumbled.

He crept into the kitchen and peered through the window, rising so he could see more than just St Bart's wall opposite. Leaning over the sink, he managed to see the front steps. A woman's expensive jacket sleeve identified the caller and his heart lurched with recognition. The sensation of the fabric moving over his bare chest was ingrained on his psyche. Anger and habit made a heady concoction and Tama forgot his promise to Hana.

"Tama!" Anka's hand rose to cover her mouth almost in self-defence. "Sorry," she gasped and turned away.

"Wait." Tama grasped her sleeve. "Don't go." He stood back and Anka paused. The fluttering of her eyelashes gave away her confusion. Fear and the thrill of danger sent her up the steps and into the small lobby. She brushed against Tama, causing his hormones to give a disconcerting surge which made him breathless and removed the last of the useful blood to his brain.

"I wanted Hana," Anka gushed. "I shouldn't have come."

She turned again but Tama blocked the doorway. His fingers scrabbled at his waist and he lifted his tee shirt over his head, inviting her to enjoy the sight of youthful muscle and supple skin. A sketchy beard covered his chin and a long fringe danced against the movement of his eyelashes. "I don't want you to go," he whispered.

Anka sighed with the memory of fulfilment as Tama parted her lips with his tongue. He began the dangerous dance with caution, picking up her enthusiasm and pushing his fingers through her short hair. Anka's tight skirt ripped as he lifted her and braced himself against the wall. She balanced and straddled his crotch, leaning back with a moan as he buried his face in her breasts. At the last minute, he remembered to kick the front door closed.

Tama's promises tumbled to the ground along with Anka's knickers. He pressed his thumbs over her erect nipples and ground her beneath him.

"We shouldn't be doing this," she moaned, her will power disappearing under the influence of the intoxicating Du Rose male.

"Shush," he soothed, marking her neck with a love bite and hoisting her bare buttocks higher. Anka ended up right back where she started. Right where she wanted to be. As her drug of choice, Tama Du Rose rendered her blissfully senseless.

Chapter 21

Hana parked at the staff units, struggling to squeeze the Honda between Tama's ute and a smart saloon. She retrieved the shopping bags from the back seat and set them on the steps, pleased with how fast she'd managed her errand without Phoenix and her paraphernalia.

The front door opened without her turning the key. "Tama!" she screamed. A bag tipped over and pasta spewed far and wide. Navigating the mess, Hana barrelled into the small lobby, a jumbo packet of toilet rolls clutched in her arms. Her jaw dropped at the sight of Anka leaping up from her new sofa.

"I'm sorry, I'm sorry." Anka's lips moved, but Hana became distracted by the pert breasts spilling over the top of a hastily fastened bra. Dropping the toilet rolls, she pointed at Anka's knickers draped over the television screen. A daytime presenter peered from beneath the gusset, demonstrating how to whisk egg whites to the perfect consistency.

"Oops!" Tama bit his lip and swore, covering his nakedness with one of the new designer cushions. Hana squealed and leapt across the room to snatch it away. Unashamed, Tama shrugged and rested his hands over his hips. He gave a cursory glance around for something else to cover himself. When his gaze rested on Phoenix's blanket, Hana bared her teeth.

"Don't you dare!" she snarled. She turned to face him and then turned away again, her cheeks flushing tomato red. "What do you think you're doing?" she gasped.

Tama quirked an eyebrow. "It has many names," he began. Hana silenced him with a raised finger.

"I'm so sorry." Anka lurched for her knickers. As she passed Tama, he reached out a hand and cupped her exposed breast in his palm. Unsated lust still darkened his expression. "Don't!" Anka hissed, her cheeks reddening more. She stepped into her underwear and Tama smirked as she bent to snag a stiletto from beneath the sofa. "Oh, shit!" she breathed at her close view of his partial erection.

Tama exacerbated the situation, turning on the spot to search for his undies. Neither woman could look at him or each other. Only Tama seemed impressed with his nude full frontal, picking through the rummage sale of clothing on the rug without shame. Anka reached across and handed him a pair of black boxer shorts. At the same time, she buttoned her blouse one handed and pushed her feet into the shoes. Hana shook her head at the precision of a practiced routine.

"Get out." She included them both in the command, stepping over Tama's jeans and scattered pasta to get to the hallway. With as much dignity as she could muster, she walked into Phoenix's bedroom and closed the door.

Hana sat on the floor for a while and waited, counting the number of splodges on the ceiling left by the wall painters. Cracking the bedroom window ajar and setting it on the security latch, she leaned her forehead against the cool glass and listened to the sounds of the school as the bell rang for morning interval. When the house settled into an eerie quiet, she returned to the lounge, expecting to find it empty. Instead, Anka waited for her, handbag and car keys at the ready. Tama fluffed around, looking for something else beneath the sofa. He'd donned his shorts but nothing else. "I'm sorry,

Hana," Anka gushed. "I came to see you, but things happened."

"And you ended up seeing much more of Tama instead." Hana's tone sounded wooden. "It must have been just like old times, having a quick shag behind your husband's back. I'm glad you've had fun with my babysitter, but I asked you to leave. Now get out." Hana ground her teeth, making a ridged line through her cheek.

"It wasn't like that!" Anka pleaded.

"Please. Leave."

Abandoning her apology, Anka sped through the open front door like a burst dam. Pasta crunched beneath her high heels. Tama found his jeans and rose, giving Hana a cheesy and unapologetic grin. "I don't believe you!" she shouted. "I was only gone for an hour! How could you break my trust? And on my new furniture!"

Tama sighed and slumped onto the sofa. He threaded one wiry foot into a moth eaten sock. "Technically," he said, "it's not your sofa. It's my bed. And you said you'd take half an hour. I'm glad you were longer, but I would've preferred an extra ten minutes." He picked up his other sock. "Then I wouldn't feel quite so cheated."

"Stop!" Hana put her hands over her ears. If she hoped to avoid the sordid details of his mid-morning romp with a woman old enough to be his mother, she lucked out. His lips kept moving and noise continued to emerge. Hana shook her head to dislodge the unwelcome images.

Tama smirked. "Another ten minutes and I could have managed a fourth time. Three's okay. I'm not angry with you." His eyes misted. "There's this excellent thing she does with her tongue." He turned to Hana and opened his mouth as though to demonstrate and she lost her temper.

"Shut up!" Tears budded in her eyes. "Shut up! She was my friend, you idiot. My friend! I don't need to know!" She swiped a hand across her face. "You always ruin everything!"

"Are you gonna tell Uncle Logan?" Tama's complexion paled as the consequences lined up before him in a worrying parade. "He'll send me away and then Flick will kill me."

"I don't know," Hana answered, her voice betraying her misery. "Get dressed! I can't think straight right now. I want you to leave, but I don't know what to tell Logan."

Tama's shoulders slumped. "I've messed up, haven't I?" The swagger left his stance as the post coital bloom waned. "Sorry, okay? I'm really sorry, Hana." He shuffled towards her with his jeans around his ankles. Half way across the rug he tripped over the other lost shoe. "Give me a hug," he demanded. He swallowed and fear back lit his eyes. "Logan's gonna kill me. Or Flick. Or both." He held his arms out in a zombie like posture and Hana tripped backwards in an attempt to duck. "Please, just hug me," he begged. "I am sorry."

"No!" Hana grunted, pushing him away as his brawny arms enfolded her. "Get off me, you randy boy!"

Tama laughed and squeezed her, his biceps squashing her cheek against his left nipple. "What kind of word is randy, anyway?" The laugh died in his throat. Hana felt his whole body stiffen and a ripple of fear pass through him. Male deodorant shrouded her head and made her want to cough.

"Get off, Tama!" she rebuked, giving him a final shove. He didn't resist and she broke free, tripping backwards as her feet tangled in his abandoned tee shirt. Tama glanced down at her, his grey eyes wide and terrified. Then he swore.

Hana knew without looking that Logan stood behind her. She clasped a hand to her chest as her heart paused its next few beats and then released a frightened clamour which sounded like rushing water in her ears. She turned with deliberate slowness to face her husband. Logan leaned against the wall of the narrow hallway. His folded arms crossed his muscular chest and his deadpan expression sent terror into Tama's brain. Hana knew the moment the latch failed on the last of his common sense because he started babbling. "It's not what you think," he began and Hana shuttered her lashes enough to peek from beneath them. A familiar warning vein ticked in Logan's neck and he unclenched and clenched his jaw. Tama put his hands up in front of him in self-defence. "Hana's innocent in all this so please, don't kill her. It's my fault. Kill me."

Logan remained motionless and Hana panicked. Footsteps crunched through the pasta in the road outside as boys used the lane as a rat run to the back entrance of the dining room. Curious faces lingered to peer into the open doorway, their eyes widening at the sight of Logan in his familiar, dangerous pose.

"Go to the bathroom," Hana hissed and Tama shot off along the hallway like a cork out of a bottle. He hauled his jeans over his backside as he went. Logan used his foot to slam the front door closed. The bathroom door clicked shut and the sound of the lock turning echoed in the hallway. So much for Tama's short lived heroism. Logan turned his head to register the sound, making no other movement. The vein continued to tick in his neck. Then he looked back at Hana.

She held her husband's gaze with as much dignity as she could muster, but nerves produced a foolish smirk which spread from her lips to her eyes. She put her hand over her mouth to disguise it, making it worse. "It wasn't me and him," she whispered. The tension in the room hiked and the giggles bubbled in her chest.

Logan shook his head and sighed. Then he unfolded his arms and nudged a pointed cowboy boot in the fallen pasta. "I'm not stupid," he said, his tone even. A smile broke out across his lips. "I saw you arrive home and your tarty friend leave. I filled in the blanks for myself." He stepped over the discarded shopping and took Hana in his arms. Her body shook as she stifled the inappropriate snorts.

"I can't control him," she said, trying to whisper, so Tama couldn't hear her.

"Join the club." Logan's voice rumbled through his chest and into her ear. "Why is he here?"

She swallowed and the mirth subsided. "You said he could stay."

"Hmmn." Logan inhaled. "He phoned and told me you said he could."

Hana tutted and ran out of responses. She hated to admit that a co-conspirator might help her precarious situation. "He might be good company," she breathed.

"As long as he keeps his pants on." Logan's sigh betrayed his exhaustion. He ran his thumbs over Hana's cheekbones and lifted her face to brush her lips, the heady Du Rose masculinity just as seductive on the older version.

"He thinks you're going to kill him," Hana whispered as Logan's lips pulsed against hers.

"I still might," he breathed. "Just for fun."

Hana gazed at the sofa. "Is it too late to get a refund? He's defiled our new furniture."

Logan's lips quirked upwards in a ready smile. "You have so little imagination, wahine," he breathed between kisses. "He's over six foot. I think the two-seater is safe." He kissed Hana once more before disconnecting. "Don't make plans to put the baby on the rug though."

Chapter 22

"No way!" Hana half shouted, desperation hiking her fury. "This isn't happening!" She put her hands over her ears, attempting to block out the bombshell news. Logan abandoned his sandwich and slipped from the stool to take Hana's hands.

"It's just a few months." His voice sounded gentle but firm, offering no debate. "There's nothing else he can do."

"You said that three weeks ago, but I'm still living in this shoe box!" Hana resisted the tears welling behind her eyes, pushing her face into Logan's chest and hearing his small grunt of pain. She drew back, staring at him in suspicion. "What have you done?"

Logan tried to push her hands away as Hana yanked his shirt from his trousers. Tama poked his head through from the hallway and his eyes bugged. "Gosh, what is it with you older women today?" His voice trailed off as Logan gave him a steely look. "I'm going out." He jabbed a finger towards the front door and snagged his tee shirt from the floor. "Out there. As a courtesy." He swallowed at the sound of Logan's hiss and grappled with the door handle.

"Don't speak to any women," Hana called after him. "I swear I'll chop it off!"

Tama fled as Logan gave up the fight and allowed Hana to see his torso. An enormous black and blue bruise spread over the right side of his rib cage and through to his back. Red, grainy patches showed where internal bleeding leeched beneath the skin. She made him take his shirt off and examined similar bruising on his upper right arm. "Why didn't you say something?" she demanded. She snapped her fingers. "That's why you've been sleeping in a tee shirt. It must be excruciating. Is this from the fall on Saturday?"

Logan muttered something under his breath and Hana raised her eyebrows. He yanked his shirt back down and tucked it into his trousers. "I'm fine," he snarled. "I don't have time for this."

"There's a blood disorders clinic today at the medical centre in town. You should see someone." Hana scrabbled in her handbag for the relevant leaflet. "I'll come with you."

"No!" Logan set his lips in a stubborn line. "I've done worse. It's healing. I'm going back to work." He pushed his arms into his jacket, trying to make the action look less painful than it felt. He snatched the remaining sandwich off the plate and stomped towards the door.

"But we haven't finished talking," Hana said, sounding pathetic. "What will you tell Angus?"

Logan jabbed a finger in her direction. "Actually, you've complained and I've listened. We're staying here until he finds a new manager. I've already agreed." He anticipated her next sentence with a shake of his head. "We won't talk later because I have a night duty. So, if you've finished telling me what to do, I'll go now." He pulled the door open and stamped down the front steps. Hana heard him crunching through the pasta.

Her shoulders drooped and she sank into the folds of the sofa. "Oh, no!" she groaned. "What now?" Logan had spent the last year learning to consult her and his split decision set her right back at the start. "What are you doing, Du Rose?" she mused. The angry slam of the front door woke Phoenix and Hana let out a frustrated sigh before answering the call.

An hour later she pushed her pram over the Claudelands Bridge into town. Amanda hadn't responded to her knock and with Tama in hiding, she locked up and headed out alone. Sunshine suited Hamilton. The city lifted its shoulders and puffed out its chest like a preening bird beneath the gold rays. Hana wandered around the shops, browsing but buying nothing.

She walked as far as the old Founders' Theatre and the dilapidated fountain there. Made of delicately wrought metal, it boasted a central spoke with a spiky arrangement of metal prongs. It used to look like a dandelion head when the water spouted from it, but it lay abandoned and rusting. Another council budget overlooked it in the annual allocation. Hana walked to the centre of town and watched a family of children play in the fountain jets in Garden Place. She caught the sound of English accents and for the first time in many years, missed home.

"Charlotte, come on!" A little red-haired girl squealed from the centre of the fountains, her clothing sopping wet and revealing a skinny body. A blonde-haired child bounced around the fringes of the water while two other children giggled and played in the spray.

The town traffic built as school pick up time approached. Tempers flared as rush hour started and parents headed out to meet their children. It got harder to cross the busy roads and Hana gave up. She grabbed a take away coffee from a street vendor and turned for home.

She set a brisk pace, weaving between pedestrians until she reached the bridge. Traffic streamed past and the pavement could only take one person at a time. When she heard quick footsteps coming up behind her, she halted the pram and pulled into the railing as close as possible, not wanting the other person to step into the road. The feet stopped behind her and she waved a hand to usher them past. "Go on," she said. "Just squeeze through."

"Now why would I want to do that?" Laval's voice held a note of victory and Hana's heart picked up pace. Before she could move, he'd trapped her against the railings and blocked her escape. A woman walking in the opposite direction tutted in irritation and stepped onto the carriageway to pass. Hana implored her for help with her eyes but aggravated, the woman didn't notice a sister in distress. Hana's coffee cup tipped from the hood of the pram and disappeared into the river below. The cardboard clanged against the railing and was gone. Her brain demanded a rush of blood and oxygen as her body readied itself to fight or run.

"Leave us alone!" she hissed. Laval's gaze slid over the sleeping child in the pram. He smiled. Cars zoomed by, taking their steady procession of exhaust fumes into the city and foot traffic dwindled to nothing. Laval's blonde hair glinted in the sunlight and he lifted a soft hand to caress Hana's cheek. The top button of his shirt gaped against a loosened tie and he carried his expensive jacket across his forearm.

Before Hana could formulate her escape, he leaned in and kissed her on the mouth. She inhaled as though drowning and pressed herself harder against the guard rail, feeling the metal bite into her rib cage through her clothing. Her right hand gripped the handle of her pram but she pressed the left against his shirt, trying to force him away. Turning her face so his kiss moved across her face into her hair, Hana let out a sob of rage. "Get off me!" Her body betrayed her and the words emerged as a pathetic, frightened squeak.

A school bus approached, wheezing diesel fuel and hot mechanical air. Laval leaned in for another kiss, but Hana collected her senses and pushed him with every ounce of her strength. "No!" she shouted. Her action caught him off guard. Laval stepped back to regain his balance and his neat shoe slipped off the high curb. It launched him into the traffic backwards. The school bus honked as Laval pitched forward onto his knees to save himself. His jacket dropped to the road spewing keys and loose change. An expensive mobile phone clattered into the gutter. The sound of air brakes filled Hana's head and small faces appeared at the bus windows.

She seized her moment and ran, forcing the pram ahead of her along the bridge. She ran until her sandals rubbed a blister between her toes and then she took them off and kept running. Phoenix slept, her body swaying with the motion of the pram and her thumb shoved between her rosebud lips. Hana didn't stop until she reached the school, pelting into the side road like a banshee.

Tama rose from the front step, his shirt untucked and beads of sweat dotting his forehead. "You left me," he said. His tone sounded sulky and Hana halted, bending her body in half and clutching her knees. Her breath came in heaves and Tama grew concerned. "Why are you running in this heat?" he demanded. "That's stupid."

Not dignifying him with an answer, Hana handed over the keys. She glanced back along the lane as Tama bumped the pram up the front steps. The Honda sat in a different position, mounted half on the curb across the street. Hana waited until she'd caught her breath to question Tama. "Did you use the car?" she asked.

He shook his head. "Uncle Logan went somewhere at lunchtime. Then he came back and dropped it off."

"Why didn't you get him to open the house then?" Hana asked, hearing the irritation in her voice.

Tama shrugged, looking miserable. "He's still mad at me. I hid. I've decided I'm too young to die."

Hana locked the front door and left Phoenix sleeping in the pram. The open blisters smarted and she hobbled to the sink and cleaned her feet, examining the raw skin and hissing as the wounds stung. She eyed Tama as she fixed plasters over the worse cuts. "Are you and Anka back on?" she demanded.

Tama leaned on the back of the sofa, watching Hana's ministrations with a distracted air. He thought for a minute and then shook his head. "Na," he said with confidence. "This time felt different. She wanted me. It was just sex. I don't think I'm infatuated with her anymore. I'm cured." He appeared thrilled with his epiphany and Hana sighed.

"If she'll jump on you that fast, her marriage rebuild can't be going well."

"Dunno," Tama answered, flicking through the television channels. He peered at the remote. "We didn't talk about it. We didn't talk about anything." A slight smirk raised the corners of his lips and Hana felt her temper flare.

"You do that in my home again and it won't just be Logan you'll need to fear, Tama."

He glanced at her and nodded, teenage arrogance in full swing. Hana rubbed at her ribs where she crashed into the guard rail and winced. "I'm going for a shower," she announced. Her gaze rested on a gift bag with her name on it. Instinct made her panic. "What's this?" she demanded. "Who's been in the house?" Tama grunted, not listening. Hana reached out a tentative finger to flip the tag and recognised Logan's neat cursive slant. She let out a groan of relief.

She opened the bag with shaking fingers and pulled out a wide box. Two more layers revealed a new smartphone. It looked expensive and she sighed in dismay. The instructions proclaimed the device could text, email, run apps she didn't recognise, take photographs and play music. A logo declared GPS and navigation tools. Hana bit her lip, guilt turning her inside out. "It's from Logan," she whispered.

"What?" Tama replied, not interested. Hana fiddled with the box, managing to extract the phone to see the screen. It displayed one cell of battery and she discovered a charger already plugged into the wall. Hana connected the phone, hearing a muted ting of satisfaction from its speaker. The screen displayed an unopened envelope in the top corner and Hana swallowed. Before pressing the flashing icon, she paused, gnawing on her bottom lip. It couldn't be Laval unless Logan had somehow transferred her old number across. She held the device in shaking hands, knowing she couldn't destroy this one too.

Hana straightened her back, gritted her teeth and pressed the envelope. Exhaling in a whoosh, she recognised Logan's number and his name appeared at the top.

'*Sorry babe,*' the message said, '*I shouldn't have accepted without talking to you first. I have my reasons and don't want to argue over it. I've been to the drop-in clinic and got more meds. Sorry for getting mad. Come and see me after dinner. I'll make it up to you.*'

Hana smiled and hugged the phone to her chest. He'd bought a bright pink case, presumably so she couldn't lose it again. An icon showed GPS as loaded, whatever that meant. "Look." She turned and showed the phone to Tama. He abandoned the cartoon to clamber up the back of the sofa and peer over the counter.

"Ooh, that's a top of the range one!" he gushed. "Lucky! Give it here." He stretched the charger cord over his head and entertained himself with a game of cards. "Love solitaire," he breathed and Hana groaned.

"I thought you'd show me how to email and stuff," she sulked.

"Later," he promised, not stopping his game. He made little grunts as he played against himself, swearing and complaining when the computerised chip in the phone bested him. Hana started to walk towards the bathroom when the baby let out a shrill wail from the pram. She sighed as her hopes of sanity grew further away.

Phoenix's tummy rose like a hill in her tiny body as she lay on a plastic change mat in the lounge. Hana had filled her to bursting with milk and she kicked her little legs around over her head and tried to eat her toes. The hammering on the front door made Hana drop the kettle in the sink. She dived behind the kitchen counter, a hand over her mouth. "He's found me!" she squeaked, her green eyes wide in her porcelain face.

Tama jumped to his feet and reached over her to peer through the kitchen window. "It's fine," he said. "It's just your idiot son."

Hana crept around the counter and knelt on the floor with the baby, taking shallow, calming breaths while Tama opened the door. Bodie stepped past with a look of disgust at the teen. "Where's my mother?" he demanded, his tone haughty.

Tama jerked his head towards the lounge and held the door as a six-year-old Jas pushed his way through like a pixie darting through trees in a forest of legs. He ran straight to Hana and hugged her around her neck in a throttle hold. "Hi, Hanny," he said, spreading wet butterfly kisses across her cheek.

He clutched an Action Man bungee jumper in his small hand, the doll wearing a pair of revealing speedos. Ball-point pen scribble covered his plastic arms and most of his body. Toilet roll spewed from the sides of the speedos and Hana reached for the action figure. "What happened to him?" she asked.

Jas rolled his eyes like she was stupid. His attitude changed at a glare from his father. "They're ta moko tattoos," he said, his voice sounding strained. "For his gynaecology. He's Poppa Logan. I done it myself." He looked down at the blue biro scribble. "But it went wrong, so I washed him with a scratchy pad in the sink. I gived him leg ones and back ones as well." He tipped the doll up sideways and a dribble of water ran through the gap where his legs joined. "He was brave in the tattoo part but he didn't like the wash. Look see, he's been peeing himself ever since. Mum says he's a continent." Jas flicked the doll upright and a jet of soapy water landed on Phoenix's bare tummy. Her body jerked and her bottom lip shot out. Hana mopped the spill with a towel and blew a raspberry on her tummy to distract her. Phoenix grinned and went back to her floor aerobics.

"It's genealogy sweetheart." Hana smiled at her grandson. "Whakapapa."

"What is?" Jas asked and Hana withheld the exasperated sigh on her lips.

"Not gynaecology, genealogy."

"Oh," Jas replied, his interest waning. He turned to watch Tama and Bodie as they postured like a couple of bantams. "Who's that big boy?" he demanded, staring at Tama.

"Logan's nephew. Tama." Hana stood, leaving Jas on the floor blowing raspberries on Phoenix's olive belly. It sounded as though there was more spit than air.

"Drink anyone?" she asked, boiling the kettle to make herself a cup of tea and fetching cold water in response to the male grunts. She jerked her head towards Tama as she clattered glasses. "Tell Bo about your agricultural course," she suggested, hoping to give the teenager credence in the policeman's eyes.

Tama stumbled through a strained narrative and Bodie listened with feigned politeness. "Yeah, Uncle Logan's offered me a permanent job on the farm."

"Oh, really?" Bodie replied. He eyed Tama with suspicion. "You don't need accounting to cook the books then?"

Tama pulled a face and sneered in derision. "Nice," he replied.

"Try not to screw it up," Bodie said and Hana winced.

"The farming or the fraud?" Tama's look of innocence was priceless and Bodie's brow furrowed. Hana snorted into her tea at Tama's wit under pressure.

She sighed and rubbed a hand over her face. "Can I trust you guys not to rip each other's heads off while I take a shower? Phoe should be fine."

Before anyone could reply, Jas let out a wail. "Oh no! I didn't mean it!"

Bodie stood and peered at his son and Tama let out a hoot of laughter. Hana jostled her way through to rescue her baby from some unknown calamity.

Jas looked up at her with tears in his eyes. "I think I'll give up tattoos," he said. "I did my bestest joined up writing but now she's leaking as well!" He began to cry.

There were lots of tears. Phoenix wasn't bothered by the words *Made in China* inscribed on her stomach in blue biro, but she didn't enjoy laying in her pee. Jas howled because everything he tattooed developed a leaking fault. Tama cried tears of mirth because he'd never witnessed anything so hilarious. Hana just felt like crying.

Instead of a peaceful shower, she bathed her daughter in the kitchen sink to wash the wee from her hair. Jas pulled a chair up to the sink and stood on it, watching Hana wrestle the soapy baby. She tried to keep her patience as he instructed her on how she could do it better, sounding just like his father. He shook his dark head and stuck a thumb in his mouth. "That's exactly what I did to Action Man and he's been leaking since yesterday!" he mumbled.

Hana bit back the urge to scream as Phoenix wriggled and kicked in the sink, spreading soapy water far and wide. Jas continued a monotonous monologue at her side. "Please can you pass the towel?" Hana asked, suppressing a groan of frustration as Jas dropped it on the floor.

Tama retrieved it and held out his arms. "I'll take her," he offered. "You can make dinner instead."

Hana shook her head. "No thanks. I'll dress her and then I'm going for a shower. You can make dinner. The ingredients for toasted sandwiches are in the fridge."

Hana got her wish, emerging from the bathroom to find Phoenix snoozing in her son's arms. The boys scoffed bread like it was being discontinued.

Hana took the baby so Bodie could eat using both hands and she sat on the sofa to feed her. Jas tried to watch, leaning backwards on his chair despite Bodie's best efforts. "What's she doing?" he demanded. "Why's her sandwich up Hanny's shirt?"

"It just is." Bodie righted the chair and pointed at Jas' plate. "Eat your dinner."

"Dinner?" Jas let his mouth hang open. "No, this is a snack."

Phoenix gripped Hana's tee shirt and moved her arm up and down, causing a draught. Hana smiled at the child's developing motor skills, revelling in the soft downy head and fragile body. Thoughts of Laval crowded her mind, robbing her sense of peace and leaving her numb. She jumped as Jas poked his head around Bodie's shoulder and demanded. "Hanny, why was you on the bridge?"

"Pardon?" Hana's blood ran cold. "What bridge, darling?"

"That bridge. You know." Jas leaned back and tipped so far, he almost toppled off his chair. He overbalanced and his knife whipped up, flicking a glob of tomato sauce into his eye.

Bodie sighed, retrieved the dishcloth from the sink and wiped Jas' watering eye. "Get on with your dinner," he told him. "Stop leaning across me."

Bodie seemed tense and Hana felt guilty for feeling unable to summon the energy to pry. She suspected he'd visited for a reason, but Tama's presence had thwarted him. Phoenix fed and Hana missed her husband, yearning for his calming influence and the sense of safety he imbued in her soul. She remembered his text message and smirked, her spirits rising in anticipation of restoring their relationship later.

"Hanny," Jas's face peered around Bodie and she looked up, popping Phoenix over her shoulder to bring up her wind. "Who was that man?"

Hana swallowed. "What man?"

"You know," he said, filling his mouth with toastie and choking as he tried to finish his sentence. "The man on the bridge what kissed you?"

Hana felt a rush of blood to her feet as it drained from her face. She busied herself with the baby, wiping the rosebud lips and switching Phoenix to feed from the other breast. She kept silent, not wishing to make a liar of the little boy but unsure how to refute his story.

"Hanny," came Jas's voice again. Hana tried not to flee from the room screaming. "Did he hurt himself when he fell into the traffic?"

She worked at keeping her composure. "I don't know," she answered, maintaining a level tone. "I didn't look. Silly man."

Bodie's body language appeared rigid and he avoided her gaze. He struggled with Jas' propensity to just say whatever came into his brain. Hana glanced up to find Tama staring at her through narrowed eyes. He sat for so long his toastie bent into an arc. Jas coughed and shot toast crumbs across the table. He leaned sideways and nudged Bodie's ribs with his elbow. "I know a song about road safety," he whispered. "Shall I sing it to her?"

Bodie shook his head but Jas burst into song, anyway. His little voice rang out crystal clear. Hana gulped and checked her watch. School had ended and Logan must have gone straight to the boarding house. Phoenix fed herself to sleep and Hana rose, heading for the hallway. "I'll just lay her down," she whispered. She wrapped her sleeping daughter in a cotton blanket, laying her on her side in her cot. Activating the baby monitor, she returned to the lounge and started cleaning the kitchen.

"Hanny?" Jas twisted his lips and stared at the ceiling in thought. "What's that man's name? The one in the road."

Hana blew out a long breath and saw the scene through Jas' eyes as Laval landed in the path of the traffic. He must have been sitting on the school bus. She licked her lips and no suitable replies came to mind.

Tama made a loud squelching noise as he sucked sauce from his thumb. "Yeah, Hana. What was that man's name?"

"Look after Phoenix for me, please?" She shot him a look containing pure agony. Before anyone else could comment, she threw the baby monitor at him. "She won't wake up for an hour or two. You'll be fine."

Grabbing her new phone, she made a run for it. The front door slammed shut behind her as she skipped down the steps. Jas gave an angry wail and Hana picked up the pace. She needed to get away. The cost of Laval's visits became higher each time and lying about them went against Hana's moral code. "I'm a bad person," she muttered to herself.

Hana found Logan in the downstairs office of the boarding house. He sorted through a pile of invoices. "Hey, gorgeous." He smiled up at her. "Where's Phoe?"

"Sleeping." Hana sighed. "Tama's there."

Logan's eyes darted over figures, copying numbers onto a scrap of paper with painstaking care. Hana watched him for a moment, admiring his dark hair flopping over his eyes and his brow furrowed in concentration. "I won't be a minute," he promised.

Feeling neglected, Hana pushed herself onto his knee. She surprised him, forcing him to scrape his chair back to accommodate her. She draped herself over his shoulder and pushed her face into his neck. "I'm sorry about before," he breathed.

Hana didn't want him to finish the sentence and kissed him, stealing his words. Her kiss felt hot and urgent, accompanied by fingers which sneaked into the sides of his trousers and parted his shirt from his waistband. Her touch against the small of his back seared his flesh and Logan's lips parted with a groan. "Bad girl," he whispered. "What's the hurry?"

Hana didn't answer, pressing her lips over his. "No talking," she ordered.

When her tongue quested with more purpose, Logan jerked back and glanced at the office door. "Not here, babe," he whispered. Hana's face expression moved between sultry and pouting in an instant. Logan ran his thumb over her lips. "I'm not on duty yet," he whispered. "So, we can go upstairs." He tipped her off his knee and gathered his papers together, taking her hand and leading her upstairs. His arm felt strong around her shoulders as they walked through the boarding house corridors and up to the staff accommodation.

Logan bolted the door of the middle bedroom off the restroom and placed his finger over Hana's lips.

"We need to be quiet," he warned, excitement and risk making his grey eyes glitter. He wrenched the tie from around his neck, but Hana pushed away the eager fingers which groped at his buttons.

"I'll do it," she insisted, narrowing her eyes. She removed her husband's shirt with painful slowness, making him wait. Hana revelled in the way he closed his eyes and gritted his teeth with every sensuous press of her lips against his bare chest, her fingers popping each button with tantalising precision.

Logan groaned as Hana stripped for him, pushing her creamy limbs between the sheets first. He made love to her, eagerness making him rough as he unwittingly overwrote Laval's advances with his own. Strong and passionate, his wife's unexpected demands emboldened him. He pressed his lips against hers to stem the groans of pleasure which carried to the staff room.

"Tea time's not your usual hour," he joked as they lay entwined on the cramped single bed.

"No," Hana sighed, snuggling closer. The physical exertion had chased all fear of Laval from her mind but as she lay recovering, the heaviness in her stomach drifted back like a rolling mist. Unaware, Logan ran his fingers in feather light movements up and down her shoulders, feeling her body tensing without understanding why.

"What's wrong, babe?" he asked, his voice a low rumble through her body. Hana closed her eyes, hating her new, dishonest persona.

"Nothing," she lied. "I don't want to go back to the unit."

Logan tutted but his tone sounded regretful rather than piqued. "I'm sorry."

She dreaded facing Tama and wondered if Bodie waited around to talk to her. She imagined Jas recounting his tale for both men and didn't know what she could say in her defence. Neither adultery nor attempted murder sounded defensible unless she confessed to Bodie about Laval. With a sigh, Hana struggled up from the bed, extracting herself from Logan's embrace. She pulled her clothes on and ran her hands through her curly tresses, her face ashen.

"Have I made you miss dinner?" she asked. Logan lay on his back, observing Hana through narrowed eyes. His olive biceps bulged against the starched pillow and the tangled sheet revealed a stomach rippling with muscle and a thigh dusted in dark hair. Hana yanked her tee shirt over her head.

"It's fine." Logan shook his head and leaned up on one elbow to watch his wife. "I'll get something from the kitchen. It was worth it."

"What were you doing before?" Hana asked, trying to distract herself. His grey eyes probed her soul and it felt uncomfortable, disturbing her equilibrium and threatening the thin veneer of lies. Logan continued his study. "Please, Logan. Stop!" Hana ran a hand over her face and reached for the door handle.

"Don't run!" Logan moved with a speed disproportionate to his height and build, halting Hana as she wrestled with the lock. His arms enfolded her and he nuzzled her long hair. He kissed the top of her head. "Stay a little longer," he whispered.

Hana breathed in his masculine scent and nodded her face against his smooth chest. She ran her finger over his raised nipple and felt a tremor run through her own body from his. His nakedness was intoxicating and she caressed the rugged scar, following it along his rib cage to the soft skin at his hip. Logan's chuckle rumbled through her chest. "That tickles," he breathed, his body jerking. "Just stay ten more minutes," he begged. "I'll get dressed and make you a drink."

Hana nodded, a tiny, reluctant movement. She watched Logan straighten the bed and lay his sleeping bag over the top, pulling on his clothes with long, scarred fingers. The bruising from the fall looked less livid and her chest heaved at the thought of losing him. Laval's words returned to dog all rational thought. *'What's your worst nightmare, Hana? Another dead husband?'*

"I was looking at the accounts," Logan said, shoving his feet into his cowboy boots. He glanced up at her. "You asked before. That's what I was doing, looking at the accounts for the boarding house."

"Oh, yeah." Hana nodded and straightened her back, forcing a look of interest onto her face.

Logan's brow knitted, but he continued. "The accountants have finished with the books and given me pointers. There are no big amounts going out, but the outgoings don't match the income. Whatever's going on, it's as subtle as an over order."

"Just put the fees up," Hana replied, her tired brain lurching for the easy answer.

Logan shook his head. "Angus did, but it made no difference. The accounts have a leak and I need to find it." He ran a hand through his hair and stood. Hana watched his muscles flex and sensed a heaviness in her groin, wanting to lose herself again for a while. Laval's blonde hair and gimlet eyes pushed at the edges of her consciousness like tight fingers around her heart.

"Hana?"

She jumped, her fingers fixed around the door handle and her green eyes wide. Laval's threat went round and round in her head and Hana's lips moved, saying nothing.

Logan put his hands on his hips, his authority washing over her. "Are you gonna tell me what's going on?" he asked.

Hana floundered and his eyes flared with a semblance of understanding, growing dark like storm water. She shook her head. "I can't. I want to, but I can't." She swallowed and eyed the door next to her.

"We promised each other last year; no more secrets." Logan sounded hurt and Hana's heart constricted in her chest. "You're pushing me away, Hana. I can feel it."

She shook her head. "I'm not." The sob caught in her throat. "I'm not, I promise. I can't do this, I can't stay here." The urge to run made her feet shift beneath her, knowing Logan read her like an open book. She scrabbled at the door handle and the lock gave with a click.

Logan crossed the room and held her, his chin resting on the top of her head. "I trust you," he whispered.

Hana squirmed, his words like a jackhammer in her head. She held his life in her hands and the responsibility overwhelmed her, pressing her body inward until it reached its breaking point. The weight bore down on her shoulders, restricting every breath and crushing her spirit. Hana sniffed and pressed her face into Logan's chest, desperate to release the burden to him but knowing she couldn't. Logan didn't push her and Hana collected her emotions into a knotted ball inside her chest, feeling unworthy of his trust. She plastered a fake smile onto her lips and tried to banish the spirit of fear playing havoc with her nerves.

Logan led Hana out into the empty restroom. She sat in a comfy chair next to the long window overlooking the soccer field while he boiled the kettle and made her a cup of tea. Hana looked at the floaters swimming around from the milk and wrinkled her nose.

Logan angled his chair sideways next to hers and stretched out his long legs. He rested his right ankle on her thigh. Hana placed her hand over it, galvanised by his nearness through the leather of his boot. "You going to be okay tonight?" he asked, his voice soft.

Hana thought about returning to the cramped unit and cringed. Logan saw and she fudged it, nodding and burning her mouth on the tea. "I should go." She placed the mug on the table even though she'd drunk hardly anything. She verged on a confession and needed to leave. Laval's kiss made her feel violated and afraid. The knowledge sent acid rising into her gullet. Looking up, her eyes met Logan's and she saw suspicion and concern in his face. She couldn't do it. If she told him the truth Laval would make good on his promise. He'd kill her husband. She smiled at Logan with bravery she didn't possess and stood to leave.

"Wait." Logan rose and ran his hand along her arm. His face looked troubled. "Hana," he began.

A slam made them both jump as Peter North shot through the door. The glass bounced back against the wall and rebounded onto his skinny body. Undeterred, he ran towards Logan with his arms outstretched and wrapped himself around his torso. "Oh, thank you, thank you so much!" he squealed.

Logan grunted in pain and sheltered Hana, fending Pete off like a one handed matador. "Stop!" he commanded, his face darkening with irritation.

"But I'm so grateful," Pete gushed. "I can't believe you said I could come. I'm so relieved! Dobbs and Watson wanted to fire me." He clutched his heart with a sense of injustice. "Me!"

Logan rolled his eyes and Hana's heart sank into her sandals. Misery made her cruel and not stopping to consider Pete's feelings, she shook her head as her face flushed with fury. "You're kidding me!" she snapped. "He's your new offsider?" She jabbed her finger in Pete's direction and he stilled, a look of pure hurt bleeding into his expression. "So when he does one of his famous disappearing acts and you end up working seven nights a week, don't expect me to still be here! That's it, I'm done!" Hana whirled around and left the room, stamping down the stairs to the front door. A group of boys stepped back for her and held the door open. She nodded at them in thanks and moved through, leaving them staring after her as a cloud of temper roiled out behind her.

Hana marched back to the unit and discovered the front door locked. She knocked on it far too hard in her temper and Tama opened it with caution, his face severe in anticipation of trouble. "Oh, it's you," he said, his eyes widening in surprise. Hana pushed past him. "Do come in," he responded with sarcasm as she blew by.

Jas snored on the sofa and Bodie stood as Hana walked into the lounge. "Mum, I need to talk to you," he began.

"Not now please, Bo!" Hana flounced to her bedroom and shut herself in, ignoring both males who came to placate her. "Please! I don't want to talk about it," she sniffed and sent them both away.

Falling asleep in a temper made her groggy and miserable. She awoke to the sound of Phoenix crying. Hana felt disoriented, getting out of bed and walking into the wall. By the time she righted herself, Tama had retrieved the squalling child and knocked on the bedroom door. "I've got her," he called, alarmed to hear another bump as Hana tripped over the bedspread and landed on her hands and knees.

"Damn it!" she raged, slapping the bed with the flat of her hand and groaning.

"What are you doing down there?" Tama demanded. He edged into the room and Hana rewarded him with a piercing glare.

"I fell," she snapped and threw herself back against her pillows while Tama waited, holding the grizzling child. He handed Phoenix over and then left.

Hana remembered her behaviour at St Bart's and cringed. The look on Logan's face chastised her rudeness, even in her memory. She sighed and played with the baby's tiny fingers as the little girl satiated her hunger. "I'm a horrible person," Hana sighed, her pretty lips downturned and her eyes filling with tears. "I'm awful."

"No, you're not," Tama reassured her, poking his head around the door. "Want a cup of tea? Isn't that the English cure for all ills?"

Hana nodded. "Yes, please. Do you know what he's done?"

"Who?" Tama's body stiffened with alarm.

"Logan!" Hana bit. "He's employed Peter North as his deputy. I could kill him!"

"Oh." Tama smirked. "Why would he do a dumb thing like that?"

"Exactly!" Hana waved her arm in his direction. "That's just what I said. I've spent the last fifteen years trying to be a good Christian around a lazy, thoughtless, self-absorbed Peter North. I've endured his bad habits, rudeness, ability to shirk any labour or responsibility with apparent ease and I've done well!" she wailed. "Do you know how hard it's been keeping my opinions to myself and hoping that deep down he was a nice guy. I frequently persuaded myself he had potential although I've no idea what with. Now I've ruined it. I've slagged him off in front of Logan like a mean girl. Matthew 7 chapter 1 'Judge not, that ye be not judged.'" Hana sniffed and closed her eyes. "Now I'll be judged too." Phoenix stopped feeding and looked up at her with knitted brows. "Sorry," Hana grumbled. "The truth is I've tolerated Pete because his behaviour rarely affected me. I did my job fine and learned to circumnavigate his laziness. He was a careers advisor, but disappeared so often we didn't bother scheduling appointments for him. Sheila and I just behaved like he didn't exist." Hana drew the back of her hand across the underside of her nose and wiped it on her jeans. "Now he's in a position to make my life a living hell."

"I'll make tea," Tama said, withdrawing his head and disappearing.

Hana let the baby grip her index finger in her tiny hand and admired the perfect olive skin and intricate nails. "Why has Logan done this?" she complained. "It's a disaster waiting to happen." A clatter against the bedroom door made her jump and Phoenix let out a frightened wail. "I can't live like this!" Hana squeezed the bridge of her nose between thumb and index finger.

Tama opened the door with caution, making his way around the bed bearing a cup of tea. "You egg!" he soothed, sitting next to her and budging her over with his hip. "Stop letting every little noise rattle you."

Hana made room and relaxed as Tama laid his arm across her shoulders. He kissed her temple. "Life sucks sometimes, doesn't it?"

Hana nodded and in her vulnerability, everything tumbled free. "I went for a walk this afternoon after

I argued with Logan and Laval followed me over the bridge on the way home. He kissed me and I pushed him. That's what Jas saw." She hid her face in Phoenix's blanket.

"Well, that explains it." Tama clicked his fingers. "The kid kept asking questions after you left. I think it bothered him. He brought something to show you; a thing he got from the trip. His class went to Hamilton Gardens." Hana let out a groan. "It's okay," Tama soothed, "he left it for you. It's a flower thing but bugs started coming out, so I put it in the sink."

Hana peeked out from the blanket. "See what I did," she whispered. "I rejected my own grandson's infested greenery. There's no hope for me."

Tama shook his head, stroking her shoulder and trying not to laugh at her self-pity.

Phoenix stopped feeding and looked up, running her cool little hand over Hana's finger as though trying to infuse her with love. "Bodie probably thinks I'm having an affair," Hana grumbled. "You have no idea how much he'd enjoy seeing Logan divorce me."

Tama shook his head. "No, it's weird because he refused to talk about it. Are you sure he doesn't know what's going on?"

Hana shook her head. "I only told Bobby, and he told you. Nobody else knows."

"You have to tell Uncle Logan though," Tama said. "If Jas lets it slip he saw you snogging some guy in town, Logan will blow a gasket trying to find out who it was."

"He wouldn't hurt me," Hana said. "But I don't want him to know yet. I'm trying to handle it."

"He wouldn't physically hurt you," Tama said with authority. "But he detests infidelity and he'd cut you off in ways you couldn't imagine."

Hana gave a hiccough of pure misery and Tama pulled her closer. "What are we gonna do?" he breathed. "How can we sort this out before it goes too far?"

"I don't know." Hana rubbed her eyes. "Laval must be watching me. What if I flush him out and trap him? I'll need you there."

"He won't approach you with me there!" Tama scoffed, flexing his biceps and pleased with what he saw.

Hana poked him hard in the ribs. "I know that! But you're meant to be a bodyguard, so you could follow at a safe distance and do some bodyguard things." She cheered up at the thought of taking positive action. "Maybe we could go for a walk tomorrow around the same time as today. You could follow without attracting attention. He intimidates me, but I know he can't openly hurt me in public. He can't find out you know anything though." Hana thought for a minute. "It's a pity I lost my old phone. He'd been texting me and I could have arranged a proper meeting."

Tama eyed her sideways. "Let's go with the first plan. You go for a walk and I'll follow and see what happens." He squeezed Hana's shoulder and laid his temple against hers. "You trashed your phone, didn't you?"

"No," Hana lied. "Yes. Sort of."

She heard Tama snuff and felt grateful for his company. "I never thought we'd be friends," she murmured and felt his head nod against hers.

"Neither," he said. "Not after the Anka thing. Circumstance keeps throwing us together. When you shared about your first husband's affair, it changed everything. I saw how vulnerable you were, but before that you seemed a bit hard ass. Being with you when you went into labour with Phoenix was incredible." He touched the fluffy head and the child's eyes flicked up at him. "She feels like my sister," he said. "I never had a sister."

"Yeah, we're certainly an unusual family," Hana replied. She patted his thigh and asked him to pass the cup of tea. "Let's see if your drink passes muster." She pretended to sample a mouthful, rolling the liquid round her tongue and swallowing. "Not bad," she agreed. "You can stay."

Tama laughed, taking the baby and putting her over his shoulder to bring up the wind. Hana drank, settling back against the pillows. "How do you feel about things," she asked and he looked at her in confusion.

"What? Anka?"

"Not just that," Hana said. "Miriam and Reuben's death and Michael now having a relationship with your mother. Kane's been thrown out of the hotel and you're starting college. It seems like heaps for one person to deal with."

"It sounds a lot when you put it like that." Tama's brows knitted in thought. "You know, Poppa Reuben was always kind to me. I knew he loved me. It made up for Kane's beatings. When I found out Michael was my real father everything made sense. But when Michael wasn't interested, it hurt more than anything which went before." He scratched at a spot on his upper arm, worrying at the scab as he tried to process his buried emotions. Then he smiled, looking every bit a Du Rose. His white teeth contrasted with his olive skinned complexion and he looked so much like Michael, Hana stopped sipping and stared at him.

"I always had Uncle Logan," Tama said. "He was constant with me. I let him down last year and when he told me not to use the Du Rose name, I walked for five kilometres bawling like a baby."

"I didn't know he'd said that." Hana bit her lip at her husband's black and white perception of the world. Logan didn't tolerate disloyalty. "Was it because you took a job with Laval Senior after what he did to me?"

Tama nodded. "Yeah."

Phoenix let out an enormous burp and grunt, followed by a happy sigh. Hana laughed. Tama gave the baby back to her and got off the bed, his long legs clad in ripped blue jeans. He reached the bedroom door and stopped, a look of concern on his face as he turned to eyeball Hana. "I don't know if you've realised, but you keep saying Laval Senior."

Hana shrugged. "So what?"

He held his arms out to his sides and shook his head. "Don't you get it?"

Hana screwed up her face. "What are you talking about?" She patted the baby's back.

"Come on Hana! You'd only call him Laval Senior if you knew there was another kind of Laval, like a Junior!"

Hana's eyes widened in horror. "Oh, no!" She tried to remember if she might have given herself away, but every conversation became a blur. "I think I'm okay," she decided. "I haven't said it to anyone else, but I'll watch myself even harder from now on."

Hana settled in the bed with the baby after changing her nappy. She missed Logan and let the child stay with her, enjoying the closeness of her small body as she lay awake in the darkness. Tama moved around in the lounge and kitchen, finally settling down late. Phoenix snuffed and moved about in her sleep and Hana stroked her soft cheeks. She worked to push the image of Pete from her mind, trying not to dislike him for being the same idle man he'd always been. She decided instead to have faith in her husband. He possessed mana and leadership qualities handed down to him through generations of French noblemen and Māori chiefs. If he couldn't inspire Peter North to behave, nobody could.

Chapter 23

Hana woke, hearing the bell for the first lesson ringing in the distance. The house sounded silent apart from Phoenix, who lay on her back in the double bed and struggled to pull the sleep suit over her feet. She had lost one leg already and the empty material hung sideways. As Hana rubbed the sleep from her eyes, Phoenix turned towards her and made delicate 'pah, pah' noises before opening her mouth in a happy grin. Hana laughed, her eyes crinkling with love.

"For such a little person, that is a very big smell!" she exclaimed after changing her daughter's nappy. She pushed the window open on its security latch and waved fresh air into the room. "Pooh, stinky! You're Mrs Bugle-bum for sure."

Contentment shrouded her and Hana felt reluctant to let it dissipate so soon. She sat in bed, feeding the baby and enjoying the luxury of reading a novel she wanted to finish. Phoenix fed and fell asleep, her little tummy rising like a hillock. Hana studied her with pride, knowing any growth was entirely through her efforts. "Maybe I'm not as rubbish as I thought," she whispered to the sleeping child. Wrapping her up, she laid her in the cot and then wandered to the kitchen for a drink.

Tama sprawled on the floor in his sleeping bag. He'd propped himself up against the front of the sofa with pillows behind him, watching cartoons. Hana picked her way past, realising her mistake as he reached out and caught hold of her leg. She wore a shirt of Logan's with knickers underneath but the ensemble showed off her slender legs. Tama winked at her and pulled the sleeping bag back with his other hand. "Fancy coming in for a cuddle?" he asked, his tone sultry.

Hana kicked out, detaching his grasp. "Don't even think about it!" she replied, her voice rising in horror. "I'm old enough to be your mother!"

Tama grinned. "You don't hear me complaining."

Hana paused, containing her indignation and playing a longer game. "Okay then," she replied. "I'll ring Logan and make sure he doesn't mind."

"No! Hana don't!" The lascivious smile slipped from Tama's face and his voice rose an octave. "Please don't. I'm sorry! He'll kill me!"

"Be quiet!" Hana snapped. "I just put Phoenix in her cot."

Tama wriggled from his sleeping bag and stood up in his boxer shorts. The flush had drained from his cheeks. He wrung his hands, knowing he'd gone too far. "I get horny," he whispered. "Women rarely turn me down."

Hana flicked the kettle on to boil and left the room, cursing her stupidity in wandering around half dressed. Tama was a mixed up, randy teenager, whose skewed moral compass was influenced by his bizarre upbringing. Logan had tried to warn her and she regretted dismissing his carefully given advice. Tama spoke the truth. If she breathed a word of his lewd suggestion to her husband, he'd dismember his nephew and bury his body under the rugby pitch.

Hana showered and dressed before returning to the kitchen. Tama's sleeping bag lay on the sofa and he'd tidied the room. He rose as she walked in, his fingers scratching at a long scab on his neck. Hana ignored him and made a pot of tea, dumping it on the breakfast bar.

Tama's grey eyes grew huge as she busied herself with the toaster. "I didn't mean it," he protested and Hana raised her eyebrows.

"You liar!" she said, smirking in disbelief. "You meant it and if that's your best pick up line, I'm not surprised you're out of luck."

"It's proved successful with the older ladies." Tama's brow furrowed with sincerity. "They like a cuddle first."

Hana raised her finger in front of his face. "Not this older lady, thanks. I'm very happy with my husband's ministrations and doubt you can improve on them."

"Bet I could," Tama protested. He quirked an eyebrow and opened his mouth.

"No!" Hana put her hands over her ears. "Stop!" She waited until his lips ceased moving. "Look, I won't tell Logan, but only because I need you here right now. But you must stop hitting on me. I'm not interested."

Tama let out such a big breath his body seemed to collapse inwards. He leant on the breakfast bar and closed his eyes. "I can't believe you don't fancy me," he grumbled.

Hana released a snort and shook her head. "That's what you took away from that sentence?"

Tama shrugged. "Thanks for not telling Logan."

Hana capitalised on his change in attitude. "I'm not Caroline and I'm definitely not Anka, so please don't confuse me with them. I love my husband and that's the way it will stay. Stop wasting your efforts."

Tama's face flushed and Hana pointed her index finger at him. "I think your relationship with Logan is more important than you pretend. So, stop sabotaging yourself."

Tama nodded. "I'll be on my best behaviour." His eyes glittered. "But can you make me scrambled eggs now please?"

Hana sighed and relented, opting to play the role of his mother for a while. Later, she picked at her toast and worried over luring Laval out of hiding. Tama inhaled his breakfast and watched her pick her food apart. "Get real, Hana," he said, making her jump. "This is too big for us to handle on our own. We need Logan's help and you know it."

Hana refused. "No! I'm keeping your secrets, so you keep mine."

"That's blackmail!" he complained, rewarded by Hana's satisfied smirk.

Amanda knocked on the door before lunch. Tama opened it and his presence seemed to dent her confidence and fluster her. "Hey," he said, his grey eyes searching Amanda's bonny face and clear complexion. He shook her hand, holding it longer than necessary and causing Hana to roll her eyes in disbelief.

"Tama! Behave!" she hissed, rewarded by the classic Du Rose lopsided grin. She marvelled at the boy's dauntless hormones.

Hana agreed to Amanda's suggestion of a walk and bundled Phoenix into the pram. Tama grew anxious. "You can't go!" he hissed. "We don't have a plan yet."

"I'm going for a walk with my friend." Hana ground her teeth and shot him a warning glare. "I'm fine."

"Why do you need a plan?" Amanda shifted on nervous feet. "A plan for what?"

"Nothing important. Don't worry." Hana waved Tama's concerns away like feathers on the wind. He stood his ground and folded his arms in protest.

"Okay, I'll grab my pushchair," Amanda conceded and left. Hana heard her clattering around next door as she gathered baby paraphernalia.

Tama tried to change Hana's mind. "This is stupid," he argued. "And now you've made it so I can't come along either without looking an idiot."

"It's fine," Hana promised. "He won't approach me with somebody else there. We'll walk a different way today and then we'll make a proper plan for tomorrow."

Tama shook his head. Hana saw he wanted to say more, but Amanda appeared at the front door with Millie lounging in a pushchair. Hana wrestled her pram down the front steps and waved off Tama's help. "Can we try a different route today?" she asked. "I fancy walking along River Road."

"What about the river paths?" Amanda asked with enthusiasm. Tama's eyes rolled like he might have an aneurism.

"They're too deserted during the day," Hana said, sounding regretful. "My son's a policeman and he wouldn't approve of me walking there."

"Tama could come," Amanda said. She offered him a coy smile and he grinned, his hormones cranking up.

"No, thanks," Hana replied with force. "He's got things to do."

"Whatever!" he hissed.

Hana slammed the front door in his face and flounced off up the road.

They walked in the sunshine, chatting away the kilometres. Amanda shared her problems as though relieved to air them. "It's hard staying married to someone whose opinion of himself is higher than it should be," she mused. "Chris thinks he's such a stud muffin when really he's a complete dick. Everyone knows it except him."

"Sounds familiar," Hana commented under her breath, thinking of her randy houseguest. "I hated having Caroline on my doorstep last year and knowing she wanted Logan. I worried about his ability to refuse her and it took a real toll on our marriage."

"At least he never succumbed, not like my idiot." Amanda grew silent and picked up her pace. Hana found herself half running to keep up.

They walked as far as Day's Landing and stopped at the reserve to stare at the water. Tourists and picnickers enjoyed their lunch on benches near the river and Hana felt less vulnerable in their presence.

"Could you hold Millie's pram for a minute, please? I need the bathroom," Amanda said. She pointed at a row of automated toilets and Hana eyed them with suspicion.

"I hate those," she said with a shake of her head. "I'd rather wait until I get home."

Amanda laughed. "It's fine as long as you press the right buttons."

They pushed the prams to the building and Hana stood outside. The ducks worked hard persuading the tourists to part with their lunch. Millie woke up and grinned at her. Hana played a game with the toys dangling above the pushchair hood. "Clever girl," she praised, righting a yellow plastic duck and watching the child bat it back into an upside down position.

Amanda reached the front of the queue and disappeared into the nearest toilet as a familiar black Mercedes slunk into the car park. Hana held her breath as it pulled into a parking space in front of her. Her gaze raked the reserve, willing someone to catch her eye and see she needed help. Nothing. Everyone busied themselves with their own activities and didn't see the look of terror which passed across the pretty redhead's face. She took deep breaths to calm herself as Laval unfolded himself from the driver's seat. Another man rode shotgun. Laval's blonde hair glinted in the sunshine and he walked straight to Hana, pushing his rumpled shirt into the back of his trousers and straightening his tie. She bit her lip and pressed herself hard against the metal toilet wall, keeping a hand on each of the pram handles.

"Hey, Mrs Du Rose," he said in a husky voice aimed at conveying sex appeal. He placed his hands either side of her waist. Hana tried to wedge herself further between the prams, feeling guilty for using the babies as a shield. She couldn't bat him away without letting go of one of the children. "You're avoiding me," he crooned. He leaned forward to kiss her and Hana dodged, banging her head against the toilet wall. He got her the second time, tasting of mint and coffee. "I can see you're busy," he whispered, peering at the babies. Phoenix slept but Millie watched him with a furrowed brow. "We need to meet and soon. If you answered your phone, you'd know how much I want that. But you don't pick up my calls, do you beautiful? So, I'll expect you here tomorrow at the same time." He held up three fingers. "Don't be late, baby. And no more games. I know you want this as much as I do. It's about time we came clean to the husband, don't you think?" He leaned forward and placed his lips against her temple. The action contained more threat than affection. "Last chance," he hissed into her ear.

He released her, his gait casual as he slid back into his vehicle. Hana tried to allow the feeling to return to her extremities, willing herself to breathe as she heard the laboured gasps catch in her chest. A flush sounded from inside the toilet cubicle and Hana's hands shook on the pram handles as she waited for Amanda to appear. As the door slid open, she sent her a look of appeal and dashed inside. Violently sick in the metal toilet bowl, Hana paused to catch her breath and wash her mouth out. A notice advised she didn't drink the water, but she couldn't help herself. The tissue felt like sandpaper against her lips and she took deep breaths until ready to face the world. Then she emerged blinking into the sunshine.

Amanda refused to look at her and the atmosphere between them cooled. They walked back to the school site in silence and Hana laboured each step. When they reached the back gate, Amanda rounded on her. "Who is he?"

Hana gulped and sensed the colour draining from her complexion. "It's complicated," she began.

Amanda raised a hand to silence her, hatred curling back her lips into a sneer. "Don't bother. I'm disgusted at you. Your husband is gorgeous and you don't deserve him. I hope you get what's coming to you." She stormed off ahead, pushing her pram out before her like a battering ram.

Nausea attacked Hana at the fear of Amanda spreading her gossip across the school site. Chris Carter would revel in Logan's misfortune. She stood where Amanda abandoned her, her shoulders slumped and tears bubbling near the surface. The rumble of voices issued through the open front doors of St Barts and gave her no comfort. "I shouldn't be here," she breathed. "I can't do this."

A hand slipped gently round her waist and Hana screamed, spinning on the spot and shoving at its owner. "Stop it!" she yelled, finding herself pushing Logan in the stomach. He grunted and dipped forward, his mouth open in surprise.

"Hana?" he said. "What's wrong?" He took her outstretched hand and turned it over as though examining it for demonic possession.

"Sorry, sorry," Hana gushed as her heart rate soared and then slumped. "I argued with Amanda and feel stink about it."

Logan's head jerked backwards. "You argued with Amanda?" He shook his head. "You never argue with anyone but me. Have I been replaced?"

"It's silly. Don't worry." Hana ran a shaking hand across her forehead and found it clammy. Logan saw the shutter come down, guarding her from his scrutiny. He decided not to press her though his expression said it galled him. He pulled her reluctant body into his side and kissed her forehead, feeling her tense under his hands. Hana sensed his concern hike.

"I missed you," he said into her hair. "Did you miss me?"

"No," she lied and then regretted it. "I let the baby stay in bed with me."

"Oh, okay." Logan sounded hurt. "Will there be room for me if I come home tonight?"

"Maybe." Hana shook herself, unable to release the spikey persona occupying her body. She needed to run away and hide from his perceptive grey eyes.

"I wanted to ask you to dinner," he said. "I need your help with something."

"That's nice," Hana sighed, craving normality. "Where do you want to go?"

"I'll walk across when I finish up here," he said. "We should talk too."

"What about Phoenix?" Hana asked as he kissed her forehead and turned to leave.

"Bring her." he said. "It'll be fine."

Hana suppressed her guilt for feeling disappointed, wanting time with Logan by herself. His allusion to talking sounded ominous. She peeped into the pram at the sleeping baby, loving her smooth olive skin and dark eyelashes. "I can't imagine life without you, Phoe, but sometimes I'd love the luxury of not having to plan my whole life around your next feed."

She trudged back to the unit with a heavy heart and leaden feet, ignoring the pulsing in her head as Phoenix woke the second the pram wheels touched the hallway floor. Hana sat on the sofa and fed her, denied the opportunity to go to the bathroom. The meeting with Laval loomed before her like a spectre of doom, chilling her to the bone in the humid lounge.

Tama tried to ask her about the walk but Hana remained uncommunicative and short tempered. He abandoned her too, joining a class on the field playing rugby with Logan.

Chapter 24

Logan attended a departmental meeting and arrived home just before the boarding house sounded the dinner bell. Hana tried to make up for her earlier behaviour by wearing a racy, light summer dress and piling up her hair. She made a special effort with her attitude and sported a tight smile.

Tama played a game on his phone in his underpants, sprawled face down on the defiled rug in the lounge. Hana eyed both offending tousled objects and wondered which she should throw out first, the rug or the boy. "I'm ready," she said with enthusiasm, holding up a baby who for once didn't wear a sleep suit but a cute sailor dress. Phoenix's bare legs and feet retracted up it, making her look like a floating white flower.

"Cool," Logan replied, appraising Hana with his eyes. His pupils dilated with desire. He leaned in and kissed her, his lips smooth against hers. "Let's go then." He shoved Tama's thigh with the toe of his black cowboy boot. "Get up, idiot."

Tama squinted up in confusion and Hana's heart sank. "A family dinner?" she asked, forcing disappointment from her tone. "Great."

"A family dinner? With me?" Tama hauled himself upright and shoved his lanky legs back into his jeans.

Bashfulness suited him and Hana rolled her eyes, finding it hard not to adore him.

She lugged the car seat out to the Honda while Tama hunted for his shoes and Logan waited to lock up. He balanced Phoenix in one arm and chatted to her. The veins stood out on his forearm and she longed to hurl herself into his embrace and fall on his mercy. Spying Amanda, her face drooped with misery. The other woman collected her washing from the communal clothes line and shot Hana a spiteful, narrow eyed look. Hana clutched the fabric of her skirt and felt her confidence deflate.

"Ready?" Logan demanded and Hana waited for him to unlock the car. The baby seat felt heavy in her arms. Logan's brow furrowed in confusion. "Oh sorry, we're walking. We don't need the car."

Hana traipsed back up the steps and dumped the car seat in the hallway, hoping she didn't break her neck on it in the dark when they got home. "Do you want the pram instead?" she asked and Logan shook his head. "It's not far. I'll carry her."

To compound Hana's misery, he strode off with Tama towards the boarding house. She clip-clopped along in her heels, feeling increasingly cheated with every step. As they reached the outer door of the reception, Logan turned to them both. "Okay, I need you to do exactly as I say. Tama, you ask for chicken curry and Hana, you ask for cabbage soup."

Hana's mouth dropped open as Tama said, "Yummy," under his breath.

With her face puckered like a small, obstinate child, she whined, "I don't want cabbage soup!"

Logan put his hand in the air, stopping her rant before she got going. "It's okay," he whispered. "I don't think you'll get it."

"But I'm hungry," she grumbled. "What will I do then?"

Logan's eyes lit up with a dangerous glitter. "Then ask for the leek pie."

Hana pulled a face and Tama offered to swap, but Logan intervened. "No, keep it that way round, please." He narrowed his eyes at Hana's pouting face. "But I don't think you'll get the pie either," he said with a shrug. He set off through the heavy front doors and Tama and Hana trotted behind. Tama waggled his eyebrows and she glared at him.

"Remind me to eat beforehand next time he asks me on a dinner date," she hissed.

The din inside the dining room sounded overwhelming. The vaulted ceiling caused the noise to collect in the apex and dive onto the heads of the occupants. A cacophony of laughing, yelling and eating filled Hana's ears. She saw familiar faces scoffing as though it was their last meal. They talked with their mouths open, waved cutlery at each other to accentuate their point and burped with abandon. It was such a testosterone fuelled environment, it made her nervous. The prefects noticed her presence and dread increased as she realised the implications of that small fact.

Cursing Angus Blair's brand of old fashioned etiquette, Hana stood shamefaced as the prefects forced every child in the room to stand to attention. "Lady present!" boomed the voice of the head student. She wanted to die on the spot. Her wooden smile acknowledged the chairs scraping back to disgorge backsides. Over one hundred faces turned in her direction, many still chewing. Hana swallowed, feeling like she'd entered a field of cows uninvited. Her mortification lessened as they sat and continued their meal, reviving as she heard her name squealed from the other side of the room. Forks stopped again and everyone stared.

"Missis Du Rose," pealed James, leaping from his seat and running towards her. He threw his arms around her neck and Logan jerked in shock. Tama grinned and gave his uncle a raised eyebrow. James unwrapped himself from Hana and made a lurch at Logan for the baby. Logan looked unsure and held her high above James' head, causing him to bounce up and down like he was trying to catch a balloon.

Hana touched Logan's arm. "James always wants to cuddle Phoe," she reassured him. "I trust him."

Logan lowered the child and James seized her, disappearing back to his table. His Korean accent squealed to his gathered audience, "See, I am with child." Sniggering issued from both the queue and the amassed testosterone at the tables. Logan's eyes widened and Tama snorted like a primary school child. Hana glared at him until he regained his composure. "Idiot!" she hissed. "Stop it!"

Tama elbowed Logan and laughed again and Hana felt her appetite desert her. Logan led them to the front of the queue and the boys accepted their superiority with down-turned lips. "I can't see any cabbage soup," she moaned, looking round the dining room. "Not a single bowl." The realisation cheered her. "Maybe it's all gone." She read the nearest menu displayed on the notice board. Cabbage soup and leek pie made an appearance and she sighed with resignation.

Tama looked thrilled with his chicken curry. A girl behind the counter appreciated his seductive wink and loaded his plate with rice. Logan chose a mince casserole and waited for Hana as she asked for her meal through gritted teeth. "I'd love the cabbage soup, please," she said without enthusiasm. The girl behind the counter ogled Logan, sending Hana's blood pressure into orbit. The name badge read, *Tahlia*, with *kitchen supervisor* scrawled beneath in italics.

"Hey, Logan," she said, fluttering her eyelashes and doing the suggestive-wiggle-thing tarty girls perfected with their hips. She turned to glare at Hana. "What?"

"Cabbage soup, please." Hana ground the request through clenched lips.

"It's gone." The girl's eyes narrowed. "Mince?" She heaped a nearby spoon with the lumpy brown mess and trailed it towards Hana's plate. Gravy leaked from its sides.

"Leek pie!" Hana squeaked. "Leek pie, please."

"That's gone too." The girl pursed her lips and with an unedifying plop, the mince hit Hana's plate and spattered up the front of her dress. "Tahlia leaned sideways and sized up Logan's rear. Her lip quirked upwards on one side.

"Pity about the cabbage soup!" Hana snarled under her breath. "I'd love to pour it over your lecherous head."

"Aye? What?" Tahlia turned her gaze onto Hana, her pretty features scrunching into a sneer.

"Nothing," Hana replied. She took her mince and followed Logan, picking her way through tables and benches.

Hana seated herself next to Tama and he leaned across to view her plate.

"Didn't you get rice?" he asked, peering at the brown mince smeared across the white surface.

"No, because I don't have a penis!" she snapped, contemplating the congealed mess.

Logan heaved out a sigh which sounded like relief. "Thanks babe," he said, squeezing Hana's fingers underneath the table. "I might get you to do that again another night."

"Get stuffed," Hana replied and snatched her hand away. She didn't want to eat cabbage soup, leek pie or brown mess. She also didn't want to witness her husband's adoring fans making free with the sight of his neat backside. The culmination of her abysmal day resulted in a fit of thinly suppressed temper and Logan's brow furrowed. Then Pete sidled up to the table and sat down on the other side of Tama. Whenever she looked in his direction, he popped backwards like a frightened tortoise. "God, give me strength," Hana begged, frustration hiking from annoyance to outrage.

She pushed the mince around the plate and quit, hiding most of it beneath her cutlery. James sat on another table, holding Phoenix under her tiny armpits and bouncing her feet up and down on his thighs. Phoenix grinned and Hana held her breath. She knew it would end in tears even before the jet of creamy liquid projected straight into James' face, because she'd only just fed her. James deposited the baby on Hana's knee amid much hilarity and headed for a shower.

Tama finished his dinner and leaned sideways, whispering into Hana's ear. "You might as well tell Logan right now," he breathed. "He knows something's wrong by the way you're behaving." He raised an eyebrow and stood, walking to the conveyor belt to dispose of his crockery.

Hana fought for control and lost the battle. With each passing second, she felt her nerve fail and the desire to pass the Laval problem over to Logan strengthened. He wrinkled his nose and turned to her. "It's Eton Mess for dessert. Ma used to make that." His smile looked wistful and he gnawed his lower lip. "Want some?"

"No!" Hana bolted upright and saw the shock cross Logan's face. "No, I don't want anything from you." Her bottom lip wobbled and she hoisted the vomit covered child over her shoulder. At that moment she hated him. Hated him for failing her when she needed him most.

Seizing the door keys from the table, Hana left. She imagined the delight of the kitchen supervisor at his abandonment. The girl morphed into a threat of Caroline sized proportions and by the time Logan arrived home with Tama, she'd convinced herself their marriage was over. She went to bed early to avoid all revealing conversation, the threat of Laval hanging over her head. Spending a cold night clinging to the edge of the bed to discourage contact, Hana woke in a worse mood.

Logan returned from an early session at the gym. Sweat beaded his brow and he clattered around the small bedroom while Tama sang in the shower. Hana knew they'd gone together and worried Tama might have confessed everything under threat of a weight landing on his head. But Logan said nothing.

Dread for her meeting with Laval occupied Hana's mind and she enacted her own personal rebellion, staying in bed and reading a trashy magazine. She counted down the hours until three o'clock and then the minutes. It didn't help. Bodie's warnings returned to haunt her and she processed the stupidity of changing location when no one knew where she was. At least in the open air of Day's Landing, she ran the chance of someone else noticing. He couldn't kidnap or hurt her in public.

Logan returned from the shower, a towel wrapped around his waist. He sat on the bed and pulled Hana into his armpit. "I love your hair," he sighed. His fingers twisted a red coil over and over. "It's why I noticed you at first, the way the harsh lights in the train caught the colours." He stroked her cheek. "Shall I tell you what I was trying to do last night?"

Hana shook her head and buried her face against his ribs. "Poison me?" she muttered. "Or give me the worst dinner of my whole life?"

Logan laughed and kissed the top of her head. Her hair caught in the bristles on his chin. "Na," he replied. "I'll tell you for a kiss."

Hana shook her head. "Haven't cleaned my teeth."

Logan discarded the towel and climbed under the sheets. "Yum, second-hand cabbage soup," he whispered.

Hana shrieked and giggled, pretending to fight him off while knowing Logan always got what he wanted. The television boomed through the unit as Tama hiked the volume, fanning himself with one of Logan's text books.

Logan's lips proved persuasive and Hana allowed him to cajole her, ignoring the voice in her head which warned it could be the last time. He showed surprise when she cried and hid her face in his downy chest. "It's nothing." She waved away his concern. "It's hormones."

Logan's brow furrowed and Hana saw suspicion in his grey eyes. She fought to distract him. "If you didn't intend me to have the worst dinner of my life last night, why cabbage soup?"

Logan's eyes glittered and he bit his lower lip. "I think I've discovered where the money's going." He sounded smug. "And I believe it's the reason the new manager quit before he started. It's not an easy fix."

"Oh." Hana's expression soured as the prospect of escaping the staff accommodation drifted out of reach. Logan smoothed away the lines of disappointment from her forehead.

"It's clever," he said, "and it's all about cabbage." Hana groaned and he grinned. "I got desperate," he continued. "Everything looked fine. So, I went back to basics and inspected everything in the boarding house. I picked a different area each time I did a night duty. I counted the cleaning products in the storeroom and then the sheets and towels."

Hana sniggered. "Did you put it back in alphabetical order or arrange by shape and colour?" She snorted as he jabbed her in the ribs.

"I put it back as I found it," he said. His tone held an edge of annoyance. "The point was not to draw attention to myself. It killed me."

Hana smiled into his chest and imagined him battling with his neat freak compulsions in the middle of the night. "Poor baby," she soothed.

"Thing is," Logan continued, "I saw an invoice last week for sixty cabbages. It's from one of the regular suppliers. So, I checked the chiller for cabbages and found none. Not one. The company invoiced at a dollar each so that's sixty dollars right there. I got curious and audited all the food and bills after the kitchen staff left at night. Some items get charged for but never arrive. I've noticed a pattern between certain vegetables."

"Cabbages and leeks?"

Logan nodded and his hair moved against the pillow. "Items like that. Legitimate things you might reasonably find on an order form."

Hana frowned. "Bodie never ate cabbage. He said it tasted of nothing." She rolled her eyes. "I think he rejects anything green or healthy looking even now."

"That's the point." Logan grinned and the light danced on his irises. "Nobody misses it. The menu needs to show it in case someone audits, but who asks for cabbage soup?"

"The Asian boys might." Hana frowned. "James likes cabbage."

Logan shrugged. "They'd only need to make it once or twice and ensure it tasted so horrible they never asked again."

"But I asked for it." Hana wrinkled her nose.

"Exactly!" Logan sounded victorious. "But you didn't get it because it never existed. I just needed to prove it."

"No, that girl said it had all gone."

"How many people did you see eating cabbage soup?" Logan demanded. "And don't you think it's weird how they ran out of the two most disgusting things on the menu? Look, the food can't be rubbish or the boarders' parents would complain. So, they make good food but put a crappy menu option in full view that nobody ever wants." He slapped the bed with his free hand. "Perfect. It's so clever you'd have to know what was going on to see it."

"So, why did the new manager quit?" Hana sighed with regret.

"Because I believe this is a city-wide thing," Logan replied. "I've made enquiries around the other boarding houses and they're noticing a similar shortfall in profits. I think someone warned the new manager off. Angus is meeting with the other school principals and will bring back copies of their food invoices and menus. But I think I've found the problem. Cabbages."

Hana leaned on her elbow and stared into his face. "Logan," she asked, her voice a whisper. "Can you stay at home with me today? Please."

Logan lifted his head and stared at her. The crow's feet around his stunning grey eyes disappeared, becoming faint cracks as his smile left. "Why, babe? What's wrong?" He ran a gentle finger along her cheek.

His scrutiny stripped her bare and Hana panicked. "Nothing, it's fine. I'm being silly." She threw the covers back and grabbed her dressing gown, bolting to the bathroom for a shower. Logan knocked on the door to say goodbye, but she didn't answer, afraid he would hear the misery in her voice.

Tama watched daytime television in the lounge. Hana emerged to find him scrubbing his teeth with the inside of an orange peel. The uneaten flesh sat on the coffee table seeping acidic liquid. "What are you doing?" she groaned.

"Doctor Oz said it works," Tama mumbled. The peel resembled a big orange grin. He removed it and a glob of dribble slipped onto his tee shirt.

"You're worse than a baby!" Hana complained, throwing herself on the sofa next to him. He budged over to make room.

"Do my teeth look white?" he demanded, waving the dripping peel at her. Hana closed her eyes in disgust. Tama threw the peel backwards, grinning as he heard it plop into the sink. "So, will you tell me what's wrong, or do I have to guess?" He turned back to the television where someone lay on the floor of the studio, swaddled in pillows as a doctor showed them how to go to sleep. Hana reached forward and pressed a button on the remote, sending the screen into darkness.

"You were right," she said with a grudging sigh. "Laval followed me and Amanda to Day's Landing yesterday. He kissed me and acted sleazy. Now she thinks I'm having an affair. She'll probably tell everyone."

Tama swore and rubbed a hand across his face. "If Logan finds out about this, he'll kill you and then he'll spread my body parts out for the moreporks."

Hana swallowed back tears. "No, he won't. He'll walk away from me without a backward glance because of all the times Caroline cheated. If I'm lucky, he'll let me have Phoenix, but I doubt it."

Tama put his arm around Hana as she crumbled. His shirt soaked up her tears. "I told you we should tell him," he said, his ignored wisdom sounding like an accusation. "What did Laval want?"

Hana sighed an awful shuddering breath. "To meet me. Today."

Tama sat up, his face suddenly far older than his years. "No way!" he snapped. "You're not going." He stood up and Hana sank into the centre of the sofa, filling the space he vacated. "I'm telling Uncle Logan now. This is serious!"

Hana stood also, not matching him for height but in courage and determination. "I need to do this," she said, meaning every syllable. "I love my husband and I can't let Laval hurt him because of me. He came after me before I even met Logan. This is my fight, Tama. Odering won't let me retract my statement, so I need Laval to understand. I'm meeting him in a public place and he hasn't hurt me yet. I'll sort it!"

"And if you can't?" replied Tama, his voice high and frightened.

"Then take care of Logan and Phoenix for me." Hana's face set in a look which Tama hadn't seen since the night on the mountain. She told him the baby was coming and she'd been right. He felt the same powerlessness.

"Hana, you can't do this," he whispered. "If anything happens to you, it will kill Logan as surely as taking a gun to his head. I can't watch that."

"I don't have a choice! Stop talking about it; it won't change anything." Hana whirled away and refused to discuss it further.

She left in the Honda after forcing Tama to babysit Phoenix. She returned carrying a steriliser unit and bottles. "This is just a precaution," she urged.

"Please, don't meet him," Tama begged. He reached for his phone and Hana glared at him.

"Do not tell my husband," she demanded. "You owe me!

She set up the steriliser and Tama watched, his grey eyes dull and his forehead creased into a frown. Hana changed the bedsheets, washing them and hanging them out in the sunshine to dry. Amanda loaded cloth nappies into a basket and Hana ignored her. Doom gripped her soul and she moved around in a fog. When the bottles were clean, Hana disappeared to the bedroom and expressed as much milk as she could manage. She wedged a chair behind the door. The clock ticked closer to midday and Tama fretted in the hallway. "I can talk to Amanda," he begged. "I can threaten her not to say anything."

"No," Hana replied. "Just leave it, the damage is done. She didn't want to know my side and I'm past caring."

"I can make her understand," he pleaded, but Hana refused.

Phoenix cried for a feed an hour later. Tama brought her to the bedroom door. "Hana, let me in. Phoe's hungry."

Hana pulled the chair away and opened it a crack. She looked hot and bothered. She couldn't look at Phoenix, handing a bottle of creamy milk through the gap. "Change her and feed her this," she said. "I'm expressing enough to last today. After that, there's formula in the kitchen."

"No, Hana no, don't do this!" Tama growled. She slammed the door in his face and leaned against it. "I'll break it down!" he threatened, but Phoenix set up a frightened protest and he felt torn.

Hana sobbed in the bedroom and expressed as much milk as she could. She heard her daughter screaming in the lounge as she refused the rubber teat. "Just do it, Phoe," she begged. "I've nothing left to give you." She pushed away the sense of foreboding and readied herself to leave.

At two o'clock, Hana crept from her bedroom and surveyed the lounge from the end of the hallway. Tama slept across the narrow gap, preventing her escape. He'd managed to feed Phoenix a full bottle and she lay in her cot. Hana stood over her, fixing the sight of the rosebud lips and dark lashes into her memory. She smelled of vomit and Hana's chest hitched with sadness. She'd heard Tama's struggle and pitied him the next feed. "I won't be long, baby," she whispered. "I need to take care of something."

Shaking her head at Tama's sleeping body, Hana walked to the laundry at the end of the hall. She took the key from the lock after opening the external door and then locked it behind her. The flat key clinked against her new phone in her back pocket. She'd closed her bedroom door in the hope Tama wouldn't miss her for a while. He'd guarded the front door but forgotten about the other exit. Her training shoes strode through the dry grass towards St Barts and the back gate. She took a deep breath and straightened her spine.

Amanda hung more washing on the communal line and paused as Hana walked past. Her brow furrowed and she let her hands drop by her sides. "That's odd," she breathed, glancing down at her daughter. Millie chatted back from the washing basket with conversational nonsense. "She doesn't have Phoenix with her." Amanda looked at the greyness in Hana's face and tensed, remembering the whispered tryst she'd overheard. Her lips twisted into a pout. "I bet she's meeting him." She turned to watch Hana walk away and something about the other woman's defeated posture confused her. "But she doesn't seem happy about it, does she?"

She turned back to her washing and finished pegging tiny tee shirts on the line. Something gnawed at the back of her mind and she kept returning to the sound of Phoenix's muffled cries through the wall earlier. She reran the overheard conversation, allowing it to take on a different perspective. "I think I might have made a mistake," she mused. "What if she's in danger?" Amanda darted a nervous look towards the units. "What if she's left her baby alone and is going to do something stupid?"

She played with Millie in the grass for a while, reluctant to overreact and cause drama if she'd misunderstood. Time passed and Millie grew fractious enough for Amanda to admit defeat and obey the overwhelming instinct that something was terribly wrong. She stuffed Millie back into the washing basket and carried it to Hana's unit, hovering at the bottom of the steps and twice talking herself out of interfering.

As Amanda lifted her hand to knock, she heard Phoenix cry and stiffened. The baby's distress grew louder and she panicked. Setting the basket on the road, she snatched up her daughter and hammered on the door. "Is there anyone there?" she yelled. "Please tell me there's someone else home."

Tama flung the door open. His hair stuck up on one side and Phoenix squalled in his arms. He clamped a baby's bottle in his fingers. "What?" he snapped. His jaw clenched at the sight of Amanda and he walked onto the top step. "Oh, have you come to do some more damage?" he demanded.

Amanda shook her head and took a step back. "No. I think something's wrong."

"Yeah, it is!" Tama raised his voice. "You accused Hana of cheating. Hana?" He made the sentence sound as ludicrous as the accusation. "What do you want?"

"I'm worried about her," she stammered, her tongue tripping over her words.

"Just leave her alone," he bit. "She's in her bedroom and that's where she's staying." He jabbed a finger in her face. "You made this ten times worse than it needed to be."

Amanda paled and swallowed. "She went out. But I'm worried about her." She blinked at the look of horror dawning across Tama's face.

"She went out?" His eyes widened. "She couldn't have." Phoenix kicked her legs and wailed as he whirled around. Amanda stood at the bottom of the steps, feeling foolish. She heard Tama running around in the unit, slamming doors and calling Hana's name. His voice competed with the sound of Phoenix's cries.

"Logan's gonna kill me." Tama reappeared, holding Phoenix one handed as he shoved trainers onto his bare feet. "I'm so dead." He ran down the steps and jumped off the bottom one. "What did you hear?" he demanded. "Yesterday, what did you hear?"

Amanda repeated the conversation, watching as Tama focussed on the time and location. He cradled Phoenix in his arms and started jogging, throwing one sentence over his shoulder. "Call the cops. Ask for Detective Sergeant Odering. Do it now!"

Tama ran to the main building. Phoenix stilled against his shoulder and he realised she'd gone to sleep. Her chest hitched, a remnant of her distress at being presented with the rubber teat again. Tama ran through an earlier conversation with his uncle, recalling Logan's timetable in his head. The familiar scent of the school assailed his nostrils and he jogged to Logan's classroom. He shifted the baby's weight in his arms and hammered on the door. A Year 12 boy opened it and peered out at him.

"Move!" Tama demanded, shoving the boy aside with his hip. He strode into the classroom and saw Logan's eyes widen in surprise. He stood with his left leg bent, the foot planted on the seat of a chair and his forearm resting on his thigh. In the middle of an explanation, his other arm remained in the air. Tama saw the lack of comprehension as he dumped the sleeping bundle into her father's arms.

"We've got a problem," he hissed. "I don't have time to explain. She's got a head start on me. I messed up. Odering's on his way."

Logan took Phoenix with a what-the-heck look on his face, but Tama bolted. Back at the unit, he thrust his car key into the ute's ignition and swore when nothing happened.

"I've phoned Angus!" Amanda called from her doorway and Tama groaned.

"I told you to call the cops!" he shouted. The ute's door slammed in his wake and he set off running.

"But I don't know what to tell them," Amanda whispered. Tama had already reached the boarding house and didn't hear.

Chapter 25

Tama ran harder than he ever had in his life, his lungs gasping for oxygen as he dodged traffic and sped towards River Road. His mind conjured up a mental image of the city and he located Day's Landing, calculating the shortest route there. Exhausted, he dropped into a steady jog, his long legs covering the ground and his body fatigued with the extreme heat. His watch ticked nearer to three o'clock and he forced terrible thoughts from his fertile imagination.

Cutting through a children's playground, Tama found his way to River Road and jumped a metal railing to land on the pavement. His right ankle complained, but he didn't stop. He ran for another five minutes and then he saw her.

Hana walked with a stiff gait, her back rigid and her arms pumping. She wore tracksuit trousers and a tee shirt and he watched her take something from her back pocket and hold it in her hand. Sunlight flashed against a pink object and he realised she carried her new phone. Relief flooded him and he patted his pockets, realising he didn't know her new number at the same moment he discovered he'd left without his phone. "Shit!" he cursed and a woman walking a dog crossed the road to avoid him.

Hana powered ahead, lifting her phone to double check the time. Tama paused for a moment with his palms on his knees, readying himself to run again. As though sensing his presence she slowed and turned, her gaze raking the sunlit road. Knowing she'd run if she saw him, Tama ducked into a driveway. He peered through the bushes and saw her resume walking.

His long legs didn't let him down and he started to gain on her. She stopped and turned more often and he saw the fear in her expression. The straight road gave him little opportunity to hide and he ran foul of neighbouring dogs and bushes in his efforts to creep up on her. He stopped and rested at the end of a curved driveway, jumping as a white tradesman's van pulled up on the grass next to him. Two men clambered out. They wore dirty tee shirts and the uniform boots and stubby shorts of builders. "Ah bro," a stocky, bald man laughed, clapping the younger man on the back. "Your plastering is shite. I've seen it!"

Tama darted behind a tree as Hana looked back again. He tried not to think about the expression on Logan's face as he dumped the baby in his arms. "Sorry, Uncle," he mouthed. "I've let you down." He increased his pace despite the exhaustion in his limbs and closed the distance. "I'm coming, Hana," he gasped under his breath. "I'll make this right."

Hana walked into the park by Day's Landing and Tama followed at a safe distance. He watched her stand by the toilets even though both cubicles displayed a green light to show their vacancy. She dragged her hand across her forehead and wiped it on her track pants before sitting on the curb. Her shoulders slumped in resignation and Tama's heart melted. He saw her glance at her phone before pushing it down her tee shirt and into her bra. His teeth ground in his jaw as he decided he couldn't watch any more. "Screw this!" he hissed. He squared his shoulders and edged from his hiding place, his eyes fixed on the back of Hana's head.

"Get down on the ground! Now!" The voice grated on Tama's nerves as the younger tradesman appeared behind him. The other one stood in front and held his hand against Tama's chest. He felt a flush of irritation.

"Get out of my way!" Tama gave a determined shove, jerking sideways to check on Hana. The older man didn't move.

"On the ground!" he said. "Do as you're told."

"No." Tama's eyes widened in horror as he processed the words. "You don't understand. I need to get to her." He jabbed a finger towards the park and the man shook his head.

"I don't think so. Get on the ground."

Tama sneaked a glance behind him. He saw a flash of carrot-orange hair which clashed with the tones of the tradesman's tee shirt. The man reached into his tool belt as Tama gritted his teeth and prepared to charge the one in front. "Stand still!" the guy urged, the warning clear. "Be sensible."

Tama saw a dark Mercedes sweep through the car park entrance ahead and knew. Laval's expensive car slid into a space next to the toilets. Hana rose and Tama watched her straighten her clothes and hold her hands before her as though prepared to negotiate. "Don't get in that car, don't get in that car!" Tama screamed, but the distance between them dispersed his warning on the gentle breeze. "No!" he bellowed as Hana took a step forward. Laval slipped from the passenger seat. "Run, Hana! Run!"

She half turned, but Laval spoke to her and she faced him instead. Tama's heart beat a frantic tattoo in his chest. Nausea roiled through his guts and his breath came in rasps. He darted a look at the ginger guy and knew he could take him. Tama drew his strength into his torso, willing his body to remember rugby first fifteen training. As his weight dipped forward, his whole body experienced a peculiar sensation and he shot backwards into the bushes. Nothing mattered but the fizzing in his nerve endings like he'd touched a live wire. His chest wall burned. His eyeballs rolled back into his head as the ginger haired man switched the Taser off.

"You didn't stay 'Stop Police' you damned idiot!" the older tradesman yelled as he checked the pulse in Tama's neck. "Can't you get anything right?"

"He ran at me," his colleague complained. "I didn't get a chance!"

"He was running at me actually!" the other man protested. "You didn't need to shock him."

Tama lay on the ground, his limbs still twitching. The voltage had ceased its rampage but someone forgot to tell his body. Sharp pains in his chest made him groan and the guy with orange hair yanked the pins out without care. Tama decided to kill him at the first opportunity. Dribble slid down the side of his cheek and into his ear. He heard himself moan without coherence as the men turned him over and handcuffed him, his face pushed into the dusty earth. Soil mixed with the dribble and made a dark paste. He vomited into the grass, unable to stop himself retching as they hauled him upright.

They read him his rights and Tama's head bobbed. He tried to say Hana's name, but it emerged as garble. The older man peered into his face, concern in his dark eyes. "You all right, son?" he demanded and Tama shook his head as the fizzing continued to spread out from his chest.

"You're an idiot!" The man turned to face his colleague. The ginger guy opened his mouth to speak and the older man shook his head. "Save it for the boss!"

The white transit van pulled up onto the grass with a crunch, riding the curb like it wasn't there. Shock from the Taser addled Tama's brain, coupled with a memory of the older man planting flower beds near the staff units the day before. The world felt surreal and his head swam with a collage of disjointed memories. "Gardener," he mumbled. "School. Hana."

The back door of the van opened and the men shoved Tama up the steps and into its darkened interior. He fell up the last stair, his legs operating like collapsing jelly.

"What did you do to him?" Blue eyes observed the bedraggled teen with suspicion. The older man shoved Tama into a seat and jerked his head backwards towards the younger guy.

"Rookie enthusiasm!" he spat. "He hit him with the Taser."

Tama observed the inside of the transit through eyes misted with pain and confusion. His cuffs dragged along the bench seat. One wall of the van contained computers and a tech sat with headphones on, speaking into a radio. His brain made irrational leaps and he closed his eyes. "Hana," he said again. Dribble dripped from his chin. "Help." His head rolled back, allowing the fizzing in his nerve endings to diminish. With it came the memory of his task and he staggered up with a garbled oath on his lips.

The new guy raised his hand to stop Tama. "Don't try it!" he warned. His smart grey suit looked incongruous against the scruffy appearance of the tradesmen and he stared at Tama hard through piercing blue eyes. Then he swore, a curse to rival Tama's. "You picked up a bloody Du Rose!" he shouted at the gardener. "You bunch of amateurs!"

"Hana!" Tama heaved out the word and the suited man's eyes widened.

"Where is she going?" he demanded. "Why did you follow her?"

"No, no," Tama groaned and lurched towards the doors, his hands still cuffed behind his back. The suited man flung them wider with a huff of exasperation, smacking the ginger cop in the forehead. Tama stumbled after him and leaned against the side of the van, peering down the hill to the car park below.

Swans marched around Day's Landing, picking up the aftermath of the lunchtime's generous visitors. The smart Mercedes had gone. So had Hana Du Rose.

Chapter 26

Tama stood on the grass and raked the horizon with frantic moving eyes, hopelessness growing in his heart. The car park looked peaceful, the ducks waddling around between the painted lines. The space in front of the toilets remained empty as though Hana's absence left a vacuum. Tama's legs shook from the after-effects of the Taser and he leaned forward and vomited, his hands still cuffed behind his back.

When he stood up straight, his jawbone jutted through his cheek. He spat and wiped his mouth on the shoulder of his shirt. The young cop watched him, relishing his discomfort with a veiled smirk. An image of Kane Du Rose flitted across Tama's inner vision, compounding his sense of powerlessness. His brain forced his emotions into well-worn tracks, as familiar as they were toxic. The cop's foolish smirk acted as the trigger and Tama dropped back into his self-destructive pattern of hatred.

"Don't!" Odering shouted. Too late.

Tama launched himself at the pale face beneath the ginger curls, head butting him full in the nose. He heard his hard forehead bend the cop's nose cartilage in a satisfying pop. The officer sank like a brick, clutching his face as blood streamed off his chin and stained his stubby shorts. Tama growled, "That's for Hana!"

A bruise began on his forehead as the other officers tackled Tama to the ground. One sat on his flailing legs while the tech rushed to examine the bleeding cop. The sound of Odering's voice cut through their grunts. "Let him go!"

The older cop shook his head. "No way! He assaulted one of ours!"

"Are you for real?" Tama saw a pair of smart shoes appear next to his face. "He was protecting a family member and you muppets arrested him. Now she's gone. Do you honestly wanna go there?"

Tama gave a nasty laugh, his chest compressed by the weight of the other man. But the memory of the empty car park induced another bout of vomiting.

"Get off him!" Odering barked. "And get that rookie out of my face or I'll punch him myself. Now let this man go!"

Tama sensed the pressure leave his legs as the cop stood. Someone released the cuffs with a metallic click and he sat up, rubbing the back of his hand across his filthy face. He glared at the bleeding cop and saw the man squirm beneath his gaze. Odering indicated Tama should get into the van and he climbed the steps, holding onto the door to support himself. Odering extended his hand. "We've never met," he said. "Which one are you?"

"Tama. And I know who you are. Can we get on with finding Hana now?"

Detective Sergeant Odering nodded. "Tell me what you know."

Logan met them at the police station with a wailing Phoenix, his face ashen. His irises looked slate grey and swirled with a torturous blackness. Tama took the baby, finding a bottle in the bag Logan had snatched from the house. He sat in Odering's office and tried to feed her. She screamed, a high-pitched wail designed to summon her mother. When hunger made her admit defeat, she sucked with a heaving chest and sporadic wails halted her progress through the milk. Logan watched his daughter with anger growing in his face. The warning vein ticked in his neck. "She made bottles? Tell me Hana didn't plan this!" he hissed.

Tama gulped and concentrated on Phoenix. The miserable hiccoughs accentuated Hana's absence as though a clanging gong pealed through the office. Logan paced, covering the carpet in four long strides before turning and repeating the movement. He resembled a caged bear and Tama closed his eyes against the dizzying, repetitive motion of his cowboy boots. Odering made phone calls, speaking into the handset in hushed tones and eyeing Logan with hurried, nervous glances.

"There's no sign of her." He released the receiver into its cradle with a click. "Everyone's looking."

Plaster split as Logan smashed his left hand through the wall. "You did this!" he exploded. "You promised this wouldn't happen!"

"What?" Tama's eyes bugged and he drew Phoenix closer. She pushed the teat away with her tongue and cranked up to a wail again. He shifted her over his shoulder and patted her back. "You knew about Laval?"

Odering cleared his throat and lowered his eyes to the desk in a look of abject guilt.

Logan strode towards him and gripped either corner. The wooden frame rocked against his fury. He leaned forward and spoke with exaggerated slowness. "I gave you the bloody sim card from her phone like you wanted!" His irises glittered with fury. "I should have dealt with this myself!"

"Then why didn't you?" Tama rose, shaking fingers smoothing Phoenix's back as she whimpered.

Logan shook his head and jabbed a finger at Odering. "He wouldn't tell me who it was." He swallowed. "I promised Hana I'd quit talking to anyone in Auckland." His eyelashes fluttered. "Anyone of influence," he qualified. "The cops came to me first and I thought they had it under control."

"And we did." Odering spread his hands. "Until this afternoon."

"Na!" Logan shook his head. "You've played us from the start. My wife is bait for your operation. You told me you didn't know who was threatening her!" Logan swore and kicked the metal dustbin. It ricocheted off the wall and hit the desk.

Phoenix whimpered and Odering winced. "Look, let's talk about this."

"No!" Logan yelled. "Find my wife!"

"Everything okay, Detective?" The school gardener appeared in the doorway. Logan looked at the man in surprise, confusion causing him to stall. A fist sized section of plaster board plummeted earthwards. A blue bruise already blossomed on Logan's knuckles as his deficient blood struggled to cope with the blow.

"We're fine," Odering assured the officer. "Any news?"

The slight shake of the man's head sent Logan into another round of pacing. "I'll sort this myself," he raved. His fingers reached into his pocket for his phone.

Odering moved fast and stayed his hand by clamping his fingers around Logan's wrist. Logan's eyes sparked as he shook him off. Odering lowered his voice. "You stay here and you talk to nobody, Du Rose. I'm warning you. You call anyone and I'll lock you up for a very long time."

"Whatever! You've failed Hana," Logan bit through gritted teeth. "And I let you."

"That's not true," Odering countered. "My people followed your wife as soon as she left this office. Two of my officers tracked her to a cafe over the bridge. They've been following her ever since." Odering pursed his lips. "She told me someone was under threat, but promised it wasn't her."

"It was Uncle Logan," Tama said. "Laval threatened to hurt him. Permanently. And it's the younger Laval, not the one in prison."

Logan sank into a chair and bent forward, his head in his hands. "I don't know anyone else called Laval," he breathed. "This makes no sense." The events of the last hour had aged him. He put his head in his hands and Tama's eyes widened with a flicker of panic. When

Caroline jilted Logan at the altar and they'd made the long, silent journey back to the hotel to change out of their stupid suits, he hadn't looked that crestfallen. Not even the night his birth parents burned alive could surpass the utter devastation on his olive face as he contemplated life without Hana. Tama watched him with fascination. Logan always coped, but he couldn't deal with this. "I can't lose her twice," Logan whispered to himself. His heels ground against the carpet.

Phoenix pushed away the teat, pulling her mouth sideways and screwing up her face. Tama peered at the half empty bottle before laying it on Odering's desk. He put the baby over his shoulder and tapped away, hearing the wind growl inside her belly. She belched and farted at the same time and Tama resisted the urge to laugh. "Bugle-bum," he murmured, repeating Hana's pet name for her. He settled her in the crook of his arm and pushed the bottle back between her lips. She sucked again, shaking her fists in disgust and looking around for Hana's more favourable alternative. "You think I'm a traitor, don't you? I've let you and her down." He fingered the bright pink fabric of her sleep suit and pondered his failure. He glanced up to find Logan staring at him as he tried to press the rubber nipple between the baby's reluctant lips. The man's grey eyes flashed as a light went on behind his irises.

"Pink!" Logan bounced up like a spring, the muscles bulging beneath his jacket.

"What?" Tama gaped and Phoenix rejected the bottle teat again. Milk sprayed up his wrist.

"Pink!" Logan repeated. He jabbed a finger in Odering's face and the other man recoiled in a fear reaction before collecting himself. "The phone." Frantic fingers dragged his mobile from his pocket. "Hana's new phone has a tracker on it. The guy loaded it for me at the shop. As long as she has it switched on I can find her." He unlocked his screen and his fingers danced across the keyboard at speed.

"You GPS track your wife?" Odering's nose wrinkled and his lips pursed as though he'd just sucked a lemon.

"He tracks her phone." Tama rose to Logan's defence like the good lieutenant he'd always been. He wiped milk from his wrist onto his shirt and balanced Phoenix over his shoulder. Placing his body between Logan and the detective, he drew his lips back in a snarl. "Good job somebody's looking out for her, isn't it?"

Chapter 27

Laval's men stuffed Hana into the back of the Mercedes. She resisted, kicking and protesting as they hauled her off her feet. "No, you don't understand!" She hit out at heads and chests with growing futility. "I couldn't retract my statement. The cops won't let me!"

The two guys had snatched her as soon as the wheels stopped rolling and Bodie's self-defence lessons didn't feature. Hana's plans to defend herself and run failed like crumpled paper against the might of Laval's heavies.

"Shut up!" A sweaty hand covered Hana's mouth. "Sit still!" the man demanded and when she wriggled because she couldn't breathe, he slapped her so hard she felt her brain rattle in her skull. The passenger door closed in her face and yanking the handle showed he'd activated the child locks

"Put your seat belt on!" The driver turned around to issue the command and Hana shook her head like a stubborn child. Laval slid into the other back seat and her blood froze in her veins. She turned her face away and cursed her own stupidity. She'd walked into this with her eyes open, but a voice in her head told her she still couldn't save Logan.

The Mercedes made the climb up to the main road and Hana screamed as she saw Tama lying on his back with strangers attacking him. "Stop! Stop!" she screeched and hammered on the window with the flat of her hand.

"Shut her up or I'll shoot her!" the driver hissed. Laval reached over and clamped both her hands in his. His eyes glinted with a hint of dark insanity.

"Calm down, gorgeous." His voice dripped with pleasantry. He leaned across Hana's body, his face close to hers as he gripped the seat belt. He drew it across her stomach in a sensuous motion and clicked it shut next to her hip. Hana froze as his fingers trailed across her thighs and he smiled. "That's better," he whispered. "Play nice, Hana."

He leaned forward and tapped the driver on the shoulder with a manicured index finger. The man half turned and Hana saw his complexion pale. "Shout at me again and I'll kill you," Laval said. His tone sounded reasonable, but she felt the tension in the car hike.

"Sorry," the man stammered. He turned his attention to the road ahead.

Michael Laval pushed a stray lock of hair from Hana's cheek, tucking it behind her ear with the care of a lover. It seemed such a tender movement, it confused her and she battled ready tears. "Who are you?" she breathed, her voice laden with terror. "Who are you really?"

He patted her hand with feigned kindness. "This will all be over soon."

"What will?" Hana begged, her words catching in her throat. "What will be over soon?"

Laval smiled and ignored her question, tapping a beat on his trouser leg with relaxed fingers.

The car headed south, the expensive engine making little sound in the interior. Hana stopped recognising the back roads or the landscape. Her breasts felt tight and painful and she missed her baby, tamping down a sob of regret. She'd underestimated Laval and sensed she'd pay the price. She turned to face Laval, the seat belt cutting into her neck. "I went to see the detective in charge of your father's case," she whispered. "You saw me in the cafe afterwards. But he made fun of me and I left. I'll try again tomorrow. Let me go and I'll see him again. This time he'll let me do it."

Laval placed his index finger over her lips and pressed hard. Hana winced. "Shush, darling Hana. It's too late for that now."

The corners of her phone dug into her flesh, causing soreness as her breasts swelled with milk. Hana longed to reach in and shift it, but common sense told her not to. She used the pain to galvanise herself, filling her brain with thoughts of determination instead of failure and regret.

"Do you have anything with you I should be worried about?" Laval asked, as though reading her mind.

"Like what?" Hana replied. She opened her empty hands and showed them to him. Her tracksuit pants contained a back pocket, but if she'd sat on anything electronic with such force, it would be toast, anyway. Her damp tee shirt clung to her waist.

Laval ran gentle hands either side of her thighs and under her bottom, his irises sparkling with a dangerous glitter. "I'll search you properly at my leisure," he informed her with an acidic smile. He turned away and she heard him say, "Without an audience."

An involuntary shudder passed through her body and left her palms clammy and cold. Hana fretted and worried alternately for herself and Phoenix. Thoughts of Logan sent a lump into her throat and she realised she needed his strength with a tangible ache. She berated herself, knowing she should have told him everything and let him fix it instead of playing the hero. Realising time spent worrying amounted to valuable minutes wasted, she turned to prayer instead. She searched her memory for helpful bible verses and remembered hearing Pastor Allen preach about the book of Daniel. She heard his voice like an echo and repeated the familiar mantra under her breath. "Despite present appearances, God is in control."

"I disagree." Laval turned his smirk towards her and his eyes narrowed. "I'm in control, Hana. Not God."

She closed her eyes and battled through the horror. Her prayers became silent, so Laval couldn't taint them and she appealed to a higher power than a twisted man with an earthly agenda. "Please make this okay," she begged over and over. "Please make this okay."

The vehicle turned onto a tree-lined driveway and bumped along a track towards a vast, rambling house. "Home at last," Laval said and smiled sideways at Hana. He stretched out his legs as though arriving after a long absence and watched green paddocks skim by through the window. An expression of satisfaction settled over his face.

"Where are we?" Hana demanded, sitting up straight.

"South of Cambridge," Laval answered, reaching across to unfasten her seatbelt. "Nice and secluded with no one to hear you scream."

Hana felt numbness descending. It stretched over her head like a stocking and her vision blurred. The sense of nothing worked its way throughout her body until a blessed freedom released her from the fear. She knew she'd gambled away her life and would lose it. The question was how Laval would do it. She tried not to think about how lengthy or painful he might make the process, focussing instead of happier images of Logan holding their daughter.

The driver pulled Hana from the car by her hair when she refused to get out. She banged her elbow on the edge of the door in the struggle, feeling the throbbing in her funny bone until it deadened. Her feet dragged against cracked pavement as they manhandled her under a covered porch and through a creaking front door. *'Never change location, Mum.'* Bodie's well-intentioned words came back to her as a reprimand and Hana regretted not getting the chance to say goodbye.

The driver shoved her in the spine to make her walk and Hana tripped over the doorstep. A wide lobby contained old fashioned furniture and he yanked her hair to force her to the right. She passed through double doors and saw Laval's shiny black shoes moving ahead of her. The feeling returned to her elbow and it ached enough to make her want to scream. Her feet moved across a mottled carpet. Once expensive, it had become a feast for carpet beetles. She held her breath and took smaller steps, imagining the bugs crunching underfoot. A lounge opened out before her. 1960s brown corduroy sofas and armchairs lined the walls like an old people's home.

"Shout when you need us," the driver said to Laval. He avoided Hana's gaze and the two men left together, closing the double doors behind them. Hana waited for the click of a lock but heard nothing.

"You can't get good staff anymore," Laval muttered. "They have a sense of entitlement nowadays. Do you find that's the case at your hotel?" Hana gaped as her heart sank. He knew too much about her. It made his threats carry more weight somehow. He'd kill her and then Logan, but what would happen to their baby?

"Make yourself at home." Laval jerked his head towards a tatty armchair and Hana sank into its torn folds. "Drink?" He lifted a shimmering crystal glass from the dusty surface of a cabinet and wielded a stylish decanter.

Hana jerked her head and then changed her mind. Alcohol might reduce the pain she sensed coming. Dutch courage. She swallowed and wondered where the term originated. Bodie's voice spoke into her mind. *'Don't eat or drink anything. It's the easiest way to subdue a victim,'* he reminded her.

Laval handed her neat whisky and she took it. Her hand trembled and she used the other to support it. She sipped, feeling it burn along her throat and into her stomach. It took the edge off her fear and another of Bodie's lessons slid into her mind. *'There's always something you can use as a weapon.'*

Laval sat and crossed his legs, holding his glass with a casual air. He swirled the contents, looking comfortable and at home in the familiar environment. Hana couldn't settle and rose, edging to the outskirts of the room for safety. Laval studied her with an eyebrow raised in amusement. "There's nowhere to run, Hana. Sit down."

"No!" she snapped, tossing her red hair and spilling whisky up her wrist. She wiped it on her tee shirt and left a gold streak. Odering would test every stain and mark on her body and the thought galvanised her. "Get on with it," she goaded Laval. "Just kill me."

He sighed and observed her as though she represented a collectible specimen. "No. Let's play a game first," he said.

Hana shook her head. "I've had enough." She waved her arm around the dowdy room and more whisky slopped from the glass. "Just kill me and then we're done."

"Find the connection first." Laval's smile showed even, white teeth. "Find that, then I'll put you out of your misery." He flicked at an imaginary speck on his trousers and uncrossed his legs; a man with time to waste.

Hana sighed, fighting the tremble in her knees as she leaned against the wall for support. Flock wallpaper peeled from the bottom up. "What connection?" she demanded. "I don't know what you mean."

Laval shrugged and studied her expression as he spoke. "He lies to you about everything, so if you find it I might be kinder."

"Who lies to me?" Hana whispered. She turned away from her tormentor's amused gaze and discovered a wall of photographs behind her. Hissing through her teeth, she moved towards the myriad faces she didn't know as though looking for solidarity with the black and white images.

"Warm," Laval called in a sing song voice and Hana gritted her teeth. She was the only player in a game she didn't understand. The drink shook in her hand and she lifted it, allowing a heady sip to pass her lips and heat her tongue.

Her free hand stroked the wallpaper as she moved around the room. The photographs made little sense and she heard Laval tap the arm of his chair behind her. The beat grew faster as his impatience increased. She moved along the wall, not comprehending the framed snaps of people she'd never met. She turned to face Laval and a frame containing a group photo caught against her hand and slanted at a dangerous angle. "I can't do this." Hana's breath rasped and she felt her throat closing. "I don't understand what you want from me."

"Keep looking." Laval rapped out the order and Hana spun to face the wall. Fear created a dizzying blindness and she couldn't distinguish one face from another. She turned the corner and skirted a dining table complete with six chairs. Her chest hurt and her breathing sounded strained.

"You drugged my drink," she breathed and Laval shook his head.

"Why would I do that, Hana?" He raised his own glass and took a sip. "I want you wide awake and looking into my eyes. This is your husband's fault and I need you to know everything."

Hana raked the portraits looking for a clue. She sensed it wouldn't help. Yet Laval continued to dangle it in front of her like a lifeline. She used the side of her hand to clear dust from the glass of a smaller frame. A young Laval stood next to a white haired man and Hana used the bottom of her tee shirt to shine the glass. "Your father?" she asked and turned to hear Laval's snort of derision.

"That's right. You never met him, did you?"

"This is pointless!" Hana whirled around as a flare of anger worked its way up her spine. "I'm fed up of your games. Kill me, come on, do it!"

"Keep looking!" Laval stood and took a step towards her, his brown eyes flashing with supernatural malevolence. Hana gulped and turned her concentration back to the photographs. "Getting hotter," Laval said as her panicked gaze took in a series of team line ups from the North Shore Grammar School in Auckland. Labels etched into the foot of each photo showed the school crest.

Hana smoothed the glass with the side of her hand and searched the nearest photograph, running scenarios through her mind. Laval's vanity suggested he wanted her to find photos of him, so that's where she directed her search. That wasn't who she found. The familiar face smiled shyly at her from the front row of a team photograph and her heart sank into her feet and stayed there.

Chapter 28

Logan's distinctive grey eyes stared at a point beyond her head and Hana held her breath. He looked the same age as the boy on the London train, but a few extra months had helped him make the transition to adolescence. A soccer ball balanced on his knees, clutched between capable hands which Hana ached to feel on her body. Her heart appealed to the wooden figure in the garish yellow strip though she knew he couldn't hear her. 'Help me,' her soul cried.

"Hot and getting hotter!" Laval laughed at his own joke and Hana's stomach roiled with the combined whisky and confusion. Her finger moved along the bottom of the glass as she searched for Logan's name as though even the typed letters might offer comfort in her last hours. The neat italics showed *Du Rose, Logan (Captain)*, reminding her of everything her stupidity would deny her in the future.

Laval chuckled behind her. He'd moved without her realising. She exhaled a ragged breath which competed for release alongside the acid in her stomach. "Is it clicking into place for you yet, my darling?" he intoned.

Hana turned, finding him too close for comfort. "I don't understand." She regretted the wobble in her voice which betrayed her and Laval shrugged.

"Perhaps Du Rose married a bimbo then. That's disappointing." He sniggered. "We never found out what kind of girls he liked because he rebuffed them all. If he hadn't been so handy with his fists, we might have called him gay!" He laughed at his own words like a regressed schoolboy telling a filthy joke. Hana turned back to the photo and stroked Logan's face through the glass.

"He waited for me," she whispered.

"Look harder!" Laval gripped the back of Hana's neck and forced her face towards the photograph. It came without warning and she cried out as the grass cracked from top to bottom beneath her cheek. "Look!" Laval shouted, smashing her face into it again. The whisky glass hit the wall, discarding its contents over the garish wallpaper and Hana saw a chip in the outer edge of the rim. She held on to the crystal tumbler, her fingers aching with the effort.

Another face next to Logan's appeared familiar and Hana peered closer. The pieces fell into place. "You were there," she said, her voice strained with tears. "You knew Logan in high school."

"Oh, he never said? Poor Hana!"

"He doesn't realise," she protested, still defending her husband with her last breath.

"Maybe not." Laval pushed her face into the photo again and Hana felt the shattered glass nip her cheek. "More Du Rose dirty secrets," he whispered in her ear.

Hana peered again at the names beneath the photograph. *Du Rose, Logan (Captain); L'Huillier, Michel (Vice-Captain.)*

"You're not Michael Laval," she gasped, a catch in her voice. "If you're not Michael Laval then I don't understand."

He touched the cracked glass with his index finger, keeping the tumbler of whisky in his hand. "Oh, but I am. I changed my name after my dalliance with the Du Roses. Your husband made sure I couldn't work again under my real name."

"You took your father's," Hana said. Relief coursed through her as Laval released her neck.

He shrugged behind her, his chest touching her shoulder. "My father's a silly old bugger," he said. "He's good with the ladies, but largely harmless. His business is small time stuff, enough to keep this old place running."

"But he lived in a retirement village." Hana turned enough to challenge him. "The cops said so."

"He worked in the retirement village," Laval corrected her. A smile added levity to his voice. "Where better to find silly old ladies?"

Hana shuddered. How many more victims lost their life savings to a nasty old man? How many felt too ashamed to tell anyone and died in poverty? "He wasn't harmless." she winced, remembering the decomposed body of Bobby's stepmother which laid in a storm drain for almost a year. "Your father killed Bobby's mother. He was a greedy, murdering conman!"

Hana cringed at the hot breath against the back of her neck as Laval spun her and pushed her face into the photograph again. She closed her eyes to avoid the look of innocence in Logan's expression. "Yes, he did get a little carried away with the woman from Northland. I think he actually liked her." He paused and pressed his lips to Hana's neck. "I like you, Hana. We could have fun together."

Hana shoved her elbow backwards, catching Laval in the stomach. He laughed and shot out his arm, sliding it around her waist before she could repeat the movement. He dragged her against his side. Hana whimpered, sensing the tug of her baby and knowing through instinct that Phoenix cried for her somewhere. It injected a frantic vibe into her voice.

"Why are you doing this?" she pleaded. "I told you, the detective wouldn't let me retract my statement. He said it was too late. I tried. You saw me coming back from the police station. It's the truth! I can't help your father." The last of the whisky slopped from the glass and stung

Hana's wrist as she tried to free herself from Laval's iron grip.

"It's not about him," he replied, placing a kiss on her neck. "It's about your husband. I never thought threatening you could stop the trial, but I enjoyed watching you try. The police detective always wanted me. It must have been a dreadful disappointment to find my bumbling old man standing at the lake with his false teeth and walking stick." A spiteful edge entered Laval's laughter. "Pity Dad didn't dispatch your husband before the police jumped him though. It was, after all the whole point of that little rendezvous. I knew Du Rose wouldn't just hand over the documents, but my stupid father didn't know that."

Hana shuddered, thinking of her gorgeous husband drowning in the wintery depths of Hamilton Lake. He didn't stand a chance with his hands tied behind his back, concussed on the metal facings as he went into the water. If Bodie hadn't jumped in after him, she would have found herself widowed a second time.

Laval's monotone churned in the background and Hana struggled to tune back in. "My mother left my father after my second birthday and raised me in Auckland as Michel L'Huillier. She married a rich businessman and sent me away to school. I excelled, especially in sport." He waved his hand in the general direction of the photographs.

"Why are you telling me this?" Hana asked, her voice flat. "I'm not interested. If you want to kill me, get on with it or let me go home. Your confessions aren't necessary."

"I met Logan during our first soccer practice," Laval continued as though she hadn't spoken, gripping her round the waist with both arms. Hana felt sick to her stomach, knowing with a sixth sense she would never survive his attentions. Laval played with her like a spider winding a fly in its web. "We became good friends, shared the same interests and hung with the same crowd. We were both raised in opulent backgrounds without love. My father reconnected with me during fifth form and introduced me to his way of life."

"If you and Logan became such good friends, why do you want to hurt him?" Hana cried out as Laval's fingers bit into the soft skin at her waist.

His face crinkled with so much spite, it took her breath away "He betrayed me!" She felt his spit on her cheek and winced, trying to take a step backwards. Laval's grip slackened, but he didn't let go.

"The more I learn, the less I understand." Hana heard the pleading in her voice and it irritated her, resonating of failure.

Confusion swirled around her, creating a fog she couldn't see through. The thought of Phoenix's pitiful cries built to a steady pulse in her head. Her rational mind took a step back and primal instinct pervaded. Hana's psyche burned like a lioness deprived of her cubs and nothing else mattered. Desperation for her baby overtook the forefront of her thinking. The pressure built in her head and heart, infusing her with a painful, powerful ache which penetrated her bones.

"I'm Liza Du Rose's husband!" Laval's confession came from nowhere and Hana shook her head to dislodge the new information.

"No," she said. She scrubbed at her eyes with rough fingers. "You're lying. Liza never married." Laval tightened his grip and forced Hana to look into his eyes. He jerked her chin back to make sure she saw the agony of failed love. She'd seen it in the mirror every day for the miserable eight years following Vik's death. Hindsight made her life before Logan appear shrouded in a dark cloud of disillusionment. But she hadn't made others suffer for her poor life choices. Just herself.

Anger burned in Hana's chest, adding itself to the hunger for reunion with her baby. "Is this what it's all about?" She raised her voice to a shout. "You make my life a living hell, you kidnap me and take me away from my baby because Liza hurt you? Did she divorce you, disown you, cheat on you, what? What justifies this?"

Hana tore herself away from Laval, stepping back to create a small distance between them before the backs of her legs hit a worn brown sofa. Her hands balled into fists. "Grow up! We've all been hurt. Logan got hurt. What's wrong with you?" The knot of fury unfurled and created a line of fire reaching from her belly to her throat.

"She chose her law career over me. I wasn't good enough! I'd have disowned my father in a heartbeat if she'd given me the chance." His eyes flashed with temper and his face creased into a sneer. Hana sensed him losing control and knew it made him more dangerous. But the word 'pathetic' swirled around in her brain like a mantra, robbing Laval of his former advantage.

He took a step towards her and Hana moved sideways, looking for a route to safety. Laval shook his head. "She came to collect her stuff and our marriage ended. No warning. No opportunity to make it better. Not only did she destroy our relationship on paper, she got her mother's fancy church to annul our vows like we'd never said them. Logan Du Rose ruined my reputation and bankrupted me. Liza tells everyone she never married. She was my wife!"

His wounds gaped deep and raw, unhealed by time's passing. Hana saw the root of the mania making him lethal. His eyes flashed as he took another step towards her and his hand trembled. He waved behind him at the broken photograph. The team image slipped sideways in answer and shards of glass tinkled to the carpet. "I greeted Logan as a brother that day. The bastard refused to speak to me. He stood by while she cut me out of her life. I'll never forgive him!"

"Did you set it up?" Hana whispered. "Was everything that happened to me about getting Logan back?"

Laval snorted, a harsh, spiteful sound. "No." He shook his head and Hana saw his mind travel back in time as an eerie smile twisted his lips. "You're my lucky break, Hana. The chance to destroy two birds with one stone."

"Me and Logan?" Her brow furrowed.

"Logan and my father." Laval grinned, a sinister, ghoulish expression. "My dad ruined my chances of ever finding happiness because of his stupid old ladies and complicated scams. He's the reason Liza left me. She chose her career over the conflict of supporting me. He can rot in prison. I don't care!" His brown eyes morphed into pieces of coal, black and impenetrable. Hana saw the sickness of his rotting soul spread into his smile. She took a gulp of air as he opened his mouth again. "Now Logan will find out what it's like when someone deprives you of your most treasured possession. I won't just kill you, Hana. I'll make sure I sully all his memories of you for the rest of his life. Every time he thinks of you, he'll be so sickened he'll wish he never met you."

The oxygen levels in the room seemed depleted as Hana gulped in the face of demonic malice. She slid her legs apart to balance herself and braced herself to run. Energy built in her legs and the chipped glass slipped in her sweating fingers. She drew her left arm back with an almost imperceptible movement, stopping by degrees as Laval's gaze settled on her and then shifted back to the photograph. When he turned to give her his full attention, Hana blanched at the mania in his eyes.

The crystal glass smashed into Laval's face with such force, it sent him staggering backwards. It shattered along the fault in its glittering construction and the dregs of alcohol burned his eyes. He dropped to his knees with a shard of glass protruding from his forehead. "Geez!" he shouted, pain pitching his voice high and tight. Hana heard the scraping of wooden chair legs against upstairs floorboards and then the sound of running feet. The bottom of the tumbler stuck to her palm and she shook her hand and dropped it to the carpet. Her fingers felt slippery and Hana looked down at them, her eyes widening at the volume of blood in her hand. Shock rooted her to the spot though she knew she should run.

The heavy tread reached the top of the stairs and echoed around the panelled lobby. Laval made a retching sound as his fingers found the jagged glass in his head. "Bitch!" he gasped. "What have you done?"

Bodie's voice clamoured in Hana's head like a memory, urging her to run. She stumbled free of her captor and weaved a circuitous route to the double doors. Her blood covered hand smeared the door handle and she fought it with growing terror. Laval staggered to his feet and lurched after her.

Late sunlight streamed through the leaded glass either side of the front doors and Hana inhaled in horror. Blood squirted from her wrist creating a mesmerising arc of colour in the air.

She heard Phoenix crying somewhere and it galvanised her brain. The two men bounded down the stairs behind her at speed, missing out steps in their haste. Smashing glass sounded from a room deep in the house and shouting accompanied it. Hana's fingers slid against the key in the front door and she battled it, pitiful sounds escaping her lips as it turned. She hauled the door wide and bolted through the gap, tripping over the doorstep and falling to her knees. Blood sprayed upwards, pulsing in time to the beat of her heart. She finally registered it belonged to her. Hana focussed on memories of Phoenix, hauling herself upright and pressing on with laboured steps. Her energy abandoned her and she begged her body for more, making it as far as the sweeping driveway and Laval's expensive truck. Her blood spattered it as she clung to the wing mirror and tried the door. Locked.

A gentle autumn breeze kissed her cheek as she saw a dark figure move from behind a magnificent oak tree. "Down on the ground! Get down now!" it shouted.

Hana's feet grew leaden as though she ran through wet concrete. She tried to speak, half turning her body to see how close Laval's men were. Ghoulish figures sidestepped towards her, their faces masked by dark balaclavas. They toted heavy guns and pointed the barrels towards her torso.

"Get down on the ground!" They shouted, voices booming even though the nearest could have reached out and touched her. Hana's shoulders slumped in defeat and her vision blurred. Laval had guards and her efforts to escape were wasted. She whirled on the spot, searching for hope through eyes no longer focussed. Her wound sprayed the driveway in a beautiful spirograph. Words of protest which sounded coherent in her head, slurred as they left Hana's lips.

"Stand still!" A hand reached for Hana's forearm and she jerked away. They wanted her on the ground, but the rough concrete seemed so far away. She lifted her left hand and stared in disbelief at the jet of scarlet blood. A shard of expensive Crystal protruded from her wrist, glinting in the evening summer sun. Every time she moved her arm it dislodged from her vein and her lifeblood spurted in a solid stream. Hana listed like a drunk. Her legs refused to fold and she couldn't manage the mental instruction to make them.

"Mum!" Hana heard Bodie's voice in her head as she staggered. Blood sprayed into her face, coating her chin and creating a metallic taste on her tongue.

"Bodie, I'm sorry," she whispered. She'd ignored every good piece of advice he'd given. She'd changed location, drunk alcohol from the hand of a madman and wouldn't get to say good bye to her children.

"Down on the ground!" The voice sounded close and Hana confessed her sins ready for the end as the concrete dipped and swayed.

"How?" she breathed and relief came. She sensed the overwhelming peace of her God as he overruled her muscles and sinews and made the ground rise to meet her instead.

Chapter 29

Hana woke to the busyness of a resuscitation room. The overhead lights dazzled her and the sound of unfamiliar voices caused her heart rate to spike. The tone of one voice resonated like a distant memory. "Hana," he whispered, his accent familiar. "Oh sweetheart, I'm so sorry. I'm so very sorry." A light touch of his lips on her forehead felt damp and Hana sensed fingers brush across her cheek. Then the voice from her past disappeared as the feeble tendrils of her consciousness reached for it.

"Get a line in!" another voice said, sounding rushed and urgent. Hana felt a sharp scratch in the crook of her right elbow, adding its pain to the other competing hurts. Cold liquid soothed the vein and she felt herself sucked down a plughole into nothingness.

When she woke again, the room seemed quieter and the lights less bright. She registered the muted sound of trolley wheels and whispered voices. The processing in heaven seemed slow and unremarkable. A cool, damp cloth passed across her forehead and she fluttered her eyelids. Her body gave no other indication of wakefulness and the darkness sucked her back into its embrace.

The next awakening contained pure agony. Hana moaned as the mental inventory of her aches grew. Her left breast approached explosion point and she forced her right hand across, feeling the tautness of the skin and the added discomfort of clumsy fingers. "Oh, *God!*" she pleaded. Pain sensors fired through every nerve ending.

Logan's face hovered above hers, misty and ethereal. "Hana?" His voice echoed around her mind

"My eyes are screwed!" she wailed. Her focus crossed over and two of him wavered in front of her. Whispered voices quieted as the pit of nothing reclaimed her. "You came to heaven," she slurred and returned to the murky depths of the pain relief injected into the drip by a silent nurse.

A few hours later, she woke to find her husband's face resting next to her right hand. Gentle, muffled snores rose from lips pressed closed against the mattress. Hana forced herself to climb an endless ladder into daylight, refusing to let the dark pit reclaim her. It wasn't heaven and she didn't want to stay there alone.

Hana moved her hand, feeling the wrench of the cannula in her inner arm. Using great concentration, she touched Logan's hair with her index finger. He started up and focussed with difficulty. He looked bleary with sleep and worry, but a light went on in his grey eyes as he saw her efforts to stay conscious. "Hana!" Logan stopped and left the words on his lips unsaid. His beard growth and mussed hair betrayed the inner turmoil of the last hours.

Hana tried to speak her daughter's name. Her lips refused to form the word and after a few tries, she managed, "Baby?"

Logan smiled and disappeared. When he returned, the little screwed-up, olive face peering from his arms oozed deep unhappiness. Phoenix's eyes looked huge and puffy and her body twitched with the aftermath of violent crying. As she hitched again and let out a wail, Hana's body responded and her left breast soaked her hospital gown. She groaned in pain.

"Should I take her away again?" Logan asked. His face creased in concern as Hana writhed.

"No. Just help me?" she begged. "I need to feed her."

A nurse appeared to crank the angle of the bed higher and offer pillows. Hana balanced her daughter across her stomach and Phoenix fed as though battling starvation. Logan changed her nappy and then Hana fed from the other side, tickling the soles of the baby's feet to stop her sleeping. As the pressure in her chest eased, she relaxed.

"Does it hurt?" Tama asked. He arrived bearing coffee for Logan but nothing for her. His brow furrowed. "Sorry, you're not allowed coffee yet. I checked."

Hana forced herself to acknowledge the state of her left arm. It lay in a metal brace swathed in bandages and gauze. Blood seeped through the outer layer and she shuddered.

"I'll clean that up later," the nurse said, fitting a temperature gauge into Hana's ear. "The surgeon removed a long shard of glass from your artery and tried to repair the damage. I'm monitoring the blood loss, but it's minimal compared to before. You were very lucky."

"My boobs hurt more," Hana answered. She studied her daughter's dark, downy hair and refused to look at her arm again. The baby's head lolled back and a double line of milk whitened the corners of her lips.

"I'll take her," Tama offered. He pushed his hands beneath Phoenix's head, but her eyes snapped open and an angry wail split the airwaves. "Sheesh!" he exclaimed and withdrew his fingers. Phoenix rooted for Hana's nipple and snuffled before settling. Her tiny fingers wound around the cord of Hana's hospital gown and tightened.

Hana dozed on an off over the next few hours. Phoenix refused all attempts at separation and fed until her stomach rounded like a rugby ball and she fell into a coma. Tama peeled her off Hana's chest and took her into the corridor where she brought up wind and vomit in equal measure. He returned with her dressed in clean clothes. She'd passed out in her car seat. "I thought babies didn't form attachments this fast." He used a damp flannel to sponge baby-sick off his shirt. "I could hold Nev's little boy until he reached ten months old. Then he bawled."

"I'm just a food source," Hana griped, laying back against her pillows.

Logan's furrowed brow chastened her. "That's not true. She hated the bottle because you make her feel secure like no one else can." He stared down at the tiled floor. "I missed you just as much. I can scream if it'll make you feel better."

"No, my head hurts." Hana closed her eyes and the voice from the resuscitation room drifted through her memory. Fear built again and the monitor attached to her pulse hiked towards the dangerous end of the graph. A nurse appeared in the doorway.

"Do you need some pain relief?" she asked.

Hana shook her head. "I want to go home," she answered. "Today, now. I want to go home."

"Yeah, like that's gonna happen!" Logan snorted. "Your surgery took hours. The surgeon got called to another emergency, but he's coming back to see you again later. He's been in a few times, but you slept through. Nice English guy."

"I'm going home." Panic rose in Hana's voice and she heard herself shouting. She tempered her fear, desperate to escape. Logan rose, palms facing her in placation. "I need to get away." A sob escaped from her throat and she threw aside the sheets and blankets. Logan tried to fight her for them and she cried out in pain. "You don't understand!" she repeated. "Please, help me get somewhere safe."

"You are safe." Logan cupped her head in his strong hands and his thumbs caressed her cheeks. "That bastard's gone. They stitched him up and took him to the remand prison, Hana. He can't hurt you."

"No, no! I need to go. I have to leave!"

Hana maintained her protest and the second the nurse unhooked the bag of donated blood, she clambered free of the bed. "You can't leave today." The nurse raised an eyebrow at Logan. "The surgeon needs to assess you. You were very sick, Mrs Du Rose. The glass in your artery plugged the hole, but whenever you moved it spurted. You lost pints of blood."

"I'm going," Hana maintained. "Where are my clothes?"

The nurse brandished a thermometer and shook her head. "The team in emergency cut them off and the police kept them as evidence. Let your husband take the baby home now and he can visit tomorrow. I understand you have health insurance, so we'll release you to the private hospital as soon as your surgeon signs your paperwork."

Logan eyed the sleeping baby and groaned. Tama rolled his eyes. "We can't take the baby. She refuses the bottle. It's been a nightmare."

"I'm sorry." The nurse shook her head and wheeled the empty blood bags and trolley towards the door. "We'll know more when your surgeon pops back." The wheels squeaked along the corridor.

"I'm not staying." Hana placed her bare feet on the floor and closed her eyes against nausea and a sense of being submerged under water. "Logan, please help me?"

"What do we do?" Tama pleaded.

Logan glanced around the room, turning his body from side to side. "I don't know. They took her clothes and the hospital won't release her wearing their stuff. I can get her out, but not naked."

"Thank you," Hana breathed, gratitude giving her courage. Logan stood and reached into his back pocket, drawing out his wallet. He pushed a credit card into Tama's hand. "Run to the nearest shopping mall and grab whatever she might need." He turned his wrist over and looked at his watch. "Go to Centre Place in town. It shuts in forty minutes."

Hana felt her body relax as Tama's footsteps rapped against the tiles. A door banged and only the ward noises remained. Logan sat on the bed next to her and slipped an arm around her shoulders. "Are you sure about this, Hana?"

"Yes," she whispered. "Please, trust me. Take me home."

"Okay," he agreed. "If you're sure."

"Is it still the same day?" Hana's lips pursed as she forced herself to view the blood-stained dressing. "You said the mall closed soon. Everything's happened so fast."

"No, Hana." Logan lifted her chin with his index finger. Pain radiated out from his dark eyes. "You disappeared two days ago."

Tama returned with the weirdest ensemble Hana had ever seen. He rocked the car seat while Logan stuffed his wife into a thong, a denim miniskirt, and a blouse which struggled to contain her breasts. "I look like a tart!" Hana grumbled from behind the curtain and heard Tama's jacket rustle as he shrugged.

"I quite like it," Logan admitted. "But maybe for private viewings only."

The wily nurse halted Hana's escape. She stood in the doorway with her hands on her hips. "You know I have to tell you how inadvisable this is, don't you?" she said. She shook her head. "The surgeon spent hours sorting out your wrist. He rang between surgeries to see how you were. At least wait to see him?"

"I'm going home," Hana maintained. She hid her right arm behind her back and stuck her chin in the air. Logan pursed his lips and eyed the cannula protruding from her vein.

"I'm a bit nervous about just pulling it out," he admitted.

"Then don't!" The nurse risked elbowing him aside and dragged Hana's arm free. "Let me do it!"

She lectured Hana for the entire fifteen minutes it took to remove the cannula, order a wheelchair and check her pulse and temperature. Hana refused to look as she changed the dressing on her wrist although Tama watched over her shoulder and made unhelpful gagging noises. She even produced makeshift paperwork to enable Hana to discharge herself and handed her over to the orderly who arrived with the wheelchair. "Any problems at all and she needs to go back to the emergency room," she stressed, jabbing an index finger at Logan. She turned her attention to Hana. "I got the doctor from the ward next door to write the discharge notice and a prescription for antibiotics. Finish the course just in case and promise me you won't hesitate to get help if you feel unwell?"

"I won't." Hana's gaze strayed to her sleeping daughter and she swallowed. "Thank you for everything."

The nurse nodded and released a sigh. "You're going to this address? Culver's Cottage, Hakarimata Road, Ngaruawahia."

Logan's brow creased but Hana nodded, the action so hard it made her neck ache. "Yes," she replied. "Definitely."

"Okay." The nurse accompanied them to the main door and waved good bye. The tracks of the wheelchair squeaked into the lift and Hana heaved a sigh of relief as the doors swished closed.

Tama carried the car seat and Logan jogged to the car, bringing it around to the front entrance. They loaded Hana into the back seat of the Honda and the orderly reclaimed both wheelchair and dignity-preserving blanket. Hana shivered and folded her arms across the skimpy blouse as Tama strapped the car seat next to her. "This isn't funny!" she snapped, responding to the smirk in his eyes. "I'll get you back."

"Sure you will." He tossed a spare baby blanket across and Hana hid beneath it for the journey through Hamilton.

"Whose blood did I get?" She peered at the bruise in the crook of her right elbow. "What if they weren't a nice person?

"Pretend it's mine." Logan negotiated a traffic jam and headed north.

"Is it?" Hana heard the hope in her voice and winced. Tears budded to the surface and she couldn't seem to control them.

"It's not Logan's." Tama's dark, glossy head shook from side to side in the passenger seat.

Logan darted a sideways glance at him. "Shut up, mate," he warned.

Tama finished his ill-advised thought. "Haemophiliacs can't donate."

"Oh." Hana gulped and the first wave of tears cascaded over her lower lids. "Oh, no."

Logan eyed her through the rear-view mirror. "Let's pretend it's Michael's, hey? He donates. Bastard's done little else for me, so a bit of blood's the least he can do."

Hana blew her nose into an inadequate tissue. "I've lost my favourite nursing bra," she sniffed.

Tama huffed out a breath. "I had enough trouble buying undies for a woman. The girl in the shop suggested I'd need a bigger size. I swear she measured my crotch with her eyes. She thought I was enough of a weirdo without me asking for help to choose bras with strange flaps!"

Hana glanced up in time to see the sign for Ngaruawahia move into view. "No!" she wailed. "No, not here."

"But you told the hospital this address." Logan pulled the Honda into a layby and killed the engine. He turned in his seat to face her. "Hana, give me a little help here!"

"I wanna go home." A tear slid down her cheek and plopped onto the frilly blouse. "I don't want to stay around Hamilton. Leslie will help with Phoenix and I'll feel safe with her. Take me to the hotel. Please, Logan."

A view of the kauri tree at the top of the mountain filtered into Hana's tired brain, the secret carvings in the aged trunk and her child's name engraved beneath her father's. "Hotel," she said, her voice sounding slurred. "I wanna go to the hotel." Logan's face drifted in her vision, so she struggled to interpret his expression. The last dose of powerful pain pills began to work.

"Okay," Logan whispered. "Suits me just fine."

Hana woke as the Honda slid through the automatic gates and climbed the steep driveway up to Culver's Cottage. She started and made a sound of confusion. Tama unfastened his seatbelt and leaned around to speak to her. "We need to grab gear for you and the baby. It won't take long."

Hana laid her head back against the seat. She lifted her right hand and jabbed it towards Logan as he studied her through the rear-view mirror. "Can you get mine?" she asked. Her tongue tripped over the words. "Don't let Tama in my undies drawer."

She heard the men snort with laughter as she released her tenuous hold on consciousness.

Hana woke to feel the Honda descending the long, darkened driveway to the hotel. Relief and a sense of safety washed over her like a warm wave. It jarred with her usual emotions about Logan's family home.

Tama drove, sweeping the vehicle around the curve to meet the wide front steps of the hotel. Welcoming lights glittered from solar bulbs flanking the handrails. "I'll take it around to the car park later," he promised.

Logan ran a hand through his hair and nodded. The sigh escaping his lips sounded laden with exhaustion. As soon as the vibration of the moving tyres ceased, Phoenix woke like a jack-in-the-box and commenced her shrill wail. Tama released a groan.

Hana swung her legs from the car, feeling cool night air against her shins and bare feet. "Hold up," Logan grunted. He dipped to lift her into his arms and Hana rested her head against his neck.

"I've got no shoes," she whispered.

"I packed some," he replied. He jerked his head towards Tama. "Please can you bring Phoe?"

"Great!" Tama stretched his arms above his head and arched his spine. "I get the noisy one."

Leslie turned in surprise, dropping a saucepan into sudsy water with a plop. Logan shouldered his way into the kitchen and Tama followed. "I didn't know youse were comin'!" she exclaimed. "Oh, Miss, what's happened?"

Three other women turned from their work, knives and slaughtered vegetables in their hands. They stared at the knot of exhausted travellers. Logan raised an eyebrow at Leslie and she dried her hands on her apron. "Out!" she snapped at the women. "Come back in half an hour."

They filed away, their eyes wide and soaking in every detail as their footsteps dragged. Hana heard their voices in the corridor rising to speculate on the nature of the new gossip.

Logan dragged out a chair with his heel and lowered Hana into it. "You need to go to bed," he said, his tone insistent.

"Bed needs making." Leslie twirled the fabric of her apron between her fingers. "I'll get someone to do it now." She scurried to the door and hauled it open, redirecting the kitchen girls with whispered instructions before returning.

Phoenix opened her mouth in a high-pitched wail and Leslie swooped to release her from the car seat. She waved the men away. "Youse look wrecked!" she declared. "Grab a drink from the bar and give the girls ten minutes to put sheets on the beds."

Hana watched her husband war within himself, knowing he wanted to challenge the old woman's order. But instead, he shrugged and moved towards the kitchen door. "I won't be long," he promised Hana. He glanced back once at his wailing daughter as Leslie hefted her over her shoulder. Then the door clicked shut behind his dragging feet.

Leslie held the squalling baby while Hana fought the buttons on her blouse one-handed. Once the child's lips found her nipple, the awful noise ceased. "She's angry," Leslie breathed as the sudden silence made her head ring. "What's happened, girly?" She pulled a chair up next to Hana's and rested a broad arm around her shoulders.

Hana stumbled through her tale of woe and Leslie interjected with small gasps of shock and the odd shake of her greying head. Her eyes filled with concern as Hana's words slurred and her head sank lower. "You're exhausted," she soothed. "You need some rest."

Hana jerked her head up and Phoenix stopped sucking. The baby's eyes snapped open in alarm. "Sorry, sorry," Hana whispered. She patted her back and the grey eyes shuttered as order resumed. "Tea. I'd love a decent cup of tea," she breathed.

"Coming right up." Leslie dug out Miriam's old teapot and used the water heater on the wall to fill it to the brim. Hana waited for it to brew and forced herself not to think of Laval. Her mind held a rawness she couldn't seem to shift and tears clung near to the surface. She tried to distract herself. "How are things with you?" she asked.

Leslie's mouth opened and closed before she busied herself stirring the browning liquid in the teapot. She set out two mugs before fetching milk from the chiller. Two of the kitchen workers filed back in and continued peeling the abandoned vegetables. "You don't wanna worry 'bout me," Leslie answered, keeping her voice low. "Youse got your own problems!"

"But I care about you." Hana accepted a drying cloth from Leslie's outstretched hand and covered as much of her dignity as she could manage beneath the worn fabric. "I know something's going on, Leslie. Is someone taking your money?"

Leslie swallowed, a loud, gulping sound. She pushed a mug of tea towards Hana with shaking fingers. "No," she replied. "I'm good. You worry about your problems and I'll worry about mine."

The woman nearest the sink released an irritated snort. Leslie glared at her as she turned around, frowning at the half-peeled carrot being waved in her direction. "Just tell her, Aunty. Everyone knows. Maybe Mr Logan can sort this out for you."

"No!" Leslie's voice rose to a shout. Phoenix sucked faster beneath the drying towel as though sensing her comfort threatened again. Hana tensed as her frayed nerves jangled in the tension.

"Just tell me," she groaned. "Please. Just say it." Exhaustion shrouded her like a cloak, the energy draining from the borrowed blood coursing through her veins.

The woman dropped the carrot onto the draining board and put her hands on her hips. "I'm speaking up," she said, ignoring Leslie's warning hiss. "Someone should've done it months ago. She's lying, Miss," she said. "Her husband died owing gambling debts and the men visit every week for an instalment. She'll never finish paying them and the longer it takes, the bigger it gets. She's been paying it for five years and she'll pay it until the day we plant her in the urupa." The woman's lips twisted into a grimace. "The usual man sold the debt just before Christmas and the new ones have no mercy. They raised the interest and started taking her stuff a few months ago. My mother saw them take her sofa last week because she needed to pay the electric bill instead of them. She's nothing left."

"Shut up!" Leslie's breath came in rasps. "It's gossip! That's all."

The woman shook her head and picked up the carrot again. "Silly old kuia," she breathed. Her companion nudged her and gave a warning shake of her head.

Hana swallowed and let her gaze slide to Leslie's face. "Is this true?" she whispered. Phoenix yanked on the cloth and exposed most of Hana's chest. She tried to contain the flailing arms and cover herself again, failing at both tasks. Leslie reached across and hefted the baby over her shoulder. The child gave a series of burps and bounced her forehead against Leslie's neck. Hana used the opportunity to cover herself.

"Yes." Tears filled Leslie's eyes and plummeted onto her olive cheeks. She turned to place the child between them as a barrier.

Hana's eyes grew hard. She shook her head. "I'm sick of men who ruin other people's lives for their own enjoyment. You won't pay them again."

"I don't have a choice." Leslie's ashen face radiated hopelessness. "The ones before this hounded my useless husband into his grave. These are far worse."

Hana gritted her teeth and gave a determined shake of her head. "They haven't met the Du Roses yet, Leslie. A few broken bones might change their perspective."

The woman at the draining board nudged her companion and grinned. "Told you," she whispered. "The kaumātua says she's the new Du Rose matriarch. He says she's got as much mana as Reuben Du Rose's mother."

"But she's British." The other woman stole a cautious glance at Hana, watching her tuck the undignified drying cloth into the neck of the frilly blouse. "I don't believe you."

"You wait and see." A snap sounded as the carrot succumbed to a sharp knife and rent in two pieces. The women switched to Māori and spoke in undertones.

Leslie helped Hana carry the baby upstairs to Logan's childhood room. She recited the code for the keypad and pushed the door open. The women had left towels stacked in a pile by the bathroom door and spread sheets and a duvet over the wide bed. Logan lay sprawled on top still wearing his work jacket and cowboy boots. His feet dangled over the edge of the bed, slewing his body at an uncomfortable angle.

Leslie tutted and switched on a lamp, bathing the room in an ethereal glow. She looked down at the sleeping baby. "Where should I put her?" she asked. "She's in a deep sleep, so you might get a few hours of peace."

Hana pursed her lips and stared at Logan. His face looked grey and sallow. Prickles of guilt sent sharp pains through her chest. "It's all my fault," she whispered. "I did this."

"No, you didn't!" Leslie's hiss sounded sharp and she nudged Hana with her elbow. "Don't go down that road or none of youse will sleep tonight." She jerked her head towards the baby. "Tell me what to do. We have two travel cots but they're in use. I didn't know youse were coming."

Hana squeezed the bridge of her nose between her thumb and fingers. "I'll put her in the bottom drawer again," she whispered. Her wrist smarted as she hauled the drawer free and tipped the few belongings onto the floor. She found an abandoned tee shirt of hers and bunched it up as a mattress for Phoenix. In desperation, she stripped off the tight blouse and replaced it with a pyjama top. Then she helped Leslie swaddle the baby in the lacy fabric, so she couldn't move her arms. Leslie gave a nod of approval.

"They enjoy that," she whispered. "It's like the womb. We changed her nappy downstairs, so maybe she'll sleep for long enough to give you a rest." Her hand strayed to Hana's cheek and she planted a kiss on her forehead. "I'm glad you survived your ordeal, Miss. Our lives would feel all the poorer for not having you in it."

"Thank you." Hana felt the unpredictable emotions build in the back of her throat and didn't trust herself to say anything else.

Leslie pointed at her wrist. "Your bandage is leaking," she said. "Want me to change it?"

Hana shook her head. "It's too complicated with the splint on and I'm tired. Looking at it makes me feel sick." Leslie nodded and with a gentle touch to Hana's arm, left. The door clicked shut behind her.

Hana tried to remove Logan's cowboy boots one-handed without waking him. She managed one but the zipper on the other defied her tired fingers. She looked up to find him watching her. "Sorry," she breathed, rolling her eyes in frustration. "I tried not to wake you."

He gave her a lazy smile. "Even injured you still take care of me." He shifted onto his side and flicked at a loose thread with his fingernail. "Do you want to talk about it?"

Revulsion coursed through Hana's nerve endings and she jerked backwards, lifting her hands as though to defend herself. "No!" she hissed. "Not yet."

"You know Odering needs to speak to you, don't you? He's blowing up my phone wanting to know where we are."

Hana released a groan. "I think I lost another phone," she murmured, watching Logan's face for his reaction. "I'm sorry."

He shook his head and tapped his jacket pocket. "No, you didn't lose it. There's no evidence on it, so Odering gave it back." He pursed his lips and looked as though he might say more, quashing the desire at the last minute. Instead, he held his arms out. "Can I hold you?"

Hana nodded and slid onto the bed, waiting as Logan took off his other boot. She braced her injured arm against his shoulder and buried her face in his chest. The steady cadence of his voice grounded her as it echoed through his ribs and she sniffed the shirt she'd ironed days ago. He smelt the same, hay and summer sunshine overlaid with a fabric softener and the faint scent of sweat. Nothing had changed and yet everything had. Hana swallowed back tears. She'd changed. Laval changed her and her perspective in a single afternoon. She'd stared into the face of pure evil and returned. "I missed you," she breathed. "I missed you so much."

She heard her husband swallow and sensed his distress. "I should have kept you safe, Hana. I let you down."

"No." Hana shook her head against his chest. "It's my own stupid fault."

"You don't need to feel afraid anymore. He's locked up." Logan kissed the top of her head. "We didn't need to run away."

Hana pursed her lips and gave a sigh which leaked sadness. "I heard my brother's voice," she murmured. "I know it was in my head, but it made me realise that you and my children are everything to me. There is nothing else." She leaned her head back and allowed his grey eyes to search her face. "I'd do it all again to save you," she whispered. She reached up, placing her lips over his. Logan responded to her kiss with a moan of pleasure. He tasted of coffee and Hana sought to borrow his strength, pressing her tongue between his lips and caressing his cheek with her good hand. "Make me forget," she begged.

Logan groaned and placed an index finger over her questing lips. "This isn't a good idea."

Hana jerked backwards, stung by his rejection. He never refused. "I want to," she whispered, hearing her own confusion. "Please, Logan."

"Well, this is awkward." Tama's head appeared over Logan's shoulder. "Unless you fancy a threesome?"

Logan jabbed backwards with his elbow and Hana's wrist slipped off his shoulder. She cried out in agony. Logan jerked upright, making certain he sent Tama headfirst onto the floorboards with a well-aimed shove. Hana sat up and cradled her wrist until the pain subsided.

"Sorry," Logan whispered. "I tried to warn you."

"Was he in bed with you?" Hana demanded through gritted teeth. The dim light showed a fresh patch of blood seeping through the bandage.

"No!" Logan sounded indignant. "He fell asleep on the rug." He peered over the side of the bed and glared at his nephew. "And now he's back there."

"I'm knackered." Tama's face reappeared over Logan's shoulder and he winced as Logan jabbed his arm towards him. "Okay, I'm going!" he protested.

"Where are you sleeping?" Hana struggled to control the burgeoning yawn which threatened to split her lips.

"Next door. Aunty Liza's room." Tama staggered to the door and rested his hand on the knob. Cocking his head, he listened to sounds through the wall. Then his face brightened and he slipped from the room.

"Oh, no!" Logan dropped back against the pillows. "The women only brought enough sheets for this room. Another girl went to fetch more stuff for next door."

"Hence him sleeping on the rug." Hana snuggled against Logan's arm and cradled her sore wrist.

"A younger girl." Logan waggled his eyebrows. "I made him wait in here and now I've let him go."

"So?" Hana halted at the sound of giggling. Footsteps pattered against the floorboards as one person chased another around the room. "Oh." Hana winced. "He wouldn't, would he?"

Something soft hit the wall behind Hana's head and she jumped. Then she recognised the sound of bedsprings creaking. Whispered giggles drifted through, female, muted and filled with nervous excitement. Logan sat up to drag his arms out of his jacket. "Great!" he muttered. "Marvellous."

"Shouldn't we stop him?" Hana whispered. "How old is the girl?"

"Old enough to know better than to mess with him." Logan stripped off his shirt and patted his chest. Moans and a muffled shriek sounded through the wall and he sighed. "I can't compete with that. Let's just go to sleep."

"You don't have to compete with anyone." Hana swallowed and remembered the teenage boy in the team photograph. Innocent and beautiful, he'd safeguarded his love for her across decades of turmoil on the strength of a single meeting. Emotion swirled like muddy water in her brain as she laid her tired head on Logan's chest. Laval had competed with Logan Du Rose. This time, he'd played the game to win.

Chapter 30

The next few days passed in a blur. Phoenix's separation anxiety lessened, allowing Hana to process the swirling emotions hidden in her heart. The darkness in Laval's eyes disturbed her sleep and many times a night she woke crying and struggling against Logan's attempts to comfort her. A numbness tainted her ability to describe the events of the previous days and she gave up trying. Leslie provided an endless source of help and the child tolerated her smothering attentions with passivity.

"A couple of months old and already in charge. You take after your father," Tama joked, lifting Phoenix above his head and squinting up at her. She grinned and kicked her legs.

"Watch she doesn't puke," Hana warned. "I just fed her."

Leslie chuckled, placing a measuring jug on the table as she passed. Phoenix spotted it and her happy expression clouded. Her bottom lip protruded and an insistent whimper began deep in her chest.

Hana snorted. "It's not for you, Phoe!" The whimper increased in volume and Tama passed her to Hana in a flying motion, adding the sounds of a diving aeroplane. She nestled against Hana's shoulder and squashed her nose into her neck. Hana straightened the tiny cardigan and patted her daughter's back. "Funny girl," she whispered into her hair.

The kitchen door opened at speed and Hana jumped and let out a frightened squeak. The baby dug her fingers into Hana's ponytail and released a high-pitched wail. Logan appeared, hands outstretched and his brows furrowed. "Sorry," he offered. He squatted next to Hana and his grey irises paled to the colour of concrete. "Didn't mean to scare you." He rested a forearm on her thigh and swallowed guilt. "Want me to take her?"

Hana buried her face in Phoenix's cardigan and shook her head. "No point. My other babies didn't care where their milk came from. This one is fussier."

"Just like her papa," Leslie interjected. She snatched up the plastic jug and whisked it across the kitchen. Logan's eyes narrowed and his jaw worked in his cheek.

Tama snorted. "Haha! I can't imagine a baby-Logan with breast envy." His brows furrowed and his expression became wistful. "Breasts," he whispered and his eyes misted. "What a good idea." He sat up and looked around the kitchen as though searching for something. Someone. "Where's that other girl from last night?" he asked.

Hana gave him a look infused with disgust. "You didn't ask her name?"

Tama offered her a cheeky grin in reply. "I'll get it next time."

Logan reached up and pressed his lips to Hana's. "I'm borrowing this kid for a few hours," he whispered. "It won't take long. Promise."

Hana swallowed and fought the temptation to mimic Phoenix's panicked wail. Logan's presence gave her security, bringing with it a tenuous sanity which offered respite from the memory of Laval's sneer. "Where are you going?" She pushed her fingers through his hair and held on. "Don't leave me."

"I have to. Trust me?" His eyes twinkled with mischief as he smiled up at her. "It won't take long."

Tama rose and pointed to his chest. "You want this kid or the crying one?" he asked with a smirk.

"The ugly one." Logan stood and clasped Hana's forearm as her fingers slithered from his hair. He pressed a kiss to the top of her head. "Get Leslie to look at that," he said, pointing to the stained bandage. He shoved Tama's shoulder and raised an eyebrow. "Ready to rumble, Du Rose?"

"Am I ever." Chair legs scraped against the tiles as Tama slouched towards the door.

Logan stared at Hana's bandage and she turned her hand over to hide the evidence against her tee shirt. She pursed her lips and avoided acknowledging its existence. As Phoenix hiked up the urgency of her crying, she fiddled with her shirt and bra and allowed her to feed again. Logan said nothing more and his boot heels sounded hollow and final in the corridor outside. His abandonment sent Hana into a pit of despair. She stroked her baby's downy head and sympathised with her separation anxiety. "This just won't do," she told her child. "We both have to get over it."

Hana recognised her Honda engine passing the kitchen window. She looked across the room to the car park filled with rays of late sunshine. Balancing the baby in her right arm, she joined Leslie at the sink. "Where are they going?" she demanded. The Honda headed for the main gate, joined by three other vehicles bulging with stock men. The farm ute laboured up the driveway, puffing out smoke behind Jack's Jeep and a newish looking truck.

Leslie's brow furrowed. "They're going causing trouble if youse ask me." She dried her hands and shook her head.

The woman next to her plunged strong hands into sudsy water and retrieved a teaspoon. "About time," she murmured. White hair snaked from a bun at the back of her head and despite her age, she stood with the poise and elegance of a dancer. Hana remembered her words from a few nights ago concerning Leslie's circumstances. She'd forgotten to speak to Logan.

A flicker of guilt worked its way from Hana's stomach into her throat and she heard her breathing change. The forgotten promise laid heavy in her chest. The baby sensed her distress and grew fractious, beating her arms as though dissatisfied with Hana's milk. Leslie shot Hana a worried glance and lifted a hand to touch her shoulder. "Nothing to worry about," she whispered. "Mr Logan's not an idiot."

Hana nodded, knowing what she'd seen but not understanding it. "Why would Logan take all the stock men with him somewhere? He's never done that before."

The woman at the sink snorted and raised an eyebrow. "Not in your time, maybe. They did it heaps in the old days. Reuben Du Rose looked like a demi-god when he rode out looking for trouble. When the whanau arrived in town with him at the front, everyone knew he meant business. Nobody dare fight him twice." A wistfulness crossed the woman's rheumy gaze and Hana wished she'd known Reuben as a young man full of promise. The woman blinked and a naughty smile etched itself on her lips. "Hottest man on the mountain," she whispered. She glanced up to find Hana studying her and sighed, pressing her memories back into their box.

"You knew him?" Hana asked. She felt the naked hunger build in her chest, needing to hear about Logan's father second hand in his absence.

"No, she didn't!" Leslie barked. The old woman's brow furrowed to darken her face. "Too young and silly for the likes of Reuben Du Rose. Get on with your work. I need those veggies in the next ten minutes." She turned to give Hana the benefit of her ire. "Let me look at that wound, Miss," she said. "It's oozing something nasty."

Hana shook her head. "I'm fine," she lied.

Seeking a hiding place, she knocked on the door of Alfred's apartment with Phoenix snoozing over her shoulder. His down-turned smile looked tired as he opened the door and stood back to let her in. "I'll take her," he volunteered, lifting Phoenix into his gnarled hands before climbing up the first of the steep steps.

"Thanks." Hana followed him up, clinging to the rail with her right hand. "I forgot how horrid it is, having one arm." She wandered into the sitting area, pausing at the sight of his belongings spread around several cardboard boxes. "You're leaving?" Her voice held an unexpected catch. "Where are you going?"

Alfred sank into a chair at the kitchen table. His gaze drifted over the view of lush green bush through the long window. "Don't take it personally, Hana. It's not about you. I wish I could stay, but I can't. There's too much history bound up in this house and I need time away." He swallowed and bowed his head. "It goes back further than what happened to Miriam. Even further than Logan's birth. I can't deal with it anymore."

"With what?" Hana sat next to him and rested her hand on his knee. She experienced a sensation of drowning as Laval's influence ruined everything around her. "Help me understand." She swallowed a sob. "Give me something else to think about, Alfred. Just for a little while."

The old man's sad smile broke her heart. A resounding click echoed through her body as she recognised the same haunted look she'd seen in Laval's face and the same potential for bitterness and hatred. Alfred patted the baby's slender back as she nestled into his shoulder. "I was born three years before Reuben. Our father died when we were boys and I remember little about him. My mother favoured Reuben, loving his creative nature and enterprising spirit. I think she saw herself in him and a chance to pass on her mana to a worthier son. She knew I was no manukura, Hana. I have no desire for leadership and she understood." Alfred sighed. "Money stuck to Reuben's fingers like honey. It runs through mine like water. When his affair with my wife blew our whānau apart, Mama sub-divided the land and gave me the house and farm. He'd hurt me, but I got his precious son and his inheritance in return. I also thought I'd get my mother's undivided attention."

Alfred paused to stroke Phoenix's dark hair. Her eyes remained open as she lay over his shoulder, her lips closing around her tiny finger joints. "In our last conversation we argued. She admitted she didn't trust me. I'd lost money at the sale yards for the fourth year in a row and disappointed her. I needed her help, but pride stopped me askin' for it. She took Logan for a ride two days later and had a heart attack at the top of the mountain. I'd left it too late to apologise."

Hana's wrist smarted and she shifted it across her thighs. Alfred stared into the distance as though seeing his misery unfolding before him like a sheet. "Logan sat with my mother's body until we found them." His chest hitched and Hana heard his voice waver. "She leaned against the old kauri tree and died. I could hear Logan talking to her in the dark, chattin' like nothing was wrong. He worried she might feel cold and covered her with his little shirt. He looked so small sitting next to her in his vest." Alfred gulped and Hana reached out her good hand to touch his shoulder. She stopped half way through the motion and let her hand fall back into her lap. The invisible wall surrounding him reminded her of Logan's emotional fortress.

"I'm sorry," she whispered.

Alfred stood and walked around the room with Phoenix, stopping to look through the floor to ceiling windows. His voice sounded distant. "Miriam chose to stay here when Mama threw Reuben out." He gave a slow shake of his head. "I told her to leave with him, but she refused. She chose me. She promised not to contact my brother again and stayed with me."

Hana swallowed and her voice sounded loud in the stillness. "You threatened to keep her children?"

Alfred's brow furrowed. "Reuben lived in a tent at first and then built a wooden shed. I didn't want Liza and my boys exposed to that life. Miriam lied about Logan but made a mistake when she put my name on his birth certificate. She gave me the power to keep him."

Hana pursed her lips and closed her eyes. Hindsight displayed Miriam's plight in a different light. Alfred cleared his throat. "You think I'm wrong." He said it as a statement of fact.

Hana sighed. "I'm not the right person to comment. I'm finding it hard to let Phoenix out of my sight after what happened. The pain of leaving her children behind would be more than punishment for Miriam. No wonder she stayed."

Alfred's brow puckered as he turned to face Hana. "You think I brought it all on myself, don't you?"

"No." Hana rose, desperate to feel her daughter in her arms again. "We make our own choices in life and Miriam chose to stay and give up Reuben. You didn't ask her to cheat on you in the first place or bear another man's baby." Her gaze dropped. "My first husband cheated on me. I spent many years blaming myself and feeling guilty for his choice and his mess. What's done is done, Alfred."

He shook his head, his eyes misting as his mind slipped back into the past. "Barry died and it hit Miriam hard. She blamed herself for Logan's illness and called it 'her curse.' She travelled to England when her brother got sick. Michael and Logan went with her, but something happened and her brother died alone. She never forgave herself. I picked her up from the airport and she never left home again. I paid the doctor's fee when I could and he visited her here every few months. He said she had bipolar disease, but she didn't always remember to take her pills. Miriam tried to kill herself more times than I remember. We'd sent the boys away to school while she nursed Barry, but I couldn't let them come home to see what our whānau had become. I left them there though I know Logan hated it."

"He turned out to be the good son though," Hana breathed. She edged closer to her daughter, her footsteps light.

"Yes." Alfred's eyes brightened. "He bailed us out, Hana. Bought everything and took it over so it could stay in the family. The perfect child. I ended up loving him the best. Ironic."

Hana reached across to take her child and Alfred relinquished Phoenix without resistance. Relief surged through her as the glazed look left his eyes. "Logan still loves you," she whispered. "You're the only father he's ever known."

It proved the wrong thing to say, heaping more blame on Alfred's slender shoulders for the years of missed opportunity between Reuben and Logan. His eyes clouded again. "How long do you think she lied to me?" he asked. He faced Hana, his cheeks sunken and ill-looking. "When I found Reuben's old guitar in Logan's room when he was a boy, Miriam assured me he found it in the attic." Alfred shook his head. "I believed her but hid it because I didn't want him playing like his father. I couldn't bear to hear him sing."

Hana pursed her lips, not wanting to compound Alfred's misery by telling him about the lessons. The lessons given by Reuben posing as a guitar teacher. Alfred squeezed his eyes tight shut and pressed gnarled knuckles into them until his fingers whitened. "I watched Logan set the lawyers onto Reuben and I admit, I thought it was funny. Reuben took back what Mama intended him to have in her will. She changed it as his penance and gave it to Logan. He loved that paddock and Logan loved it just as much." Alfred let his palms slide over his cheeks. "I liked seeing Logan take him on, but it was wrong. I got my punishment, didn't I?"

"Oh, Alfred," Hana whispered. "Life isn't like that. What Miriam and Reuben set in motion brought all of this about. You were the victim. Maybe you made mistakes along the way, but you didn't wish them dead, did you?" She regretted the question as it left her lips, but to her relief Alfred shook his head.

"No," he breathed. "I loved my wife and though I hated what my brother became, I loved him once."

Hana nodded. A memory of the fire and Miriam's screams cut through her reverie. "Everyone lost something that night." She shivered. "But Logan lost the most."

"It's why I need to leave." Alfred inhaled and drew himself up straighter. He fingered a pile of newspapers next to his hand. "I'll clear my gear out and get on the road."

"You'll destroy Logan," Hana whispered. "Please don't abandon him."

Alfred ignored her, picking up the first newspaper and then setting it back on the pile. The vacant look in his eyes told Hana she'd lost his attention. The mountain compounded his sense of inadequacy as a son, husband, father and businessman.

She clutched Phoenix and backed away. "Don't slam a door you might be unable to open again," she warned, knowing the consequences from bitter experience. She turned at the top of the stairs but Alfred bent to retrieve a pile of laundry and ignored her. With a sigh, Hana picked her way downstairs, using her good hand to support her daughter's weight. At the bottom of the steps, she grappled with the door handle and her wrist smarted.

Hana sought Jack in the stable yard. He'd worked for the Du Rose family for so long, nobody remembered where he came from or when. She found him in a stall, sifting through the straw and throwing soiled bedding into a wheelbarrow. His gnarled body bent at strange angles and his head popped up and down over the door. Profound deafness masked Hana's approach and she waited until he sensed her. He stilled as her presence obscured the shafts of sunlight and threw the stable into darkness. The yellow glow shone from behind her, turning Hana into a fiery, beautiful silhouette.

Jack tipped his cowboy hat and straightened his back, leaning on the pitchfork and cocking his head. Hana resurrected her rusty sign language to greet him. He ventured squinting into the light, pushing his hat further back on his head with a gnarly forearm. He beckoned her to follow him to his untidy office at the end of the stable block and she turned in obedience. While her boot soles clattered against the floor of the stable yard, the old man moved with silent, stealthy steps. Inside the office he yanked out a seat and shifted papers onto the floor, waving at her to sit.

Hana's left wrist ached and diluted blood seeped through the bandage. Jack held out his arms and demanded the baby, using a series of grunts. Hana relinquished her, relieved as she supported her painful wrist in her lap. Jack flopped the sleeping girl over his shoulder, smiling at the obvious surprise in Hana's face. "Mokopuna," he mouthed. Grandchildren. Hana blushed at the amusement in his eyes. Deaf, not inept.

With confused and halting sign language, Hana explained Alfred's plan. A few times Jack cocked his head before reading her lips and understanding. "He's leaving," she mouthed. She finished her tale and held her hands open in front of her, asking, "What should I do?"

He furrowed his bushy brows into deep lines as Phoenix slept over the torn shoulder of his aged farm shirt. Rheumy eyes stared at the faded rug on the concrete office floor. When he rose, Hana jumped and followed him outside. She trotted behind as he strode across the stable yard and turned the corner towards the shed where the farm vehicles lived. He handed Phoenix over and tapped the side of the old red Jeep parked outside, its keys still dangling from the ignition.

The vehicle started with a puff of black smoke and Jack pushed it into gear and revved hard. When he let out the clutch, it lurched forward. Hana gripped the side rail and the child with shaking fingers, the stitches tugging in her wrist.

Jack drove up to the bunkhouse, a low cedar building where the farm workers lived. The pen still stood out the front where Flick had walked the colicky horse in circles and argued with her. The only women who ventured into the testosterone laden environment were the maids who cleaned up after them once a week. Leslie told her they took days to get over the trauma. Hana balanced the baby over her shoulder and expected Jack to stop outside but he didn't. He drove past the bunkhouse and continued along a hidden driveway to the right. Confused, Hana peered around her at the thick native bush interspersed with an incongruous array of bright hollyhocks.

Jack halted the Jeep beside a low building. The red cedar panelling shone from recent treatment. Jack took the baby and smiled as Hana slithered down from the foot bar. "Mon, mon," he grunted, indicating she should follow him. He reached into his worn jeans to retrieve a door key. Hana followed him into the house, stepping over the threshold and expecting a rugged bachelor pad. Instead, the scent of bathroom cleaner and air freshener greeted her.

Photographs lined the hallway showing a much younger Jack. Tall and upright, he stood beside a bride and groom in black and white wedding photos. In others he held a series of small babies and children in ascending order. Hana peered closer, recognising the same child in each. She turned to ask a question, but Jack shooed her away, his face darkening with an emotion which frightened her.

"I don't understand," Hana said, confusion showing in her face. "It's a lovely home, but why am I here?"

Jack waved an arm in the doorway of an empty guest room. An old blanket sat on the bare mattress, folded into a neat square. He pointed at Hana and then at the bed and she drew her shoulders up towards her neck. "Oh!" The realisation came like a breaking dawn and her lips parted into a smile of relief. "Not me. Alfred. Are you saying he can stay here with you?"

Chapter 31

Jack and Hana conspired over a cup of tea back at the hotel. Leslie sat with them, understanding nothing of Hana's hand movements. The old woman held the baby and watched as Hana revived her dormant skill. "How'd youse learn that?" she demanded.

"My mother was deaf," Hana replied, between signs.

"Well! Who knew!" Leslie exclaimed.

Slamming doors and loud male voices sent Leslie scurrying to the window. She stood on tiptoe and peered through the glass. Her chins wobbled as she provided a running commentary. "Them boys is back," she hissed. She shot a sly glance at Hana. "It don't look good, Miss. Your tāne's wiping his hands on his jeans."

"Why?" Hana rose and Jack gripped her forearm with a sudden movement. His brow furrowed and she forced herself to sit and finish their conversation. She couldn't think straight and he kept leaning forward to read her lips. "Logan," she mouthed and jerked her head towards the window and Leslie's bobbing figure. She rubbed her knuckles and words abandoned her.

Jack patted her shoulder and gave her a smile. He made the motion of a fist pounding into his other hand and when he saw the panic in her eyes, shook his head and tried to smooth over his silent tactlessness.

The first of the men barged into the kitchen and the heavy door hit the cupboard behind. "Did you see that left hook?" he demanded and a peal of laughter followed him.

"Is that what you call it? Loser!" Tama entered next, a cut leaking from his chin onto his shirt. Sickness roiled in Hana's stomach and worked its way into her throat. She stared at the door as the men filtered through, desperate to assess Logan's health for herself.

"Out!" Leslie shouted. Phoenix's head bounced against her shoulder. "No boots in here! All of you. Out!"

Hana heard the groan leave her lips as the men drained away like water down a plughole. The delay sent her heart rate thudding higher. It seemed an age before the men returned, passing through the doorway in their socks.

Logan appeared last and Hana's gaze raked his body for signs of injury. He sought her and padded across, touching Jack's shoulder as he passed. Relief coursed through Hana and she felt tears push towards the surface of her equilibrium as her tight muscles relaxed.

Flushed and excited, the men tucked into juice, platters of fruit and muffins. Leslie produced items from the chiller one-handed and kept Phoenix over her shoulder. Tama washed his hands and made a beeline for the baby, repatriating her without debate. "Hey, sis," he whispered. "Ya miss ya bro'?"

Phoenix sought his eyes and beamed, her lips moving in response as she cooed and kicked her legs. An uncoordinated hand rubbed at her eyes and clasped the greenstone tied around his neck. Jack gave Hana a smile of encouragement and rose, joining the men's impromptu feast.

Logan saw the exchange and narrowed his grey eyes, hefting an apple and taking a bite. He pulled out Jack's vacated chair and sat next to her. Hana's lips parted with an enquiry and he gave her a warning look. "I'm fine," he said, leaning close enough to whisper in her ear. "I'll explain everything in a while." Hana nodded, but her eyes widened at the sight of the knuckles of his left hand. She made a grab for it and Tama pointed in their direction.

"Enough, you two!" he chastised, turning away with a smirk as Logan glared at him. The men stared and Hana blushed and her teeth found her lower lip.

"Where did youse lot go?" Leslie demanded. The sounds of chewing ceased. The room became silent as all eyes turned to Logan for explanation. He shook his head in a movement almost imperceptible. The men shifted from foot to foot and went back to eating and talking in low voices. Tama bounced the baby on his hip and ate one-handed. He stuffed a muffin into the hole in his face without biting into it and Phoenix blinked as though surprised.

"Thanks boys," Logan said as the last apple core disappeared into the dustbin. "Good job."

The men nodded and left in single file, moving along the corridor in silence. Hana heard them retrieving their work boots from the front door step. Jack left too. The farm vehicles moved off the driveway, but the Honda remained at a jaunty angle in front of the steps. Tama eyed the expression on Logan's face and made an excuse to leave. "I'll take Phoe outside and show her the roses," he said, moving towards the door at speed.

Logan stood up and threw his apple core in the dustbin, awkwardness shrouding him as he eyed Leslie's back. She clattered dishes in the sink and the other women grew nervous. "Ladies?" Logan cleared his throat. "I'd like a word with Leslie, please." He made it sound like a question but Hana heard the mana and authority in his tone. It left no room for discussion or disobedience.

The three women present shot sideways glances at Leslie before drying their hands and removing their aprons. They too left in single file. Hana watched Leslie's spine stiffen as she hefted a saucepan onto the draining board and pretended not to notice.

Logan stepped behind Hana's chair, slipping his hands beneath her hair and gathering it into a ponytail. He moved the tresses from hand to hand, feeling its silkiness against his coarse skin. "Leslie." Hana watched the old woman turn with exaggerated slowness. "Sit with us," Logan demanded.

Leslie's movements appeared laboured and her cheeks infused with an uncharacteristic ruddiness. She looked older in that moment like a woman who hadn't slept for too many nights on end, a woman who heard noises outside and feared the worst. "I know I'm not the missus," she began. "I'll try harder, I promise. I really need this job, Mr Logan. Please, don't take it away from me."

"It's not about your work, Leslie," Logan replied, patting the seat next to Hana. "It's about the debt collectors."

Leslie remained standing, posturing with her arms outstretched. "Please don't finish me because of them!" Her voice rose. "I'm dealin' with it."

Logan reached into his pocket and threw two fifty dollar notes onto the table between them. Misunderstanding, Leslie's eyes widened and she flapped her arms in panic. "No! No, please don't finish me!"

"It's the money we gave you for babysitting my daughter," Logan said. "With their apologies."

"They took it." Leslie's bottom lip trembled. "But the debt still grew."

"Well now they've returned it." Logan's voice sounded soft, the tone the same one he used to suppress the horses' fear. "Just sit down, wahine."

Leslie sat on the edge of her seat. "All right," she said, her brow furrowed with worry. "Say it."

"The boys and I paid a visit to the debt collectors," Logan said. "They won't bother you again."

Leslie's eyes widened and her mouth opened and shut like a goldfish. Hana could see she didn't believe him.

"Na," she said with a shake of her head. "Their kind don't go away."

Logan stopped playing with Hana's hair and leaned over, his hands either side of her. His shirt front touched the top of her head and she saw the tautness of the tendons in his forearms. His scuffed knuckles bled into a wad of paper towel wrapped around them. Hana swallowed, sensing the debt collectors took some persuading.

"They won't come back!" Logan said with certainty. "They're a little indisposed." Leslie's jaw dropped again and Logan continued, "We'll drive you home after the baby's next feed. Then Hana can help you pack. We'll move you into one of the motel units for now. Your landlord doesn't expect you back."

Hana tipped her head to stare at the underside of Logan's chin. She saw his jaw work in his cheek, pulling the skin tight. She sighed, reaching out to touch the makeshift bandage around his bleeding knuckles. Her dance with Laval had been about taking care of Logan and sparing him more pain. Yet he walked into the next battle, regardless. She wondered if her subconscious buried Leslie's confession to prevent her involving Logan. Part of her regretted it. A bigger part of her didn't. A line of bruising spread into the back of his hand as the haemophilia hindered his blood's ability to clot. Hana swallowed, knowing it hurt but understanding he'd never admit it.

Leslie put her head in her hands and a sob issued from her throat. Hana slipped from her chair, crouching beside her and patting her knee. "It's okay, Leslie. But this is good, isn't it?"

Logan bit his lip in confusion. He ran his hands through his hair and shifted on his feet, leaving it to Hana to mop up the mess he'd made.

"I'm all good, Miss." Leslie rose and settled her uniform dress over her ample hips. She reached into her apron pocket for a tissue, dabbing at her eyes and nose with its frail remains. Logan poked around in his jeans pocket and produced the ever-present-handkerchief, a fond legacy of his mother's sense of etiquette. He held it out and she took the plain white cloth as though selecting a delicacy from a tray.

"Shit," Logan whispered under his breath. Weeping women left him clueless. Hana caught his nervous glance and her heart softened. He looked vulnerable and unnerved.

"I'll be forever grateful," Leslie choked. She reached for Logan, her body so short she wrapped her arms around his stomach. Her breasts spread either side of his waist. "You're a good boy," she whispered.

Logan peered over the top of her head and winced at Hana. His arms hung loose by his sides and he appealed to her with his eyes. "Help," he mouthed.

Leslie sniffed. "Youse never did like to be touched, did you?" She released him and dabbed at her cheek with the handkerchief.

"Nope." Logan's body remained as rigid as a plank of wood. Hana watched the interaction with interest. Her husband's miserable expression struck at her heart and she realised she'd witnessed a side of him he kept hidden.

"Ah well." Leslie straightened her shoulders and pushed Logan's hanky into her apron pocket. "Best get on," she said, patting Hana on the arm. "Youse let me know when you wanna leave. I don't have much to take with me."

With the worry gone from her face, Hana saw a striking woman, her brown skin healthy and her dark eyes sparkling. She held her portly body with grace and poise as she left the room with a skip in her chunky calves.

Logan deflated like a balloon and sank into Hana's vacated seat. Hana pushed herself onto his lap, forcing him to widen the gap between her and the table. Her bandaged wrist rested in her lap and she ran a finger along his cheek and kissed his neck. "So, Mr Du Rose, you don't like to be touched?"

He moaned as she bit the soft skin beneath his ear lobe. "Only by you," he whispered.

"Just as well." Hana entwined her fingers through Logan's and settled her lips over his, running her tongue along his bottom lip.

"Come to bed with me, wahine," he whispered and Hana shook her head.

"No time," she breathed. Phoenix's grizzling echoed along the corridor as Tama brought her back. Logan released a series of unpleasant swearwords driven by frustration and Hana smirked and rose, so he could straighten his jeans before Tama appeared.

As Tama handed the baby over, he jerked his head towards Hana's bandaged wrist. "That looks nasty."

"It's fine!" Hana heard the lightness disappear from her voice. She sat down and accepted the kicking baby, keen to distract the men from the weeping bandage. "Phoe's gaining the weight she lost," she commented, latching the child onto her nipple beneath her tee shirt.

Leslie bounced back into the kitchen and beamed at them all. She squeezed Tama's waist and stood on tiptoe to kiss his lips. The action made a smacking sound and Tama stepped back, horror widening his eyes. "Thanks for helping with them debt men," she said, seizing a damp cloth off the draining board and leaving the room.

Logan snorted with laughter at the sight of Tama's scowl. "She's old enough to be my granny!" he complained. "Great great granny!" He raised his hand and wiped his mouth on his sleeve.

"Oh, do you normally ask their age?" Logan asked, his face blank. "I hadn't noticed, tāne."

Tama's face darkened as his mind strayed to his love affair with Anka. Hana changed the subject. "I went upstairs to see Alfred," she said. "I caught him leaving and managed to stop him, for now."

Logan breathed out and rolled his eyes. "Am I meant to care?" he demanded and Hana hid her dismay at his detachment. "You should have just let him go."

Hana's face fell and anger swelled in her breast. "How many times have you visited him since we arrived?" she snapped. Logan's sneer held his answer. "Well, Jack says he can live with him for a while, until he sorts himself out. I stupidly thought you'd prefer him to stick around."

"I don't care." Logan shrugged, reaching for the newspaper in the centre of the table. "Do whatever suits you."

"I shouldn't get involved." Hana shook her head and looked at Phoenix to avoid her husband's piercing grey eyes. "I'll stay out of your business from now on."

Tama grew still in the awkward silence. He sank into the chair next to Hana and the heavy atmosphere subdued his words. "I think Uncle Logan feels betrayed," he said. He stammered over the halting sentence as both adults stared at him. He quailed, but continued. "Everyone knew Reuben was his papa except him. I get it. Everyone knew Kane wasn't mine. Nobody said anything. It takes time to forgive the people who didn't care enough to tell you the truth." Tama picked at a knot in the wooden table and the air hung like lead around him.

Logan's dark lashes brushed his olive cheeks. Tama held his breath, knowing he had nowhere left to go. Reuben's nomadic family had been billeted by the insurance company wherever it could find room, but Tama had no rights to their consideration. Apart from Logan's charity, he'd have nothing but the clothes he wore on the night of the fire. Logan huffed out a breath. "Yeah," he conceded. "That's exactly how I feel."

"I'm sorry." Hana's brow furrowed. "I was one of those people."

"Yeah, nobody ever said anything but I kinda figured it out myself. The things you said and your mannerisms matched his." Tama sighed and the tick of the clock occupied the silence. Phoenix fed herself to sleep and the chiller whirred to itself. "I loved the old bastard."

"About Leslie," Hana began, her voice sounding too loud. She felt responsible for chasing away the ghosts.

"Should we renovate Alfred's apartment and let her live there? You don't want to lose income from a motel unit for too long." She couched her question in a veiled concern for profit, knowing she could hook Logan best that way. He folded his bottom lip over in thought and cocked his head.

"This bloody hurts," he said, unwrapping his knuckles and watching his deficient blood drip onto the table.

Tama waggled his eyebrows. "That's what happens when you make a guy eat his own teeth."

Logan heaved out a sigh and leaned back in the chair. He turned to face Hana's gaze. "Do what you think, Hana. I don't really care."

"Then why did you help her?" Hana leaned forward, her eyes reaching in to search Logan's soul.

He swallowed and looked away. "You're making me soft, wahine. I did it for you. She made my life a misery when I was a kid. I owe her nothing."

Hana swallowed and searched her mind for some useful comment. Nothing came. Logan rose and reached out to drag a stray curl behind her ear. "We'll move her into Kane's motel unit and she can stay there until the builders finish upstairs. I'll get them to renovate when they take down the kitchen wall." He pressed a kiss against Hana's forehead and spoke over her with words she didn't understand. "He aha haere a tawhio noa mai a tawhio noa."

His footsteps padded from the room and the closing door left a draught in his wake. Hana turned to Tama. "What did he say?"

Tama swallowed. "He said what goes around comes around. And he's right."

Hana sighed, understanding the way of the Du Roses was littered with glass. She would need to harden her delicate feet.

Chapter 32

"Your stitches need to come out, wahine!" Logan said. His brow furrowed and he released Hana's wrist back into her lap.

Her face crumpled. "I won't go back," she whined. "Please, I'm not ready!"

Logan faced her, seriousness drawing his eyes into narrowed slits. Hana tensed, expecting more bad news. "Odering is threatening me with obstruction," he said, forcing his voice to remain light. "I've ignored him for days. Bodie tipped me off last night. He says he's lost patience and I'm in the firing line."

Hana shook her head, closing her eyes against the growing sense of unease. "He can't arrest you, Logan. It's my choice."

"But it's not, Hana." Logan's lips quirked up on one side. "And you know it."

"I'll talk to him," she whispered. "Just not yet. He doesn't know we're here, does he?"

Logan chewed on the inside of his cheek, his eyes flashing as he forced himself to stop. "Not yet. But the receptionist turned away a cop car earlier, so he's got a fair idea. He's checked everywhere else."

"Sorry." Hana hung her head and refused to look at him. Misery and terror created a tight, painful band around her head.

"It's okay, babe. I'll hide you and go to jail if I need to, but doesn't it seem a bit pointless? Speak to him."

"I will, I promise." Hana licked her lips, feeling her tongue sticking to the roof of her mouth as her throat dried. Her gaze darted around the kitchen and her mouth moved as though wanting to say more.

"Angus called me too." Logan intended the new topic to soothe her ragged nerves, but Hana tensed. He slipped an arm around her shoulder and pulled her closer. The chair legs scraped across the tiles and she sighed into his chest. "I know you don't want to go back," he acknowledged. He dipped forward so his lips brushed against her forehead. "I'm sorry, Hana." She squeezed her eyes closed, her hands knotted in her lap and her body tipping forward at an uncomfortable angle. "It seems Pete's found his niche." Logan's voice rumbled through his chest and reverberated against Hana's ear. "Angus is raving about him. He's done all his night duties without prompting and moved into the unit behind ours. Angus has alerted the fraud department about the invoices and they've seized the accounts." Logan shrugged. "I've already checked the process, so I'm not sure what they think they'll find. It only works if the delivery company is in on it." He pursed his lips and Hana read concern in his grey eyes. She voiced the conclusion for him.

"And if someone at the school is part of the scam."

Logan raised an eyebrow and gave a shallow nod. "Exactly."

"I don't want to live next door to Amanda." Hana spat the words which bothered her most, the sentence bubbling from far beneath the surface.

"Any other stipulations?" Logan smiled but his grey eyes held a glint of caution. It irritated something deep in Hana's soul and she rebelled, her reaction too hot for the situation.

"You can't make me!" She stuck her nose in the air and ground her teeth.

"Can't I?" Logan's dark hair bounced against his eyelashes and his eyes sparkled with challenge.

"No!" she snapped. She shot backwards from her chair and skirted Logan's flailing arms. She heard his chair legs screech against the tiles as he gave chase.

Running upstairs wasn't her best idea and he caught her at the first bend of the main staircase. The woman behind reception looked up in alarm as they barrelled through the quiet foyer. Hana squealed as Logan caught her under her thighs and lifted her into the air. "Watch my arm," she wailed, holding it above her head.

"I have no intention of looking at it." His voice sounded hoarse with lust. "Not when you own more interesting parts." He pushed her into the lift on the first floor and chased her into their bedroom in the private wing.

"But Phoenix might need me." Hana's face creased with concern and she faltered, the game in danger of running out of steam.

"Leslie's got her." Logan skulked around the bed and lurched for her as she darted across to the other side. The bed springs twanged as he thudded onto the mattress. His outstretched fingers caught the bottom of her tee shirt and he reeled her in. Hana gasped as the stitching made tearing sounds, wailing in dismay.

Logan clambered across the bed without releasing her, knee walking with his boots raised above the bedspread. He ignored her pleas and gasped as his soles slid against the bedside rug. Hana stopped tugging and waited for him to right himself. Her hands lifted to assist and she noticed the oozing mess on the bandage as though seeing it for the first time.

"Oh." She turned her wrist over and inhaled. "It looks bad."

Logan rested a hand against the mattress to pull off his boots. "No distraction techniques." His voice rang out in a tone laden with authority. "I've got an hour with my wife and I intend to make the most of it."

He slipped her clothes off while she hesitated, lifting her tee shirt over her head without disturbing her wrist. His fingers caressed the tender skin at her waist and his eyes begged for acceptance. Hana spied the darkness in his eyes, the remnants of a worry which ate away at his peace and sanity like an ulcer. She let him lift her and lay her in the wide bed, enjoying the sensation of his warm skin covering hers. When he hesitated, she felt the papercuts of Laval's interference in their marriage and leaned up to kiss Logan's full lips, needing to banish the blonde man's spiteful influence.

"I thought I'd gone to heaven," she whispered afterwards. Logan's strong arms enfolded her and he'd hauled the blankets over their legs. His fingers tightened on her ribs.

"What? Just then? I think I did."

"No. When I woke up after the operation. I heard voices and the lights confused me. I thought I'd gone to heaven."

Hana felt Logan's body stiffen and used her right hand to push herself up. She drew her knees to her chest and clasped her arm around them, letting her sore wrist trail on the mattress. Logan blew out a sharp breath. "You thought you'd died?"

Hana nodded, the motion shallow and non-committal. She wrinkled her nose and sighed. "I prayed and God saved me. I didn't deserve it."

"Geez, Hana! He sure didn't do it for me, even though I promise I asked a million times." He covered his eyes with his left forearm. "I couldn't think straight when you disappeared. It's not something I suffer from unless you're involved." His other hand reached for her and his fingers fluttered against her thigh. "Everything happened in slow motion. I can't settle, Hana. It feels unreal."

She rocked back and forth, the mattress dipping beneath her. "I hear you in the night. You pace around. I wake up panicking and you're not there."

"I'm never far away." His fingers tightened around her thigh. "I won't leave you."

"But you will when we go back to Hamilton." Hana squeezed her eyes closed. "You'll do night duties and I'll have to manage alone again." She pressed her forehead into her knees and Logan's fingers traced the ridges of her spine as though they reminded him of guitar strings. Her body looked thin and fragile against the backdrop of the wide bed.

"If you want me to back out, then I will." Logan's words cut through the silence and Hana jerked her head up. Her green eyes settled on his face and she saw the cost written there in the background wince. He hated the idea of breaking a gentleman's agreement. But she sensed he meant it. He'd break it if she asked him. Hana sighed, knowing she couldn't ask.

"Don't," she whispered. "I'll come back to Hamilton with you while you fix the problem at St Bart's. Then we go home."

Logan watched her face for a moment before giving a definitive nod. "But you stay at school with me," he added, an eyebrow raising in question. "At the staff unit?"

Hana felt the last of her energy deplete like a spent firework. She left it long enough to watch the stress lines appear in Logan's forehead before nodding. "Okay."

The tension left his shoulders and he relaxed, pulling her into his side. His phone buzzed on the nightstand and he reached sideways to snatch it. The text message drove the worry lines back between his eyebrows and Hana watched as Logan's fingers flew over the keypad to send a reply. She blinked as he glanced up at her. "That's not how you spell that swear word," she said and Logan jerked to the side to hide the screen. He sent the message and slammed the phone face down on the cupboard.

"Don't care." He lay down and pillowed his arms behind his head. His biceps bulged.

"Who was it?" Hana demanded.

Logan caught her around the waist and pulled her into the bed, his actions too fast for her to resist. "Nobody," he lied.

Hana snuggled into his downy chest and closed her eyes, exhaustion washing over her. She didn't ask again, having recognised the name above the message. Supercop. The name Logan called her son.

A visitor greeted Hana in the kitchen the next morning. Leslie's daughter rose from her chair with a smile. "Hey, Mrs Du Rose," she said. "I'm not sure if you remember me."

Hana shook her head and winced as Leslie snatched Phoenix from her arms. "I remember," she said. "You helped me after the birth."

Isla nodded and sank back into her chair. A mug of coffee cooled on the table in front of her. Hana eyed the rigidity of Leslie's spine and frowned. "This isn't a social call, is it?"

"Told you she'd guess." Isla rolled her eyes at Leslie's back. She turned her attention to Hana. "No. Mum asked me to check out your wrist. She's worried about it."

Hana sighed and hid the stained bandage behind her back. "It's healing." She pursed her lips. "I'm not supposed to mess with it."

"Liar." Tama stepped from the chiller with a chicken drumstick clasped in his fingers. "They told you to keep it clean and go back if it didn't look right." He pointed the fleshy end of the bone at her face. "And that doesn't look right."

Hana gritted her teeth and glared at him. He ignored her. Tipping his head upwards in thanks to Leslie, he left the kitchen. She screwed her head round once to observe Hana's defensive stance and returned to whispering nonsense to Phoenix.

Isla held her hand out, her dark eyes radiating kindness in the green glints which lit the brown. Hana relented, sitting on the edge of a nearby chair and laying her wrist along her thigh. The action pained her but she couldn't bear to admit it. Thoughts of the wound took her back to Laval's lounge and the beetle eaten carpet. She smelled the musty scent in her sleep at night and woke crying.

Isla unwound the bandage and removed the gauze. She made no comment about what she found underneath. Hana kept her eyes fixed on Phoenix's bobbing head and refused to look. "Thanks for your kindness to Mum," Isla whispered.

Hana jumped and winced as stinging liquid seeped through the stitches and into the ragged wound. "It's fine," she answered. She swallowed. "I couldn't have managed without her these last few days."

Isla's smile faded and her eyes became glassy. "She didn't tell me or my sister what was happening. I just found out she borrowed furniture from a neighbour at Christmas when I visited and took it back the next day." She shook her head. "Stubborn old woman." She pursed her lips and stared at Hana's wrist. "This is infected. Why don't we drive to the medical centre in Rangiriri and see Dr Seuli? I'll come with you."

Hana shook her head. "No thanks. I'm fine." She withdrew her wrist and gasped as Isla kept hold of her fingers. The stitches tugged and Hana glanced down, seeing black thread and a ragged flap of skin pulled closed over her swollen vein. Nausea rose into her throat and she forced herself to swallow.

Isla's eyes narrowed. "I'll try an old remedy for now. Manuka honey and a fresh bandage." Her eyes narrowed. "But you need antibiotics soon, so you must see a doctor when you get back to Hamilton."

She busied herself with a tub of the expensive honey, daubing it over the stitches until they stuck flat to Hana's wrist. Then she covered it with clean gauze and a new bandage.

"Thank you." Hana gave her a fake smile and withdrew her hand as soon as she could without snatching it.

"Please don't tell Logan." She sensed Leslie's gaze on her and held her ground until Isla gave a reluctant nod.

Hana thanked Isla and escaped from the kitchen as soon as she dare. Leslie refused to relinquish Phoenix and Hana felt the conspiracy against her grow. She ventured outside into the sunshine and discovered Logan sitting on the front steps. His hat dangled from his fingers and he stared at the stone between his knees. He smiled as Hana halted next to him and nodded approval at her clean bandage. Clearing his throat, he voiced his main concern. "My mother wouldn't leave here after we arrived home back from London," he said. "Looking back, I think I missed the signs."

"You think I'm crazy?" Hana's voice rose and she took a step back. Her feet tangled with a man's suitcase and he apologised and continued down the steps.

Logan rose with more speed than she credited him with and grabbed her right hand. "That's not what I'm saying," he hissed. "But trauma can trap you and make it hard to get out."

"I'm not trapped." Hana wrested her hand free. "Don't you understand? I feel safe here. Why is nobody listening?"

"I'm listening." Logan's voice soothed and cajoled. He stepped close enough to wrap his arms around her rigid body. "But you're not talking."

Hana closed her eyes and allowed her brain to run a check over her body. Her chest felt tight and her wrist smarted from the cleanser and honey. She groaned. "I just want to be left alone. I'm only asking for a little while, Logan."

"What's this about Amanda?" His change of tack confused her and she floundered.

"What?"

Logan's arm tightened against her back. "You said you didn't want to live next door to her. I asked Tama about the argument you had with her, but he said to ask you. Did you know she raised the alarm?"

Hana rested her forehead against Logan's shirt. His heart beat a dull thud into her head. It felt strong and real and comforted her. "No, I didn't," she muttered. "She accused me of having an affair with Laval when he threatened me by the river."

Logan heaved out a breath. "Okay. That's why you were pissed off the night before."

Hana lifted her head and rested her chin against Logan's muscle. Her arms hung by her sides like a rag doll. "Why didn't you tell me about him? Why didn't you tell me about Liza and him?"

Logan swore and his eyelids shuttered. Open. Close. Open. Close. Hana watched as he made the internal decision. He glanced at the top step and tugged on her sleeve until they sat there together. "I need to speak to her but she's on a trial. She isn't responding to my messages." Tension drew his lips into a tight line and his dark fringe bounced against his eyelashes. "This is gonna mess her up real bad, Hana." He blew out a breath. "He changed his name twenty years ago. I knew him as Michel L'Huillier. It's why I didn't recognise the name Laval. It meant nothing to me." He squeezed the bridge of his nose between thumb and forefinger and released a sigh. "I'm sorry. I let you down."

"Not if you didn't realise. But what happened between him and Liza? He said they got married." Hana watched colour flush into Logan's cheeks, driven up his neck by an unseen flame.

"Don't make me tell you," he whispered. "Trust me, you don't wanna know."

Hana's lips parted as Logan rose, unable to explain the darkness she'd seen in Laval's eyes. The sound of hoof beats plodded from the direction of the rose garden. "Where are you going?" She heard the hurt in her own voice and straightened her spine.

"I need to go up the mountain." Logan leaned forward and pressed his lips over hers. He tasted of chewing gum and coffee. He rose and his palm sent a single stroke across her hair before he turned.

"Will we talk when you get back?" Hana's voice rose and hysteria laced the fringes. He'd opened up the can of worms and left her to face it alone.

Logan turned as Jack limped around the corner leading Sacha. He shook his head and clamped his hat down over his ears. "Not about that, Hana," he replied. "Anything but that."

Other horsemen joined Logan as he mounted up, holding their reins one handed and sitting deep in their saddles. Toby waved to Hana and she smiled, lacking the energy to lift her hand enough to return his greeting. His brow furrowed, but he touched the brim of his hat and let his horse surge after Logan. Gravel spat from their hooves as five horses trotted from the driveway onto the grass. The men cheered as Logan jumped the low stone wall dividing the gardens from the paddock. They opted for the gate instead and let him keep his growing lead. A wedding party stopped to watch the scene. The bride struggled from the car unaided as her bridesmaids giggled and pointed at the raw masculinity on show. A ripping sound heralded the bride's heel going through the hem of her dress and they jumped into action. But their collective gaze strayed towards the handsome figures galloping up the long slope of the foothills.

Hana carried Phoenix's drawer to the family room and reclaimed her child from Leslie. She threw the French doors open to clear the mustiness and lifted Miriam's abandoned knitting from an armchair. The room looked untouched since the night of the fire and held a listlessness which resonated with her. Hana remembered the cosy winter evenings spent in front of the hearth. Miriam knitted and Alfred wound wool from a skein while they watched something mindless on television. She ignored the ghosts and settled her child in the drawer on the coffee table. Then she curled up on the worn red sofa to read a novel borrowed from the ground floor library.

The sound of her book thumping onto the floor woke her up with a start. She reached for it but sent it skidding across the floorboards instead. Hana wiped her left hand across her face, confusion muddling her tired brain. The hard edges of the splint stabbed her eye and she hissed and let her hand fall into her lap. "Damn it!" she grumbled. A yellow stain leaked through the white surface of the bandage and mixed with diluted blood. Hana winced and turned her hand over so she couldn't see it. The tendons ached and she counted the hours until her next dose of painkillers.

A knock at the door made her jump. Her wrist twitched and she swore.

"Mrs Du Rose?" Leslie's voice sounded formal and strange. Hana's brow furrowed as she rose to turn the handle, wondering why Leslie didn't punch the number into the keypad.

"What's wrong?" Hana stood back to let her in, but Leslie shot a nervous glance to her right.

"I'm sorry, Miss. But the po-po wants ya," she hissed.

"Pardon?" Hana peered in the gloomy corridor and squinted. "The what?"

"Cops." Leslie waggled her eyebrows and a flicker of fear shot through Hana's breast.

"Logan?"

"No, Miss, no!" Leslie reached for her, her eyes rounding as Hana trembled. "No, Mr Du Rose is fine, I just heard him on the radio. They've rounded up the stock and he's headed back." Hana put her hand to her mouth and Leslie saw the state of the bandage. She searched for something to lighten the mood. "Mr Tama fell off his horse. I heard them all laughing."

Hana fought for control. She couldn't think straight.

"Mum?" Bodie stepped from the hallway and Hana felt a sensation like her heart restarting. Her good hand fluttered to her chest.

"Bo," she managed, her voice catching. "Bo." She opened her mouth but no other words emerged. Her lips crept upwards into a relieved smile until another shape slid into view.

"Hello again, Mrs Du Rose." Odering's voice sounded clipped and he held out his right hand in a formal handshake. Hana stared at it and her world began to tip.

"Mum? Mum?" Bodie's arm shot around her back as Hana wobbled. She ran a shaking hand over her face and saw Odering drop his arm in her peripheral vision. Bodie couldn't look her in the eye, his treachery raw in every angle of his clenched jaw.

Hana staggered backwards into the lounge and her calves bashed against the nearest armchair. Leslie pushed between the men and widened her eyes. "I'll fetch tea," she said out loud, but her face communicated something different. She leaned in close and whispered, "I'll get him here."

Hana nodded and backed further into the room. A fog shrouded her as though Odering's appearance had summoned Laval's pervading sense of evil. It locked up her lungs and robbed her of oxygen. She forced her legs to take her across the room to the French doors and debated her escape.

"Mum, don't." Bodie's warning cut through her confusion and she bent her knees and dropped into a chair. She stared in surprise at the novel by her feet. The men watched as she reached for it with trembling fingers. The dust cover tore across the spine and she cursed her clumsiness.

Phoenix stirred in the drawer on the coffee table and Bodie looked down. His olive cheeks flushed at the sight of his sister. "She's grown," he said, stating the obvious. He drew the collar of her cardigan away from her chin and stared at her fluttering eyelashes. Odering grunted as he sat without invitation and rested a clipboard on his knees. A skilled sleight of hand produced a black dictaphone from his breast pocket. Hana blanched and pushed herself back into the squashy armchair.

"Let's get started," Odering snapped. He raised an eyebrow at Bodie.

Hana's son leaned forward. "I'm sorry," he said. "I didn't want to do this."

"Ambush me." Hana stared at her hands and spoke the words. Her voice sounded flat. "You didn't want to ambush me."

Odering's face twitched and his colour flushed red. "You were the victim of a crime," he snapped, his tone bordering on aggressive. "I used valuable resources finding you, Mrs Du Rose. You have a duty to provide us with a statement."

"Valuable resources." Hana closed her eyes. "I'm sure my husband can refund it."

"Mum!" Bodie's lips parted and Hana saw him move towards her from beneath her lashes. She drew back further into the chair.

Odering dipped his body forward. The tape recorder teetered on his knee. "Mrs Du Rose," he began, "I understand this is hard for you. It's not my intention to make matters worse, but I need to take a statement and I insist we do it now."

Hana raised her head and forced herself to get eye contact with him. "I know, let's play twenty questions." She put fake enthusiasm into her tone. "And then I could treat your concerns like a joke too."

Bodie dropped into an armchair. His jaw fell open with comical effect and a sane part of Hana's brain fought the urge to laugh out loud.

"I'm sorry for that," Odering began and Hana held her hand up in front of her face.

"Save it. You're a bunch of amateurs. I have no faith in you or the court system and don't wish to waste my time. Please leave." Hana opened her novel to the page most bent from its plunge onto the carpet and traced a sentence with her forefinger.

Bodie's cheeks pinked with embarrassment. "Mum!" He sounded shocked. "We drove for two hours to see you. The least you could do is talk to us!"

Hana looked up and her lips curled back into a snarl. She jabbed her finger in Odering's direction. "Did he tell you?" she demanded. "Did he tell you what he said when

I went to see him? That was after the first time Laval threatened to kill my husband. Did he tell you?"

Bodie shook his head and glanced across to Odering. He tried a different tack. "You probably misunderstood, Mum. He detailed a whole team to watch you around the clock."

Hana snorted and shook her head. "Where were they when he kissed me on the bridge? What did they do when he assaulted me at Day's Landing? What about poor Tama? He tried to help me and your goons electrocuted him."

Odering's left eyebrow hiked. Amusement back-lit his eyes. "We didn't electrocute him, Mrs Du Rose." Exasperation filled his sigh. "My officers Tasered him in error."

Bodie's eyes widened in shock. "They Tasered the kid?" he exclaimed, darting a look at Odering. His superior ignored him.

Odering answered with practiced calm. "I think my decision not to prosecute him for an assault on police is apology enough. By the way, the officer's fine, thank you for asking. He's on sick leave after a nose job. Perhaps you'd convey to Mr Haewi that head-butting a police officer is a serious offence."

Bodie sat back in his chair and the down-turned slant of his lips communicated defeat. He resembled a man very much out of his depth. He shook his head.

Hana's gaze flicked to her son and she pitied him. Odering made him his pawn and ambition would keep him there. He caught her eye and winced, his brow furrowing at the sight of the yellowed bandage. He saw her at the scene, spraying blood from an arterial bleed. Paralysis took over his legs as the paramedics slipped a drip into her vein and plasma pumped into her limp body. They pressed gauze so hard into the wound her hand turned blue. Bodie forced himself to focus on the infant sleeping in the drawer. He craved a connection with her but didn't know where to start building it. He opted out, leaving Hana and Odering to stare each other down in a pointless stalemate. Odering spoke first, breaking the leaden silence with a question. "Will you ever give me a statement, Mrs Du Rose?"

He didn't seem surprised at her answer, but Bodie's lips parted in shock. "No," Hana said with conviction.

"Can I ask why?" Odering replied. His tone sounded calm as though he soothed a dangerous animal.

Hana sighed and relaxed as he offered no resistance. She gazed through the open doors towards the stables. The sun beat down on the mountain range without respite, withholding the rain as a silent punishment for past offences. Hana knew her husband planned for a drought. She turned her green eyes on Odering's face and the breeze blew her red hair across her cheek. "I want to forget how you used me as bait. Twice. You caused the perfect storm and did it with forethought and planning. You got your man, Detective Sergeant. Now leave me alone." Hana searched for more words but came up empty. There were none. Her mind drifted to the memory of the tatty lounge with its old fashioned carpet and endless photos decorating the tired walls. It induced a feeling of suffocation and she couldn't bear the thought of reliving it. Even Logan hadn't asked her for details. She spoke the truth. She needed to forget.

Odering put his head down and stared at his shiny shoes. "His men claim he intended to keep you prisoner. There was a room upstairs." He paused, unable to describe the room kitted out for torture. "The lawyers will need to show you photographs and corroborate your version of events." He squinted as sunlight turned Hana into a fiery silhouette. "It's best you don't see it in court without warning."

Hana shook her head and flapped her hand in front of her face. "I don't want to talk about it." Her mind drifted to Liza's critical eyes and she wondered if they knew she'd married Laval. She owed the spiteful judge nothing, but Logan's relationship with Liza demonstrated the only normal family bond she'd witnessed. The urge to protect it for him overrode her natural sense of justice.

"I need you to tell me what happened." Odering's fingers poised, the ball-point pen ready to jot notes and the recorder set to capture every wobble and waver in her voice.

"I don't remember," Hana lied.

Bodie saw her floundering and betrayed her in an instant without a second thought. "Mum!" he snapped. "Is it Logan? Is he forcing you to lie? I know he's mixed up in this somewhere."

Hana's gaze slid to his face and she gripped her fingers together in her lap. It pulled at the stitches in her wrist and the pain reminded her she'd survived. "You'd like that, wouldn't you?" she whispered.

"Just say the word." Bodie leaned forward in his seat, sweat beading on his forehead.

"You know nothing about this family." Hana's chin wobbled. She remembered the haunted look in Alfred's eyes and cringed at the memory of it in her own. She'd seen it in Laval's. Rejection. Not good enough for someone to bother loving. She would help Alfred. Someone else could heal Laval.

Odering shot from the chair at speed, his knees locking with an audible crack. His fists bunched at his sides. "So, let's make sure I understand this correctly. A criminal I spent the last three years of my life chasing will get the opportunity to enjoy seeing you called as a hostile witness. He's made your life a living hell through harassment, kidnap and actual bodily harm, but you'll overlook it." His lips curled backwards to expose shiny incisors. Bodie groaned and ran a hand over his face.

"Yes," Hana replied through gritted teeth.

"Why?" Odering looked tired and sweaty. His shirt stuck to his torso to reveal the white vest beneath. His big career break unravelled before his eyes. Years of late nights and covert surveillance and the stuffed files on his desk told him nothing. "Why?" The repeated question emerged as a hiss and Hana twisted her fingers tighter.

Bodie exhaled. "It's this bloody family. I just know it. Let me take you out of it, Mum. I'll do it today. Right now. Pack the baby's stuff and we'll leave."

"This family." Hana squeezed her eyes closed and Miriam ran across the screen in her mind. Her hair streamed out behind her as a silhouette until the fire engulfed her. "This family." Her eyes snapped open. "This family is ruthless and selfish. It consumes you until there's nothing left and spits your bones into the gutter. But this family is my family now. I'm not leaving."

Bodie's lips parted to argue and then his complexion paled. Odering's eyes widened and Hana knew without looking that her husband occupied the doorway behind her. He'd approached from the garden, silent and unseen until he chose to make his presence known.

Logan moved and the light changed, casting a long shadow which stretched across the hearth rug. He stepped over the threshold, his hands pushed deep into his front pockets. Dirt streaked his left cheek and his fringe tumbled into his eyes. His cowboy boots wore a layer of dust from the hard downhill ride and his shirt had slipped from his waistband on one side. He stepped in front of Hana's chair and blocked her view of the policemen. His arms folded over his chest and his legs slid apart in a combative stance. "Do you have a warrant?" His voice sounded calm, but a sinister note hovered in the background.

He glanced back at her and Hana watched the muscles either side of his back flex. She bit hard on the inside of her cheek. He'd heard her. The rigidity of his neck told her he'd heard her spiteful summary of his whānau. Inwardly she kicked herself over and over, frightened she'd revealed something about herself even she hadn't known. She sounded like she hated them. It occurred to her that perhaps she did.

Logan removed his gaze from Hana and she sensed the coolness of its absence. He turned back to the policemen and jerked his head towards the door. "Get up," he snarled. "Time to go."

Hana kept her eyes down, burning a hole in the rug beneath her feet with the intensity of her gaze. She heard the men stand and ignored them both. Her fingers itched to catch hold of Bodie's pants as he sidestepped her but she kept them twisted in her lap. She doubted his loyalties of late, seeing a darkness in his eyes she remembered from his youth. It pained her to avoid his gaze, fearful of betrayal. Bodie's proximity to Odering gave him a career driven focus which seemed to obscure family loyalty. It frightened her. He would never accept Logan or understand their relationship.

She listened to their footsteps recede outside and track along the back of the hotel. Odering's voice rose and ended with abruptness. Hana wondered what Logan did to shut him up within earshot. Leaning forward, she put her head in her hands as nausea rode through her system. She bumped her fist against her forehead. "Idiot! Idiot!" Phoenix stirred in her drawer and Hana forced herself to stand. She concentrated on breathing and not imagining the hurt in her husband's face. She'd trashed the family name he loved and she'd done it publicly.

A series of clicks heralded Leslie with the tea tray. She trapped it between her hip and the wall of the corridor and pressed numbers into the keypad. She jerked in surprise as Hana opened the door, almost dumping the tray onto the carpet. Hana recognised Miriam's favourite teapot and sighed. "I don't deserve the best china," she whispered. "I think I'll find myself divorced before dinner time."

Leslie plonked the tray on the coffee table next to the makeshift cot. "What you done?" she asked, her voice a low hiss. She twisted her body around to survey the empty room. "You killed the po-po and buried the bodies?" She winced, remembering too late that one of them was Hana's son. The spare skin on her upper arms hung like bat wings as she wrapped them around Hana's torso. She patted her back like a child and made soothing noises.

The clearing of a male throat made both women jump and Leslie scooted to the door without a backward glance. Hana felt the sense of abandonment spread out wide in every direction, sealing her fate. She slumped into the nearest chair and bent double, hooking her arms around her shins. Waiting for the hatchet to fall seemed to consume her remaining energy.

Logan's hand rested on her back and she heard him grunt as he squatted next to her. "Hana, don't." His voice sounded calm, the vowel sounds dragging in their usual twang. He pressed a kiss to the top of her head.

Hana blew out a breath which contained more sorrow than she imagined it could. "I'm sorry." The words wrenched from somewhere deep in her soul and she knew she meant them.

"Oh, Hana." Logan sighed and inched forward until her forehead rested against his shoulder. "What's going on in that beautiful head of yours?"

"Not much." Her chest hitched and hot tears pattered against Logan's shirt. Hana pressed her face into his collarbone and squeezed her eyes shut. Her right arm wrapped around his neck while her painful wrist languished in her lap, honey mingling with a bloodstained discharge.

"Everything will be okay," he promised, his voice muffled against the side of her head. "Just trust me."

Hana forced herself upright, her cheeks sticky with tears. She used the hem of her tee shirt to dry her eyes. "Why are you so nice to me?" she breathed. "I thought you'd be angry."

Logan winced at the cramp beginning in his calves and stood. His nose wrinkled as his blood made its way back into his feet. He dipped his body and scooped her into his arms, spinning before sitting in the chair he rescued her from. Strong arms kept her pinned in his lap and he placed a large hand against the right side of her head to press her face into his neck. Hana felt his shrug of dismissal ricochet through her body. "I didn't know you thought about my family that way."

Hana swallowed. "Neither did I." It seemed wrong to admit the insult took her as much by surprise.

Logan bent his head to place a kiss on her forehead. He used his left hand to lift her chin and gave her a sad smile. She saw the creases in the corners of his eyes and the tired greyness of his complexion. "Hana?" he asked in a whisper. "Do you think I'll consume you and then spit your bones out?" The sentence sounded ludicrous and childish on his lips, not the dramatic statement she'd heard burst from her own.

She shook her head, separating Logan from the Du Roses in her mind and seeing something fresh in the resulting picture. "No," she sniffed. "You're just another victim of the family, not the aggressor."

Logan leaned back so he could study her, confusion narrowing his eyes. "What do you mean?"

"Who are the Du Roses?" Hana demanded. "You carry their name but you don't act like them. Do you cheat and deceive to get what you want? Your mother, Kane, Michael, all of them; they do what's best for them and nobody else. You're not selfish like them, Logan. They make my flesh crawl with their petty rivalries and their damaging secrets. You're nothing like them. They take what they want and everyone else be damned."

"What about Tama?" Logan's fingers clamped around her waist as she shifted in his lap. He wouldn't let her go.

Hana closed her eyes. "I don't know. He's different, like you." Her wrist ached and a powerful tiredness moved through her bones, threatening to drop her where she sat.

Logan sighed. "Bodie texted me last night. I told him to stay away. I love how he listened and respected our space."

Hana let out a laugh which held no mirth. "That's my boy."

Logan's heels tapped the floorboards and his knees rocked beneath her. "I said they can speak to you later. Odering refused to leave, so I found them the shittiest room we have for the night. It'll be late when we're done."

Hana tensed. "I'm not talking to them again."

"Yes, you are." Logan's voice held steel and his grip on her waist tightened. He raised his left hand in front of her face as she opened her mouth to protest again and she fought the irrational urge to bite his fingers. "You need to talk about it to someone," he said. "You don't eat, you wake up thrashing most nights and what if he gets off on a technicality and comes after Phoenix?"

Hana squeezed her eyes shut. "I won't do it," she whispered. "I can't."

Logan's fingers pulled her chin towards him, waiting until she opened her eyes and faced him. "Who are you protecting now, Hana?" he asked. His voice softened and his eyes implored her to tell the truth.

She swallowed and cocked her head. "You. Always you."

He sighed and his stunning grey eyes narrowed. His index finger traced a line along her jaw and he blinked, his long lashes grazing his cheek. "Hana, I don't need your protection. Talk to Odering. It's my job to protect you. I don't understand why you deny me the chance to show you how much I love you."

Hana tipped sideways and pushed her face into the space between his collarbone and neck. "He said he'd kill you," she mumbled. "I couldn't let it happen."

Logan sighed and ran his hand up her spine to cradle her shoulder. "Hana, I can take care of myself. I ended up in the lake because I let Odering use me as bait. Being haemophiliac has taught me not to let someone get the jump on me. I don't have enough good blood to lose.

"What about Liza?" Hana rubbed her nose with the underside of her hand. "I don't think he knows about her marriage to Laval."

Logan kissed the top of her head. "She doesn't deserve your protection either, Hana. But don't worry about Liza. We covered our bases at the time. Odering will struggle to find any link."

"How did you do that?" Hana popped up, curiosity overriding her misery.

"Never you mind." Logan bopped her on the nose and grinned. He lifted his knees one at a time and wobbled her in his lap. "Speak to Odering tonight, babe. Tell him about the threats to me and what happened. I'll sit with you."

"But the photographs." Hana swallowed. "They'll see the link between you."

"So what?" Logan shrugged. "I knew him in school by a different name, perhaps his mother's or stepfathers. But I'm not sure Odering can link L'Huillier to Laval, anyway. I doubt he changed his name legally, babe. It's more likely he assumed his birth father's name. Who cares? It's not your problem. Say what you need to say and let me worry about clearing up any mess."

Hana twisted her lips between finger and thumb. Logan hid his frown at her resemblance to a tiny, fragile girl. His arms tightened around her. "Did you really give them a crap room?" she asked. She turned to face him and blanched at his grin.

"Hell, yeah!" he exclaimed. "It's a double bed in a cupboard which backs onto the laundry room."

Hana narrowed her eyes. "Logan Du Rose, you are a very wicked man."

Chapter 33

Alfred ate in the kitchen with Phoenix balanced over his shoulder. He kept his large palm against the flat of her back and she sucked at her fingers and made sighing noises. She burped a couple of times and farted once, making him chuckle. "Funny moko," he breathed. He pushed the remnants of a buttered scone between his lips.

Hana smiled at the domestic scene. Alfred looked less frantic, an aura of calm surrounding him. He'd moved his gear into the attic and decamped to Jack's spare room. His head seemed clearer away from the ghosts of his family.

"She's like her papa." One of the kitchen girls leaned over to stroke the child's hand as she passed, smiling at Phoenix's fluffy dark hair which sprouted from the crown like Logan's. Her eyes had settled into a stormy grey and showed no signs of darkening.

Alfred winced at the comment and Hana watched as he fixed the emotional wall back around his heart. He'd confessed to her that sometimes Phoenix's eyes held such profound wisdom, he felt he stared into Reuben's soul. "Awesome kai," he muttered with his mouth full, lifting his head to search for more.

"Tēnā rawa atu koe." Leslie beamed, thanking him for his compliment and bristling with importance.

A wedding banquet continued in the ballroom with guests dancing like maniacs in unsuitable shoes and dresses. Only the newlyweds and a few chosen guests had booked rooms, so normality would resume by midnight. Logan arrived in the kitchen still fastening the buttons on his clean shirt. He kept the door open with his foot and raised an eyebrow at Hana. The colour drained from her face and a tremor began in her knees. She scrunched her body as small as possible as though trying to make him overlook her. Logan's nostrils flared and he turned to Alfred. "Please can you keep the baby for a little while? We'll be in the restaurant."

"No problem." Alfred's eyes glittered as Leslie dumped another warmed scone in front of him. A knob of butter slid onto the plate and the fingers of his left hand twitched.

Hana groaned as Logan held his hand out and curled his fingers to beckon her. She closed her eyes to block out the ordeal looming and felt the air shift as he released the door and strode across the tiles. "Come on." He leaned down and his kiss brushed against her cheek. "You promised."

Hana dragged her feet into the restaurant and slid into the booth where Bodie and Odering waited for her. She offered them mute nods of acknowledgement. Logan pushed himself in next to her like a formidable rear guard. "Use a recorder," he advised. "She won't be repeating it."

Odering narrowed his eyes and stared at Logan. "You don't get to boss me around, Du Rose," he snarled.

"Don't I?" Logan's tone sounded loaded and Hana tensed. "If you don't like it you can crawl home to your real boss and explain all your stuff ups to him."

"Her." Bodie dipped forward as Logan's gaze turned to him. "The chief is a woman."

Mischief sparkled in Logan's eyes but before he could open his mouth, Odering delivered his threat. "One of these days, Du Rose, I'll lock you up so tight you won't see the sun until you're an old man."

Hana gasped and Logan's jaw tightened. "Give it your best shot," he growled. "I'll be waiting."

"I can't do this." Hana rose so fast the tablecloth caught in her writhing fingers and the salt crashed into the pepper at the centre of the table. She turned to face Logan, urging him with her eyes to let her escape.

Bodie stood and reached across the distance between them. His hand felt warm on her forearm. "It's okay, Mum. They're just posturing. You can talk to me if you'd rather. Just pretend it's you and me." Hana looked down at his olive hand and drowned out everything else in the busy restaurant. Her knees shook and she gave a shallow nod. An expression of contrition flashed across Logan's irises and he pursed his lips in a silent apology. A hand snaked behind her knee and he tugged her closer until she plopped onto the bench.

"How's Amy?" he asked, making conversation while Hana settled herself again. He reached out his other hand and righted the fallen condiments.

"Away seeing her parents in Wellington with Jas," Bodie answered with a swallow. "I don't think it's going well."

"Amy?" Odering turned his head to observe, his eyes narrowed. "Our Amy from the custody suite?"

Bodie closed his eyes and gritted his teeth, resenting the overlap between work life and personal. He nodded and slammed a lid on the small talk, allowing the silence to envelop them like a shroud.

Logan ordered for Hana and when it arrived, she pushed it around the plate without eating the delicate crumbed fish. The bandage on her wrist hid beneath a cardigan sleeve but numerous times she gripped a spot above it with her other hand, her face a mask of pain. Bodie glanced across the table at Logan, uniting them in concern. Logan gave a slow shake of his head to warn him to ignore it.

"Did Izzie tell you what happened the other day?" Bodie asked. His voice strengthened at Logan's smile of gratitude.

"No. What happened?" Hana's voice drifted as though another place occupied her mind.

"She took the boys shopping in a double buggy and got the thing wedged in a shop doorway. They couldn't dismantle it and the shop owner had to call a tradesman to remove the door frame. Nobody could get in or out."

Hana smiled, imagining her beautiful Indian daughter in her high heels, posturing and denying any blame.

"Izzie called Marcus but he was in the middle of a funeral. He said when he got there, Izzie was fuming and the buggy is a write off."

Logan snuffed a gentle laugh but when he stole a sideways glance at Hana, her glazed look told him she was only half listening. He took her writhing fingers under the table and squeezed, attempting to inject his love into her spirit.

"Thanks for dinner," Bodie said as the staff cleared away dessert dishes.

"Yeah, thanks," Odering grumbled.

"Fancy a walk, Mum?" Bodie glanced at Logan and received a small nod of permission. Hana shook her head and pressed the spot on her wrist again, her face blank.

Odering's brow furrowed and he placed his napkin on the table. "You look tired, Mrs Du Rose." His voice sounded soothing. "I think we should have our talk tomorrow morning." His gaze flicked to Logan. "Does that suit you both?"

Logan took a good hard look at Hana. He remained silent for a moment. "Okay," he conceded. "Tomorrow. After breakfast."

Bodie gave Hana a lame smile and raised his arms above his head. "I might go for a look around," he said. "See you in the morning."

Odering rose and gave a tiny bow, before following Bodie from the restaurant.

Hana turned to her husband. "I need to feed Phoenix," she stated. A hand pressed across her breasts and then the right one pressed at the bandage. It looked like a reflex action, as though she didn't realise she did it.

Logan nodded and rose, waiting for her beside the booth. They left the restaurant and headed back to the kitchen for Phoenix. "Is everything okay?" he asked. His voice echoed in the empty corridor.

"Yeah." Hana shrugged and shook her head at the same time, sending confusing mixed messages.

"Don't worry about the meeting tomorrow." The certainty in Logan's tone offered reassurance. "I'll be there."

Hana stopped in the middle of the corridor, staring at a point on the floor. "I don't understand," she said, her inner turmoil creasing her brow. "How can I talk about something I don't understand?"

"You don't." Logan kissed her forehead and pulled her right hand away from its death grip on the bandage. "You tell the facts and leave out all speculation. It's their job to pick through it, not yours."

"But what if I accidentally mention Liza? What if she loses her job over it?" What if I say something you don't want me to?"

Logan rested his hands on her shoulders. "There's no proof of his connection to Liza." He glanced behind him to ensure they weren't overheard. "Everything got destroyed and a little cash donation made sure all legal documents disappeared without trace. They still used paper records back then and she hadn't gotten around to changing her surname anywhere important. Don't worry. The 'what ifs' are my department."

Phoenix slept over Alfred's shoulder while he read the newspaper. Kitchen staff picked their way around the wide table and he seemed oblivious. "Thanks," Logan said, reclaiming his daughter with gentle hands. "I appreciate your help."

"No worries," Alfred replied but the emotional void still hung around in his eyes.

Hana walked upstairs and stretched out on the bed to feed a sleepy baby. She played with the tiny fingers which clutched her nightshirt. "It's Phoenix," she said, meeting her husband's watchful eyes. She stared at her daughter's miniature nails and knuckles, reliving the dread of separation. "I thought I'd never see her again and the pain's still here in my chest." She touched her breastbone. "My mum didn't watch me graduate from university. She didn't see me married or meet my children. There's a void in my chest and it's opened wider. It feels like I might fall inside whenever I think about what happened." Hana stroked the downy black hair and stared into the penetrating Du Rose eyes glittering from the delicate olive face. "I understood how Reuben felt in that moment. My mum was there one minute and gone the next and I figured it would be the same for Phoenix. She wouldn't even remember me except from photos. But Alfred forced Reuben to watch your whole life play out from a distance. I think it's what hell must feel like."

Logan rubbed his eyes with the heels of his hands and turned away, something clicking inside his chest. Hana's words echoed in his mind. "I know exactly what hell feels like," he whispered. "I experienced it in Odering's stuffy office. It's life without you, Hana." He rose to make coffee, busying his hands to stop his thoughts punishing him.

"Sorry." Hana spoke the word into the silence. "I'm not losing the plot, I promise. Reliving it for Odering's benefit tomorrow fills me with dread."

"I know." Logan flopped the tea bag around in the mug, adding milk and cursing as the bag broke and he needed to start over. He winded Phoenix over his shoulder while Hana sipped the tea, his thigh resting against hers in the wide bed. She'd lost weight and her bones looked as fragile as a bird's. Phoenix gave a sigh which ended in a hiccough, protesting at the delay before dessert. She whimpered and jerked as the air in her stomach fought for release. Logan cleared his throat. "Would you rather

I stayed out of the interview?" he asked, watching Hana sideways. "I'll do whatever makes it easier for you."

"Until I start talking tomorrow, I won't know," Hana said, her eyes unfocused and distant. Then she turned to face him, looking into his dark grey irises. "Can I ask you something?"

Logan pressed his lips together and bowed his head, knowing the question before she asked. "You can ask, but I might not answer. It's not my secret."

Hana lay back against the pillows. "Fair enough," she said. "But Laval claimed you were friends once. Is that part true?"

"L'Huillier, yes." Logan nodded, shifting the wriggling infant on his shoulder.

"Did Liza meet him through you?"

Logan took a deep breath in and shut his eyes before answering. Hana struggled to hear it. "Yes."

"Did she have a good reason for divorcing him?"

"Yes." Certainty dominated Logan's voice.

"Can you tell me what it was?" Hana pressed.

"No." Logan gritted his teeth, giving his face a harsh, angular shape. "I won't."

Hana looked stung as she reached the impasse. He hadn't said he couldn't, but he'd refused because he wanted to. She hated the idea of Logan and Liza sharing secrets she couldn't access. After a long silence she asked, "Am I doing the right thing, talking to Odering tomorrow?"

Logan's expression darkened. "Hell yeah! We need to make sure he doesn't get out, at least for a while."

"A while?" Hana blinked. "You think he'll get out, anyway?"

Logan twisted his lips and released a tense breath. His jaw tightened against his cheek. "Let's hope he leaves in a body bag," he growled.

Odering conducted his interview with formal precision the next morning. He seemed determined not to have his intentions thwarted again. Bodie produced the recorder and it lay on the table between them like a threat. Alfred took a sleeping Phoenix for a walk in the pram and Hana felt redundant without her. She sat on the edge of the sofa in the family room, twisting her fingers and hiding the stained bandage beneath her cardigan sleeve. The fingers of her right hand strayed to her left wrist and she squeezed at a spot above the bandage. Pain crossed her face as a grimace and then she released it.

"No disturbances," Logan told Leslie as she delivered the tray of tea. He closed the door on her retreating back.

Bodie worked the recorder and made notes while Odering teased information from Hana she hadn't realised she possessed. "From the very beginning, Mrs Du Rose," he said, a deceptive gentleness in his voice. "When did you first meet Michael Laval?"

Hana told her story, unable to look at Logan as she recounted how Laval touched her, kissed her and behaved with unnerving familiarity. She enjoyed Odering's embarrassment as she recalled her visit to his office and his game of twenty questions, noticing the look of horror on Bodie's face. She glanced sideways at her husband's expression, seeing a look of dark menace brooding there. He fidgeted as she described the snatch, Laval's conversation in the car and how she'd concealed her phone. She touched a sore spot on her cheek. "One of his men hit me in the face when I tried to stop them taking me from the car." She sighed and her brow furrowed. Forging on through halting sentences, she revealed every detail of their subsequent conversation except any reference to Logan's relationship with Laval.

Then came the question Hana anticipated with dread. She'd punished herself enough for her foolish decisions but sensed Odering would compound the guilt. "Why did you agree to meet Laval alone?" he asked. His eyes glinted with hidden enjoyment as he hunted answers and Hana felt Logan's thigh tense on the seat next to her. She took a deep breath in and resisted dressing her stupidity in nobler clothing.

"I thought I could reason with him. If I could make him believe you wouldn't let me retract my statement, I thought I could stop him hurting Logan. If I couldn't do what he wanted, I figured he'd leave us alone."

Odering's lips pulled back in a gleeful grin. "You were protecting your husband?" His eyes flicked to Logan and back. "You expect me to believe that?"

"Yes." The last of Hana's confidence pooled around her feet. "We've had enough tragedy. We don't need any more."

Bodie's gaze fixed on Logan and he frowned. Then he returned to his notes. Odering sniffed as though looking for loose ends that weren't there. "The idea of Logan Du Rose needing protection from his wife is almost unbelievable." His eyes flashed. "Are you sure there wasn't something else you were afraid of? He wasn't planning to blackmail your husband?"

"No." Hana jerked her head back, the notion odd and thrown at her from nowhere. "He wanted me to withdraw my statement against his father otherwise he'd kill Logan. He gave no other reason." Hana avoided her son's gaze, sensing he'd see the lie swirling above her like a neon sign.

Odering dipped forward. "So, the presence of high school team photographs in the house have no bearing on the kidnap? Despite the fact your husband was in some of them." His gaze slid to Logan. Bodie's lips twisted and he looked from Odering to Hana as though wanting her to confess to some awful crime and bargain away Logan's freedom. Sadness filled her heart along with the understanding he'd never accept her husband. Three backward leaps accompanied each tiny step forward.

"I don't want to do this anymore." Hana shot to her feet. Her right hand clamped down over her bandaged wrist and squeezed as though needing the pain to galvanise her.

"But Mrs Du Rose!" Odering stood also, raising his voice in frustration.

"I've told you the facts." Hana parroted Logan's instruction. "I've nothing else to add. Are we done now?" As all three men gaped, Hana left the room.

The door clicked and she heard shouting behind her. The angry voices rose for a moment and then dulled as the door opened and closed once more.

"Mum!" Bodie sounded angry. "What the hell are you doing?"

Hana stopped and turned, her movements slow. "I'm stopping you from making this all about Logan. It's just a distraction, Bodie. Laval wanted the statement retracted and Odering wouldn't let me." She spread her hands before her. "I need to get on with my life. Just let me forget."

"Like hell I will!" He took angry strides towards her. His dark face radiated fury and Hana shrank back against the wall. Her late husband's eyes glared at her from her son's face, accusing and cruel. She'd loved Vik but paid a terrible price, losing most of herself in the yawning pit of his dissatisfaction. Something in her snapped and she held her ground despite wanting the wall to suck her in and hide her.

"You seem to have forgotten I'm your mother!" She jabbed her index finger into his chest. "I've given my statement, Bodie. Accept it and move on."

"You're hiding something." His eyes flashed a dangerous, glinting brown. "I'll find out what."

Hana sighed. "You do that." Exhaustion laced her voice and the energy from her anger pooled around her feet. "Forget I'm the victim in your thirst to prove Logan's some criminal mastermind. You're as bad as Odering. I'll refuse to sign any statement I've given you if you persist, Bo. Tell that to your boss." He blanched, the colour leaving his cheeks as fast as it had risen. But he rallied.

"You gave a tape recorded interview. We don't need a signature, Mum."

"Well, good for you." Hana took a step forward and Bodie winced as the flat of her hand stroked the front of his shirt. "You can hound my husband until the day I die and it won't change how I feel about him. But it will change how I feel about you. I will always love you, Bodie, but right now I don't like you very much."

Hana turned and marched along the passageway, her floral dress swinging above the backs of her knees. She heard a slow clap begin as she rounded the first corner and Logan's praise straightened her spine, though she wished he'd chosen a more private setting for congratulations.

Bodie found her in Miriam's garden. "I looked for you everywhere," he said, his shoes pressing into the grass as he shifted from foot to foot. "We're leaving now."

Hana knelt next to the flowerbed plucking ugly weeds from the baked soil. She looked up at him and a streak of dirt marred her porcelain complexion. "Nobody takes care of the roses anymore." She sighed. "Miriam would hate seeing them like this."

Bodie swallowed and offered his hand to help her stand. Hana pushed herself upright using her right hand but accepted his outstretched fingers. "You've changed, Mum," he said and Hana heard the accusation hidden in his tone.

Hana moved backwards to sit on the bench. "I've found myself. I lost the person I was before Vik and now I've found her." Hana brushed hair from her eyes and stared up at the mountain ridge. "She's more selfish than I remember but she has balls. I forgot those attributes."

Bodie slumped next to her, hitching the legs of his smart work trousers before he settled on the wooden seat. "I didn't know you'd lost yourself." He leaned forward to rest his elbows on his knees, staring at the dusty ground beneath his feet. "Was it so very soul destroying being our mother?" He avoided her look of surprise and concentrated on the shiny toes of his shoes.

"I love being your mother," she whispered.

"Then what?" Bodie spun to face her. "What does Logan give you that my father didn't?"

Hana sighed. The game exhausted her, skirting around the sainted Vikram Johal's memory. She'd protected his honour even after death when he had destroyed her. She reached the end of the road and stepped into the unknown, sensing things would never be the same again. "Logan hasn't lied to me. I'd trade every moment with your father in exchange for that."

She waited for the wave of realisation to hit, doubting her motives for destroying her son's world. But he gave nothing in response. She'd expected questions followed by fury and denial. Nothing. Bodie kept his head down and his shoes scuffed a pattern in the dirt.

"You knew?" The knowledge hit her like a side swipe, robbing the oxygen from her lungs. She wrapped her arms around herself as though trying to block out the pain.

When Bodie raised his head, his dark eyes glittered with a decade old disappointment. They carried everything she once felt; guilt, betrayal, anger and dismay. He nodded. "I found out by accident. I didn't know how to tell you. But it's why I didn't cope with his death." Hana leaned closer as his voice lowered. "I saw you grieving and I wanted to tell you hundreds of times. All that pretence of a great family and all those church people who spoke at his funeral. It was a lie. Our lives were a big fat lie." He rubbed a hand under his nose. "How long have you known?"

"A woman came to see me, the day after the funeral." Hana swallowed. "She told me Vik planned to leave the day before he died. He'd booked a holiday with her and planned to let the dust settle before filing for joint custody of you and Izzie."

"Shit." Bodie rubbed a hand over the back of his neck. "I sensed it coming. They looked pretty serious."

"You knew her? How?"

Bodie snorted with derision. "I walked to his office every Monday and Wednesday after basketball practice for a ride home, remember. One time I walked in on them kissing. I pretended I didn't see. I've spent the last nine years wanting to tell you but then so much time passed, it seemed too late. Bodie shook his head. "I wish I had. We might have comforted each other."

"Sorry." Hana reached out and stroked his rigid bicep. "Vik was dead and it seemed wrong to rob him of everyone's respect. I kept quiet for you and Izzie."

"I wonder why he didn't leave." Bodie blinked. "You said he planned to leave the day before he died. I wonder what stopped him."

"We'll never know." Hana sighed and withdrew her hand. "But he loved you and Izzie. He cheated on me, not you. Don't forget that."

Bodie shook his head. "He cheated on all of us. And then he left permanently." His tone sounded laden with resentment.

Hana rubbed a hand across his back and felt the tension in his spine. "I've played the loser in every possible scenario in the last nine years, so I can't trust my own memories anymore. Meeting Logan woke me from a nightmare and I'll never stop being grateful for that. But mistrust colours even this relationship and I worry that one day, he'll decide I'm not good enough for him either."

"Oh, Mum, we're a pair of damaged morons." Bodie sighed. "When I fell in love with Amy at work and discovered too late she was married, it nearly killed me. I gave her an ultimatum because I couldn't do what Dad did to us. She chose her marriage and I left Hamilton to get away. I know you didn't believe me but I knew nothing about Jas. Her husband walked out on her before she had the baby, so the kid's had no male role models. I'll marry her and make it right one day. Otherwise, I'm repeating my father's mistakes."

Hana picked at the bandage. "We're emotional refugees." She stretched her arm around Bodie and he permitted the contact. His spine relaxed enough to sit with her in the sunshine. They sat in silence as the warm rays stroked their faces and their minds ticked through shared memories.

Odering clattered round the corner, his face pink and sweaty and his shirt creased. He glared at Bodie. "Sergeant!"

"Oh, oops!" Bodie grimaced. "I came to say goodbye but got distracted. Sorry sir. I forgot you were waiting in the car."

"Keys!" Odering snarled. He held his hand out and Bodie leaned back and dug in his trouser pocket.

"Ah, yeah. Sorry. I guess the air conditioning wouldn't work." He lifted the keys for Odering to snatch. "And the electric windows wouldn't open either."

Odering grunted as though about to blow a gasket and Hana reined in her laughter. "Thank you for waiting," she managed. She turned a gracious smile in the blustering detective's direction. Leaning forward, she smoothed her son's fringe back from his face. "Friends again?" she whispered. Bodie nodded but as he turned to leave, Hana snatched at his hand. "Izzie?"

Bodie's eyes grew wide and he shook his head. "No!" He blinked and clamped his jaw shut. Hana saw his agony laid out before her and it gave her understanding. He'd worked so hard to maintain a facade for Izzie, shielding her from additional pain. Hard enough to drive himself insane. "Just my pastor." He made the confession with a faint smile and Hana rolled her eyes.

"Bloody Marcus," she breathed. "I should have guessed." Her mind recalled a recent conversation when he'd urged her to trust Logan. Hana shook her head.

"Can we leave now?" Odering demanded. He marched towards an archway created by trimmed camellia bushes. He skidded to a halt as a shape cut off his exit. Logan stepped through the gap trailing Sacha behind him.

"Are you still here?" he grunted, not waiting for an answer as he strode towards Hana. The white mare tossed her mane, moving her head from side to side to take in the strangers. She lifted her head and examined them through a brown eye and then a rolling blue one. Odering took a step back, a look of distaste curling his upper lip. He pressed himself against a rose bush. Sacha snorted, grinding the metal bit in her mouth and lifting her stunning Arab tail. She followed Logan to Hana's side. "Will you be okay?" He dropped to his haunches and let the rein trail over his left shoulder. "The spring in the fortieth isn't flowing and Toby can't spare anyone to go and look. I'm riding up to see what's wrong, but I'll hurry back. Give me about three hours."

Hana felt the trepidation budding in her heart and tensed. "Is Alfred still pushing Phoenix around in the pram?" Her hand fluttered over her chest.

"Na, he's back in the kitchen stuffing his face." Logan bopped the end of her nose with a gentle index finger. "I've got a radio so you can call me unless I'm out of range." He kissed her forehead and turned to leave.

Sacha shook her head and blew out a long breath. The click of Logan's tongue sent her backing up. Bodie took refuge behind Hana's bench which left Odering exposed. The detective avoided the dinner plate hooves near his shoes and pressed himself against the rose bush. Sacha nudged Logan's shoulder and tossed her head. A squawk followed the sound of liquid hitting a hard surface.

"Sacha!" Logan growled. "You know better than that. Don't crap in your workspace." He turned her in a tight circle and headed under the arch. Her eyes rolled at the space restriction but she followed, swishing her tail from side to side.

Odering stared down at his legs and Hana covered her mouth with her hand. Logan showed no sign of having done it on purpose and staring at the back of his head gave Hana no answers. The rich, sweet grass from the lower slopes of the mountain covered Odering's suit trousers as slurry. Sacha flattened her ears and snaked her neck in his direction.

Bodie's eyes watered as he stifled a laugh.

"Oh, gosh!" Hana rose and pinched her nose between finger and thumb. "I'm so sorry." She avoided making eye contact with her son as silent tears dripped off the end of his nose. "Would you like a tissue?" Odering ignored her, peering at his splattered trousers. His jacket draped over his forearm and his eyes widened at speckles of manure dotting the fabric. Hana swallowed. "A dustbin bag, perhaps?"

Bodie leaned in and placed a kiss on her cheek. "Bye Mum." His chest heaved and his eyes watered. Turning aside, he dashed a hand across his cheek before facing Odering. "If you're ready, Sir?" he said.

Chapter 34

The quad bike left the concrete driveway and bumped over a ridge onto the grass. Logan glanced sideways at Hana and raised an eyebrow. "Okay?" he asked. Hana nodded and clutched the baby against her chest. "Not far now," he promised. The lush paddock rolled into view and Logan got off to open the gate.

"Why are we here?" Hana demanded. She closed her eyes to savour the sea breeze on her face. The vast Tasman Sea glimmered in the distance beyond Port Waikato.

"Let's wait for Tama," Logan said, measuring the time by the sun. "Bloody boy's late, as usual."

Tama appeared on horseback, sweating and whining. "You can't just text me and tell me to get up here! Not when I'm half an hour across the valley." He dismounted in a single bound and bent to rest his palms against his knees.

"Get a move on," Logan said, ignoring the barrage of complaints. "And close the gate."

He led them to the cliff edge and looked out over Port Waikato, the sea breeze counteracting the stifling heat.

"What's this about?" Tama asked. "Are you gonna push me off the mountain?"

Logan shook his head, his expression serious. "Not today." Hana's eyes widened and she pressed Phoenix closer to her chest. Logan turned to face them both, the sun putting his face into shadow. "We're building a house right here. It's a new start for all of us." His grey eyes searched his nephew's face. "It'll be a different Du Rose legacy because we're different to them. The tangata whenua messed up. We'll put it right."

Tama's smile appeared forced, his lips curving upwards but his eyes projecting a wistfulness. He slid his gaze to the sleeping baby and Hana saw envy reflected there. "Lucky little girl," he whispered.

Logan huffed out an exasperated breath. "Don't be an egg, Tama!" he snapped. "We want you with us."

Tama shook his head and shrugged. "I know nothing about building," he replied, his forehead creasing. "I'll labour for youse if it keeps the costs down."

Hana reached out and laid a hand on Tama's solid shoulder. "That's not what he meant," she said. "We want to offer you a home and a family. But only if it's what you want."

"What? Me?" Tama swallowed and touched his chest. He licked his upper lip and shook his head. "But my name is Haewi. It's the only thing my mother left me when she shot through."

Logan raised an eyebrow. "And you said you hated it."

"I do, but I'm not a Du Rose, am I?"

Logan pulled a piece of paper from his back pocket and it fluttered as he handed it over. Tama unfolded it, peering at the printed form in his hands. "What's this?" he asked. "I don't understand."

Logan pointed to the title of the form and cleared his throat. "We want you to change your name legally to Du Rose. I'll pay for it. Hana filled the form in so you just need to sign it."

Tama kept his head lowered and his finger tapped a beat against the page. His voice softened. "You said I couldn't use your name," he whispered. "Last year, you said so."

Logan inhaled and avoided Hana's look of surprise. "And I'm sorry," he said. "I had no right. You're Michael's son and that makes you a Du Rose. Changing it by deed poll is faster than all the paternity crap, but we can take that route if you'd rather. I just don't know if he'll be obstructive."

"No." Tama clutched the paper to his chest. Hana's cursive script decorated the flimsy surface. "This way is fine."

Logan righted Phoenix's bonnet and gnawed on his lower lip. The moment turned awkward as both men struggled to show their feelings. Hana rolled her eyes at their identical walls of bravado, knowing both hid behind them like emotional cripples.

"Group hug?" She sought to break the deadlock and shuffled closer. The contact seemed less strained with her and Phoenix at the centre.

"So, nobody can take the name away if I sign this form?" Tama stepped back and patted the paper.

"Only if you post it." Hana smirked and he narrowed his eyes and beeped the end of her nose.

"Yeah." Logan nodded and looked away. "You need to post it and then it's yours."

Phoenix startled as Tama kissed the top of her head. Her eyes widened as she tracked his movements. His voice sounded croaky and his hand flapped as though he needed to check every small detail of Logan's offer before he could snatch it away. "So, you're my legit family? Forever?"

"We want you to live with us." Hana added the promise and watched the colour rise into his cheeks. Sweat dotted his forehead and he whipped off his cowboy hat to run his forearm across it.

"For real?" he whispered. "No more sofa surfing?"

"Not unless you choose to." Hana's brow furrowed, his excitement giving her a fresh insight into his disadvantaged existence. "No more sofas."

"Shit." He faltered and stared at the ground. "Shit." Logan backed away, the rawness of Tama's heart too naked for him. He shot a covert look at Hana and winced. She held the baby in her right arm and waited while Tama regrouped. Tears shone in his eyes when he looked up at her. "I don't know what to say," he whispered.

Hana shrugged. "Then say nothing," she replied. She narrowed her eyes and lowered her voice. "No more looking at my butt."

Logan kept backing, his chest rigid and his posture showing discomfort. "We should head home," he called to Hana.

"Okay." She gave him a smile and waited for Tama to catch up his horse's reins. "Did you notice Phoenix's name on the tree?" Tama shook his head, towing the gelding behind him. "Logan did it." Hana gave him a stunning smile. "It's beautiful."

They reached the gate and stepped beyond it. Tama stared up at the familiar family names etched into the ancient bark and followed their genealogy. Hana took the reins and nudged him around the other side to where Logan had begun his new legacy. Still joined to the old, it stood out fresh and crystal clear. Tama stared and then blinked. He lifted his index finger. "That's my name," he said, his tone filled with wonder. "Tama Du Rose." He swallowed and his chest hitched. "You put me next to Phoenix."

Logan's eyes widened in alarm as Tama sank to his knees in the dust and ferns. He covered his eyes with his hands and leaned forward. Tears dripped from beneath his hands and Logan screwed up his face. He caught Hana's eye and jabbed a finger towards Tama's bowed head, begging for help to soothe the broken teenager. Hana smiled and shook her head, stepping over the ground cover and leaving him to cope alone. They needed each other. They just hadn't realised it.

Hana held her baby and towed the horse back to the quad bike. She lay a sleeping Phoenix on the bench seat and tied the horse to a tree. A tui bird hopped up on a nearby branch, his fluffy white bow tie wobbling at his throat. Cocking his head, he stared at Hana. Low voices carried through the bush and Hana listened to the sound of Tama's ragged tears. She ached for him in his nomadic world and prayed he'd accept their offer. "Everyone needs someone," she whispered, keeping a light hand on Phoenix's chest in case she woke up and panicked.

Twigs cracked and Hana jumped as the sound grew closer. It moved fast through the undergrowth and she tensed, opening her mouth to shout for Logan. Tama moved downhill at a run, his cheeks pink and tear stained. Fear of rejection shone from his grey eyes and she sensed he might never settle or find his equilibrium in life. He trusted no one and she saw the same reflection of hopelessness she'd witnessed in Alfred. The downhill pushed his feet faster than he intended and he barrelled past the horse. The gelding jerked his head from the ground and turned to stare as Tama hurtled past him. Hana held her arms open and Tama almost bowled her over, righting her at the last minute with a gargantuan effort. His tears dampened her shoulder and his chest heaved against her face. "Promise you won't leave me," he whispered. "Promise you won't get tired and leave me."

High above sea level on an ancient, sacred tapu piece of ground, Tama Du Rose found peace and thoroughly lost himself.

Chapter 35

Phoenix played with her toes, grumbling when they slipped through her fingers. Hana sat in the back of the car watching. She wondered who her tiny daughter might become in life. "It's not the same without Tama," she said with a sigh.

Logan wrinkled his nose in the rear-view mirror. "I need him at the farm. And you're safe now. We don't have to worry."

Logan drove through Huntly and Hana sat up as he ignored the turn towards the Tainui Bridge. Her nose pressed against the side window. "I wanna go to Culver's Cottage," she protested. "I need to check something."

"Liar! I wouldn't get you out again," Logan snorted. "You'd hide up there and avoid life forever."

"Please, can we go back?" Hana begged. Her breathless voice held panic. "I can't stay at the unit without Tama while you do night duties. Not yet, please Logan? I thought you'd give me a few days to get used to being back in Hamilton." Her heart clenched with anxiety as Logan drove through Hamilton and made the turns towards Fairview Downs. He glanced in his mirror and saw her draw her knees into her chest and rest her feet on the seat. She scrunched herself into a ball and he winced.

"It's gonna be okay, Hana," he promised. "But I can't leave you at home alone. At least at the staff unit I can check in on you. Culver's Cottage is too far away."

"But I'll still be alone," Hana breathed. "Twenty metres or twenty kilometres away. It's all the same to me."

It felt strange walking up the narrow steps towards the front door. Hana kept her right fingers clenched over the spot on her left wrist and her jaw clenched. A mental block seemed to keep her frozen in position. Logan stepped up behind her. "Take Phoe." He handed the car seat to her and she clasped the handle, holding on as though nothing else mattered. Logan gave her a nudge. "Get it over with, babe. Don't let the fears build themselves. Face them."

"Is that what you do?" She gritted her teeth and remained stalled on the top step.

Logan exhaled. "No, Hana. I avoid them, but it's what I should do."

The lounge looked unchanged and Hana took a tentative step over the threshold after Logan ground the key in the lock. She never expected to return and the realisation hit her like a punch to the stomach. Placing the car seat on the floor, she brought both hands up to her face and covered her mouth. Logan's hand on her shoulder made her jump and she released a squeak of fear. She whirled around and pressed her face to his chest. "I thought I could convince him to stop." Her voice hiked. "But I knew I couldn't. In here." She tapped her chest. "I left, Logan. How could I do that? I just left. I couldn't let him hurt you and I went to meet him knowing it was futile. What was I thinking? What's wrong with me?"

Logan brought his arms up to wrap around her shoulders. His chin pressed on the top of her head. "You reacted, Hana." He lowered his voice to a whisper. "You let him isolate you. It coloured everything you did from the moment you decided not to come to me for help. You can't make good decisions based on fear. We're a team, Hana. I protect you, not the other way around."

She swallowed and let his words wash over her. How would it feel to let someone take complete care of her? A flicker of anxiety began at her tailbone and spread as heat through her ribs. It involved more trust than she knew how to give. Hana pushed her hands around Logan's waist and dragged the bandage across his stomach. "I can't stay here," she whispered. "Don't make me."

Logan's sigh communicated a ripple of disappointment. She sensed him biting back a retort. Her wrist sent a dart of pain to wake up her brain and she felt a tremble begin in her knees. "Hana, relax." He whispered the words and bent to scoop her into his arms. He navigated the car seat and pulled her on top of him on the sofa. Tama's scent rose up around them and the ache of separation added to Hana's confusion. Logan squeezed the back of her neck and her face pressed against his collar bone. "You're so bloody hard on yourself," he sighed. "Too hard."

"I'm not enough." She repeated the mantra of her unworthiness as though it offered a flawed security. "I wanted to be enough," she murmured. "Enough for my baby, my husband and my God. Just this once."

"Don't do this, Hana," Logan soothed. "Please, babe. Let it go." He kissed the side of her damp face and realised his mistake. "We shouldn't have come back." He sighed. "I'll ring Angus and call it quits."

Hana pressed her face into his hard collarbone and closed her eyes. "Now I made you a quitter," she hissed.

"It doesn't matter." Logan ran his hand through his hair. "I'll clear up here. Why don't you go for a walk?"

"By myself?" Hana's eyes widened in terror.

"Make it right with Amanda?" he suggested. "Otherwise it'll bug you forever. She raised the alarm despite what happened before."

Hana cringed against his chest. "Don't try to get rid of me. I don't want to see people. They'll want to know all about it and I don't want to talk anymore." Her eyes darted around the unit and she put the back of her hand to her lips, the gory bandage lathered in dried leakage and manuka honey.

"Okay, then stay here. I'll make a drink and we'll work everything out." He tipped her onto the seat next to him and rose.

"Kua riro katoa kua whaiāipo, Logan," Hana whispered. Her pronunciation sounded terrible and Logan jerked back in surprise. He rested his right palm over his chest and his cheeks flushed pink.

"I fell in love with you too, babe, the first time I saw your beautiful face. Please trust me, wahine." He bent to kiss her and she shivered as though needing more. His biceps flexed and she gasped as he lifted her from the sofa. His kisses covered her face as he navigated along the short hallway to the bedroom.

"Phoenix." Hana's brow furrowed and Logan laid her on the bed and stepped back. He gave her a sultry wink, the action slow and filled with promise.

"Hold that thought," he said. "He smirked. "The one before you mentioned my daughter."

It took a minute to settle Phoenix in her cot and he returned to find Hana had stripped and climbed beneath the sheets. His fingers trailed along her soft shoulder and a fire ignited in his belly. "Are you sure you're okay with this?" he whispered against her skin. He joined her beneath the bed clothes and curled up behind her.

Hana turned over to face him and her expression held him at arm's length. "He didn't touch me," she said, her tone dismissive.

Logan ran an index finger over her top lip and let her beat her demons back behind the familiar portcullis. Then he set about rebuilding their fragile peace, starting with a kiss which made her forget everything.

The sound of hammering on the front door later woke Hana with a start. She sat up in bed and pushed her hair from her eyes. "Logan!" Her voice croaked as she called his name, splaying her fingers across the empty mattress next to her. "Logan!" The sheets tangled her feet and tripped her as she tried to run. She couldn't work out where she was and as the low ceiling of the unit crowded her, she panicked at her inability to escape the dream. Her fingers clutched the soft fabric of a tee shirt and Hana snatched it up and pushed her head through the neck. Her arms caught and when she hauled it down, she realised she'd put it on back to front. She fought her discarded underwear one-handed, hauling her knickers over her thighs.

The bedroom door crashed open so hard, it hit the wardrobe behind it. Hana screamed and pressed her hands over her ears.

Jas clambered onto the bed, his face a mask of distress. "Hanny," he cried, his eyes as wide as oranges and his little lips formed in a delicate 'o.' "Mummy said you got hurt and I needed to see you." His fingers reached out to touch the dirty bandage on her wrist and he looked guilty when Hana pulled it away from his clumsy ministrations. "Did your hand fall off?" he asked in a whisper. "Mum said I mustn't ask but she can't hear me." He gazed at her with conspiracy sparking in his eyes. "Did the bad man get you again?"

"Hana?" Logan put his head round the door and Hana's mouth opened and closed with nothing sensible passing through her lips. Logan rolled his eyes and bent to retrieve her jeans and blouse from the chair near the door. "Turn around buddy," he said to Jas. When the child resisted, he placed a hand on the boy's head and turned him. Logan flicked his earlobe with his other hand. "You give ladies respect, Jas. Understand mate?"

"Yeah." Jas sighed. "But it's hard. There are things I need to know."

Logan raised an eyebrow and hid his smile. "You'll know when you need to know," he said. His touch felt tender as he dropped the clothes on the bed and pulled Hana's hands away from her ears. He hooked a curl away from her eye. "It's okay," he whispered. "It's okay." He gave her a push until she sat on the bed and then twisted his lips as he pushed her clothes towards her.

Hana reclaimed a sense of decency and shot Logan a grateful look. He kept Jas facing in the opposite direction but watched every move Hana made, giving her an upward jerk of his head as she hauled her jeans over her butt. His full lips formed a kiss and he winked. If he noticed her shaking fingers, he didn't mention it.

"Is the lady done yet?" Jas grumbled. "I need to interrogate her."

"She's done." Logan released him as Hana sank back onto the bed. Her bare feet stretched out over the covers.

"Hanny would like tea with four sugars," Jas informed Logan. He knee walked across the mattress and waved a hand in dismissal.

"Would she now?" Logan narrowed his eyes, but the effect channelled more amusement than irritation. He smiled at Hana and left the room, taking with him her sense of security.

"Right." Jas rose on the bed and performed a twirl, almost pitching off sideways. "Look at my uniform, Hanny. I'm handsome, aye?"

Hana made appreciative noises in all the right places. But she'd noticed something. The shorts Jas wore were for a much bigger boy and the grey material hung past his knees. His yellow polo shirt dangled like a dress over the top. "Beautiful," she concluded, confused by the lack of fitting. "Does Mummy expect you to grow into a man by Easter?"

"Guess what?" Jas whispered.

"What?" Hana mustered as much energy as she could find in her depleted reserves.

"Guess!"

"I don't know." She laughed. "Give me a clue?"

"I'm gonna be a bridesmaid."

Hana's jaw hung slack and her brow furrowed. "Oh. Are you sure about that?"

"Am so!"

Hana chewed her lower lip before forcing her mouth to curve upwards. "Right." She grappled for a safer subject. "Has Action Man stopped wetting himself yet?"

"Well," Jas began. He settled into a cross legged position ready for a complete documentary. "Mummy and me put band aids on the leaking slits so he could meet the grandparents in Wellington. But they started peeling off and the new granny couldn't bear to look at him. She said he smelled rank." His shoulders slumped and his lower lip sank to join them. "She didn't like him. I don't think she liked me much either." He twisted his lips into a fish face and eyed Hana sideways. "Mum said if I'm good and stop wearing my uniform all the time, then I can get a new man. Maybe Action Man Paratrooper or Policeman." He beamed and his fingers picked at a snag in his shorts. Hana tensed as Phoenix wailed from her cot. Jas' eyes became round and bobbly and he shot from the bed. "It's okay, baby, Uncle Jas is coming!" he shouted.

"Nephew," Hana called after him. "She's your aunty."

Jas poked his head back through the gap, a grimace already spoiling the effect of his stunning genetics. "That's messed up," he grumbled and withdrew his head.

Hana staggered around the bed but Logan reclaimed his daughter first. He gave her a smile and retreated to the lounge. Phoenix wailed as Logan changed her nappy, kicking her legs and protesting. Jas offered useless instructions as the volume increased. Silence descended as Logan handed Phoenix over and she disappeared up Hana's tee shirt. Jas sat on the arm of the chair, trying to work out where the child's head went. "Did it come off?" His eyes widened in horror. "Where'd it go?"

Amy sat at the dining table, her nose red and her eyes puffy. She blew loudly into a tissue. "Sorry," she said with uncharacteristic gruffness. "I didn't want to come, but Jas insisted. I've got the window open so the germs should go outside."

"It doesn't matter," Hana replied with a smile. "Nothing could make the last week any worse."

Amy cringed. "Bo said what he did and I'm appalled. He used his personal knowledge to invade your space with Odering. That's not okay."

Logan released an exasperated breath and Hana heard his teeth grinding. He kept his opinion to himself though and she shot him a grateful smile. She sighed. "I don't think Odering gave him much choice." The memory of Sacha's diarrhoea shower quirked her lips upwards. A sideways glance at Logan witnessed him running over the same thought.

"Did you have a nice day at school?" Hana turned to Jas as he played with the baby's toes.

He shook his head and cackled. "Nobody goes to school on Saturday!"

Hana ran a hand over her forehead. "Is it Saturday already?" She narrowed her eyes in confusion and pointed to Jas' shorts. Her lips parted to draw attention to his uniform and Amy shook her head and rolled her eyes. The flash of desperation in her face begged Hana not to ask. "I've lost track of the days," she said with a frown.

Logan watched her fall silent. Worry creased his brow. He felt the atmosphere grow heavy and sensed Hana's mind taking her back to memories she would do better to leave alone. His face brightened. "Hey, who wants to go to the dining room for dinner?"

Jas leapt to his feet with a whoop of excitement, his eyes bugging and his fingers twitching. He hopped from foot to foot. Amy looked unsure, checking her watch and screwing up her face. "Mum, Mum, please can we? I wanna eat with the big boys!" Jas squealed, sensing his treat in peril.

Logan cringed. "Sorry, I should've checked with you first."

"No, it's fine. Bodie is still working, so we've got another couple of hours." Amy blew her nose and Jas ran to the door, eager to leave.

"Hey." Logan caught the child's hand. "We'll go to my office for a while. There's stuff I need to check. The girls can come over later."

Jas reached explosion point, his face alight with glee. He ran to the bedroom and reappeared with Logan's cowboy boots, one in each hand. They dragged his spindly arms past his knees and bent his spine with the weight. Amy shook her head with resignation at his comical antics. Logan sat on the sofa next to Hana to put them on while Jas got in the way. His tiny fingers itched to fasten the zippers. Amy writhed in discomfort, letting out a series of frustrated puffs. "Jas! Leave the man alone!" she snapped.

"Grab my wallet from the bedroom, please?" Logan asked. He raised an eyebrow and Jas raced off on his errand. When the front door closed behind them, the women heard Logan instruct Jas how he must behave. The child's squeak of agreement held pure sincerity.

Amy sighed and rested her head in her hands while Hana burped the baby over her shoulder. "I had the worst time with my parents," she said. Her shoulders slumped low and she fumbled for another tissue. "They've never met Jas. I thought visiting them would be an olive branch but I couldn't have been more wrong."

Hana patted the baby's back. "Jas said your mother didn't appreciate his leaking Action Man."

Amy released a sound like a low growl. "She didn't appreciate much about him or me. I won't bother again. We came home early. They liked my first husband and can't let go of what happened between us. I didn't intend to detonate my marriage and get pregnant by another man but I've paid the price. I lost everything and understand that's only fair. They punished me all over again when I thought we might reconcile."

Hana tipped her head to the side. "Perhaps don't write them off yet. Our children's choices can be difficult to swallow sometimes." Her mind strayed to Phoenix Du Rose and she wondered how she coped with Reuben's grenade in her family. Her retribution had been swift, but the ramifications still played out. "I miss my mum," she whispered. "If I could see her one more time, I'd just hug her and not try to explain my past decisions. But I guess the reality is different. We romanticise things and it never happens like in the movies." Her down-turned smile appeared sad. Amy's eyes glittered with unshed tears and misery shrouded her like a cape. Hana switched Phoenix to the other side and held her free arm out to Amy. "I don't have a mother, but it doesn't stop me being one."

When Amy slumped next to her on the sofa, Hana put her arm around the slender shoulders and felt the shuddering of her body. Wisdom advised Hana to say nothing and she gave Amy comfort, drawing some for herself from the uniqueness of female unanimity.

Phoenix farted with such force she frightened herself. Amy giggled as the baby jumped in a fear reaction and splayed her arms wide. When Hana stroked her cheek and gave her eye contact, Phoenix smiled a lopsided expression which matched her father's. "You're done little girl." Hana said. She glanced down at Logan's tee shirt and pulled a face. "Could you hold her for me, please? I can't go to St Bart's looking like this."

Amy took the baby, holding her at arm's length as though afraid. In the bedroom, Hana donned a pretty shirt and lightweight skirt, tidying her hair and fastening it back in a clip. Her wrist felt tight and painful and Hana peered at the bandage. The soreness seemed deeper as though even the bone had set up a protest. Hana pulled a sleeve over the mess and ignored it.

She paused at the end of the hallway to watch Amy with the baby. The younger woman gazed at the child with such longing, it rocked Hana. Her eyes contained a strange sadness as though she contemplated an unreachable goal. "Ready?" Hana asked softly.

"Yep." Amy got to her feet, masking her sadness with a wooden smile.

They walked to the dining room, Hana carrying Phoenix. She asked a question with extreme caution, not wishing to tread where she shouldn't. "What's the story with Jas? I can't work out if he's rebelling or just enjoys behaving like a cantankerous old man."

Amy laughed. "He's always been precocious but I can't cope with him at the moment. He won't take his damn school uniform off and he keeps telling everyone he's coming to our wedding as a bridesmaid. I've told him a hundred times he's a groomsman. It's embarrassing. Bodie says to ignore him, but Jas presses my buttons and I snap. It felt worse at my parents' place because I couldn't make a scene and he knew it. He exploited it to his advantage and made me look stupid. How can a five-year-old make an adult feel so dumb?" Amy kicked at a pebble on the ground in front of her, sending it skittering across the road towards the soccer field.

"What can we do to help?" Hana turned to face her and Amy halted.

"I don't know," she replied. "Nobody ever asked me that before."

Hana patted Phoenix on the back as the child peered over her shoulder. Her tiny head bounced. "You're not alone in this, Amy. We're family and I'm happy to support you. Bodie was fine until Izzie came along and then he turned into the proverbial monster child. I'm sure Jas can't pull much out of the hat I haven't already seen!"

They arrived at the boarding house as the bell clanged for dinner. Boys appeared from everywhere, charging to the dining room and queuing up outside the entrance. When Hana's nemesis pushed open the door and clipped it back, the queue appeared to lean back as one to give her room. A mass of bodies surged after her as she disappeared into the dining room. "Great," Hana breathed, her heart sinking at the prospect of another meal spent watching her letch over Logan.

Amy pointed along the corridor. "Oh, there they are." Logan stood in the mirrored office in the lobby and Jas perched in a swivel seat.

"The girls are here," Jas squealed, spotting them through the open door.

Logan looked up from the computer screen and pressed the keyboard to log out. "Come on then, whānau. School dinner awaits," he said with a smile.

Jas skipped along the corridor, his eyes wide with awe at the huge boys he passed. He clutched Logan's hand and stared at them with open curiosity. Amy raised her eyebrows at Hana and they shared a quiet laugh at his innocent wonder. Logan led them to the front of the queue and the boys stood back without question. Jas wasn't tall enough to see over the counter, so Logan hoisted him in his arms and pointed out the choices.

The kitchen supervisor materialised from the chiller and her eyes widened as she spotted Logan. She elbowed another server out of the way to get to him. Hana released an audible groan. Logan appeared immune to the girl's charms and gave her a polite nod before turning his attention to Jas. The girl beamed at him and leaned further over the counter. Her uniform shirt hung low enough to show her breasts bursting to escape. Silence rippled through the queued boys as they craned their necks to see better. Hana gripped her daughter and felt her heart rate rise.

"Bloody hell!" Amy hissed. "She's got it bad for your husband."

"I know." Hana's colour hiked and she sensed the boys' attention turn to her. They looked eager to gauge her reaction and start the gossip train rolling. "What can I do?"

Amy eyed Logan and then shook her head. "He doesn't look interested, Hana. I shouldn't worry."

Jas deliberated too long over his choice and Logan pointed to the queue behind them. "Choose quickly, mate, or I'll do it for you."

"He's gorgeous," the girl simpered and Hana gritted her teeth and cuddled Phoenix into her shoulder. "Is he yours?"

"No." Logan's face remained impassive and he raised an eyebrow at Jas. The child pouted and chose chicken pie with mashed potatoes. Logan praised him in a quiet voice and set him down on his feet. "Good man," he breathed.

The girl screwed her face up in appreciation of their adorability and Hana suppressed the angry growl threatening to burst from her throat. Logan picked up two plates of chicken pie and led Jas to a long table. Hana glanced at the menu over the warming cabinets and her brow furrowed in thought. Amy chose a salad dish with quiche and Hana's gaze fell on an item at the bottom of the list. "Cabbage curry please," she said to the girl.

The young woman paused with her spoon raised above a tray of mashed potato. Her eyes narrowed. "It's all gone," she replied, as though Hana might be intellectually challenged. Her attitude made Hana grateful she held the baby, otherwise the urge to insert the spoon somewhere inappropriate would have proved less manageable.

A large hand rested on her shoulder and she looked up to see Logan's eyes flash a coded warning. "The chicken pie tastes great," he said, his tone conversational. He turned to give the girl a warm smile and held his hand out for a plate. She delivered it, simpering and fluttering her eyelashes.

"Cabbage is great for breastfeeding," Amy said. She gave Hana a smile and turned to locate Jas.

They sat side by side along a table for twenty. The boys avoided them until the room filled, packing the adult free zones first. Except James.

"Miss, hello Miss," he said, hurling himself onto the bench next to Hana. He looked with longing at Phoenix balanced over her shoulder. "I take baby?" He held his arms out.

"I'll keep her until you finish eating," Hana replied. She gave him a warm smile which faltered when she noticed the fluffy turquoise slippers on his feet.

Jas sat between Amy and Logan, his curly head popping backwards to peer at James. As the dining hall filled, other boys gathered at the table. Jas stared at the boys with his mouth open, watching every move they made. Logan leaned forward to speak into his ear. "Get on with your dinner, mate. The next sitting starts in fifteen minutes."

"What's a sitting?" Jas' eyes were wide with wonder and pie crust dropped from the prongs of his fork without him noticing.

Logan leaned close again. "Boys from the prep room and those playing sports come to dinner later. We need to get out so they can have their kai."

Jas nodded and piled food into his mouth. He gave a massive swallow and choked. His next question appeared soon after. "What's a prep room?"

Logan bowed his head and Hana saw the care he took in his explanation of the boarding house homework routine.

James inhaled his food and held his arms out for Phoenix. "I take baby now."

Hana waited until he'd settled the child in the crook of his arm before using the opportunity to eat her food two-handed. She adjusted her sleeve to hide the bandage. Jas ate everything apart from his carrots and asked permission to move seats, so he could sit with Hana. Logan gave him a nod and continued his conversation with the prefect opposite. Jas ducked behind him and squirreled his way onto Hana's knee. He cuddled into her, watching James hold Phoenix over his shoulder. "How do you know what to do?" he demanded. "She's wiggly." Hana jerked in surprise, wondering why she'd never asked.

"I have much brother and sister in Korea," James stated. "My father die so mother work hard to feed children. We take care of each other." He smiled. "I miss family. It's expensive to go home for holiday, so I not see them long time."

Jas looked down and reached in the pocket of his shorts. He wiggled around, pulling out a ball of fluff, a paperclip and a golden coin. He held the dollar out to James. "You have it." He placed it in front of the older boy. "Now you can go home."

James looked at the five-year-old's earnest face. Hana held her breath, feeling tension in the moment as the boy fought not to decline the child's kindness and cause offence. James reached out and took the dollar carefully in his fingers. "Thank you, Logan-son," he said, effecting a regal bow. Jas smiled back, importance in his serious expression.

James looked up, acknowledging another boy with a sharp incline of his head in greeting. As Jas copied James' gesture, the teenager played a clever sleight of hand and dropped the coin onto Hana's plate. It made a slight clang as it landed. She put her fingers over it and slipped it into her pocket, having found out more about James in five minutes than in the previous five years. His joviality and desire to be the centre of attention was a carefully constructed front. The boy was lonely.

Jas screwed himself around to watch Logan. A group of younger boys in the far corner grew rowdy. One of them noticed Logan's raised eyebrow and a hush fell on them like an automatic volume control. The boys at Logan's table watched him with covert skill, deceptively in tune with every change in face expression. They appeared not to care, but the opposite proved true. They missed nothing. Jas pointed to the long scar beneath Logan's right eye and spoke to the teenager opposite him. "My poppa's like Action Man," he said. The table occupants sniggered and shot quick glances at each other. Irritated by their unbelief, Jas whipped Action Man from his hiding place in his shorts pocket. He narrowly avoided Hana's right eye with the doll's legs. The plastic limbs bent at jaunty angles, making him resemble a crazy gymnast.

"Jas, no!" Amy reached out and missed, lurching without precision. Jas pointed to a scar drawn onto his doll's face with gaudy penned stitches.

Logan stopped eating, his fork halfway to his mouth. He peered around Jas' shoulder at the doll. "Geez I'm ugly," he sighed.

The audience at the table stared at the doll with interest. And then it happened. Jas flipped Action Man the right way up and a trail of rancid, slimy liquid shot from his groin, landing in snotty blobs around the table. "Oh no, not again!" he cried, peering into the gaps between the legs, "I thought I cured him."

The hideous smell killed dinner with as much success as a ripe stink bomb. A Year 12 hovered over his plate in a standing position, trying to scoff the last bite of pie as his friends abandoned him.

"What is that?" Hana demanded, watching the white, jellified mess slip down Action Man's legs. Jas dangled him over her plate, ending any hope of finishing her dinner.

"It's glue!" He tipped the doll and more oozed free. "Flour and water like we make at school. I thought it might bung up his holes, but it didn't."

Amy apologised, looking as though she wished the ground would open up and swallow her. James rubbed the baby's back as Phoenix leaned over his shoulder and watched the unfocused shapes hurtle from the dining room. Her little eyebrows moved up and down like piano keys.

The snotty stuff covered Hana's skirt and Jas became distressed. He shook his doll and more stuff slid out. He began to sniff, signifying an approaching meltdown. Hana watched Amy tense her jaw.

"Keep it in, mate," Logan whispered. He shook his head in warning and Jas struggled to regain his composure with loud deep breathing. Hana's bandage glued itself to the table and she sighed in frustration.

James leaned sideways to get Jas' attention. "Wrap him in a napkin and I'll fix him."

"Oh," Jas whined, screwing his face into a pout. "But he doesn't know you. He might not want to go." He looked at the leaking toy in his hands and conflict radiated from the boy's body.

"Logan, my legs have gone to sleep," Hana hissed. A grimace accompanied her words. "We should leave."

Logan unwound his tall frame from the bench and disappeared, returning with a roll of industrial blue kitchen paper. He placed a few squares on the table and rolled the doll inside. Jas flapped and panicked until Logan made holes in the paper. "He can't breathe!" he insisted.

A vein twitched in Logan's neck, a warning of depleting patience. Hana unstuck herself from the table and grabbed Jas' hand. "Leave him with James," she said, asserting her authority. "He'll fix him." She pulled the child towards the door, leaving Logan to collect the baby from James. "I've no bloody idea how though," she whispered.

"No, Hanny, no!" Jas dug his heels in as Logan relieved James of the baby. He released Hana's hand to run back. He put one hand on the mummified doll and leaned in to whisper something to the teenager. James listened, bowing his head and closing his eyes. He looked like a benevolent king humouring a courtier. Jas nodded his fluffy dark head and threw his arms around James' neck. He returned to Hana and took her hand. "Just some last minute destructions," he explained.

His curly hair wobbled in the breeze from the doorway and his enormous brown eyes stared up at Hana. "You're adorable, but I'm not fooled for a second," she whispered. She smiled and looked back towards the serving hatch, her heart sinking in misery. The kitchen supervisor stared at Logan without shame and Hana's pie lurched in her stomach. She resigned herself to spending a lifetime watching other women throw themselves at her husband.

Jas yanked on her hand, his face filled with childish concern. "All right, Hanny?"

She wrapped her fingers around his slender fingers and nodded. "I'm fine, baby. Thanks for asking."

"Ready?" Logan raised his eyebrows, appearing oblivious to the lecherous glances from the girl behind the counter. She leaned sideways for a better view of his butt. Hana's green eyes blazed and Logan cocked his head with a frown. "What's up," he whispered. "You jealous, Mrs Du Rose?"

Hana inhaled and shook her head. As Logan's eyes narrowed, she saw another dimension to him. His situation awareness meant he knew exactly what the girl was after but ignored it. There wasn't much he missed in a crowd and she'd made the mistake of forgetting it. Hana pursed her lips not daring to lie further. She changed the shake to a nod at the last minute. Logan's lips parted in a smile and he pressed them over hers. "Then it's a good job I only want you, isn't it?" he whispered against her mouth. Phoenix squeaked between them and he released Hana.

They caught Amy up half way across the soccer field. "I'm so embarrassed!" she hissed, her face ashen. She chewed her lip and eyed her son like he was a feral bear. Producing a tissue, she gave another nose blow which carried far enough to make a distant group of boys turn to face her.

Hana pursed her lips. "It was an accident. And James promised to fix it."

Jas skipped along next to Hana, a small smile on his face and his eyes glassy. He recited something which sounded like a battle plan from the Second World War and Hana heard him mention Hitler a couple of times. Amy flapped her hand and lowered her voice. "I didn't know he stuffed it with glue. I can't keep track of him, he's too smart for me." Tears budded in her eyes. "No offence, Hana, but your son is useless as a role model. I asked him to speak to Jas about the whole bridesmaid thing and refusing to wear anything but his school uniform. He hasn't got around to it." She raised her index fingers and put air quotes around the end of her sentence to infer Bodie didn't want to. Hana tried not to cringe.

Swallowing, she glanced down at the dark curls bouncing next to her. "Go home with Logan," she said to Amy. "We're going for a little walk."

Amy's forehead creased and she hesitated. "You don't have to," she began.

Hana shook her head. "I made you a promise. Du Roses don't break promises." She saw Logan's head turn and watched as a smile broke across his face. He clicked his tongue to Phoenix to hide his eavesdropping and she gave a gummy grin.

Hana walked Jas across the soccer field to watch the group of boys training. When the ball rolled out to Jas, he kicked it back and then hid behind Hana. A tall boy collected it with a smile of thanks and ran to his teammates, passing it sideways with expert accuracy. Hana relaxed, reminding herself she was outside without Logan and Laval couldn't get to her. She let the sense of safety surround her and focussed on dampening the ready panic in her heart. The sensation of eyes boring into her from a distance no longer seemed real. "I can do this," she whispered. "I can stay here."

"What?" Jas watched the boys in fascination, still holding Hana's hand. When she didn't answer, he yanked it to get her attention. "I'd like to play soccer." He stood up on tiptoes and his gaze strayed towards the boys' expensive boots. Each wore a different fluro colour. "In shoes like that."

"You could play it here," Hana replied. She watched one boy nutmeg another and dash away with the ball. He shot at goal but missed. Jas tensed enough for Hana to dart a covert look.

"It's spensive," he answered. "I'd like to, but Mummy and Daddy won't ford it."

Hana frowned. "You're five, Jas. It's not your job to worry about money." She changed the subject. "Are you excited about Mum and Dad's wedding?"

"Not really." Jas scuffed at the dirt with his sandal. "I like Mummy by myself and Daddy by myself, but I don't like us all together."

"Oh, that's a shame." Hana couldn't think of a suitable retort. She left the statement hanging.

"Yeah," Jas continued. Sadness crept into his voice. "Mummy was screaming about dollars yesterday and Dad said he couldn't help it. Mummy wants a party like you and Poppa Logan's wedding but Daddy wants a church and a party. And Mummy doesn't want to live at our house no more and Daddy does." His concerned face tilted upwards at Hana. "What will happen to me? Where will I go?"

Her heart clenched. "Oh, Jas," she sighed. She pulled his curly head against her hip and cuddled him close. The soccer team ran around the field at a steady pace, their coach calling instructions from a distance. Hana chose her words before bending down to the child's level. "Jas, whatever happens in your life and I'm praying it'll be good things, you'll always have me, Poppa and Phoenix. Do you understand?"

He nodded, leaning into her and wrapping his thin arms around her neck. She knew it was a promise she couldn't keep. Too many things stacked up against her as Jas swallowed the lie. Hana thought about the promises Vik made to her children and how death broke them for him. She cringed at how she almost didn't return to her own child and hoped God would help her keep her pact with the little boy. She kissed the side of his face and rose. "Why do you insist on being a bridesmaid?"

Jas splayed his hands in front of him as though giving a lecture. "My friend, Jacinder has a dress from last year. She said I can borrow hers. Less dollars for Mum to worry over." He shrugged as though he didn't care about turning up to his parents' wedding in girly clothes. Hana saw through the act in the twist of his puckered lips.

"Okay." She left it, not wanting to burst his facade wider open. But something else bothered her. "Why won't you take your school uniform off?" she asked.

Jas looked around him before revealing his big secret. He made sure the soccer boys were at the other end of the pitch. Cheers drifted back to them as a goal scorer celebrated. Jas lifted his polo shirt and revealed the waistband of his shorts. Threads dangled loose and the lining stuck out between the band and the shorts to display the elastic of his underpants. Reaching into his pockets, he almost detached the left one. "I'm a bit hard on my clothes," he said with regret. "I've stopped playing tag rugby with the big boys now, but it's too late. They pulled my clothes instead of the tags. Mum's gonna kill me because she can't ford new shorts. So if I wear my uniform all the time, she can't see what I did to my pants."

Hana sighed. She swallowed. "I'm sure Mum would understand," she said. She squeezed his hand.

"Nuh uh!" Jas snorted. "She'll go mental. Dad sets her off when he says dumb things." He sighed. "I wish sometimes he didn't come back." His brow furrowed. "But I love him. It's all mixed up in my head." He tapped his temple and Hana forced herself to maintain an even expression. The best she could do was mend what she could of the little boy's life, one knotty issue at a time.

They walked back to the staff unit and heard Phoenix wailing from outside the front door. Logan let them in and raised an eyebrow at Hana. "Tell you later," she whispered. She hefted the squalling infant over her shoulder and pleaded for a cup of tea. "Come sit with me in the bedroom for a while, Jas," she said, giving him a sweet smile. "We can finish our conversation." She widened her eyes at him, grateful when he took the hint without debate.

She fed Phoenix and under the pretence of Jas reading a story from his library bag, she darned his shorts. The baby snoozed across her legs.

"That's not bad, Hanny!" Jas' voice rose at the end of his sentence in surprise, "Them's real neat now!" He sat cross-legged on her bed in his briefs and Hana flapped the finished shorts at him. Logan brought a mug of tea and laid it on the bedside table nearest Hana. He noticed the sewing kit spewed over the bedspread but said nothing. He closed the door behind him.

"Please let Mum wash these tonight, Jas. They stink! Don't be that poor smelly kid everyone feels sorry for." Hana frowned.

He smiled and pointed to her stained skirt. "You got sticky on you. You stink."

Hana picked at a crusty piece of glue, frowning as it crumbled beneath her fingernail. She lifted Phoenix over her shoulder, gratified when the baby burped without fuss. "Can I make a suggestion?" she asked.

Jas cocked his head and considered her for a moment. Then he nodded. "You may."

"Perhaps you and I could go shopping for a smart groomsman's outfit one day. Would you like that?"

Jas' eyes widened like saucers. "Are you rich, Hanny?"

She shook her head. "No darling," she whispered. "But I could raise enough for a suit. It'll need to be an off the peg one. What do you think?"

Jas pondered for a long while, his brain ticking and his fingers smoothing the pages of his unread book. "What's off the peg?" he asked.

Hana wrinkled her nose. "I can't afford someone to measure you and make something special. We have to get something from a store."

Jas blinked. "Not like Poppa Logan then? Jacinder's mother says he'd look hot in a dustbin bag."

Hana gritted her teeth. "No, not like Poppa Logan's suits. They're Italian. But we won't get something which looks daft."

"Daft." Jas tasted the word and grinned. "Daft. No, I don't wanna look daft. I'd like a peg suit, please. I didn't really wanna go as a bridesmaid."

Hana relaxed. "I didn't think you did." She settled Phoenix under her tee shirt to feed her from the other breast. She clicked her fingers at Jas' face as he tried to lift the shirt to peek. "Not your business, Mr Nosy," she said.

Jas stood up to wriggle into his shorts. The mattress tipped around him. "I'll need to pay you back for the peg suit." Hana began to protest but as she opened her mouth, Logan stepped into the room. He pulled his phone from his back pocket and plugged it into the charger. Jas turned towards him. "I should pay Hanny back, aye?"

Logan stood up straight and stretched his arms above his head. His fingers stroked the ceiling and his shirt rose to display tight abdominal muscles and a line of dark hair which disappeared into his waistband. "Yep," he replied. "Always."

"But you don't know what for." Hana's brow knitted in irritation and she saw a shadow cross Logan's face.

He shook his head. "It doesn't matter. You always pay your debts."

"But he has no money or any way of getting some." Her eyes flashed and Logan faltered, understanding what she didn't say. He gritted his teeth knowing without a doubt Bodie had stolen from her during his rebellious teenage years. He read the pain in her eyes. She didn't want to put Jas in a position where he became tempted to use theft to solve a debt problem.

"Let him pay you back in jobs." He placed a hand on the top of Jas' head and kept it there. "Agree a fee and keep an account. It's still paying a debt." He threw a smile at Hana over his shoulder and opened the door. "Amy left to grab some cold medication. She'll be back soon and then she wants to get Jas home."

They spent the next half an hour ironing out which jobs might qualify as payment. Jas had grand ideas of chauffeuring for Hana and his fingers twitched around an imagined steering wheel. She brought his grandiose plans back down to earth, making him understand that emptying the dishwasher or other small chores would suffice. "But how will you know when it's paid off?" Jas' earnest face leaned closer. "How will I know when it's paid? You could work me until I'm an old man." He slapped a hand to his forehead and his eyes widened. "I could die from exhaustion."

Hana fought tiredness. The child made life more complicated by the minute. As soon as she solved one problem, he invented another. Hana laid Phoenix on the bed for a moment and searched in her dresser drawer for a small notebook. She found it, added a pen and filled in the first page with date, cost and job columns. "Logan said to keep a log. This is a log." She dropped it in front of him. "Each job pays off fifty cents."

Hana ran a bath for Phoenix and held her wiggling body in the shallow water. The baby kicked her legs with glee and her fists pumped in a rhythmic motion. Hana heard Logan and Amy chatting in the lounge, the steady hum of her husband's voice inducing a feeling of safety. A splash made her shift to the side and Jas sent a spindly leg over the edge of the bath. Stripped naked, he plopped into the water at the plug end. He lathered up his hands with soap. "I'm in charge of washing," he insisted. He dabbed a finger under each armpit and wrinkled his nose at Phoenix's rounded stomach. She blew a bubble from her rosebud lips and Jas recoiled. "That's enough," he declared. "She's clean."

Hana shook her head and took over the washing. Jas laid flat so his chin touched the watery surface and wriggled his toes in front of Phoenix. Her eyes flashed and she made noises of amusement. Her thrashing made Hana nervous and she lifted her out and folded her into a towel. Jas floated around on his stomach, sending up occasional splashes which soaked the bathmat. "Careful," Hana advised, putting the toilet seat down and perching on it.

"I'm careful." Jas performed a barrel roll and put his face under the water. He came up spluttering and pursed his lips, refusing to catch Hana's eye.

Back in Hana's bedroom, Jas snuggled into his towel and seized the notebook and pen. He scribbled something on the first page.

"What are you doing?" Hana stuffed Phoenix's feet into her sleep suit and lunged for the book.

"I washed the baby in the baff." Jas made an illegible scrawl. "That's fifty cents."

"Rip off!" Hana muttered. She fastened the buttons on the sleep suit. "I know whose son you are."

Chapter 36

"I'd like to go to church." Hana leaned her head against Logan's chest and listened to his steady heartbeat. "I haven't been for a while and I miss it."

Logan kissed the top of her head. "Just stay here with me in bed," he replied, sounding sleepy. "I love having my wife in my arms and my daughter in the next room." He stopped his brain straying towards what might have been and squeezed Hana tighter. When she wriggled against him, he clasped her around the waist. "I'll drop you up there," he promised. "Just five more minutes."

Hana shook her head. "I'll drive myself."

"Not after wrist surgery." His tone discouraged argument. "While you're in church, I'll call at the Gordonton House and sort out the last of my stuff. Now Pete's gone, Angus wants to rent it to someone else. I still have my old Spitfire in the garage."

"You won't come to church with me?" Hana sat up and watched the discomfort drift across his expression like a rain cloud. Logan grabbed at his throat and mimicked a lightning strike. Hana shook her head. He'd dipped in and out over the last few months, drawn to Pastor Allen but intimidated by the older women. He found them intrusive, misunderstanding their caring for prying.

Logan drove to the church in Horsham Downs before the ten o'clock service. Oadby Church sat in the middle of nowhere. Surrounded by green paddocks, it boasted an awesome view of Mount Pirongia. He helped her lift the car seat out of the back and her bandage caught his eye. "Geez, Hana!" He winced and jabbed a finger at it. Hana cringed and pulled her sleeve lower.

"It's fine." She spoke through gritted teeth and refused to look at him.

"Fine my ass," he muttered.

Hana pursed her lips and hefted the car seat with her good hand. "You have a very fine ass, Mr Du Rose," she retorted, slinging him a look of defiance over her shoulder.

"I'm serious, Hana," he called after her. "We're getting it looked at." His voice carried and he saw the instant it reached her ears in the stiffening of her spine. She shoved her phone into her jacket pocket and grappled with the car seat, change bag and bible. Logan watched as she lumbered over to the arched front doors, greeting people on the way with false bravado and a wooden smile.

Logan leaned against the car and watched the congregation file in. He unwrapped a stick of chewing gum and folded it into his mouth. He'd always thought Christians were a strange bunch. They faked an illusion of a loving family but if anyone slipped up and fell from grace, they turned like a pack of feral dogs. Logan folded his arms and leaned his head back to enjoy the warm sun on his face. "At least with the Triads I know what I'm getting," he murmured.

"And what is that?" The car bumped as Pastor Allen joined him leaning against it.

Logan jumped and turned to shake the pastor's hand. "Honesty," he answered.

"If you say so, my friend." The sound of an organ rent the air and Allen cringed. "Ah, Mrs Brown is on the organ this morning. Tone deaf but a willing heart. Sure you don't want to come in for a bit of screamo?"

Logan shook his head. "No, thanks. I'm too busy for the proverbial lightning bolt. No time for a headache."

Allen laughed. "You and me both, mate. None of us is spotless."

Logan looked sideways at the pastor and his eyes narrowed. "You are. You have to be. It's part of the job description for a do-gooder."

Allen raised an eyebrow. "Then I should recheck my CV. I shouted at my wife this morning because she made a small error of judgment through pure exhaustion. I was tempted to drop my eight-month-old baby from a second-storey window at midnight because teething kept him crying the last two nights. Issues of lust assail me every time I drive past the mall and see poster girls advertising bras and knickers. The sin of overindulgence got me yesterday at the MacDonald's drive through when I went around twice for another sundae. It's tempting to fiddle my tax return each year because I tell myself nobody would notice and halfway through this morning's service, I will fight the temptation to slam the organ lid on the lovely Mrs Brown's fingers just so she can't play the final hymn in G Major."

"Oh." Logan wrinkled his nose. "It's been nice knowing ya. There's a lightning bolt with your name on it." He looked up at the blue sky soaring overhead. Not a single cloud marred its azure beauty. "You might be lucky today though."

"I'm human, Logan." Allen squeezed his shoulder. "Just like you and the other faulty souls who just walked through that door. If there was a God throwing lightning bolts today, our little church would be toast before lunchtime."

Logan looked into the distance at Pirongia. A dusting of snow speckled its highest peaks. It felt like a fantastic day to gallop Sacha across the crests and valleys of home. "I'm still not coming in." He shifted his feet and ignored Allen's snort of laughter.

"That's fine, my friend." He slapped Logan's shoulder. "It can't be me who makes you." He stuffed his hands into his pockets and sauntered across the rough car park towards the front doors. A blast of music hailed him as a cat died somewhere in the organ pipes. Logan watched, chewing his gum and feeling isolated from this part of Hana's life. Allen wore nothing to indicate his clerical status. His ordinary shirt and smart black jeans disappeared through the doors.

Logan remembered the Catholic priests his mother dragged him to see as a small boy. Swathed in black cloth, they resembled forbidding blackbirds uttering words he couldn't understand. Their churches held no love or compassion for him. Miriam sought healing for his haemophilia alongside her own absolution. She wanted someone to tell her that loving Reuben would be okay and birthing his illegitimate child acceptable. Nobody could tell her that.

Hana talked about the Father heart of God, but Logan couldn't comprehend it. His own experience of fathers worsened with each nasty revelation. Alfred had dropped any pretence at fatherhood and Reuben was gone. Orphaned at forty one. Logan felt it like a physical ache, shrugging off the pain when it threatened. The first hymn ended, the music grinding to a screeching halt before the singing trailed away. Logan had a vision of his guitar teacher and the motel room where they met. Large, scarred hands pointed to the strings and a gentle baritone corrected Logan's wrong notes. The guitar seemed huge at first, shrinking as his body grew to fit. He heard Reuben's voice in his head and the words held more meaning with hindsight. "Not quite right, tamāroa. Stretch your fingers further, then the note will sound clearer. The greater the challenge tāne, the stronger your sense of achievement." They'd sung together, Māori songs from their combined heritage, tikanga and kawa.

Logan looked at his hands, recognising the similarities. A strange, empty ache spread across his heart. Tamāroa meant first-born son and the one to whom a father passed his knowledge and mana. Logan breathed out a ragged exhale. No wonder Kane hated him. He squatted on the ground next to the car and fought a wave of nausea. It bubbled up from his feet and threatened to overwhelm him. The emotional cavern yawned in his chest and he fought against the filth inside, running interference and knowing it must never escape. He forced himself to his feet and climbed into the Honda, pushing down fear, regret and loss as he pulled out of the car park.

Church helped Hana. It plugged her into something bigger than her own problems. Phoenix stayed asleep for most of the service, cheerful when she woke. As soon as her eyes opened, the older ladies fought over her and she bounced around the congregation. The songs sounded safe and familiar but Pastor Allen's preach rattled her.

"We choose to be offended," he said. "It's a choice we make about how we want to live. It's easier to react to a hurtful comment with defence or aggression and harder to let it pass us by. I struggle with this issue too. It's a gut instinct to defend myself and I do it all the time. It's centred in my need to make everything about me. I choose to get nasty in response to an offhand comment, instead of acknowledging they're having a bad day, bad year or bad life. Maybe they didn't mean to say, 'Hey Pastor Allen, your preach today sucked.'" The congregation sniggered at the analogy but stopped on cue. "Why do I take offence? Because it feels great to be justifiably angry. I can keep my grievance going for years, telling anyone who'll listen and sympathise. Where's the mileage in letting something go? Where's the fun? What am I gonna complain about if I let that opportunity pass?"

Hana's mind wandered. She began with the names of people who'd offended her but ran out of fingers. She switched to thinking of those she'd upset over the years. It formed a frighteningly long list. She thought about Peter North and Amanda, convicted by Allen's words.

She'd dismissed two friendships just because she could. It seemed so much easier than apologising.

"Un-forgiveness," continued Pastor Allen, "is the cup of poison we pour for another and drink ourselves."

Hana chided herself as they sang the final hymn. The organ struggled valiantly with the timbre of the notes and at the high points, the whole thing shook on the wall. The elderly organist hammered away below its elegant brass tubes. Pastor Allen used a wooden smile to cover his grimace.

Hana made small talk after the service but crept away to a quiet corner to feed Phoenix when a lull in conversation allowed. Allen sat in his office checking emails and nodded to her as she plonked herself on his sofa. He waited for her to speak and when the silence continued, he looked up from his computer. "What is it, Hana? I'm sure there're lots of places you could feed your baby around the building without causing heart attacks among our oldies. Are we going to talk about something interesting or can I get my lunch?"

Hana narrowed her eyes at his mischievous smirk. "You're an infuriating man."

"Not taking the bait I see." He smirked. "I hoped you'd stomp off and then I could lecture you about taking offence after my wonderful preach."

Hana snorted. "Like I'd fall for that gag." She lifted the baby to burp her.

"What is it, Hana?" Allen indicated the oozing bandage at her wrist. "I can see you've been in the wars again."

"It's a really long story," Hana sighed. "I'm not sure I have the energy to tell it."

Allen's lips quirked into a grin and he rose and dragged his car keys from his pocket. "Would a fine Sunday lunch give you enough to get you through?" he asked.

Logan clattered around the garage of the empty house. His fingers coasted across the dusty chassis of his Triumph Spitfire and he pursed his lips at the prospect of selling it. He glanced at his watch and noticed the time, panicking as he rang Hana's phone. The call dropped before connecting and he swore, cursing the limited cell coverage out in the rural black spot. He locked up and slammed the rear door of the Honda. Dustbin bags crammed into the space, filled with items he no longer wanted and a number containing Pete's abandoned gear.

Flooring the gas pedal, Logan bumped the truck over the rutted driveway until he reached the main road. As soon as he turned onto Thomas Road, his phone signal boosted to two bars and he dialled Hana's number.

She answered and he heard a cacophony of sound in the background. A baby wailed and a television blasted, forcing Hana to step outside. A door closed and muffled the noise. "I'm fine. Sorry, I tried to call you but remembered how bad the signal was out there. I'm at Pastor Allen's. He said you should come over." She sounded brighter and dismissed his apologies.

"I feel bad." Logan swallowed and made the turn towards Allen's house in Rototuna. "Bloody Pete left a right mess. I've got the trunk stuffed full of his crap. I'll drop it all at the city dump tomorrow."

"It's fine." Hana sounded like she meant it. "See you soon."

Allen's house was in chaos. His two teenage stepsons fought a virtual battle on a games console and kept bumping into each other. As Logan removed his boots, he saw Hana wielding a third remote control. A smaller boy played in the centre of the action with a pile of Lego and a boy-baby slumped in a high chair, almost asleep in his lunch.

Phoenix snoozed by the partly open ranch slider in her car seat, oblivious to the testosterone laden atmosphere.

"Drink?" Allen closed the front door on the quiet suburb. "I won't offer you a beer. My wife's still grumpy after our last bender!"

Logan smiled and had the decency to look guilty. "Yeah, heck of a night, wasn't it? I don't usually drink, but you kept them coming."

"Next time you think Hana's broken up with you, go somewhere else." Allen frowned and nudged Logan's shoulder with his.

Logan opted for coffee and leaned against the counter as his host spooned instant caffeine into a mug. "How are you?" Allen turned to eyeball Logan. "And before you give me a load of bullshit, be aware your wife told me the whole story."

"Which story?" Logan watched Allen's wife push mushy stuff between the baby's lips. He pushed it back out again and it landed on the tray of the high chair.

"How many stories are there?" Allen smiled, shutting the fridge with his foot and handing Logan the coffee. Logan took it, nodding a thank you. He refused to get drawn into a contentious conversation, knowing Hana would never betray his emotional agonies. She couldn't. She didn't know half of them.

"I'm good," Logan lied. Allen narrowed his eyes but didn't probe further.

"Hana needs that wrist looking at," he offered. "Sue was a nurse but Hana refused to let her see."

Logan nodded. "I'm sorting it." He sipped his drink, knowing before it touched his lips it was too hot. "Please don't tip her off, though. She's gonna go nuts."

"We had a little chat," Allen said. "She's carrying lots of guilt, but you know that, don't you?"

"Yeah." Logan sipped his drink, his chest tightening as the thing inside him shifted. "She's not the only one."

Allen's littlest boy wandered into the kitchen carrying a Lego man. In the lounge, his brothers stumbled over his buildings in their efforts to beat Hana at the car racing game. "I can't get him to stay on, Daddy," the child said, handing over the man and a brick. Allen fiddled around while the boy watched his brothers trip over his creation. "They're gonna break it, Daddy!"

"Boys!" Allen called. "Watch your feet, please!"

"Does it matter," Logan stammered, picking his words with care. He eyed the child, not wanting to break a confidence. Allen's fingers stilled and he stared at him. "I mean when they have different genetics?"

The Lego-man clicked onto the brick and the tousled haired child grabbed it with eager fingers. Allen stood up straight, the perception in his eyes making Logan squirm. "Sometimes yes," he said. "But mainly no."

Logan thought of Alfred, hiding his guitar to prevent the only contact with Reuben he would ever know. He swallowed. "Would you stop your older boys seeing their father?"

Allen read Logan's desperation in his eyes. He watched his youngest stepchild move out of earshot.

Logan waved his hand and coffee slopped over the side of the mug. "Hey, don't answer that. It's personal, I shouldn't be asking."

"It's fine, you can ask me anything. And their father isn't in a position to make demands yet." Allen sighed and ran a hand across his chin. "It would cause me terrible conflict. Brad is the youngest and doesn't remember his father. He calls me 'Daddy' and I let him. But I'd have to deal with it, for their sake. One day he might want contact and I don't have the right to deny him."

"Where is their father?" Logan resented his own question, but the awful ache drove him to find answers.

"In prison." Allen folded his arms. "Sue and I married when the boys were young. Brad was one. Now we have Noah too. I think of them as my boys."

Logan's hand shook as he peered into the mug of coffee. "My father lived next door and I never knew. Not until after his death. Nobody told me."

"Ah." Allen's blue eyes reflected understanding. "And you're trying to work out who to hate."

Logan's head shot up. "What?"

"It's natural to look for someone to blame. I would." Allen smiled with encouragement.

"Maybe I am." Logan's brow furrowed. "But my mother died in the fire with him and the man who brought me up can't look me in the eye. There's nobody left to blame. I could shout and scream, but no one is listening." He put his mug on the counter, the coffee unfinished. "I should wait in the car," he said. He took a step towards the hall.

"Now this one's stuck!" Bradley wailed, storming into the kitchen. He handed his dilemma to Allen and waited for him to extract the female Lego person from the yellow brick. He gave it back, but the child looked up at Logan. "Do you have the Lord Jesus in your heart?"

"Pardon?" Logan sent a panicked look towards Allen, for once at a loss. Allen smirked, but his wife gave a sharp intake of breath and stopped pushing food into the baby.

"Do ya then?" the child persisted, posturing with his hands on his hips. "Do ya know Jesus?"

"Maybe." Logan hedged, hoping the child would go back to his bricks. He looked to Allen for assistance and got nothing. "I know he exists," he said, his agitation growing. He counted the steps from the kitchen to his boots and from them to the door.

"How?"

"Because he helped me out recently." Logan cringed, wondering how a six-year-old could put him under more pressure than a Triad.

"That's cool!" The child turned on his heel and strode away, "Just making sure," he called over his shoulder.

Logan glared at Allen, who spread his arms in a gesture of innocence. "Brad's our little evangelist," he said with a laugh. "He seeks out secret believers."

"Yeah, whatever!" Logan replied. Anger budded in his heart and he needed to leave before it escaped.

He peeled Hana away from the video game, surprised by how much she enjoyed thrashing the teenagers. "But I'm winning!" she complained.

Allen fastened the belt around the car seat as Logan wiped his sleeping daughter's mouth. The pastor leaned forward as they shook hands. "Blame and hate are overrated, my friend. They deliberately draw us backwards and never let go. You've too much to get on with here." He waved a hand at the car containing Logan's most precious possessions. "For now, concentrate on enjoying what you have and leave other people to atone for their poor decisions. We will all need to one day, Logan."

Hana became quiet on the way into town and Logan attempted to distract her. "I taught Allen's eldest boy last year. Neat kid. Did the younger boy not want to go to our school?"

"It's expensive." Hana picked at a loose thread on the bandage. "Angus gave Roderick a scholarship to play rugby, but Ben's good at art and there's never any funding for that."

Hana's mood worsened as Logan pulled into the driveway of a house in Hamilton East. "Who lives here?" she asked. Her brow creased. "I'm tired, Logan. Will you take long?"

"Nobody lives here." He climbed from the vehicle and reached in for Phoenix. "And we're all going in."

Hana shrank back into her seat. "I don't feel ready to meet new people." Her right hand gripped her painful wrist as a reflex action. "Don't make me."

"Out." Logan held the handle of the car seat and hauled her door open. "Now." The warning vein ticked in his neck and Hana scrabbled to get away from his outstretched hand.

"No!" she exclaimed, refusing to undo her seatbelt. "You can't make me."

Logan's anger made his eyes flash like storm water. "Can and will." He reached in and hooked strong fingers around her elbow. "Do I have to put you over my shoulder?"

"You wouldn't dare!" Hana's jaw dropped open. Her eyes widened at the sight of a woman waiting under a covered porch. Logan's fingers twitched and she drew back, the fire in his eyes warning he meant to see it through. An image flashed through her mind of her over Logan's shoulder with her underwear on show to the residents of Hamilton East.

"Get out, Hana." Logan's voice lowered to a growl and her heart rate hiked. She blew out through pursed lips and fought to breathe. Logan paused and licked his lips.

He motioned over the roof of the truck and the woman stepped off the porch.

Hana cringed against the seat as she appeared in the doorway. But the woman lifted the car seat into her arms and turned away. "No!" Hana squeaked. She shot Logan a look of accusation and followed, clicking the seatbelt and almost falling out in her haste. His eyes narrowed and he took her elbow, slamming the car door behind her. She stole a covert look back and he smirked before activating the central locking.

Hana baulked in the reception of a small private clinic. She turned to run and met Logan's rock-hard chest. He placed a firm hand on the top of her head and turned her to face an open doorway ahead of him. "In!" he growled.

Hana sulked like a teenager as the woman unwrapped her wrist in a sterile looking surgery. A finger clad in a surgical glove poked at the soggy mess unmasked beneath the bandage. "I think it needs re-suturing." She glanced up at Logan.

Hana's heart sank. "Please, no!" she begged, snatching her hand back. "This is why I didn't want to come." She glared at Logan.

He ignored her protests, rocking the car seat with the toe of his boot and folding his arms. The woman glanced up at him and gave him a smile. "Dan should look at this," she said. "I'll get him."

"See what you did?" Hana's eyes filled with tears. "I don't want to talk about it! They'll want to know how it happened and I'll have to tell them! I don't want to talk about it!" Raised veins stood out in her neck and her cheeks flushed.

"Is that what this is about?" Logan gave a nod and walked towards the door. He jabbed a finger at Hana. "Stay right there. If you run, I will find you and drag you back. Do you understand?" Hana pursed her lips and nodded. Logan glanced towards the right arm hidden behind her back and his eyes narrowed. "I mean it, Hana." He disappeared, closing the door behind him.

With a murmured curse, Hana uncrossed her fingers. Her eyes shot towards the window and she imagined herself clambering out through the narrow aperture. "Ohhhh!" The groan left her lips and she realised how irrational her behaviour must appear. Within seconds, the door opened and a small man walked in, a stethoscope hooked around his neck. His grey hair stuck up on end and he smiled at Hana. "I didn't expect to meet the famous Mrs Du Rose under such circumstances," he said. His eyes tracked to Logan and back to her.

Logan's eyes narrowed. "You weren't meant to meet her at all," he growled.

The man smirked. "Am I allowed to tell her my name, or is that not allowed either?"

Logan sighed. "Don't push it, Dan."

"Oops." The man bit his lip and winked at Hana. He lifted her wrist in gentle fingers and peered at it with a frown. "Don't worry, I'm a qualified doctor," he said, ignoring Logan's grunt of warning. "I've patched up your husband a few times." He waggled his eyebrows.

"Dan!" Logan's eyes flashed and the man laughed. He tested Hana's fingers, bending each of them in turn.

"Some slight nerve damage," he muttered. He glanced up at her and sparkling blue eyes glinted from behind hooded eyelids. "It's infected for sure. Did your surgeon prescribe antibiotics before discharging you?"

Hana swallowed. "I took whatever they gave me."

The doctor twisted his lips into a grimace and wrinkled his nose. "I'll give you some more. I could take swabs, but they'll need to go to the laboratory." He glanced across at Logan. "Do you want that?"

"I'm not a doctor," Logan replied. He folded his arms across his chest. "Do what you think."

The man shrugged. "You're the boss." He sighed. "I'll take swabs and get them analysed. In the meantime I'll give you more antibiotics. What's this yellow stuff?" He touched the mess with a gloved finger.

"Manuka honey." Hana pursed her lips, hearing her heart pound in her ears.

"Smart. Natural antibiotic and antiseptic." The doctor smiled. He turned his body to block Logan from view, demanding Hana's full attention. "If this doesn't work, you must go back to see your surgeon. It'll need to be reopened and washed out under general anaesthetic. I think there's still glass in there." He turned her tender wrist over again and bent it backwards on the joint to expose the tight stitches.

"Ouch!" she gasped and pulled away. The doctor eyed Logan's serious expression.

"Because it involved an opened vein, there's a strong risk of blood poisoning. You look healthy enough so I don't think that's a factor right now." He narrowed his eyes at Hana and held onto her hand. His head jerked towards the car seat and Hana's daughter. "You're the first mate of this ship. If you're not on deck, what happens to those who rely on you?" His eyebrows waggled again and he gave Logan the side-eye. "Besides, if I let you die now that I've examined you, your husband will kill me and ensure nobody finds the body. Isn't that right, Logan?"

Logan twisted his lips and his folded arms bulged. Hana blanched, focussing on her daughter's reliance on her. She hadn't realised Phoenix even cared who fed her, but recent events showed she did. She cared very much. The fear of separation haunted Hana like a ghoul, making her ache for all her children. She pushed it out of her mind but it swirled back like flood waters, the guilt of leaving them. She nodded. "I know. Believe me, I know."

The woman bustled around with items on a trolley, handing the doctor whatever he requested. He sluiced the wound over a plastic tray with saline, then he inspected the stitches. "I don't want to mess with this." He cocked his head. "For now, hit it with the antibiotics and keep it clean and dry. Leave it open and see if it dries out. If it carries on weeping, you must see your surgeon."

Hana nodded without looking at the spiteful gash or stringy brown stitches sticking out at odd angles. Surgery had widened the opening and the scar stretched over ten centimetres to end at the heel of her hand. She knew what it looked like. She'd seen a similar thing on a boy who tried to slash his own wrists. Hana withdrew her arm from the doctor's grasp and turned her hand palm down, out of sight. Thoughts of Laval rose without warning, seeing his tortured face as he spoke of Logan's friendship and the malevolent stare he reserved until the end. Bodie told her she must prepare herself for the court case, mentally and emotionally. Laval's plans for killing her were feral, but nobody would elaborate. Logan promised there were good reasons for Liza cutting herself off from Laval and Hana possessed no evidence to the contrary. She stared at the doctor without seeing him.

"Mrs Du Rose?" The doctor's voice cut through her thoughts, making her jump. She dragged herself back to the present and nodded in the right places, earning herself a smile and a pat on the hand. When she stood up, trying to regain some semblance of control in her life, everyone seemed surprised. Logan looked at her long and hard, assessing and summing her up like he did when he didn't understand her. Feeling like a bug under a microscope, Hana decided she'd had enough.

"Thanks then," she said. Picking the car seat up with her right hand, she pushed her way through the bodies and focused hard on the exit door. The balmy fresh air hit her, encasing her in the comfort of summer. Logan met her by the Honda, waving a piece of paper.

"You didn't wait for him to print off the prescription," he snapped. "You agreed to counselling and then walked out."

"Counselling? I didn't!" Hana's eyes widened in confusion. "Please can we just go?"

"No!" Logan shoved the prescription into his pocket. He took the car seat and held onto her hand. "I need coffee!"

Logan drove into town and found an open cafe. He settled Hana at a table and ordered drinks. "Stay there!" he ordered. "I'm taking this prescription to the pharmacy next door. Move and there will be trouble!"

"I'm fine!" Hana pulled an irritated face. "Stop looking at me like I'm about to flip my lid."

Logan grunted and disappeared next door, arriving back with the antibiotics before the coffee came. He leaned forward in his chair with his elbows on the table, rocking the car seat with the toe of his boot. Hana relented as he twirled his wedding ring, reaching out with her right hand and winding her fingers through his. "I'm not happy in this town anymore," she said, looking around at the other customers. "Not happy and definitely not safe. He ruined it for me."

"I know." Logan's eyelashes fluttered. "Thinking it was over after last year made it worse for you. You had to start hiding again."

Hana nodded, hearing understanding in his voice. Logan gritted his teeth and struggled to form his next sentence. "Hana, I need you to know I liked Michel L'Huillier at school. He was an awesome soccer player and my best friend. It went wrong when his father came looking for him. Michel changed. The marriage thing with Liza was a huge mistake for her and she realised too late. I had to go with her to pick up her stuff because Michel terrified her. Because of him, she'll never trust another man to get close to her again. Not ever."

He gripped Hana's fingers in his, twisting and turning their entwined hands. "We will get through this," he promised. "Let me take care of you. Trust me."

Chapter 37

They walked around Hamilton Gardens, Phoenix asleep in the sling with her face pushed against Logan's broad chest. The warm day brought out the tourists and Hana connected with the English accents around her. She showed Logan the haunts where she took her older children and the bank they sat on each year to watch 'Shakespeare in the Park.' Logan talked about the hotel and the section where Reuben's old house used to stand. "What do you think we should do with it?" he asked. "I think the tapu should stay."

"You want it to remain sacred?" Hana reached for his hand. "Then what about a memorial garden?"

Logan wrinkled his nose. "I've still got Ma's rose garden. But Reuben's place was so high up the mountain, it might be too hard to nurture new plants without running water. The fire destroyed the tanks."

"Why don't we build a maze?" Hana twirled a camellia bud in her fingers. "They filled their whole lives with such confusion, why don't we represent it with the design? Find some hedging that won't require fussing over."

Logan shielded Phoenix from the sun and cocked his head. "Yeah, I like it." His eyes brightened. "You have all the best ideas."

"What about Alfred though?" Hana asked. "We don't want to offend him. He might hate it."

"I don't care." Logan's tone sounded harsh. "You stopped him leaving, Hana. Not me." He set off through the regal Indian garden and Hana struggled to keep up. She caught his hand, a ragged catch in her voice.

"Logan, please!" She bent double, winded.

Pain crossed his face. "Sorry. I'm sorry," he gushed. They ducked out of the garden tour and he walked her to the little cafe opposite the pavilion to recover. His lips puckered with concern at the whiteness of her face and he didn't let go of her hand. His thumb caressed the backs of her fingers, but his brow remained furrowed. They sat outside under umbrellas and watched the ducks diving on the lake. Their coffees arrived and Logan calmed. Hana's equilibrium returned by degrees. He reached for her hand across the table. "You okay, now?" he asked, guilt still edging his words.

Hana nodded and sipped her coffee, feeling the spike in her heart from the caffeine. "I'm fine. Seeing you striding away with Phoenix gave me this massive sense of isolation." She gulped and touched her chest. "I need to stay close to you both for a while."

Logan nodded and stroked her fingers. "It'll take time to get it out of your head. I'm sorry. I won't do that again."

She nodded. "I've been pondering what you said about Alfred. Do you feel displaced?"

Logan gulped and shuttered his emotions. The instant disappointment in Hana's face stopped him. "I don't know, Hana. Maybe. I built my understanding of myself on my whakapapa but it was all lies. My brothers weren't my brothers and my sister isn't my sister." He laughed with a nasty undertone. "Hell, my father isn't even my father!"

"The sins of the fathers," Hana whispered and sighed. "Bodie knew about his dad's affair. All these years I've guarded the secret and tried to protect Vik's image. I wouldn't have needed to if he'd kept his pants on. Don't these men realise what they cause when they give in to temptation? Their children grow up fatherless. Just look at poor Tama and Jas. What a mess!"

Logan reached down and stroked the tiny fingers curled against his chest. Phoenix slept with her head lolling back and her mouth open. Logan sighed and stared out across the lake. "Well, for Reuben the wages of his sin was death." He deliberately misquoted the old scripture referring to eternal death and Hana didn't contradict him. He stretched his arm around her shoulders. "We're never splitting up and I won't lose sight of my daughter. She'll know exactly where she came from and who she is."

Hana smiled. "Even when she wants to stay out all night drinking?"

"Especially then!" A dangerous glint flashed in Logan's eyes. "I'll be loading my gun to greet any interested parties."

Back at the staff unit, Logan seemed restless. He kept walking onto the front doorstep and looking over to something happening at St Bart's. Hana felt his agitation and tensed. "What's wrong?" she asked. "Stop pacing and just tell me."

"Sorry." Logan pursed his lips. "I need to check something in the office but dragging you both over there seems extreme." A line appeared between his eyebrows. "The delivery van is hanging around in the front car park and I didn't think it came at the weekend. Maybe it broke down. I didn't see it there when we came home."

"Just take a look and come back." Hana frowned. "I hate it when you're brooding. I feel as though you're only half with me, anyway."

Logan kissed her cheek. "Promise I won't be long," he whispered.

"Are you still obsessing over the cabbages?" Hana raised an eyebrow.

Logan wrinkled his nose. "It won't take long."

Hana lay Phoenix in the cot after her feed. Then she vacuumed, polished and restored order to the small unit. Her wrist felt better without the gaudy bandage. When

Logan still hadn't returned after an hour, she walked across to the boarding house to find him. Irritation burgeoned in her heart and she intended to make him feel guilty for going missing after promising he wouldn't. Phoenix flopped over her shoulder, swaddled in a blanket and still sleepy.

Finding the office locked, Hana climbed the long staircase to the restroom. The door stood open but silence greeted her. Her fingers fluttered against Phoenix's blanket. She wanted to text Logan but her phone still charged in the bedroom of the staff unit. As she turned, she heard muffled voices from the middle bedroom. A beeping sound from the window drew her attention and she looked down on the rear driveway of St Bart's. A delivery truck backed towards the kitchen beneath. Its wing mirrors brushed the bushes as the driver negotiated the side of the building. It halted and air brakes gushed, followed by the grinding of a roller door.

Talking and laughter filtered through the open window and Hana heard the clatter of crates being dragged across a gritty surface. The noise went on for a while as she enjoyed the bizarre satisfaction of watching someone else work. Phoenix grew heavy in her arms and Hana's wrist hurt. She lay the baby on the sofa, stuffing cushions to one side to stop her rolling. With a sigh, she lay her forearms on the edge of the metal frame and peered at the scene beneath, her breath fogging up the glass. Logan had said he'd seen the delivery truck out the front. She wondered if he watched from a vantage point as it sneaked in behind the kitchen. Curiosity budded in her chest and she pressed her nose to the glass, craning forward but unable to see anything but the roof of the truck and a little of the pavement.

The activity stopped and the tops of two heads appeared standing close to the truck door. A male's bald white crown showed tufts of hair and his muscular shoulders looked strong from lifting. His shirt matched the blue of the truck roof so she guessed he was the delivery driver.

"We got cabbages this week?" The other head turned from side to side and a woman's voice dropped an octave. The driver's head nodded forward and back. "Because that new manager's onto us. People are asking for the things we don't have, so we need to stay one step ahead of him. We'll swap it for something else."

The driver nodded again. Hana leaned forward to identify the woman. Desire to solve the mystery meant she leaned out further than she should. Logan searched for an insider and if Hana identified the woman, he could clear up St Bart's financial mess and leave.

Logan said the fact all the food appeared on the menu, even the cabbage and leek, caused confusion. The head chef in the boarding house formulated the menu and the school typist produced the sheets. Neither seemed to realise there was any discrepancy, operating under a well-oiled formula. The head chef claimed he made up the menu himself years ago and it hadn't changed. He'd worked at the boarding house for over thirty years and threatened to quit when Logan challenged him. Logan told Hana he backed off, not wanting to arouse suspicion. He'd questioned a kitchen worker about the cabbage and she'd shrugged, looking around before answering. The head chef couldn't read. He'd dictated the menu and that's why it hadn't changed. She hadn't wanted to tell the chef's secret and Logan had needed to promise he wouldn't repeat it to Angus. Hana pursed her lips, remembering his account of the conversation as the possibilities moved through her mind.

Hana leaned out as far as she dared. She recognised the woman's voice but without seeing her face, couldn't name her. She reached out further, teetering with her stomach balanced across the metal windowsill. The top of the woman's head showed greying hair and Hana frowned, knowing it matched half the women in the school. Cut into neat curls, it eliminated only a few more.

She jumped as the bedroom door opened behind her and pulled her head back in. Turning, she saw the dark haired kitchen supervisor close the door. The girl stood with her back to it, fastening the buttons on her uniform with a smug smile plastered onto her lips.

Feeling Hana's gaze on her, she looked up and let out a small gasp. Her face radiated guilt which slipped with ease into obstinacy. She sneered, adding an unpleasant slant to an otherwise pretty face. "What are you staring at?" she spat, glaring at Hana.

It felt as though the world stopped turning and Hana gaped. It didn't take a genius to work out she hadn't been using the bedroom as a changing room. Hana's brain locked, Logan's mysterious absence sending damaging thoughts through her mind. As fast as she put out one mental fire, another rose to overwhelm her. The girl pulled her phone from her skirt pocket and shook it at Hana. Her face creased into a smirk. "Tell your husband to give me another call," she said, her tone filled with implication. "I'll be waiting." She reached behind and adjusted her underwear. Hana heard her heart pounding as she watched the intimate action and understood the inference. Her eyes flicked towards the closed bedroom door and then back at the girl's face. An image of Logan drifted across her inner vision, strong, dependable and dangerous. But hers.

Hana straightened her spine and stuck her chin out. She forced the words into her mouth. "My husband wouldn't touch you with a barge pole," she hissed. "He has standards." She trusted he wouldn't repeat Reuben's mistake. It cost his father everything.

The girl started as though Hana slapped her, the statement stinging as though she had. "Whatever, bitch!" she retorted. Her footsteps sounded loud on the stairs.

Hana trembled, her world collapsing in on itself. She plucked her daughter from the sofa, letting the cushions fall to the floor and leaving them there. "Come on, baby," she whispered. "Time to go." Phoenix stretched and bent her body backwards like a banana. Hana strode towards the stairs, resisting the urge to kick the bedroom door as she passed. She reached the fire door and glanced back, barrelling into the stairwell. She squealed as she crashed into something sideways.

Logan righted her, keeping her at arm's length to avoid squashing Phoenix. "Whoa babe. Sorry I'm late. I got roped into dealing with a broken arm." Logan looked at her rattled expression and narrowed his eyes. "What's wrong?"

"Nothing, I'm going home." Hana tried to push past, prevented by Logan's strong grip on her shoulders. Guilt assailed her for having doubted him and the urge to escape fought for prominence. She couldn't face him and pulled away, but he wouldn't let her go.

"Hana?"

"Sorry," she whispered. "It's nothing."

His eyes narrowed. "I saw the kitchen supervisor on the stairs. Did she say something to you?"

Hana shook her head and then nodded. "Yes. She said you can call her again. She'll be waiting."

Logan grimaced. "No thanks. She knows nothing about what's going on. Even Angus thought that interview was a complete waste of time."

Hana chewed the inside of her cheek and felt her colour flush with embarrassment. "You met her with Angus?"

"Yeah." Logan frowned. "What crap is she telling you?"

Hana sighed and lowered her voice. "She was in that bedroom with someone else." Her eyes widened and she jerked her head towards the door. "They're still in there."

"What?" Disbelief shrouded Logan's face and Hana took a step back from his anger. Something sinister descended and she saw a click as his mind ran over scenarios. His lips curled back in a snarl. "Figures!" he snapped. "No wonder he's not answering his phone."

The door burst open at the single kick from Logan's boot. It smashed back against the cupboard behind it. Hana heard a howl of alarm from the room's occupant. Hugging Phoenix closer, she stepped into the doorway to discover Logan holding Chris Carter by the throat. Phoenix jumped at the loud noises and gave a whimper of concern. Hana pressed her lips to the baby's temple to reassure her and held her breath as Logan forced Carter against the wardrobe. "You make me sick!" Logan gritted his teeth and snarled into Carter's face.

"Get off me!" He aimed a kick to Logan's shin and sliced his hands in a faint imitation of a karate move. Logan's head butt drove him down onto the carpet.

"I warned you!" Logan stabbed a finger into Carter's face and whirled around. He knocked the fallen desk chair aside with his knee. Hana backed up, the expression on Logan's face terrifying. In the absence of his usual calm, he epitomised the very nature of fury. His grey eyes flashed black like storm clouds and his lips curled back to bare his teeth. Hana's eyes widened and she backed up as far as the kitchen counter, petrified of her angry husband.

Logan halted in the doorway at the sight of her. She sidestepped away from him, her lips parting in a silent moan. He'd bowed to his anger and it made him reckless, displaying the harshest side of his character. Hana saw regret in the flickering fire dying in his eyes.

"I'm calling the cops." Chris Carter struggled to his feet and staggered towards the door. Blood dripped from his nose.

"Do it!" Logan turned to face him, satisfaction in his tone as Carter shrank away from him. He took a step nearer and raised his left hand. "Call them right now, 'cause I have things I'd like to tell them."

"Dude!" Carter shook his head and his complexion paled. "No, please don't. I don't want my wife to know."

"I bet you don't." Logan jerked his head towards the stairs. "Get out, Chris. Take your stuff and go. I'll ask Angus to send your termination letter to your parents' place."

"Not my job!" Chris lifted his arms and clasped his hands behind his head. "Don't do this, man. Please, not my job." Hana saw a tuft of blonde hair below his navel as the misaligned buttons of his shirt parted.

"Get out!" Logan's dismissal sounded final. "I warned you what would happen if I caught you again." He turned to face Hana and his pupils dilated. His brow furrowed as he watched her flounder, his temper the catalyst for her falling apart at the seams. He ignored the man dragging at his sleeve and strode towards his wife.

"Don't walk away from me!" Carter lunged after him and Hana watched as Logan sent an elbow into his face. He groaned and dropped to the carpet.

She backed up against the counter clutching Phoenix as Logan approached. He dwarfed her, casting her into shadow. Every muscle and nerve ending shook as she clamped Phoenix to her body. The baby thrashed against her shoulder and wailed. "Hana." Logan's voice sounded level as he fought to restore order.

"You hit him!" Her incredulous tone cut him and his lips parted.

"Hana." He repeated her name, not prepared to justify his actions while Carter still lingered in the bedroom.

"You hit him." She backed up as far as the sink and Logan caught her around the waist.

"Hana, let's get out of here." He tugged Phoenix free and she settled over his shoulder. Logan pulled Hana towards him and edged her away from the sink unit. She resisted, but only for a moment.

"You hit him," she whispered again. "Twice."

Logan sighed. "And I'll do it again if he opens his mouth. I warned him, Hana." He edged her towards the stairs. "I know Amanda isn't your favourite person right now, but she doesn't deserve that jerk dropping his pants at every opportunity." He glanced over his shoulder and narrowed his eyes at Carter. The other man watched Logan from around the door frame. He popped his head back in at the threat he saw in the narrowed grey eyes.

Hana's body trembled against Logan and words evaded her. She struggled with the stairs, her legs weak and uncooperative. Pete emerged from the downstairs office, leading a pale Year 10 boy whose face creased in pain. The boy wore a white sling and looked sick. Pete glanced at Hana as though she was a dangerous spider and skirted around her. Logan spoke to the boy. "Hop into the school van. Mr North will take you to the hospital." He nudged Hana's arm, asking her with his eyes to comply and sending her towards the front doors. Then he turned back to Pete. "Carter's packing his gear and won't be back. I'll ring Angus and ask him to send someone else to cover while you're at the hospital."

Pete's brow furrowed. "Can't you stay?" His gaze slid to Hana's face and back again. She forced herself to smile and banished the sense of terror governing her face muscles.

"No." Logan's answer sounded certain and he dragged his phone from his pocket one-handed.

He stood outside and made a difficult phone call to Angus, leaving it on speaker phone as Hana stood next to him. "Oh, bloody hell!" The principal's deep Scots accent rumbled through the handset. "I'll finalise the termination of his contract in the morning. Gross misconduct should do it although we have the other warnings on record if he wants to argue. I'll not tolerate his shenanigans anymore."

"There's one other thing." Logan shot a sideways glance at Hana and let Phoenix slide into a more comfy position in the crook of his arm. "I kinda roughed him up a bit. After all the drama with that underage girl he brought back last week and the nights I spent covering for him when he did his disappearing acts, I lost the plot a little."

Angus sighed. "How little did you lose the plot, Logan? What's the damage?"

Logan narrowed his eyes at the sight of Carter emerging through the front doors. He shot Logan a fearful glance and scurried away, a duffle bag over his arm. "A bit," Logan replied. He winced. "Just the usual."

"If he can still walk, get rid of him," Angus snapped.

Logan trudged next to Hana as they returned to the staff unit. Her shoulders slumped and she struggled to look at him. They walked through the front door and Logan waited for her to settle on the sofa before handing the baby to her. "I'll make you a drink," he said.

Hana listened to the sounds of the boiling kettle and processed this new facet of her husband. He made no secret of his tendency towards violence, but seeing it in action presented something very different. She closed her eyes and wondered if the shattered pieces of her life would ever fit back together again. Logan set a cup of tea on the coffee table in front of her and sank into the seat beside her. His arm rested across the back of the sofa and he propped his boots on the table.

"You hit him." She let the words hang in the air and Logan sighed and rubbed his eyes with the heels of his hands.

"Yeah."

"Why?" Hana turned to face him, sliding one leg beneath her so she could turn and watch his expression. "He's no match for you."

Logan shrugged. "I have no excuse. It just happened."

"It just happened?" Hana's voice rose at the end. "I thought you would kill him. Something like that doesn't just happen."

Logan's lips quirked upward. "If I meant to kill him, I'd have shut the door behind me first." His sideways glance met Hana's stony expression and he sighed. "He got caught twice with Caroline last year and let her take the fall. That's the second time I've caught him in the last month. Pete covered me while we were away and came back late to find him in his bed with some teenager. I looked into his eyes and just lost it. I'm sorry. He's the reason for those last minute night duties. He kept disappearing. If he'd done his job, I'd have been home more and known something was going wrong. I looked at him and saw he didn't care. You almost died and he didn't care." Logan's fingers scraped across the bristles on his chin. "Now he cares about something, even if it's only his pretty face getting messed up."

Hana tapped a beat on the baby's back and swallowed. Phoenix stopped feeding to stare up at her. "Is that what happened when you went to fix Leslie's problem?" she whispered. "Do you have anger issues?"

Logan snorted. Hana jumped and faced him. "It's not funny!"

"Oh, Hana." He stretched backwards and his fingers touched the counter behind him. His shirt rode up to reveal his tense abdominal muscles. "No, I don't have an anger problem. I take care of myself and I want to take care of you."

"You're scary." Hana dropped her chin and pursed her lips. "Terrifying. Your eyes blazed and I thought you might go on the rampage."

"On the rampage!" Logan's face creased with laughter and he tilted next to her. "That's hilarious!"

Hana glared at him and pursed her lips. "Violence isn't the answer," she protested. "You need to stop. What if Phoenix saw you bashing someone?" She pointed to his forehead. "You should be more careful because of your haemophilia. There's a big bruise starting on your face."

Logan heaved out a breath and the laughter died in his throat. "Okay, Hana. No more bashing people." He reached an arm around her shoulder and pulled her in close. "Unless it's in self-defence. That's okay, aye?"

Hana rolled her eyes at him and accepted her tea when he passed it from the table. "Maybe." She sipped and her hand wobbled as the realisation hit her. Logan grabbed the mug before she spilled it. "What?" He leaned closer, his eyes dark and searching.

Horror shone from Hana's face and she groaned. "No! Amanda just moved in. What does this mean for her?"

Logan blinked. "She'll need to leave. You should talk to her."

"I'm not telling her!" Hana's body stiffened and she lifted a trembling hand to her lower lip. "I can't."

She lay awake for hours after she climbed into bed. Logan slept from the moment his head hit the pillow, his body still. His fingers twitched against her thigh as the day's events played out in his dreams, but his breathing remained constant and heavy. Thoughts of Amanda disturbed Hana and she wondered when Angus would break the news. Pastor Allen's advice about letting things go returned to haunt her and she regretted missing the opportunity to make things right. Amanda's accusation had hurt, but in the light of Chris Carter's infidelity it was understandable.

When Hana's fidgeting disturbed Logan, she got up and padded across the hallway to check Phoenix. Her baby lay on her back with her arms in the air and she'd kicked the blankets off. Hana covered her up and rested her hands on the cot, pausing to enjoy the sound of her soft breaths. A sense of gratitude rippled through her and she felt her chest lock.

A sharp clunk made her gasp and she froze with her hands gripping the cot. When another one followed it, she lifted her fingers to her chest. The sound came from the far wall and she waited to see if it happened again. Something scraped across the surface and Hana realised she could hear Amanda in the adjoining unit. She relaxed and waited for her heartbeat to return to normal.

Painful sobbing carried through the thin partition and Hana bit her lip. Amanda knew. Another bump against the wall sounded like a suitcase flipping open. Hana looked down at Logan's old shirt which she used as a nightdress. If she returned to the bedroom and tried to dress, he'd wake and talk her out of going next door in the middle of the night. She curled her lips back at the sight of the pale thighs sticking out of her knickers. Her bare feet looked white in the faint moonlight and she hesitated.

"Come on, Hana," she breathed, giving herself encouragement. "Get it together, woman!" She lifted her keys from the breakfast bar and locked up behind her, treading on grit and painful stones along the small road to next door. She knocked on Millie's bedroom window, waiting until Amanda's face appeared. A cool breeze whipped around her thighs, but Amanda didn't acknowledge her. Feeling like an idiot, Hana turned to leave.

She heard the front door click as she picked her way back along the road. Light flooded the narrow street. Amanda's face poked from her porch and the shadows highlighted her puffy eyes and down-turned lips. "What?"

"Amanda," Hana whispered. She turned, the breeze nipping at her bare legs and icing her bones. "I heard you banging around and came to see if you were okay."

Amanda gulped and the painful sound carried along the quiet street. Hana frowned and retraced her steps to Amanda's front door.

"You're freezing," Amanda said, her voice wobbling. Hana looked at her shivering legs and nodded, knowing the reaction had its root in fear. Amanda stood back for Hana to enter and she climbed the steps before brushing her feet on the prickly doormat.

The unit looked like a tip. Hana's brow knitted as she stepped over a suitcase with its contents disgorged across the floor. She rubbed her tired eyes and avoided standing on a pair of trousers and a large bra.

"I'm moving out," Amanda said. She waved her hand around the room and tried to look as though she didn't care. "Tomorrow."

Hana looked for somewhere to sit, finding nowhere. Baby items littered the floor and a bag of nappies sat on the sofa. A dress hung over the television. Hana retrieved the dress and rolled it into a sausage, kneeling by the suitcase and viewing the haphazard contents. After a moment's thought and a tired sigh, she took everything out and started repacking it. Amanda watched. "Chris said you knew." Her voice wavered and Hana saw her wringing her hands in her peripheral vision. "He said Logan hit him because he said something about you."

Hana gaped. "About me?"

Amanda nodded. "He made some smart ass comment about the guy who took you. I think he panicked when Logan kicked the door open. Chris said he regretted saying it the second it left his big mouth, but it was too late." She gulped. "He's told me everything. There are so many other women he can't remember their names. He said he can't seem to stop." A tear left a track down her cheek and she swiped it away. "We talked. He said he loves me but doesn't know how to let anyone love him back. He knows this is the end and promised to get help. I can't go back to him though. Not after this."

Hana rolled the clothes, making space on the surrounding floor. She nodded to acknowledge Amanda's revelation, but sensed easy platitudes would sound false. "I'll make a drink," Amanda said, drying her eyes on the bottom of her pyjama top. "I think I'm done crying." She busied herself in the kitchen making tea after retrieving cups from a cardboard box on the counter.

"Here." She handed Hana a cup of tea with a trembling hand. Then she sank into the sofa, her energy sapped. The clothes beneath her creased into a ball and something plastic snapped.

"Thanks." Hana looked for somewhere safe to put it. "Haven't you slept?" she asked, her voice soft.

Amanda shook her head. "Can't." She leaned forward and lowered her voice. "I'm sorry I accused you of having an affair with that man. When I heard what happened, I felt awful. I gave your son a statement of what I heard through the toilet wall. You should've told me he threatened you, not let me jump to stupid conclusions."

"I couldn't." Hana focussed on the tiny socks in her hand. "He said he'd hurt Logan and I wouldn't take the risk. But I understand what cheating does to a marriage and the legacy it leaves. When I saw that girl come out of

Chris' bedroom, I doubted Logan just for a minute. He's done nothing to deserve it and yet I still can't trust him. Because of Vik, I punish someone who doesn't deserve it. At least you got to talk to Chris and asked him why. Vik didn't give me that opportunity. I couldn't shout or scream because he died and left me with nothing but hurt and questions. When I think I've forgiven him, I discover I haven't." Hana ground her jaw and closed her eyes, Amanda's pain mixing with her own.

She felt a light touch on her arm. "I'm sorry, Hana. Wish I'd trusted you more," Amanda breathed. "I enjoyed having you as a friend. The isolation has been killing me."

Hana put her hand over the other woman's as a sign of solidarity. "Where will you go?"

"I don't know," Amanda said. Tears sprang into her eyes and surged onto her cheeks. "I can't go back to my parents. I need a job and someone to look after Millie for me. Chris will struggle to get another teaching job. Angus won't give him a reference."

Hana shifted onto the sofa and put her arm around Amanda. "I have no answers for you. But I'll pray for you," she offered. "Something will come up." She gulped, expecting a knock back and waiting for it.

"I don't believe in God," Amanda acknowledged. "I'm desperate enough even for that."

Hana relaxed and gave her a smile which drooped at the edges. She fought a yawn. "Well, the Lord helps those who help themselves," she said. "So, we should get packing."

Chapter 38

Desperate knocking on the front door dragged Hana from her nap and she sat up with a start. Running a hand over her face, she wondered where she was. She groaned at the stabbing back ache and felt dribble on the cushion she'd used as a pillow.

"Okay, okay!" Hana wiped her face on her sleeve and tried to get her feet to move. The knocking began again and she stumbled to the front door and fumbled it open.

Amanda burst through the gap, her eyes bright and her face alight with excitement. "You said something would come up," she said, switching Millie onto the other hip. "You'll never believe this!"

"Sorry, what?" Hana slumped back onto the sofa and rubbed her eyes, trying to get her brain to catch up. "How can you look so awake? Neither of us slept." She shifted in her seat, pulling her legs up next to her as Amanda jiggled her daughter on her hip. "We packed until six this morning. I'm shattered! Have you been licking the coffee canister again?" Hana groaned and closed her eyes.

"About the packing," Amanda said. She winced. "Can you help me put it all back?"

Hana shook her head. "I hate dreams like this," she murmured. She squinted at Amanda and imagined she wasn't there.

"Angus came to see me," Amanda gushed. "He fired Chris but asked if I was interested in a job at the boarding house. He got rid of the kitchen supervisor and promoted another woman to her role. I can have her hours in food preparation. Then he spoke to a friend who owns the day care centre up the road. They'll take Millie while I'm at work for a reduced fee."

"Wow, that's incredible," Hana breathed. She thought about leaving Phoenix with strangers and her heart quailed.

"You don't look pleased," Amanda said, her brow furrowing.

"I am," Hana said, pushing aside her own separation anxieties and struggling not to yawn.

"This will work out great for me." Amanda bounced Millie. "I'll lose weight, regain my focus and maybe my self-esteem. I know it's only chopping veg and making meals for the boys, but it's a start. And the best part is I can still live here. Angus will take the rent out of my wages, so you were right. God was looking and made something happen. Just like you said."

"Where did you work before?" Hana asked, her brain still foggy.

"I was a real estate agent," Amanda said. "So, from house deals to meals on wheels."

Hana burst out laughing. She put her hand over her mouth and apologised, but still the giggles poured out. "It's not funny, I know it's not funny," she snorted.

"It is." Amanda threw herself onto the sofa, her eyes bright with energy. "Wait until they figure out I'm a rubbish cook and I burn water."

Tiredness swept through Hana's body and she felt crowded out by emotions she couldn't control. Healing laughter spilled from her lips and her eyes watered at Amanda's continued analogies. "I cooked broccoli once," she confessed, rolling her eyes. "Even the cat stank of it for a week!"

Tears of mirth poured down Hana's cheeks as she gave up seeking dignity or control. Millie joined in, hauling herself up on the furniture and letting out giant whoops of fake delight. Amanda sniggered and Millie's eyes widened as she put her whole tiny being into a ferocious cackle. Her fists balled and she gritted her teeth. "Mills, you look like a maniac," Amanda snorted.

Without warning the child let go of the coffee table and with little hands held high in the air, she took her first steps. They were precious, faltering footsteps on bare feet and the baby stopped for balance, holding out her fat little arms to her mother. "Oh, my days!" Amanda breathed and pressed her fingers to her lips.

She caught the wavering arms and Millie's momentary panic turned to satisfaction. "Clever girl!" Amanda told her and the child beamed, her graduation from baby to toddler complete. She used the stability of her mother's grip to walk the rest of the way to Hana's knees.

Hana's eyes shone with delight and she turned to enjoy the little girl's achievement. But she found Amanda weeping. "He missed it," she sobbed. "He's gonna miss everything from now on. I'm alone."

"Not necessarily," Hana soothed. "You and Chris can still work together. It'll be okay." She lifted Millie onto her knee. "Nobody can take this from you, Amanda, so don't destroy it for yourself."

Hana fed Phoenix while Amanda made sandwiches in the kitchen. Millie slept on the rug in the middle of the floor after wearing herself out with repeats of her cleverness. Hana took the cheese sandwich with a grateful smile. Amanda sat next to her. "Did Logan mind you spending the night packing my crap?" she asked.

Hana blanched and the bread stuck in her throat. "He was fine," she lied. She pursed her lips, surprised Amanda didn't hear their heated argument when she let herself in the front door. Logan greeted her with his arms folded across his bare chest and fire in his eyes. He'd called her irresponsible and left for work in a temper.

"Do you fancy a walk?" Amanda asked as she cleared up their empty plates.

Hana groaned. "Aren't you tired?"

"No way! I'm wired!"

Hana pushed her pram towards the river, hoping the fresh air would wake her. They didn't make it, collapsing into seats outside a coffee shop. Amanda stepped inside to order and a pretty barista followed soon after. She smiled, her blonde ponytail bouncing at the back of her head. "I want to be that gorgeous," Amanda mused as the girl held the door open for an elderly couple before disappearing inside.

"I'd just settle for her energy," Hana grumbled. "Or her body. Mine's falling apart."

Amanda eyed the open wound at her wrist and nodded. "How's the infection?" she asked.

"The antibiotics are working," Hana conceded. "It still hurts, but at least it's stopped oozing. I'm scared there's still glass inside." She flexed her wrist and winced.

"There won't be," Amanda reassured. "It's just the stitches pulling."

The walk east seemed endless in the heat and Hana felt an overwhelming gratitude upon passing the Fairview Downs sign. They entered the front gate in time for the final bell and Amanda begged her for a detour to the main building. "Please, Hana? I won't be long, I promise. If I don't sign my contract today, I'm scared Angus might change his mind."

"He wouldn't," Hana grumbled. "Just do it tomorrow."

Losing the argument, she waited in reception with both prams. Phoenix slept, so she played a game with Millie. "You're so clever!" she cooed. Hana turned a red teddy bear upside down and waited for Millie to spin him on her activity rail. The little girl squawked with delight. Hana avoided the receptionist's glare, feeling the woman's animosity through the back of her skull. Angus' open door allowed Amanda's excited tones to carry from his office. "Thank you, God," Hana whispered under her breath. "Your timing is much better than mine. With your next miracle, please can you make sure I don't need to double pack someone's belongings?" She stood the red bear on its head again and watched Millie bat it with an infantile precision.

The telephone rang in reception and the receptionist answered in crisp tones. "Oh yes, I'll put you through to our principal's assistant." She bobbed her brunette page-boy cut and pressed buttons on her switchboard. Hana heard the phone ring in the office next to Angus' and the click of the handset.

She cringed and Millie watched her face and giggled. Hana put her finger to her lips and the little girl shrieked at the new game. "No, no," Hana begged as the receptionist tutted.

"Principal Blair's office. How may I help you?" Angus' assistant sounded officious as the caller stated their business. "He's in a meeting," she snapped, her voice drifting through the flimsy partition.

Hana's blood chilled. The heat of the day abandoned her as realisation flooded through her muddled brain. "No!" she gasped, covering her mouth with her hand. Millie dissolved into peals of laughter at Hana's obvious alarm.

Hana reached into her pocket to search for her phone, panicking when she couldn't find it. Millie giggled and copied her. "What should I do?" Hana hissed and Millie giggled again.

Hana listened as Angus' assistant made the person on the other end of the telephone miserable. She didn't need to see their reaction to understand their humiliation. "Well, I can't help that," the woman bit. "Mr Blair is unavailable for the next two weeks. Sir, that's not my problem. Yes, I suggest you do that!"

Hana sighed as nausea roiled in her stomach. "Hurry, Amanda," she muttered. "Please hurry." The mastermind of the boarding house fraud slammed her receiver down and shuffled papers on her desk. Hana wondered how well she knew the delivery driver at the heart of the cabbage plot.

Amanda emerged from Angus' office, waving her contract in victory. "Oh yeah! Celebration time," she declared, bouncing on the balls of her feet. "Wine or champagne?"

"Maybe later," Hana replied. "I don't feel well. Sorry."

"Oh, okay." Amanda's tone sounded flat. "It's my fault for keeping you up packing all night. I'll pop in and see how you are in a while."

"I'm fine. I just need a nap," Hana promised. "Congratulations on the job."

She found her phone charging in the kitchen and dialled Logan's number. "Please pick up, babe, please," she begged. The call went to voicemail after five rings. In the upset of Chris Carter's indiscretion, she hadn't told Logan about the conversation between the delivery driver and the woman. "Where are you, Logan?" she panicked, ringing again and receiving no answer.

Hana pushed the pram down the front steps and slammed the door behind her. The heat wave had bleached the soccer field to an unhealthy brown and dust rose beneath her hurried steps. Pete looked up as she strode into the office. He pursed his lips and frowned. "I owe you an apology, Hana," he began.

She shook her head and guilt prickled at the back of her skull. "Where's Logan please, Pete? It's urgent."

He shook his head, not sure. "I think he popped in fifteen minutes ago on his way home."

"He didn't arrive!" Hana snatched Phoenix from the pram and hurried into the corridor. Her body swayed with the baby's awkward weight. Boys swirled in and out of bedrooms getting showered after sport practice. Hana charged past a boy in a towel and another in boxer shorts, not caring as she headed for the stairs.

She didn't realise Pete had followed her until she heard his heavy breathing. He lagged behind as she burst through the restroom door. The space appeared deserted, the three tiny bedrooms empty and a breeze carrying through from their open windows. "Hana," Pete puffed, "what's wrong?"

"I don't know but something is. I can feel it!" She kept Phoenix in her right arm but Pete spotted the mess on her other wrist and his eyes bugged.

"Geeze, Hana!" He pointed and his chest wheezed, defeated by two flights of stairs.

"Stop!" Hana heard a sickening sound drift through the open window behind her and she recognised the sound from the day before. Her blood pumped hard through her veins and her wrist throbbed. She hefted Phoenix into Pete's inexperienced arms. "I'm trusting you to keep her safe, Pete!" she breathed. "Don't let me down!"

She moved at speed, finding her way downstairs through the myriad corridors until she discovered the kitchens. Hana blasted through the swinging doors, taking a smack to her forehead as her enthusiastic thrust returned to meet her. She felt the breeze from an open doorway and heard again the unforgettable noise of bone on bone. With running feet, she crossed the smart industrial kitchen and spotted the dark blue lorry in the narrow driveway. Its shadow blocked the light through the huge windows and bathed the room with a blue hue.

Hana's breath caught in her chest at seeing Logan facing the open doorway. Two tall men held an arm each while the bald man beat him around the head and stomach. Only Logan could see her. Blood ran in rivulets down his face from an open wound on his temple. His left eye looked swollen shut. His body slumped against another fist to the stomach and he leaned forward retching. Blood and mess heaved onto the concrete. "Hold him!" the delivery driver ordered. He drew his arm back for a final punch to Logan's face. "Go on! Stand the bugger up!"

Hana seized a metal frying pan from the draining board, hefting it in her right hand as she ran through the open door. She didn't give herself time to think. Her sacrifice to Laval seemed pointless in the face of Logan's fate and rage burned inside her breast at its futility. The skillet bent her wrist under its iron weight and she saw Logan's right eye shutter in defeat at the sight of her. His attempt to communicate with her generated only blood stained air bubbles.

The man drawing his fist didn't see it coming. He went down like a stone under the heavy thwack to the side of his head. Hana put everything into the blow, her rage, her disappointment and her need for justice. The men holding Logan dropped him and it took him out of the range of Hana's next blow as he slid down the side of the truck. She swung her arm and scored twice, making the man to her right bang heads with his companion. A misty red rage left her dissatisfied with the result as the men rallied and stepped towards her. One rubbed his ear and the other his forehead. "Put it down!" the man on the right growled and reached for the pan. Hana ducked sideways out of range and aimed a kick to his shin, waiting until he bent forward in pain and then cracking him over the back of the head as she popped upright.

"Shit!" The other man swore and raised his hands. Hana missed the defeat in his eyes, seeing only Logan's blood staining his fingers. She feinted right and as he dodged to avoid her, brought the pan up from underneath and heard his jaw crack.

Hana stopped and stared at the weapon in her hand, realising why fishwives allegedly beat their husbands with them. The hopelessness in Logan's eyes hadn't done her and her trusty frying pan justice. She hefted it and watched the delivery driver stagger upright. He wobbled on his feet, towering over her and holding his ear. He looked too tall and too close for her to get a decent swing but adrenaline fuelled her. Her face registered panic as Logan spewed up a volley of bright red blood. He tried to get up but bent with one hand resting against the side of the truck. He looked spent, his body sagging and his legs bowed.

Something flared inside Hana's chest, a savage copy of the anger she'd turned on Kane Du Rose. She'd felt disgust at seeing it in Logan's eyes as he vented his rage on Chris Carter, but felt the same need surge in her breast. She knew in that moment Laval unleashed something terrible during her captivity and she channelled it into a stream of hatred. Like a pressure cooker valve it released and Bodie's lost instructions returned to her as a battle plan. '*Stomp to the shin, a fist to the face, knee in the nuts and shout your bloody head off, Mum. Yes, I know it's embarrassing, but shouting is your best defence!*'

She opened her mouth and shouted. Her unusual weapon swung through the air and she screamed to embolden herself. "Shin stomp!" she yelled. She dug the toe of her shoe into the delivery driver's shin and sensed it drag skin away with it. "Skillet to the face!" She bashed him with a competent tennis backhand and watched his head spin. "Skillet to the nuts!" Skillet to the nuts sideways. With the hard edge slicing upwards, she killed any future plans he might have entertained about fathering children.

With a scream of agony, the man sank as the iron pan crushed his groin. He knelt on the bloodstained concrete and squeezed his hands between his legs, bending low in a bow. But the unleashed thing in Hana's chest still burned. In her nightmares, she didn't escape Laval. He came after her to the front door and she reached a different point each night. Sometimes the handle wouldn't turn and sometimes it did. Often, he followed her, still mobile with the glass sticking out of his face. Despite the delivery driver appearing incapacitated, some part of her brain slipped into the realm of nightmares and a murderous spirit emerged. Hana spun the skillet in her right hand as though it was a tennis racquet and cracked him over the back of the head. His forehead hit the concrete as his curled body tipped and he put a hand out in self-defence. "Stop!" he screeched. "I'm done. Stop!"

"Hana!" Logan gasped her name through his bloodied lips and he raised an arm towards her. Her lips parted and the skillet dropped to the ground with a clang.

"You bitch!" The delivery driver sensed her giving up and rose, one hand still between his legs and the other reaching for her. Hana's mind replaced Laval's eyes for his and the anger flared again with full force. He staggered upright, still bent over and she saw Logan try to leave the safety of the truck. Logan's legs buckled under him and he tried again, his good eye fixed on the back of the delivery driver's head. His jaw gritted with determination.

Hana shook her head. Everything she'd done in the last few weeks centred on protecting Logan and despite what he said, Hana believed he needed her. Her attention flicked to the delivery driver's lips pulled back in a snarl and she raised her right hand, flattening it before jabbing him in the throat. Her fingers overlapped and the bones jarred as her chopping action caved against his Adam's apple.

He gagged and his knees found the concrete as Logan seized Hana's left forearm and hauled her sideways. He'd missed the painful stitches and aimed higher but it still sent a dart of pain up her arm and into her shoulder. "Stop, baby," Logan hissed, blood and saliva spraying onto her shirt.

"He can't do this to you!" Her voice sounded ragged and hurt laden and he gave a shallow nod. Laval's cruel image swam in front of her vision. Logan snatched up her other hand, gaining a better grip of her wrist.

"It's okay," he hissed. "You stopped him, Hana. You stopped him. It's over. Know when to leave it alone."

The delivery driver's foot twitched and Hana's jaw ground her teeth together. She tried to drop and collect the skillet, but Logan gripped her arm and stopped her bending to retrieve it.

"Oh, my freakin' days!" Pete's voice rose like an opera singer's as he popped through the back door. Phoenix bounced in his arms, her face pushed into his greasy neck. He bent in half as though nursing a belly ache and his feet moved on the spot. Phoenix slept on without concern.

A Year 13 boy appeared behind him, his eyes widening at the wounded and the wide arc of blood. He hauled a phone from his blazer pocket and dialled, unable to take his gaze from the massacre. He started as someone on the other end of the call spoke. "Yeah," he gushed. "There's been a murder. Bodies everywhere. Fire brigade, ambulance and cops. Send them all."

Logan clasped Hana around the waist and rested his forehead against her shoulder. His body shook and he sought more support than he felt able to give. Hana lifted her arms and clasped his head, her chest heaving though her lungs felt deprived of oxygen.

"Oh, shit!" Angus stepped into the gathering crowd and surveyed the scene, a hairy hand stretching up to run through his depleted ginger curls. "What the hell happened here?"

"Hana beat everyone up." Pete's eyes widened to the size of espresso saucers, the pupils obscuring his watery blue irises. "She's a ninja. Who knew?"

Angus turned with a growl as boys appeared from every angle, gawking through windows and crowding in from the kitchen and dining hall. He dispatched two nearby prefects to restore order, insisting nobody should access the rear driveway. Logan's knees sagged and Angus moved to assist, dragging one of his arms around his shoulders and helping to prop him up. He leaned close to Hana's shocked face, noting the clamminess of her skin and the white, deathly pallor. "Are you okay?" he whispered. "Is that your blood?"

Hana stared down at her sleeve and saw the crimson splotches dotting the fabric. She recoiled and made a sound like a sob. "I don't know!" Her voice rose. "I don't know!"

"Hana!" Logan's voice rasped and he coughed before continuing. Blood trickled from the corner of the lip nearest her. "Hana, look at me. Don't think about anything else. Just look at me."

Hana's chest locked and a sob caught in the back of her throat. "They were killing you!" Her words stuttered like a gunshot. "I couldn't stop it. I couldn't stop Laval."

"But you stopped this." Logan's arm rested heavier across her shoulders. "It's okay, Hana. I'll fix this."

Hana's foot kicked against the fallen skillet and the clang made her jump. She slid it sideways with the toe of her boot. "I don't want it anymore." She skirted the abandoned kitchen implement and Angus gripped her left shoulder as they supported Logan into the building.

Angus unlocked the sickbay and helped Logan onto a bed. Blood stained everything they touched. Hana alternated between squeezing her husband's fingers and pressing against the stitches on her wrist, as though hurting herself might atone for her violence. Pete hovered nearby, patting the baby's back and staring wide-eyed at Hana.

"Hana." Logan spoke her name and squinted up at her. She bent down to listen and heard him apologise. "I'm sorry," he whispered. "This is the last thing you needed."

"What happened?" Hana reached up and pressed her fingers to her lips to hold in the shock which made her body tremble. Angus stepped up closer and slipped a steadying arm over her shoulders. Logan hauled himself upright and swung his legs over to touch the floor. He wobbled but remained seated.

"I went downstairs to the kitchen after something Pete said. St Bart's kitchen served cabbage soup last night for dinner."

"Yeah. Disgusting." Pete wrinkled his nose and swung Phoenix in a rough arc. "It gave me diarrhoea."

Logan wiped his mouth with the back of his hand and sirens sounded in the distance. "I checked the chiller and found cabbages and leftover soup. I figured they'd moved on to a different item and knew I'd need to keep looking at the invoices. Something stank in the kitchen and I tracked it to the dustbin. Someone left meat in the bottom and the heat had got to it. I took it out the back to the trash and saw the delivery van reversing along the driveway. They delivered yesterday so I couldn't understand why they'd come back. I didn't see the third guy and he took me by surprise." Logan rubbed at a space across his abdomen. "He jumped me from behind and I didn't see it coming."

Hana's voice sounded small as she blinked back tears. "I can't keep rescuing you," she whispered. "I'm no good at it."

Logan choked back what sounded like laughter and Hana frowned. "You need to go to the hospital."

"Oh, no." Logan forced himself to a wavering position on his feet. He kept one hand on the mattress. "I don't think so."

"Don't be ridiculous!" Angus spat. "You've broken ribs by the looks of it and you need your head checked in more ways than one. You bleed like a stuck pig and I don't want your death on my conscience."

Hana's eyes widened and she turned to stare at Angus. "You think he'll die?"

"No." Logan blew out a breath through pursed lips. "I won't. The hospital gave me a Factor 8 infusion last week while Hana was sleeping, so I know the bleeding will stop. I've had worse." He glared at Angus. "You know I have."

The sirens grew closer and Hana stepped back to allow Logan to limp to the doorway. Angus shook his head and let his hands slap against his thighs. "You're a bloody idiot, Du Rose," he called after him.

"I need to look at the last invoice," Logan replied. "But I need a cup of coffee first."

Pete, Angus and Hana followed Logan in a slow procession up to the staffroom. He led with his left side, his right eye swollen shut. "There's someone on the inside," he said, turning his head to eyeball Pete. "Any clues before the cops swarm in?"

Pete sprang up behind him with Phoenix draped over his shoulder. Awake and curious, she watched Hana coming up behind her and sucked her fingers. Hana froze on the stairs and Angus ran into the back of her, halting with a painful grunt. "I know who it is," she said. "I know who's running the scam. We need to speak to Bodie."

Logan continued coughing up blood in the staff restroom and Hana dispatched Pete to their unit for his medication. "It's in the bathroom cupboard," she told him, handing over the front door key. Pete obeyed without question, fear and respect mixing in his eyes. He handed Phoenix back to Hana and his arms hung limp by his sides as though he missed the infant.

Bodie arrived with his uniformed colleagues and called an ambulance despite Logan's refusal. The paramedics fussed, demanding he at least let them conduct tests. "I have my own doctor," Logan insisted. Hana pursed her lips and remembered the kind man in the Hamilton East clinic. She relaxed, knowing Logan trusted him and that he'd patched her husband up before. They left under protest and only after the matron covered Logan's body with ice packs from the sports club freezer.

Hana waited to speak to Bodie, wanting to make up for her obstructive behaviour at the hotel. Logan sat on the sofa with his back to the window and dripped blood onto the carpet. The flow stemmed as he'd promised and his medication started to work. Pete sat next to him and Hana turned Phoenix to face her battered father. She noticed nothing different, wringing her hands and cooing.

"Look, I know who's behind this," Hana whispered. "It's Angus' personal assistant. I heard her talking to the delivery driver yesterday. She's been stealing from the boarding house by paying invoices for items they haven't delivered. It's possible she's running the same scheme in all the other hostels in town. I recognised her voice but couldn't place it. Today in reception I heard her on the phone and knew. I walked over to tell Logan, but the men were already here."

Bodie disappeared to use his radio and spoke to a controller. Logan sank back onto the sofa, his shirt open and his torso a mess of bruising.

The boarding house buzzed with excitement, affecting Phoenix like a drug. Her wide eyes and tiny head darted in every direction, her brain working overtime. The head prefect snatched her from Hana as Logan clutched his side and made a gurgling sound. He rolled sideways, moaning in agony. He coughed blood onto the carpet and Angus reached for his phone. "I'll get the paramedics back," he stated.

"No!" Logan choked. "Don't!"

Hana squatted next to him, her brain on overload. "Logan! Please go to the hospital?" she begged. "I need you, Logan." Her hands shook and without the rage and adrenaline, guilt for her actions weighed on her like a stone. "I shouldn't have done it. Help me cope with it. Tell me what to do."

Logan put his head between his knees, his body doubled forward. "Oh, my days," he groaned. "Oh, my freakin' days."

"What are you saying?" Hana demanded. She fought tears and her chest heaved. "What do you need?"

"Skillet to the nuts," Logan rasped and coughed again. The sound morphed into a gurgling laugh. He repeated it. "Skillet to the nuts, wahine?"

"Ohhhh, is that what she said?" Pete frowned. "I wondered what she was shouting about."

Bodie reappeared and stood behind Hana. "Is that what you said, Mum?" She turned to see his face creased in amusement. "I never taught you that."

Hana stood back as her son sniggered. She glared at Logan, her temper flaring again. "If that's your dying sentence, it's crap!" she snapped. "I'm not impressed!"

Bodie's colleagues smirked among themselves and he grinned as someone passed him an evidence bag. Hana saw the skillet sealed into it and winced. "Hey, Mum," Bodie said, his tone light. He waved the bag in front of her face. "I don't suppose you'd like to autograph this?"

Hana took Phoenix from the prefect and stalked away. Her hands still shook and the withdrawal of adrenaline seemed to leave an emptiness she couldn't dispel. Logan gave a statement and Bodie sought Hana in the downstairs office. She fed Phoenix behind the mirrored glass and watched the boys filtering past. He slipped through the door and sat in Pete's swivel chair. Hana winced as dandruff floated onto the carpet, but she said nothing. "You did great today, Mum," Bodie said, his voice soft. "Those self-defence lessons were worth it." He cocked his head and furrowed his brow. "I never imagined you sconning someone with a frying pan though. I kinda thought you'd use your bare hands."

"Ha ha." Hana sighed and rocked the baby. She looked up and her serious gaze settled on Bodie's dark eyes. "It was beyond reasonable force though, wasn't it?" She chewed her lip. "I could be in big trouble, couldn't I?"

Bodie shook his head. "Not on my watch! You defended yourself and a group of school children against three unknown attackers. The chief might give you a medal."

Hana shook her head. "I don't want to go to prison. But after all that agony with trying to keep Logan out of Laval's way, he got beaten up on our own doorstep." She ran a hand across her face and her fingers still trembled. "I've never felt that angry, Bodie. I didn't just want to kill them, I wanted to smash them into the ground."

Bodie leaned forward and rubbed her shoulder. "Maybe it's okay to snap occasionally, Mum. Whatever I think of Logan, I respect you for defending him. A husband can't ask for any more than that."

"Skillet to the nuts," Hana muttered. "I'll never live that down."

"Probably not." Bodie grinned and pushed a red curl away from Hana's face. He tucked it behind her ear. "You look exhausted all the time. Is it just because of everything that's happened in the last few weeks?"

"Yep, I'm just tired." Hana dismissed his concern and watched her daughter barf milk onto the office carpet.

She sighed and dropped a tissue over the mess, pressing it with the toe of her boot. Her forehead creased in a frown and she winced. "Hey, you won't tell Jas about this, will you?"

Bodie shook his head, but a smirk hid in the corners of his mouth. "I'm not allowed. But he'd love it. Ninja Hanny with the assault skillet." He bit his bottom lip to control the grin spreading across his face.

"Please don't," Hana breathed. She looked so fragile and desperate, Bodie reached across to squeeze her fingers.

"I won't. His behaviour improved heaps after you spoke to him. He's let Amy wash his school uniform and stopped saying he's a bridesmaid."

Phoenix beamed at Hana and she smiled back. She missed the gist of Bodie's next sentence. "Sorry, what did you just say?" she asked.

"Yeah, bit worrying." Bodie rubbed his eyebrow with the edge of his notebook. "He says he's leading Amy up the aisle in some kind of suit, but reckons he hasn't decided what sort yet. We've had dragon suit, bear suit, Smurf suit and this morning he decided on a Darth Vader suit." Bodie's radio chirped on his breast and he reattached his ear piece and strode from the room.

"Oh, no!" Hana groaned. "I didn't mean that kind of suit!" Phoenix gave her a gummy grin and threw up some more.

Angus drove Hana, Logan and Phoenix back to the private clinic in Hamilton East. The nurse greeted them outside in the same way and the doctor conducted a similar conversation to the day before. Hana excused herself and sat in the waiting room with Angus while Logan got treatment in the doctor's office.

Angus took a phone call from Bodie and listened outside. Hana watched him pacing along the driveway and cuddled her daughter as Phoenix sucked her thumb and drifted off to sleep. Angus' shoes crunched through a border covered in forest bark before realising and redirecting himself back onto the drive. He brought cool air inside with him when he returned. Hana gave him a tired smile. "Bodie?" she asked.

Angus nodded. Then he tapped his temple with a long finger. He looked as though his age had caught him up. "It seems the delivery driver returned today to drop off a delivery of leeks. How did I miss such antics?" He sighed. "It must've been going on right under my nose. She's been my assistant for years. I think I inherited her from my predecessor. Do you suppose it's been happening for that long?"

Hana shrugged. "Not sure. The cops will work it out. Perhaps they just got greedy this last couple of years."

"And they didn't factor in Logan Du Rose, did they?" Angus ran a hand through his sparse red hair.

Hana smiled. "Nobody ever factors in Logan Du Rose. You should know that by now."

Logan's face appeared ashen as he limped from the doctor's office. Angus gave Hana the car keys while Logan paid. He stood at the window and watched her strapping Phoenix into her car seat. His fingers clasped behind his back and he rocked on his heels.

"I should have seen that coming," Logan grumbled. "I'm getting soft in my old age."

"You and me both!" Angus replied. Then he smirked. "I suspect that fragile Du Rose ego is wounded because your dainty, flame-haired wife had to rescue you."

"Whatever!" Logan snapped. "I'm sure that will comfort me in bed tonight when I can't find a body part to lie on that doesn't hurt!" His dark eyes flashed the colour of grit. "I told her I didn't need her to protect me. I've made a liar of myself."

Angus grinned and shot Logan a sideways look. "I think you've bitten off more than you can chew son," he said, his voice soft.

"You pushed me into it," Logan retorted. "You didn't tell me this might have been going on for years."

Angus looked back at the car and watched Hana clamber into the back seat. She leaned over and he saw her kiss the baby's forehead. He raised his eyebrows as the doctor took Logan's wad of cash and gave a satisfied nod without counting it. Angus sighed. "I didn't mean the issue with St Bart's," he said. "I was referring to your wife. I think our beautiful Hana marches to her own wee drum, don't you?"

Chapter 39

Hana relaxed after the sermon, sipping a cup of coffee as the older ladies passed Phoenix around like the collection plate. She jumped as Allen's middle son bounced in front of her. "Guess what, Aunty Hana, you'll never guess!" he whispered. He glanced around him and she saw the secret burning in his eyes.

Jas perked up and stopped to listen, biscuit crumbs dropping from the custard cream he'd had to chase the biscuit tray to secure. His eyes sparkled. "I know it, you got a puppy!"

Ben looked smug. "Even better!" he said. His face broke into a grin.

Jas frowned. "There's nothing better than a puppy," he grumbled.

"I'm going to the Waikato Presbyterian School for Boys," Ben announced. "I got into the art academy. Dad picked up my new uniform yesterday from the menswear shop because I start tomorrow." He hugged himself, excitement bursting from his eyes.

Hana smiled. "You lucky boy! Congratulations." She gave him a side hug.

Jas narrowed his eyes and his brow furrowed. "Maybe that is better than a puppy," he admitted. "Do you think that might happen to me?" He peered up at Ben as though the boy might predict his future.

Ben nodded his encouragement. "Yep, sure could."

"Marvellous things happen when people pray to Hanny's God, don't they?" Jas looked at Hana and Ben grinned.

"My dad says so," he confirmed.

Jas nodded. "Yeah, because when I asked Jesus if I could go to my mum's wedding without a dress, Hanny said she would buy me a suit." Jas scratched at a scab in his hair but Ben's eyes opened wide in horror.

"You're going to a wedding in a dress?" His face creased in concentration.

"Not anymore," Jas replied. He sounded absent as though his mind already strayed elsewhere. His lips moved as he murmured the names of superheroes. "Superman, Darth Vader. No, Superman."

Ben raised his eyebrows at Hana and then distracted her with more details of his good news. "Principal Blair came to see my dad yesterday. On a Saturday!" Ben hopped from foot to foot as though he couldn't contain himself. "He said there's a space for me. He created it specially."

"Wow." Hana maintained her smile, but something didn't sit right about the story.

"It's all paid for," Ben gushed. He wrapped his arms around his stomach and hugged himself as though containing his excitement with physical barriers. "My uniform and everything is paid for. It's a new scholarship, look." He yanked a well-thumbed leaflet from his pocket and Hana took it. She unfolded the creases and stroked the glossy cover as understanding filtered through her tired brain. The leaflet bore the school crest, but the composition looked hurried and sloppy. Whoever slapped it on the photocopier hadn't lined up the edges with any degree of accuracy. She sighed and realised it didn't matter. There would be no more copies made.

She paused, waiting for the wave of emotion to subside so she could drink in the details. The writing sounded familiar, the style and language something she heard every day. Jas tugged at her sleeve. "Read it, Hanny," he demanded. "I wanna know if I can get one the same."

Hana paused and licked her lips. Then she turned to the front of the leaflet. "'The Reuben Scholarship,' is for the pursuit of dreams and is awarded to boys who would not otherwise have the opportunity to follow them." Hana glossed over the details about grade point averages and the requirements for continuation of the scholarship during a boy's school career. She read a note at the end of the first page beneath the funding provisions. "Recipients of the scholarship will engage with a mentor to facilitate their continued success."

"Guess who my mentor is?" Ben's eyes bugged as though he hoped Hana couldn't guess. She opened her mouth to speak, but he couldn't wait. Jas leaned closer, his body almost touching Ben's in case the good news rubbed off on him too.

"Mr Blair himself!" Ben said, pursing his lips. His eyes shone with the glitter of delight

"Whoa!" Jas inhaled, thinking of the formidable Scotsman with the bright orange hair and the loud tartan tie. "Lucky!"

The leaflet shook in Hana's hand as she turned it over to the final folded page. She read the inscription tacked onto the bottom in italics and her voice trembled. "For Reuben," she whispered. She struggled to read the quote, but forced herself. "Where words fail, music speaks. *Hans Christian Andersen.*" She swallowed and handed the leaflet back to Ben. "Congratulations," she said and turned away.

Her gaze settled on Logan as he chatted to a group of admiring women on the other side of the church. Hana bit her lip as she appraised his muscular physique and the arrogant tilt of his head which hid his fears from public view. One eye was half closed and shrouded in purple and black bruising. He moved with uncharacteristic stiffness to avoid jarring his broken ribs. The cut to his temple healed with frustrating slowness despite the passage of a week. Everything about Logan healed slowly.

Hana saw him glance at her, a plea for rescue in his glittering grey eyes. A sense of mischief made her smirk and wave, leaving him to the mercy of the pensioners. Logan turned enough to produce an obscene gesture behind his back. "Naughty!" Hana mouthed and turned her back on him.

"Where did you go while I was in church?" she asked later as they fitted Phoenix's car seat into the back of the Honda. "You only just made it for coffee at the end."

"You really wanna know?" Logan's lips quirked upwards and he caught her around the waist.

"Careful of your ribs," Hana chided. She narrowed her eyes. "And yes."

Logan lifted the sleeve of his tee shirt to reveal his muscular shoulder, exposing a white medical dressing on his upper arm.

"What happened?!" Hana's eyes widened and her heart sank. "What now?"

"This." Logan peeled off the white gauze and showed her his morning's work.

Hana pressed her fingers to her lips. The tattoo which swirled around his shoulder looked different. It extended further down his arm, hugging the bottom of Logan's substantial bicep. The names, *Hana-Phoenix-Tama-Du-Rose*, nestled beneath the swirls and whirls representing Logan's whakapapa. Logan smiled, his expression betraying a peace she hadn't seen there for too long. "My heritage," he whispered. "I'm okay with it now."

Hana smiled and kissed the empty space above his elbow. "Does it hurt?" she whispered.

Logan shook his head. "No. Not anymore." His words held many meanings and Hana sighed.

"Good," she replied.

"You shall not bow down to them or worship them; for I, the LORD your God am a jealous God, punishing the children for the sin of the fathers to the third and fourth generation of those who hate me, but showing love to a thousand generations of those who love me and keep my commandments."
Exodus 20:5

One Heartbeat

IF YOU ENJOYED THE NEW DU ROSE MATRIARCH, CHECK OUT THIS SAMPLE CHAPTER OF THE NEXT NOVEL.

A crowd gathered in a fast-food restaurant on Greenwood Street in Hamilton, loud, hungry and covered in slick brown mud. The staff looked unhappy, descended upon without notice by the group of twenty.

"Amazing win!" a thick-set man beamed, slapping the back of a spindly blonde male who almost fell over. "I love this team. We might win the staff and old boys' league."

The blonde man grimaced and moved away from another debilitating slap to the back. His tracksuit pants dripped mud onto the tiled floor. "That hurt," he grumbled to the dumpy man standing next to him. "Pete, did you see him sit on my head during the game?"

"Shut up or he'll do it again just for the hell of it." Pete gave the thick-set man the side eye. "He isn't safe outside the chemistry lab. A Bunsen burner is the only thing he should be allowed to play with."

"And even then only under supervision." They smirked with a sense of shared conspiracy and Pete stepped up to the counter to take his turn. He shot a glance over his shoulder and scanned the queue. Then he leaned forward and whispered his order.

"What, sorry?" The teenage boy behind the counter leaned closer. "Was that a supersize burger or normal?"

A shriek sounded from behind Pete and his eyes rolled heavenward. "Damn it!" he cursed.

"Peter North!" a woman yelled, jumping the queue to slap the top of his head. "Have you forgotten our diet?" She ordered him a chicken salad with a fruit bag and he came away from the counter with a frown on his face.

"I ran around for ninety minutes, Henrietta," he whined. "I've burnt the calories in advance."

She shook her blonde curls and put her arm around Pete's shoulder. Chunky fingers ruffled his sandy hair and disturbed the parting at the back of his head. "Let's sit and share your fruit bag," she soothed, dragging him away from the promise of a cheeseburger.

The team gathered at one long table where they continued their excited conversation. The players resembled swamp creatures and the unpleasant brand of orange soil on their clothes and skin carried a rank smell. Other customers wrinkled their noses and moved away. Pete sniffed an armpit. "Do I stink, Henri?" he demanded, forcing his arm into her face. "They need to look at the drainage on our home pitch."

"You smell of rose petals, my love," Henrietta lied. She turned her face aside and pushed a finger underneath her nose.

"It used to be a flax swamp." The chemistry teacher sat next to Pete and gave him a back slap which made him choke on a grape. "Our school is the oldest in the city and started when the first settlers came from the garrison. This rain isn't helping though. The water table is too high. I'm sorry they called the game off before full time. It's a good job we got ahead enough for the other team to concede the win."

"I'm not sorry the referee called it off," Pete grumbled. He lifted a piece of apple to his lips and the chemistry teacher jabbed his elbow, sending the fruit skittering across the table. Pete wrinkled his nose and looked at Henrietta for help.

"Here come the Du Roses." Her attention remained fixed on the sliding doors and her blue irises sparkled. "Hana looks soaked to the bone." She stood up and waved to the woman dashing through the doors and her hip banged into Pete's shoulder. Another grape left his fingers and rolled away. "We're over here, Hana!" she yelled, deafening everyone in close range.

Hana Du Rose's auburn hair reached her waist and flickered under the harsh strip lights. Thin and elegant despite the waterproof jacket burying her under layers of warmth, she waved in return. Her eyes sparkled with enough green to contain a hint of emerald. The baby girl in her arms looked dry, observing the lights and bustle with interest. Her Māori genes dictated a healthy olive skin, but some ancient European influence gifted her unusual grey eyes which glittered and shone as she studied her surroundings.

Henrietta hollered, bouncing on the balls of her feet. "Get your food and come over!"

Hana smiled as the whole restaurant winced at her companion's volume. "Okay," she mouthed. "Logan's just parking the car."

Appearing through the sliding doors came a giant of a man of six foot three or four. He carried an authoritative presence which caused several other customers to stop eating their burgers and stare. Ruggedly handsome with dark hair and features, his impressive physique betrayed a man not afraid of physical labour. His Māori heritage translated into confidence and satisfaction; his mana grounding him in an ethereal reassurance. He shook his dark head and rain droplets scattered around him in an arc. The baby laughed, her rosebud lips parting to show tiny front teeth. Logan Du Rose wore the same soccer strip as the others. Black shorts with a black-and-white striped shirt displayed the letters of his team, '*WPSB Staff and Old Boys*.' A round red insignia graced the front left while the back of his shirt read 'Du Rose' and a number four.

"You're soaked." Hana reached up and wiped the water from his brow. Her English accent differed from the cacophony of New Zealand vowel sounds. "Pity Larry didn't turn up to open the changing rooms. You all needed a good shower."

"Yep. Dunno where he is." Logan turned a hundred-watt smile on Hana. He leaned closer to her and pressed a kiss against her forehead. "Shall I just order drinks? I don't want to eat fast food." His hand strayed to pat his muscular stomach and he wrinkled his nose.

"Good idea." Hana left him to order at the counter and drifted across to sit with the raucous crowd.

"Hana, did you see my goal?" a young man shouted from next to Pete.

She smothered a laugh and nodded. "Yes Tama, it looked spectacular. I didn't know you'd been practicing scoring with your bum!"

Everyone on the table laughed and spoke at once.

"Did you see Pete's goal?" cried Henrietta, patting him on the head with a meaty hand and dunking his face into his salad.

"That was an own goal!" Tama jeered and Pete pinked with embarrassment, muttering into his lettuce leaves.

Henrietta bridled in her boyfriend's defence. "Well, really!" she huffed. "My Pete only covered for the groundsman not showing up. Don't be so ungrateful!"

Murmuring began as the team conceded their muted thanks to Pete for standing in as a defender. Curiosity surrounded the mystery of Larry Collins' absence. "He might have forgotten," someone suggested.

"Or had too much wacky baccy last night," Pete snorted.

Tama kicked him under the table and shot a nervous look at Logan as he put the cups of fizzy drink on the table next to Hana. "Shut up, Pete!" he hissed. "Uncle Logan hates drugs."

"Maybe he's somewhere on the school grounds measuring the height of the grass and yelling at everyone to get off it!" shouted a huge man with a streak of orange mud across the bridge of his nose. He performed a superb impression of the groundsman, standing up and yelling in his best Larry Collins voice, "Get off that bloody crease!"

"Drama teachers," Logan whispered in Hana's ear. She clamped her teeth over her lower lip and smirked.

The gathered crowd laughed and moved on to other topics. Tama rose and stole the baby from Hana, cuddling her into his broad chest. She smiled up at him and made a gurgling noise. "Come on Phoenix, let's have some fun away from the rents." He returned to his seat and ate one-handed, feeding her ice-cream sundae in secret and snorting at the dreadful face she made against the coldness. Despite the faces, she waved her little arms and opened her mouth for more. Hana gave a sigh and leaned sideways against her husband, her fingers reaching out and twirling the wedding band on his finger.

"Did you enjoy your secret deodorant shower, Logan Du Rose?" She smiled up at him, scenting the strong maleness hidden beneath the haze of spray.

He shrugged and his gaze flicked to her lips and back to her eyes. He released a frustrated sigh. "No. The truck stinks now, so don't hurry your drink." His eyes flickered shut as he pressed his lips over hers. He released a groan. "Having Tama living on the sofa is killing me." His lips traced a line along her jaw and he sighed into her hair. "He's like a human contraceptive."

Hana laughed and her fingers coasted across the tattoo peeking from his sleeve. It ended above his elbow with italic script swirling through it like a lace fringe. Mud stained his face and neck, but he smelled good.

"Sorry we're late." A man with Indian heritage slotted himself onto the bench opposite and faced Hana. "Hey, Mum." He turned to help a tousled haired boy lift a laden tray onto the table. The child seized a packet of fries and plonked himself on Logan's knee without invitation. He swung lime green soccer boots back and forth under the table.

Logan nodded to his stepson. "Bodie." He turned his attention to the child in his lap. "You don't want to eat that crap, Jas," he said. He winced at the grease coating the boy's fingers.

"It's tasty." Jas dangled a bunch of fries in front of Logan's face and grinned when he jerked backwards. "You played great, Poppa Logan." He reached up and kissed the underside of Logan's rough chin. He wrinkled his nose at the feel of stubble. "Daddy didn't play so good though." He looked sideways at his father. Small fingers stuffed another handful of chips between his lips despite the limited space. "You're not s'posed to let goals in Dad."

Hana leaned across to run a hand through her son's dark hair. "But Jas, he kept heaps out. He only let one in!" She gave Bodie a conspiratorial smile.

"Yeah, thanks Mum. I'm glad someone appreciated my efforts." He eyed his wrapped burger. "This won't help my game much though."

Hana looked along the table, shaking her head as she saw Tama still feeding ice-cream to her baby. "Stop it," she mouthed, seeing him bite his lip and carry on. With a cross exhale, Hana excused herself from the table, heading to the toilets near the back of the restaurant.

"Wait for me, Hanny!" Jas hopped off Logan's knee and followed, grappling at his crotch and sliding on his tiny boot sprigs. She waited at the door and held her hand out. "I don't need it," Jas reassured her, though he didn't let go of the front of his shorts.

"You obviously do," Hana retorted. She pushed the door open and gave a shake of her head as the child opened his mouth to protest. "No, I'm not going in the men's toilets. It's this or nothing, mate."

Logan sipped soda through a straw and stared around the restaurant. He missed nothing, his watchfulness a lifelong habit born of necessity. As Hana and Jas disappeared through the toilet door, a couple in their late-seventies arrived. They ordered at the counter before sitting nearby. The woman limped and the man carried the tray containing coffees and a muffin each.

"Tourists," Bodie said, nodding towards them. He moved with Hana's slender grace, but shared his features with her late husband.

"Yeah." Logan observed them with interest. "Poor buggers. Do you think their travel agent forgot to tell them autumn is wet and winter is cold?"

Bodie rolled his eyes. "Probably. Everyone in the northern hemisphere assumes New Zealand is hot all year around."

"Where do you think they're from?" Logan slipped his straw between his lips and took another sip of his drink.

"Policeman's intuition," Bodie said with a smug grin. "Their clothes look European. Not expensive, but different."

Logan's eyes narrowed. "I can see that. I wanted specifics."

Bodie snorted. "No idea, mate." He blinked. "Why, what do you think?"

"English." Logan jerked his head upwards. He pointed his straw towards the woman's coat. She'd taken it off and let it fall backwards over the chair while she leaned forward to sip her coffee. Her hand shook. "Look at the tag in the back of her coat. Marks and Spencer. That's an English brand."

Bodie's lips parted and his brow furrowed. "Oh." He swallowed. "You're good, man. You'd make a good cop if you weren't so dodgy." He smirked at Logan and the other man ignored his veiled insult.

He concentrated on the elderly couple, perplexed by something. A familiarity in the man's movements made him doubt himself. Thin and distinguished looking, the man sat as though the crowded restaurant didn't faze him. His calm contained a hidden authority which Logan recognised as one leader to another. His grey hair ran to white in a gentle, even way, cropped and neat above bifocal glasses.

"Do you know him?" Bodie asked. He reached across and snagged one of Jas' chicken nuggets. "You look like you do."

Logan shook his head and paused. "No. But yes. The man seems familiar." The sense of déjà vu rippled through him like a warning bell.

Bodie shrugged and helped himself to more of Jas' abandoned food. "They look harmless enough."

Logan nodded and went back to his drink, shuttering his eyelashes so he could watch the woman without detection. She looked delicate boned and seemed more uptight, jerky movements betraying her anxiety. She'd pulled her greying hair into a severe bun and she flapped and fidgeted while her companion perused the free newspaper.

"Hana's a long time." He shot the comment sideways, reluctant to remove his attention from the couple. "I might send Henrietta in after her."

"She's got Jas with her," Bodie replied. He rolled his eyes. "He's fascinated with the hand dryer. The motor blew up at the one in the cinema when I let him go in alone."

"Then don't let him go in alone." A darkness infused Logan's grey irises and he risked a sideways glance in Bodie's direction. "You need to rein him in, man. He's getting unmanageable."

Bodie shrugged. "I can't. Amy won't let me." He grinned as sauce dribbled off his chin.

Logan shook his head. "Don't leave it too late. He's a good kid, but he needs boundaries." He turned away, his gaze flicking towards the elderly couple and then the toilet door. Hana's absence sent a prickle of unease up his spine and he pushed his drink away.

In the toilet, Hana struggled with Jas. "Everyone's waiting, mate. We need to go," she argued.

"But it's eaten Action Man's hair!" he wailed. "He just wanted to see inside and it's stolen his hair!"

Hana poked her hand in the dryer and it activated itself, the powerful mechanism devouring the rest of the black mop. "It's sucked it into the filter," she said. "It won't come back out." She tried to fit her finger into the drain hole and failed.

"He doesn't like being bald!" Jas wailed and Hana fought her growing irritation.

"Then you shouldn't have stuck his face inside the dryer," she replied. It took a mammoth effort to keep her tone even. "Look," she hunkered down next to him, "why don't we get help? The staff might know how to get the filter out. I'm sure Daddy can speak to them."

Jas allowed Hana to lead him into the restaurant. She kept hold of his hand, noting how he pushed his Action Man inside his coat. Pale plastic legs protruded from a naked bottom but his bald head remained hidden. "Now?" Jas pleaded. "Can Daddy get it back now? He can arrest them if they won't help, can't he?"

Hana saw Logan's face light up with the special smile he kept only for her. She rolled her eyes and tried not to betray her inner annoyance as the grumbling child trailed after her. She stopped so fast, Jas ran up her heels and Action Man escaped his coat and skittered across the tiles. Jas yanked his hand free and went after him.

The sight hit her like a physical blow, taking her breath away so she froze on the spot. The colour drained from her face and her body refused to obey the simple instruction to run. Her legs trembled beneath her as the realisation struck her like a vehicle collision. Logan moved in her peripheral vision, rising from the bench and picking his way towards her. But he wasn't the only one.

The male tourist rose from his chair, his eyelashes fluttering over vibrant blue eyes. He lifted his glasses up and sat them on his head. He peered at her and

Hana shook her head. "No," she gasped. "No." Her brain did mental somersaults as it tried to offer reassurance. She'd spent a lifetime imagining the moment only to discover it would never happen. Her mouth opened and closed as though she gulped for air and her gaze flicked towards the doorway as a family entered and brought in a breeze from outside. Hana craved the fresh air like a healing balm, promising herself if she could just get outside she'd be okay.

"No, Daddy! Ask them now!" Jas protested. Action Man's backside mooned to the restaurant as oblivious, Jas covered the bald head with his fingers.

"Mum?" Bodie ignored him, rising and watching Logan's journey through the scattered seating. "What's wrong?"

The tourist struggled with the extra chairs near his table, his face ashen and unreadable.

Hana's lips moved as she murmured to herself. "This isn't happening, Hana. Get a grip. It's a coincidence."

Logan reached her. "Hana, babe, what's wrong?" The anxiety in his eyes hiked her panic and words failed her. She gripped his hand to reassure herself. The bizarre hallucination would end if she could just hold on to him. "Hana?" He looked down at their joined fingers, seeing her knuckles showing white through the skin. The tourist kept coming, picking his route with determination as a new spring entered his step.

Hana's eyes widened, imploring Logan for help. His other hand closed over her shoulder and he squeezed life into her frozen bones. "I'm sorry," she breathed. She'd gone before he could catch her, fleeing the restaurant with her jacket billowing out behind her. She put her hands over her ears and focussed on the doors sliding open and closed before her, picking up enough speed to make it through the narrow gap. They hissed closed behind her and she dodged moving vehicles, drawing an angry horn blast in her wake. She became the broken teenager of almost three decades ago and shame washed over her. Panic made her abandon her baby and guilt mingled with terror. But she couldn't go back. Fear pinned her to the gritty floor of the car park.

Logan found her crouched next to their truck with her face in her hands. Rain fell on her head in sheets and soaked her hair. "What's wrong, babe. Tell me?" he begged.

Hana opened her mouth and then closed it, knowing she sounded crazy. He'd never believe she had just stared into the face of her dead father.

Dear Reader,

I would love it if you could leave a review at your usual retailer.
I find the opinions of readers helpful and constructive. Reviews are the Holy Grail to an author as they cause our work to sink or swim. It is the bench mark for other readers and can determine whether our work will be successful and reach many or none. It doesn't have to be an essay or a literary criticism. A few words about what you liked would be most appreciated. The shortest review I ever received for my work was, 'Great,' accompanied by five stars and the longest was a whole video from a gorgeous woman in the USA. My favourite to date has to be the lady who said, '*I read until my eyes fell out.*' I keep looking at that one because it makes me laugh.
You can review on my website, ktbowes.com.
Go to the book's buy page where you can follow through to your own retailer and leave a review for me.

And hey, let me know when you've done it. I'd love to hear from you.

About the Author

K T Bowes is a bestselling teen and women's author. Her novel, *A Trail of Lies*, was the winner of the genre award for Author's Cave in 2014.

Phoenix Du Rose was considered for the prestigious Ngaio Marsh awards for 2021 and *Her Quiet Legacy* in 2022.

K T Bowes is an Englishwoman in exile in New Zealand, swapping rugged cosmopolitan for mountain ranges and terrifying rivers. She loves Māori culture and has learned to weave flax using traditional methods. Her other passion is Rongoa Māori, which involves creating medicines from native plants. She is a student of Te Reo Māori.

You can find her hanging out on social media in the following places.

Check in and say hello. Maybe suggest she gets back to writing and stops watching cat videos.

FACEBOOK
https://www.facebook.com/NZauthorKTBowes/
TWITTER
https://twitter.com/ktboweswrites
INSTAGRAM
https://www.instagram.com/k_t_bowes

Also by this Author

The Hana Du Rose Mysteries Series:
Logan Du Rose
About Hana
Hana Du Rose
Du Rose Legacy
The New Du Rose Matriarch
One Heartbeat
The Du Rose Prophecy
Du Rose Sons
Du Rose Family Ties
Du Rose Vendetta
Phoenix Du Rose
Wiremu Du Rose

The Calculated Risk Series:
The Actuary
The Actuary's Wife
The Actuary in Trouble
The Heart of The Actuary

Troubled series for teens:
Free from the Tracks
Sophia's Dilemma
A Trail of Lies

Gone Phishing

Escaping the Back Country NZ Series:
Pirongia's Secret
Deleilah

Standalone novels:
Artifact
Demons on Her Shoulder
All Saints
Her Quiet Legacy

Humorous Cozy Mystery Series from New Zealand
Dead Straight
Bad Hair Day
Side Parting

www.ingramcontent.com/pod-product-compliance
Lightning Source LLC
LaVergne TN
LVHW040746250326
834688LV00034B/482